Mesmerized

Also by Candace Camp
in Large Print:

Secrets of the Heart

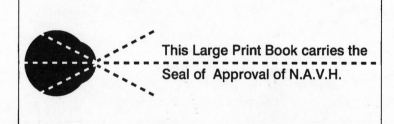

Mesmerized

Candace Camp

WHEELER PUBLISHING

Published in 2004 by arrangement with Harlequin Books, S.A.

Wheeler Large Print Romance.

The text of this Large Print edition is unabridged.
Other aspects of the book may vary from the original edition.

Set in 16 pt. Plantin by Christina S. Huff.

Printed in the United States on permanent paper.

Library of Congress Cataloging-in-Publication Data

Camp, Candace.
    Mesmerized / Candace Camp.
       p.   cm.
    ISBN 1-58724-565-5 (lg. print : hc : alk. paper)
    1. Parapsychology — Investigation — Fiction. 2. Large type
books. I. Title.
PS3553.A4374M47 2003
   813'.54—dc22
                                        2003062168

Mesmerized

As the Founder/CEO of NAVH, the only national health agency solely devoted to those who, although not totally blind, have an eye disease which could lead to serious visual impairment, I am pleased to recognize Thorndike Press* as one of the leading publishers in the large print field.

Founded in 1954 in San Francisco to prepare large print textbooks for partially seeing children, NAVH became the pioneer and standard setting agency in the preparation of large type.

Today, those publishers who meet our standards carry the prestigious "Seal of Approval" indicating high quality large print. We are delighted that Thorndike Press is one of the publishers whose titles meet these standards. We are also pleased to recognize the significant contribution Thorndike Press is making in this important and growing field.

Lorraine H. Marchi, L.H.D.
Founder/CEO
NAVH

* Thorndike Press encompasses the following imprints: Thorndike, Wheeler, Walker and Large Print Press.

1

1876

The oil lamp in the center of the long table was turned low, eerily lighting the faces of the people around it, throwing eyes and hair into deep shadows and dancing along the sharp lines of brow and cheekbone, making the silent attendees look gaunt and mysterious. All eyes turned toward the large wooden box a few feet from the table, dark and looming. There was no sound from inside it.

Then the lamp went out, and one of the women gasped. Blackness enveloped them. Hands turned cold, and pulses sped up. Everyone waited. There, in the dark hush, it was easy to imagine a ghostly finger trailing coldly across one's shoulders, to think, with a heart-pounding combination of fear and anticipation, that someone might speak from across the black void of death.

Even Olivia Moreland, despite the fact that she was there for a far different purpose, could

7

not help but feel a little thrill dart up her back. But it was not enough to keep her from her business. Slowly, carefully, using the tricks she had learned from the very people she intended to expose, she eased backward, shielded by the blackness surrounding her, and separated herself from the ring of people around the table.

She paused for a moment, giving her eyes a chance to adjust to the lack of light; then she started forward slowly. It was still difficult to see, as the only light in the room was the glow from the hallway creeping in around the door. She did not want to alert anyone to the fact that she was up and walking. It had to be a surprise to everyone when she reached the medium's cabinet. All her attention was on the dark box before her; every nerve in her body seemed to quiver, tense with expectation. She was almost there. . . .

A hand lashed out and wrapped around her arm, fingers digging painfully into her flesh.

Olivia shrieked and jumped. A deep masculine voice cried out, "There! I have you!"

All around the table, women echoed Olivia's shriek, and there was the clatter of a chair overturning and a general hubbub of voices and movements.

Whatever instinctual, primitive fear had flooded Olivia at the sudden grasping of her arm, it subsided at the sound of a very real and human voice.

"Let go of me!" she snapped, trying to pull her arm away.

"I think not — until you have explained your-self."

She continued to struggle, hissing, "Stop! You are ruining everything!"

"No doubt I am," he replied in a faintly amused tone. "It is always so unpleasant to have one's duplicity revealed."

"Duplicity?"

As the two of them exchanged words, there was the sound of a thud, followed by a muttered curse, and at last a match flared into life at the table. A moment later, someone lit the oil lamp and there was light in the room. Olivia found herself staring down into the cool gray eyes of her captor.

A faint shock passed through her, a feeling almost of recognition, though she realized immediately that she had never seen this man before. She was certain that, if she had, she would have remembered him.

He was seated at the table, his chair pushed a little away from those on either side of him, and he was half-turned and leaning back in order to grasp Olivia's arm. His shoulders were broad, and Olivia could well attest to the strength of his hands and arms. His face was lean, with high, wide cheekbones so sharp they looked as if they could have cut paper. It was a hard face, a look emphasized by the cold intensity of his eyes. Only his mouth — wide, with a full lower lip — would have softened his face, but it was at the moment pulled into a thin line. His hair, thick and dark, nearly black, was shaggily cut, as if someone had taken a pair of scissors to it — or, perhaps, a knife. The ungentlemanly appearance of his hair was echoed in his clothes — made of clearly fine materials, but just as clearly sewn by someone other than one of the well-known London tailors, as well as being a trifle out-of-date. She would have thought him foreign on an initial glance, except that his voice had been un-mistakably that of an upper-class Englishman.

There was a moment of silence as everyone else in the room stared at the tableau.

"I don't have to explain myself to you!" Olivia retorted, desperately searching for a good reason for her to have been walking about. She twitched at her skirts, which had managed to become twisted, showing an entirely inappropriate ruffle of her petticoat on one side. There was a lock of hair that had escaped from her neat bun, as well; she could feel it curling down beside her face. She realized that her appearance put her at a disadvantage, and she was made even more uncomfortable by that steady silver-gray gaze on her face. But she refused to let this man cow her. Olivia was quite aware that she was small and unremarkable in appearance — a little brown wren of a woman, she had more than once thought of herself, especially when compared to the other, more peacocklike members of her family. But she had learned to counter that impression with a steady and stubborn refusal to be intimidated.

She cast a disdainful look down at the stranger's hand, curled around her upper arm. "I demand that you cease this bullying at once."

"I think you have to explain yourself to the company in general," he countered, but he relaxed his grip enough that it was no longer actually painful. "Exactly what were you doing sneaking about the room? Were you about to manifest yourself as a 'visitor from beyond'?" His deep voice was laced with cynicism.

"Of course not!" Color flared in Olivia's cheeks. She was painfully aware of the gazes of everyone else in the room fixed on her. "How dare you?"

"Sir, this is scarcely the behavior of a gentleman." One of the other men in the room spoke up, a portly fellow with a great curling mustache and plentiful muttonchop sideburns — such hirsute magnificence grown, Olivia suspected, to compensate for the man's shiny bald pate.

Olivia's tormentor did not so much as even glance at the other man; he simply continued to look straight into Olivia's face. "Well? Why were you tiptoeing about the room?"

Another guest chimed in. "It is odd, Miss . . . um . . . dreadfully sorry, but I am afraid that I cannot remember your name."

Unfortunately, neither could Olivia, or, at least, she could not remember the name she had given these people tonight when she had arrived. It had not been her own, of course. She knew that what she called her nondescript appearance was a blessing in that regard, allowing her to pass unknown through these gatherings as long as she used an assumed name. It was sheer bad luck that the excitement of the past few minutes had driven her evening's nom de guerre right out of her head.

"Comstock," she blurted out, the name coming back to her suddenly, but she could see by the expressions on the others' faces that her hesitation had been too long. They would not believe her now.

"How convincing," the man who still held her arm drawled sarcastically. "Now, Miss 'Comstock,' why don't you tell us about your plans to — what, put a sheet over your head? Or were you simply going to make piteous moans?"

"I say," said one of the men thunderously, rising to his feet. "What the devil are you saying, man? Are you implying that I would allow some . . . some damnable *chicanery* in my house?" He turned immediately toward the woman at his side. "Pardon me, my dear. Ladies. I forgot myself in the heat of my indignation."

"St. Leger . . ." the man who was sitting beside Olivia's captor said with distress, "whatever are you doing?" He turned toward their host, who was standing and staring with grim dislike at the man holding Olivia's arm. "Colonel, I beg your pardon, Lord St. Leger meant no disrespect, I'm sure."

"Of course not," Lord St. Leger said shortly,

glancing toward the colonel. "No doubt you were being duped, as well."

"Duped!" squawked the colonel's wife, her eyes bulging.

From inside the large box there came a moan, rising in volume when no one responded. The colonel's wife let out another noise, this one more a bleat, and jumped to her feet. "Mrs. Terhune! Mercy! How could we have forgotten about you?"

One of the men rushed to open the door of the medium's cabinet. There sat the gray-haired Mrs. Terhune on a stool, hands and feet bound just as they had been minutes earlier when they had closed the medium inside the box. The colonel's lady and the man who had opened the cabinet rushed to untie her. Olivia watched with a cynical eye as the ropes fell easily away. She felt sure that the medium had herself untied the ropes, then hastily retied them when she heard the hubbub break out in the room. But, of course, she could not prove that now.

"There! You see what you've done!" Olivia snapped at Lord St. Leger. He turned toward her, his eyebrows rising lazily.

"What *I* have done?" he repeated.

"Yes! You've ruined everything."

He smiled then, and it was astonishing to see the change it wrought in the man's face. Looking at him, Olivia felt as if her stomach had just fallen to her feet, and she drew an involuntary breath.

"No doubt I have," he agreed. "I apologize for interrupting you, Miss . . . *Comstock*. I should have let you play out your masquerade before I exposed you."

"You didn't expose anything, you dolt!" Olivia bit back, too disappointed and angry to worry about manners. "I was about to prove —"

"Who are these people?" the medium asked in a die-away voice that somehow brought everyone's attention back to her. "I feel . . . so strange. I was deep in a trance, then these angry voices pulled me back. It makes me feel quite tired. Did I speak? Did the spirits come?"

"No," barked the colonel, casting a flashing look toward Olivia and Lord St. Leger. "There was no visitation, no words from beyond. Nothing but these two people disrupting the séance."

"Disrupting —" St. Leger gaped at the man. "I caught these people about to perpetrate a fraud upon you and all of us here, and all you can say is that I disrupted this little farce?"

"Farce?" The colonel's face turned an alarming shade of red.

"Oh, dear," moaned the man beside St. Leger, hastening to say, "Colonel, please, forgive him. Lord St. Leger has been living in America for years. I'm afraid that he has forgotten his manners." The man turned and cast Lord St. Leger a significant look. "I am sure that he meant no insult."

"Of course I didn't mean any insult," St.

14

Leger replied. "You have been hoodwinked by this so-called medium and her partner, Miss 'Comstock.' "

"I am not her partner!" Olivia cried.

"Sir, I assure you, I have never seen this woman before in my life," Mrs. Terhune said, looking at Olivia blankly.

"Then what was she doing walking about during the séance?" St. Leger asked.

"I have no idea," Mrs. Terhune returned calmly. She fixed a stern gaze on Olivia. "Miss, I specifically told everyone not to leave the table. It is very important. Our friends from the other side are very particular about such things."

"Yes, no doubt they are," Olivia replied dryly. She wondered if there was any hope of somehow managing to pass this off as her having to get up because of an unmentionable emergency.

But at that moment, one of the other women at the table said suddenly, "Wait, I know you. You aren't Miss Comstock at all. You are that woman who dislikes mediums. My brother was telling me all about some symposium he attended —"

"Good Gad!" the colonel exploded. "The two of you came here purposely to cause a disruption! How dare you enter my house under false pretenses? I've a good mind to thrash you, sir."

St. Leger released Olivia's arm and rose to face the other man, his height and the breadth of his shoulders rendering the colonel's threat rather empty. "Don't trouble yourself, sir," he said coolly. "I will leave now. It is clear that everyone here would prefer to retain their delusions."

He strode from the room, and, as the colonel started toward Olivia, she decided it was best to follow St. Leger rather than be forcibly escorted from the house. The host was on her heels, calling for his servants. A stone-faced footman handed them their coats and hats and swept the door open, closing it with a snap as soon as they were outside.

St. Leger stopped abruptly on the stoop, and Olivia bumped into his back, letting out an annoyed "Oof."

He turned and met her glance. She glared at him, but she knew the look was rendered ineffective by the fact that she was struggling to hold her bonnet and put on her cloak at the same time.

St. Leger took in the struggle over her cloak, which had inexplicably gotten turned inside out, and a smile tugged briefly at the corners of his mouth. Naturally he had already popped on his top hat and shrugged into his light coat.

"Allow me," he said, reaching out and taking the cloak from Olivia's fingers. A quick shake straightened it out, and he placed it around her shoulders. His fingertips brushed over her shoulders, and even through the cloth of her cloak, the touch sent a shiver down Olivia's spine.

When he reached for the ribbons of her cloak, as if to tie them, she grabbed them herself, saying, "I can do that myself. You have done quite enough already."

He raised an eyebrow, then said, "Is it true what that woman said? You are an enemy of mediums?"

"I am an exposer of charlatans," Olivia responded tartly. "I stand ready to believe anyone who can prove to my satisfaction that they have contacted the otherworld, but as I haven't yet found a medium in London who can do that, I cannot label them as anything but frauds."

"So you were not helping out Mrs. Terhune tonight?"

"Of course not!"

"Then why were you sneaking about in the dark?"

"I was not 'sneaking.' I was walking quietly and carefully," Olivia corrected with a haughty look, "to the medium's cabinet to expose Mrs. Terhune, untied and about to hold up this silly daguerrotype that she displays over the top of the cabinet door and pretends is a spirit. I had a sulfur match ready to strike."

She sighed at the thought of the opportunity lost, and Lord St. Leger looked slightly abashed. "I beg your pardon. I thought I had caught a conspirator."

"Yes, well . . ." She turned and gestured, and a carriage down the street began to roll forward.

Olivia started to descend the steps, and St. Leger followed her. "Tell me, do you do this sort of thing often?"

"Get into séances and try to expose their frauds?" Olivia sighed again. "No, unfortunately. If a medium knows me, they will not let me attend. My 'lack of belief' disturbs the spirits. And few people hire me," she admitted candidly. "I find that almost no one wishes to 'let go of their delusions,' as you pointed out tonight."

He stared at her. "Hire you? What do you mean?"

"I have a business," Olivia told him, reaching into her reticule and pulling out one of her cards. She was rather proud of them, really, and never failed to hand one out, though the response she received was more often one of shocked disapproval than admiration.

St. Leger took the card and glanced down at the neat black script: *Miss O. Q. Moreland, Investigator of Psychic Phenomena.*

He looked back up at her in amazement, a hundred questions buzzing through his brain. But the first one that came out was, "*Q?*"

Olivia's mouth tightened. "It is a family name," she said, and reached out to snatch the card back, but he quickly pocketed it.

"And does your family not mind that you —"

"My family is quite open-minded," Olivia told him tightly. The carriage had pulled up in front of the colonel's house, and she went to it, waving the coachman to stay on his high seat.

St. Leger, following her, reached out to open the carriage door for her, but she grasped the

18

handle before he could. Turning to him, she said significantly, "My family is not so archaic as some and see nothing wrong in a woman exercising her mind in pursuit of a career."

"They see nothing wrong in your chasing ghosts?" St. Leger asked mildly, reaching toward her to help her up into her carriage.

Olivia narrowed her eyes and started to reply, but stopped as she saw realization dawning on St. Leger's face. He looked at the carriage door, on which her father's ducal crest was tastefully drawn, then pulled out her card to look at it again.

"Good God!" he exclaimed, with some amazement. "You're not — you're one of the 'mad Morelands'?"

Olivia jerked the door open and stepped up into the carriage, shrugging off his helping hand. She turned and sat down, leaning forward and saying, "Yes! I am definitely one of the 'mad Morelands.' Indeed, I am probably the maddest of the lot. If I were you, I'd burn that card, lest some of it rub off on you."

She slammed the door on his hurried words: "No, wait! I didn't — I'm —"

Olivia rapped sharply on the carriage roof, and the driver started like a shot, cutting off the rest of her companion's words.

"— sorry," Stephen St. Leger finished lamely. He looked down at his polished leather boots and elegant silk trousers, now splashed with dirty water from the carriage wheels. He suspected that the driver had been well aware of what he had been doing.

Of course, Stephen thought ruefully, he could scarcely blame the man. His words had been clumsy and boorish. His cousin Capshaw was right: he had spent too long in the United States, or, more accurately, he had spent too long in the lonely wilderness of the Rocky Mountains. He was no longer accustomed to being in polite society or, indeed, much of any kind of society at all.

He had not really meant anything bad about the woman's family. He had merely been shocked when it registered on him that the young lady he had thought he caught red-handed aiding a medium had in fact been the daughter of a duke, a gently reared young woman of good lineage and a hefty fortune. He had simply blurted out the name by which her family was largely regarded in London society. The "mad Morelands" . . . they must be mad, indeed, he thought, if they found nothing wrong with letting one of their daughters traipse about London alone at night, attending séances and confronting charlatans. It seemed a risky business.

Her having a business surprised him less. He had seen enough wives and daughters helping to conduct family businesses — or widows left to run one on their own — in his time in the United States. It was, however, somewhat startling to find a young, unmarried lady in England doing so, especially one from one of the most noble families in the country. Her family, he would have thought, would have moved heaven and earth to keep her from doing so.

But, he supposed, the reason they had not lay in the very epithet that had slipped off his tongue. The Morelands, while not actually legally mad, were generally considered to be, well, *off*. The old duke, Miss Moreland's grandfather, had been famous for his various bizarre and intense "health treatments," which had ranged from mud baths to foul-smelling restorative drinks to being wrapped in wet sheets for hours at a time — the latter of which was generally considered to have been what sent the man at a relatively young age into his last, fatal bout of pneumonia. He had spent much of his life traveling in England and the Continent, consulting with quacks and chasing the latest fads. His wife, it was said, had a peculiar tendency to talk about her ancestors as if she had daily conversations with them. The duke's younger brother, the present duke's uncle, was reputed to spend much of his time playing with tin soldiers.

The present Duke of Broughton, Miss Moreland's father, was obsessed with some sort of ancient subject — Stephen wasn't sure what, though he had it vaguely in his mind that the man collected statues and broken bits of pots and things. And he had married a woman well-known for her unusual views on social reform,

21

women, marriage and children. Even more horrifying to London society was the fact that the
current duchess had not been born to the nobility, being merely the daughter of country
gentry. There were several Moreland children,
most of them younger than Stephen was, and he
did not know much about them, having left the
country before most of them were old enough to
enter society, but from everything he had heard
from his mother and friends, he had gotten the
impression that they were an odd lot.

What he had seen of Miss O. Q. Moreland
certainly had done nothing to change that impression. She was decidedly peculiar — going
out alone in the evening to attend séances,
sneaking through darkened rooms to pounce on
a fraudulent medium and expose her practices,
even carrying on a business of doing such
things!

Stephen idly rubbed his thumb over the engraved letters of her card. *Investigator of Psychic
Phenomena.* He couldn't help but smile a little,
thinking of her feisty stance, hands on hips,
looking up at him with those big brown eyes
that looked as though they should be soft and
melting but were instead fierce. Small and
dainty, yet looking as if she were ready to take
on any opponent.

He remembered the odd feeling that had gone
through him when the light had been turned on
and he had first looked at her. He had thought
her a part of the medium's act, helping to hood-

wink an innocent public. Yet when he looked at her, something had shot through him, some strange current of emotion and physical attraction that jarred and surprised him. It had been something like desire . . . and yet something more, as well, something he could not remember ever feeling before.

Frowning, he turned and started to walk away, but the man who had been beside him at the séance came out the front door at that moment and hurried down the steps toward him, saying, "St. Leger!"

Stephen turned, surprised. "Capshaw. I thought you must have decided to stay."

The other man made a face. "I doubt that I would have been welcome, frankly, after the scene you made. But I had to do what I could to calm down Colonel Franklin. I told him that you were my cousin and a gentleman and would not spread scurrilous lies about him."

"I don't give a damn about that pompous colonel," St. Leger said, grimacing.

"What were you doing, by the way?" Mr. Capshaw went on curiously. "Did you go there to expose the medium? I must say, I didn't think it sounded like your sort of entertainment."

"Hardly. But I wasn't planning to do anything. It was just that when I heard her rustling about in the dark, I could not resist the opportunity to catch one of the charlatans red-handed." He shrugged. "I went merely to — I don't know, see what sort of thing they do. Try to understand what their hold is on otherwise rational people."

"There are more than a few who believe in it," Capshaw commented. "I've seen one medium who did things that, well, frankly left me wondering." He glanced over at his friend. "Don't you ever think that maybe it's a possibility? That people can speak to us from the other side?"

"It strikes me as highly unlikely," Stephen said shortly. "If they could, surely they would tell us something more important than the wretched pap these mediums put out. And why do they spend their time knocking on things? One would think that they would have better things to do with their time than play parlor tricks."

Mr. Capshaw chuckled. "That sounds like you."

"They are playing on people's grief," St. Leger went on grimly. "Using it to gain money."

His friend glanced at him. He had heard that Lady St. Leger, Stephen's mother, had been attending the séances of a popular Russian medium, and the anger in his friend's voice confirmed his suspicion. Stephen's older brother had died almost a year earlier, and their mother was said to be still mired in grief over his death.

"Sometimes," Capshaw said carefully, "it helps a person get through it, thinking that they can contact their loved one."

"It helps the damned medium acquire money," St. Leger growled. "And how do you know it

24

helps them? What if it just keeps them in that same painful place, constantly mourning their loss, never getting on with their lives?"

He stopped and looked at his companion. "I thought Mother was getting better, that she was not so wrapped up in sorrow as when I first came home. And when she wanted to take Belinda to London, it seemed a good sign. But then she fell in with this Valenskaya woman, and now she seems deeper in mourning than ever. I told myself the same things you said, that it didn't matter if it wasn't real, that it would help soothe her. What did it matter if she went to a few séances? But when Belinda wrote me and said that Mother had given this medium her emerald ring out of gratitude for all she'd done . . . Father gave her that ring! I have never seen it off her hand until now. Obviously this woman is exercising great power over her. That's why I came to London. And it didn't help my fears any when I saw Mother, either. She is forever talking about what this woman says, she and Belinda both, and it all sounds like the most blatant nonsense. Yet they seem to swallow it without a moment's thought."

Capshaw gave him a sympathetic glance, but, as Stephen knew, there was little he could say to help him.

"If only I could prove to her that the woman is a fraud!" Stephen went on. His thoughts went then to Miss Moreland of the snapping brown eyes and the business card, but he pushed her aside immediately. A man could hardly ask a woman to get rid of his problems for him, after all, and, besides, he could not expose his mother to the embarrassment. Besides, the woman was probably as peculiar as everyone said all her family were.

They continued for a moment in silence; then Stephen said, with studied casualness, "What do you know of the Morelands?"

"Morelands? Who do you — oh, you mean Broughton's brood? The 'mad Morelands'?"

"Yes."

Capshaw shrugged. "I don't know any of them personally. Although the eldest was at Eton at the same time I was — some damned peculiar name, I remember that. They've all got peculiar names. Roman or Greek or something. Broughton's always been mad for antiquities, you know."

"Yes, I remember that much."

"He was a daredevil — the one at Eton when I was there. Always into some scrape or other. Not the sort of chap I was mates with. It was enough to make one tired just hearing all the things he'd done. Theo — that was what we called him. His real name was something longer, Theodosius or some such. He's an explorer now, I've heard. Always off paddling up the Amazon or trekking through Arabia or something."

"Ah. Even more peculiar than haring off to the U.S., I suppose."

Capshaw glanced at him, then gave a rueful grin. "Well, yes, I guess he would be someone you might get along with. If you and I weren't cousins, we probably wouldn't be friends, either. He was a couple of years behind you at Eton, though." He paused, then said, "There are several others, all younger, though. The girls, I think, tend to be bookish. Don't go out in society — well, except for The Goddess."

"The who?"

"Oh, some poetic sort gave her the name years ago when she came out, and it rather stuck. Suited her, you see. Lady Kyria Moreland. If ever anyone could carry off such an epithet, it is she. Tall, statuesque, flaming red hair . . . she's a beauty, right enough. Odd, though — she could have married anyone, had suitors begging for her hand right and left, still does get plenty of offers, so I've heard, though she's been out for eight years, at least."

"She's still unmarried?" St. Leger asked, surprised.

"Yes. That's what I'm saying. All the women say she's the maddest of the lot. She could have been a duchess, a countess . . . Even some prince or other asked for her hand — foreigner, of course, so no surprise she didn't accept him. But still . . . she turned them all down, says she enjoys her life just as it is. Doesn't plan to ever marry."

"Definitely one of a kind," St. Leger commented.

"Oh, and one of the daughters blows things up."

"I beg your pardon?"

"Burned down one of the outbuildings at Broughton Park a couple of years ago. Caused a bit of a stir."

"I see. For any particular reason?"

His cousin frowned. "Not sure, really. Just heard it round at the club, that Broughton's daughter burned it down, and it wasn't the first time she'd blown something up. Oh, and that Broughton was in a flap about it — it was next to some shed full of his pots or something."

"Interesting." St. Leger wondered if it was another daughter or his own medium-chaser who had engaged in the pyrotechnics.

"Why are you so interested in the Morela — oh, wait!" Capshaw's brow cleared. "Don't tell. Is that your 'ghost'? She was one of Broughton's brood?"

"Apparently." Stephen nodded.

"Good Gad," Capshaw said, much struck by the revelation. "Well, not really a surprise, I suppose."

"No. But, you know, she didn't seem that peculiar, really." He paused, then added, "Well, maybe a bit odd, but quite sharp and — somehow appealing, for it all."

"Appealing?" His friend narrowed his eyes in speculation.

"Yes. In a general way, you know."

"Mmm-hmm."

Stephen grimaced at his companion. "Don't give me that look. I have no interest in Miss Moreland. Believe me, the last thing I am looking for is a woman, particularly a peculiar one. Between the estate and my mother falling into some charlatan's clutches, I have enough on my plate."

The two parted soon after that, Capshaw hailing a hansom to take him to his rooms and St. Leger turning to walk the last two blocks to his family's home.

It was a pleasant town house, narrow and tall, built a hundred years earlier in the Georgian style by a St. Leger ancestor. Stephen stopped at the foot of the steps leading up to the elegant front door and looked at the house for a moment. This house held some of his sweetest and bitterest memories, for it had been here where he lived when he came to London as a young man. When he had fallen in love . . . and later lost her.

Shaking off the memory, he trotted up the steps and opened the door. A footman came forward promptly to take his light coat and hat.

"My lord. I hope you had a good evening."

"Not as productive as I'd hoped."

"Lady St. Leger is in the drawing room."

"They didn't go out?"

"I believe that she, Miss Belinda and Lady Pamela did go out earlier, sir, but they returned a few minutes ago. Her Ladyship asked me to tell you that she would like to see you if you came in early."

"Yes, of course." Stephen turned and went down the hall to the formal drawing room, a narrow elegant blue-and-white chamber. Pamela had redecorated it, of course, as she had the rest of the house, after Roderick had come into the title. Stephen preferred the warmer, darker colors of the room when he had lived here years ago.

His mother was sitting at the piano, playing a quiet air, when he came in. Belinda, his lively younger sister, was seated beside her, turning the pages of the music for her. Pamela, he was sorry to discover, was also there, sitting on a pale blue velvet love seat, a bored expression on her face. It changed when Stephen entered the room, turning into the slow, faintly mysterious smile that she was well-known for, a smile that promised a wealth of secret pleasures.

"Stephen," Pamela said in her husky voice. "What a pleasant surprise." She laid her hand in silent invitation on the seat beside her on the love seat.

"Pamela," Stephen replied stiffly, giving her a brief nod, then going to his mother at the piano. He bent and kissed her lightly on the cheek. "Mother. I am surprised to find you home so early."

Lady St. Leger gave him a sparkling smile. She was dressed, as always, in the complete black of mourning, although tonight a pair of diamonds dangled at her ears, catching the light. White hair curled softly around her face, gentle and still pretty despite the years and sorrow that had visited her.

"There were really no parties of any consequence," his mother explained. "The season's all but over, really. And Belinda was tired. So we just visited friends."

Belinda jumped up from her seat, belying any indication of tiredness, and came around the piano bench to greet her brother. Her hair was dark, like his, arranged on her head in a cascade of curls, and her eyes were also gray, though softer than his silvery brightness. She was a pretty girl, with the light of intelligence and curiosity in her eyes, quick to smile and laugh.

"Stephen!" she cried now as she reached out to give him a hug. "Are you going riding with me in the park tomorrow? You said this morning you might. Mother won't let me go without an escort." She made a face, annoyance tempered with fondness.

"In the morning?"

"Of course. That's when everyone goes."

"Everyone meaning the Honorable Damian Hargrove?" Pamela asked in a tone of lazy amusement.

Belinda wrinkled her nose, saying, "No. Mr. Hargrove is simply a friend." She looked up at her brother pleadingly, "Please, Stephen, say you'll go?"

"Of course I will. If you can manage to get up early enough, of course."

"Of course." Belinda looked affronted at the idea that she could not.

Lady St. Leger arose from the piano, taking her son's hand, and led him around to the sofa across from Pamela. She sat down beside him, beaming, her hand still tucked in his.

Stephen smiled back at his mother, then said in carefully neutral tones, "Whom did you visit this evening?" He had a pretty strong suspicion who it had been.

"Madame Valenskaya — and her daughter and Mr. Babington, of course." Howard Babington, Stephen knew, was the gentleman who had opened his house to the Russian medium and her daughter during their stay in London. "It was such a pleasant evening," his mother went on.

Her smile was enough to make Stephen wonder if perhaps Capshaw wasn't right, after all. Maybe it was better for his mother to believe in this nonsense if it lightened her heart. She had been plunged into grief at his older brother's death almost a year ago. It had taken Stephen some time to settle his affairs and return to England to take up the title and estate left to him by Roderick's demise, so it had been four months after Roderick's death before he reached their ancestral home. But his mother had still been in the depths of despair. He had wished many times over the months that he could lighten her sorrow somehow. Even if it took the ministrations of this Russian medium, perhaps it was worth it. They would, after all, be leaving in a few days to return to the family estate, leaving Madame Valenskaya in London. Hopefully, by the next season, his mother would be past this nonsense.

"The most wonderful thing happened," Lady St. Leger went on, excitement tingeing her voice. "Madame made contact with Roddy."

"What?" Stephen looked at her, then glanced over at Roderick's widow, Pamela.

Pamela nodded. "The spirit rapped out 'Roddy.' "

"His nickname!" Lady St. Leger went on excitedly. "You see? Not St. Leger, or even Roderick, that anyone might know. But the pet name I called him since he was a baby! It must mean it was really he, don't you see?"

"But, Mother, you must have spoken of him as Roddy sometime when you were around this woman," Stephen could not keep from pointing out.

Lady St. Leger made a disapproving noise. "Oh, Stephen, you are so suspicious. What does it matter if Madame Valenskaya knows his name is Roddy? It was the *spirit* who rapped it out."

"Of course." It was pointless, he thought, to try to reason with her. She thought the sun rose and set on Madame Valenskaya.

"It was the first time he's actually spoken to us, although of course Chief Running Deer has told us that he knows Roderick is well and happy." Lady St. Leger's eyes welled with tears at the memory. "You can imagine how thrilled I was."

"Yes."

"But I couldn't help but be sad, too, because we are leaving London soon. And it was so unlucky that Roddy should appear just now, when we are about to leave."

"Yes, wasn't it?" Stephen commented dryly.

"I said so to Madame, of course, and she agreed. She was very tired, as she always is after a visitation, but she is so kind. She stayed and talked to us for a long time afterward. Madame is certain that Roderick wants to speak with us again. She says she can feel his eagerness. It is just that when they are so new to the other side, as he is, it is a trifle difficult for them to communicate. But she knows it is coming soon."

Stephen could well imagine that the woman would hate to lose such a generous client; no doubt that was why Roddy's "spirit" had been trotted out. But Stephen kept his lips firmly shut against such words. His mother would not believe him, and it would only anger and hurt her.

"She suggested that we remain in London, but of course I told her we could not, what with you coming here to escort us back to Blackhope. You could not be away from the estate too long, I said. I could hardly ask you to twiddle your thumbs here in London when there is so much needing to be done. And, of course, the season is over. But it all turned out quite wonderfully! I realized that although we had to leave London, that didn't mean I could not see Madame Valenskaya. She could come to Blackhope Hall to visit us!"

Lady St. Leger beamed. Stephen stared.

"What? You invited her home with us?"

His mother nodded happily. "Yes. And, of course, her daughter and Mr. Babington. I could scarcely leave them out, especially after Mr. Babington has so kindly opened his home to us time after time. I cannot believe I never thought of inviting them before."

Stephen clenched and unclenched his jaw, at a loss for words. He wondered exactly who had come up with the idea for the visit — his mother or Madame Valenskaya.

"I am sure that Madame Valenskaya can communicate with the spirits just as well at Blackhope as she can here in London," Lady St. Leger went on. "Indeed, when I told her about the house, she was ecstatic. She says she is sure that someplace as old and as full of history as it is must be very well suited to communications from the spirit world. I had never thought of it, but that does make sense." She paused and looked at Stephen. "I know I should have asked you first, dear. It is, after all, your house now. But I was sure you would have told me to invite whomever I wanted."

"Yes, of course. It is your house, always has been. I would not forbid you to invite whomever you wanted there."

That was the problem, of course. Despite the fact that he was lord of Blackhope now, Stephen would not think of telling his mother who she could or could not invite to the home that had been hers from the day she married his father.

He glanced over at Pamela, who was watching him with a faint smile on her lips. There were times when he wondered if Pamela encouraged his mother on this foolish course just to arouse his ire. She talked about Valenskaya and her "spirits" as his mother did, but he had a little difficulty believing that Pamela really believed such things. She was a woman who was ruled by her head, not her heart; she had proved that much years ago when she married Roderick. Perhaps she was fond of Roddy in her fashion, but Stephen didn't believe that she had ever been passionately in love with his brother, certainly not enough to be overwhelmed by the torrent of grief that had inundated his mother. He knew that Pamela's heart had been more scored by the knowledge that she inherited nothing but a widow's share at her husband's death than by the death itself. He knew firsthand that hers was a cold and calculating heart, and he found it hard to believe that she wished so much to communicate with Roddy.

Lady St. Leger patted Stephen's hand. "I know. You are such a dear son, just like Roddy. I knew you would not mind, and, anyway, you are always locked up in your office or out riding the estate or something. You'll scarcely notice that we have guests."

Stephen sincerely hoped so, but he said only, in a neutral voice, "How long are they staying?"

"Oh, I didn't ask them for any specific time. I don't know what will happen, you see, or how long it will take. And three guests will scarcely tax the resources of Blackhope."

"No. Of course not." He paused. He could think of nothing to say about the matter that would not upset his mother. Life had been easier, he thought, when all he had to worry about was locating silver ore and bringing it out of the ground.

He cleared his throat. "Well, then . . . I suppose we will be able to leave soon."

"Yes, of course. The sooner the better, really. I must make sure that the house is ready for guests."

Stephen left his mother happily making plans for her guests and started up to his room. He had reached the stairs when he heard the sound of light footsteps behind him.

"Stephen!" Pamela's voice sounded behind him, and he turned reluctantly.

"What?" His voice was formally polite, his gaze devoid of warmth.

Age had changed Pamela little. Golden haired and blue eyed, she was still beautiful, her pale features a model of perfection. She walked toward him in her habitual slow way, as though certain that any man would willingly wait for her. It was the way she went through life, confident and cool, sure of getting her way. And, indeed, she had every reason to think so: she had rarely been thwarted.

"Must you run away so quickly?" she asked, her voice lowering huskily. "I only wanted to talk to you."

"About what? This nonsense that you are encouraging in my mother?"

"Nonsense?" Pamela raised an eyebrow. "I am sure Lady Eleanor would be shocked to hear you call it such."

"You are not, I see," he retorted. "Why the devil do you go to these séances?"

"I am not shocked to hear what you think about them," Pamela explained. "It is clear to anyone, even your mother, though she tries not to admit it. That does not mean that I agree with you."

Stephen's mouth twisted into a grimace, and he started to turned away.

"Why do you run from me?" Pamela asked again. She smiled, her eyes alight with knowledge. "Once you were quite happy to be near me."

"That was a long time ago," he replied shortly.

Pamela came closer, moving up onto the step below him. Leaning toward him, she placed a hand on his chest. Her cornflower-blue eyes gazed earnestly up into his. "I hate that things are so awkward between us now."

"I see no other way for them to be." Stephen wrapped his fingers around her wrist and removed her hand from his shirtfront. "You chose this. You are my brother's wife."

"I am your brother's widow," Pamela corrected huskily.

"It is the same thing."

Stephen turned and went up the stairs, not looking back.

Sleep did not come easily that night, even though he drank a snifter of brandy as he paced the floor of his bedroom. His head was too full of thoughts of mediums and heartless chicanery — and a small woman with a compactly curved figure and huge brown eyes that seared right into a man.

It was a long wait in the dark, tossing and turning, eyes opening and shutting, before at last he drifted down into the blackness. . . .

There was the smell of smoke and blood in the air, and the castle rang with the clash of iron against iron, underlaid by the moans of the wounded and dying.

He blinked his eyes against the acrid smoke; sweat trickled down into his eyes and dampened the shirt on his back. He had had no time to do more than don his hauberk of chain mail and grab up his sword.

He was on the stairs, close to the bottom, making his slow retreat up the curving stone steps to the tower room above. It was, he knew, the only slim hope for her safety. The lady of the castle. His love.

She was behind him now, her body shielded by his, inching up the steps as he did. No coward she, she had not run up the stairs to the safety of the tower room with its heavy barred door; instead, she stuck with him, turned to face out to the side of the stairs, the dagger pulled from its sheath at her belt and held to the ready.

His heart hurt with love of her — and fear.

"Go!" he barked at her. "Get up to the room and lock yourself in."

"I won't leave you." Her voice was calm, a silvery pool underlaid by iron.

He continued to swing his sword, holding off the rush of men who pushed up the staircase. There were two in front, for the staircase was no wider, and at the edge of the steps there was no rail, only empty space to the great hall below. Here, only a few steps above, some tried to climb up onto the steps or to grab at his legs to pull him down. One had managed to land a hit with his sword, but fortunately only the flat side had slammed into his calf, hurting even through the thick leather of his boots but not cutting him. He had taken care of each of them with a hearty kick that broke one man's jaw or a swift downward slice of his sword that left another without a hand. Lady Alys, behind him, had dispatched another by hurling at him the poker she had carried. The man had fallen like an ox, but unfortunately, the poker was now lost to them.

His arm was weary, yet still he swung. He would

fight, he knew, till he was bleeding and on his knees, and even then he would fight. Even though he knew they were doomed, he would fight. It was all he had of hope.

Stephen's eyes flew open, and he sat up, a gasp torn out of him. He was drenched in sweat, his hair lying wetly against his skull, and he still felt the heavy ache in his arm, the sting in his eyes from sweat and smoke.

"Bloody hell!" he said. "What the devil was *that?*"

2

Olivia Moreland sat back against the comfortably cushioned seat of the carriage. Her spine was ramrod-straight with irritation. The nerve of that man!

"Mad Morelands, indeed," she muttered.

It was an epithet she had heard all her life, and it rankled. Her family was not mad in the least; it was simply that all the rest of England's upper crust were narrow-minded, set-in-their-ways snobs.

Well, perhaps her grandparents had been a little strange, Olivia acknowledged in the interest of fairness. Her grandfather had been somewhat obsessive about some rather bizarre medical cures, and Grandmama had insisted that she had "the second sight." But her father was simply a scholar of antiquities, and her great-uncle Bellard was a shy, sweet man who loved history a great deal and stayed away from strangers with equal zeal. There was nothing odd in either of those things, she thought. Nor was there anything wrong with Aunt Penelope going off to France to sing opera, though everyone in society had reacted with as much horror as if she'd been transported to a penal colony.

The problem, she knew, was that her family thought differently and acted differently from the rest of society. Her mother's greatest sin in society's eyes, Olivia knew, had been to be born to minor country gentry instead of the nobility. Personally, Olivia suspected that this attitude was prompted simply by jealousy over the fact that she, a virtual nobody, had managed to snare the prize bachelor, the Duke of Broughton, when none of the titled debutantes had been able to. Olivia found her parents' meeting and subsequent marriage a charming love story. One of her father's many holdings upon his own father's early demise had been a factory. Her mother, an ardent social reformer, had managed to burst in upon a meeting between him and the manager of the factory, somehow evading all the minor clerks outside, and she had passionately put forward to him the rampant injustices in the treatment of his workers. The manager had moved to toss her out, but the duke had refused to allow him to do so and had heard her out. By the end of the afternoon, he, too, was seething at the plight of the workers and even more passionately in love with the redheaded, shapely reformer. She had also grown to love him, moving past her strong dislike of the nobility, money and power. They had married two months later, much to the dismay of the dowager duchess and most of the British peerage.

Olivia's mother, who held decided and innovative views on women's place in society, held equally unusual views on the education of children, and all seven of her children had been educated by tutors under the duchess's careful eye. The girls had received the same education as the boys, and all had been allowed to explore every manner of subject as their interests dictated, though their father had insisted on a basic grounding in Greek, Latin and ancient history. As a result, the entire brood was a well-educated lot, as well as an independent one. It was this combination of bookishness and independence that had caused most others in society to term them odd. Caring little for society's strictures, each of them had gone his or her own way.

Theo, the heir to the duke, had followed his passion of exploring, whereas his twin sister, Thisbe, had pursued the area of science, conducting experiments and writing papers on them. It was true, Olivia had to admit, that a few of Thisbe's experiments had gone awry. There had been a small shed on the country estate that had blown up during a study of explosives, and there had also been one or two fires, but, after all, it was in the interest of science and little damage had been done. It was excessively wrong, Olivia thought, to label Thisbe a pyromaniac, as some had done.

The younger twins, Alexander and Constantine, had gotten into a number of scrapes, but, really, what else could one expect from two lively, intellectually curious boys? It was a nuisance, of course, to find one's clock did not run because they had taken it apart to find out how it worked, and even Mother had been a trifle upset when they had ruined the Carrara marble floor in the conservatory trying to build a steam engine. It was an endeavor, the duchess had pointed out, that was better suited to one of the outbuildings behind the house. But the hot-air balloon incident, in Olivia's opinion, was entirely the fault of the owner of the balloon. Anyone with any sense would have known better than to leave two ten-year-old boys alone with one's empty-basketed balloon. And, anyway, they had managed to bring the thing down with a minimum of damage, hadn't they?

Kyria's "madness" in the eyes of society was that she refused to marry. And Reed — well, Olivia could not imagine how anyone could find Reed odd. He was the most normal and down-to-earth of them all, always the one to whom one turned in trouble, the one who would step in and right things. He took care of the family's finances and reined in their extravagances and kept the admittedly erratic path of the family ship somewhat straight.

Olivia knew that most would consider her profession a strange one. Indeed, most would consider it bizarre that a woman would have an occupation at all. But Olivia had been intrigued by the possibility of communication from the spirit world since she was a child and had listened with a combination of horror and fascination to her grandmother, the dowager duchess, tell her that she was possessed of second sight and suggest that Olivia was similarly inclined. Although Olivia was quite certain she possessed no such ability at all, she had wanted to study the subject. She saw no reason why one could not apply the tools of science, such as research, logic and experimentation, to the more nebulous world of spirits. Several scientists, indeed, were also exploring the claims of mediums and the possibility of communication with the dead, although it seemed to Olivia that they were all strangely inclined to ignore evidence of fraud and to seize upon any evidence that seemed to support the existence of spirits.

There was nothing wrong with any of the Morelands, Olivia thought staunchly as she got out of her carriage and marched up the front steps of the grand Broughton House. It was the rest of society who was wrong.

As she stepped inside the massive front door of the house, she was met by her twin brothers, who were taking turns jumping off the steps of the main staircase onto the black-and-white squared tile of the entry hall.

"Hallo!" Alexander called cheerfully, bending down to place a marker where his brother's feet had landed, then hurrying up to the same step from which his brother had jumped.

Constantine gave her a cheerful wave as he bounced up from the floor and went over to get a silver candlestick to use to mark his twin's progress.

"You might be careful," Olivia told them mildly. "You could crack your heads on that marble."

"We don't land on our heads," Con remarked scornfully.

Since her brothers had been jumping from the steps onto the marble since they were toddlers, Olivia had to admit that they were, in all likelihood, experts at it. "What are you marking?"

"How far we slide. You can't accurately measure your jumps from the stairs because you always slide. We've tried factoring in the slide, but one really cannot."

"Sometimes one slides a lot, and other times hardly at all," Alex put in. "Here I go, Con."

He jumped and slid, coming up short of Con's marker. "Blast!"

"Language, Alex," Olivia reproved automatically.

"So we thought, why not see who could slide the farthest?" Con finished the tale.

"I see." Olivia was well used to her brothers' competitions. Theo and Reed had been much the same, although to Reed's disgust, Theo had nearly always won, being two years older. "But why are you up so late?" Though her mother believed in freedom, she also had definite views on health, and her children, when young, were bound by early bedtimes. "And where is Mr. Thorndike?"

"Oh, him." Alex shrugged, dismissing their tutor. "He's sound asleep." The twins found sleep a boring and useless pastime and were seemingly able to run endlessly on sheer energy.

"I am sure he is exhausted after a day trying to keep up with you two," Olivia noted. "But that doesn't explain why you are up. Your bedtime was an hour ago."

Con grinned. "We have permission. Thisbe is going to take us out back for an astronomy lesson. We're just waiting for Desmond." He named Thisbe's husband, also a scientist. "He has an experiment running, and he won't be through until ten o'clock."

"Ah, there you are," Thisbe said as she came into the entry from the back hall. "I thought you were working on your Latin upstairs."

Con's mouth twisted in a grimace. "It made me sleepy. I hate Latin."

"Well, you can't get out of it," Thisbe said. "You know Papa insists on it. And, besides, you have to know Latin if you hope to be a biologist. Or a doctor," she added, turning her gaze to Alexander.

"On a more immediate note . . ." said an amused voice from above them, and they all looked up to see Kyria, in an elegant emerald-green gown, her flaming red hair done in an intricate pattern of curls, descending the stairs. "If either of you hopes to live past ten and a half, you might want to retrieve your boa constrictor. It was traveling down the hall toward the back stairs when I stepped out of my room just now. You know what Cook will do if it enters her kitchen."

The two boys, who had a healthy respect for Cook and the great metal cleaver she had threatened to use on the next "devilish serpent" that entered her domain, cast an alarmed glance at each other and started off at a run toward the kitchens.

"Hallo, Thisbe. Liv. Have you been out this evening?" Kyria cast a glance at Olivia's hat.

"Yes. How did you — oh!" Olivia realized that she had not removed her cloak and bonnet. She glanced back at the footman, who was still hovering behind her. "I'm sorry, Chambers. I quite forgot."

"Perfectly all right . . . miss." The footman had to force out the last word. He had not been here long, and it was still difficult for him to address Olivia with the egalitarian "miss" that she preferred instead of the "my lady" to which she'd been born.

Olivia handed him her cloak and hat and turned back to her sisters. Kyria had sauntered down the last few steps to the bottom of the staircase, but she still towered over Olivia by several inches, as did the willowy, dark-haired Thisbe. Olivia was dishearteningly accustomed to it. She was the only one in her family who was not tall, except for her great-uncle Bellard.

"Where are you off to?" she asked Kyria, who carried an elegant satin evening cloak over her arm.

"Lady Westerfield's soiree," Kyria answered. "It will probably be quite dull, but it was the best of the offerings tonight." She sighed. "The season is almost over."

"Oh, my, and whatever will you do?" Thisbe said with a large dose of sarcasm.

Kyria raised a brow at her sister. "Really, Thisbe, one doesn't have to mess about with chemicals to lead a worthwhile life."

"Of course not. But with your abilities, one ought —"

It was a long-standing argument — or discussion, as their mother preferred to call it — between the sober-minded Thisbe and her flamboyant, fun-loving younger sister, and Olivia cut in quickly to ward it off. "Kyria?"

"Yes, dear?" Kyria turned back to Olivia. She never minded her little tussles with Thisbe; in fact, she rather enjoyed them. But she was well aware that Olivia hated to see anyone in her family quarrel.

"Do you know — have you ever met Lord St. Leger?"

"Do you mean the new one? Or Roderick?"

"I — the new one, I suppose. Who is Roderick?"

"He was Lord St. Leger, but he died, oh, about a year ago. A hunting accident, as I remember."

"Well, no, this man was very much alive."

"You met him? Tonight?" Kyria's brows went up with interest. "Is he handsome?"

"Well, yes, I suppose one could say that. He has, well, rather devastating gray eyes, almost silver, one would say, if one were inclined to say things like that."

"I see." Kyria's eyes turned speculative. "Well, I'm afraid I don't know much about him. I have never met him. He came back to take over the title after his brother died, but he's been living on the estate ever since he returned. There has been a great deal of speculation about him, of course, because he is unmarried and something of a catch. Apparently he has been living in the United States for the past few years and made a fortune there. I didn't know he was even in London. How did you meet him?"

"He was at a séance that I went to tonight."

"He's one of those?" Thisbe asked with scorn.

"No. He doesn't seem to believe in it at all. I'm not sure why he was there, really, but he mistook me for an accomplice of the medium!" Her voice rose in remembered indignation.

"No! Why?"

"I had gotten up to go to the medium's cabinet and open it to show her untied and holding up those silly pictures she does — but then he grabbed me, and of course it was all ruined."

"He grabbed you?"

"Yes, by the arm. You see, he thought I was going to put on a ghost act myself. And of course there was a tremendous hubbub about it, and they ejected us from the séance."

Laughter bubbled up from Kyria's throat. "Oh my. That must have been quite a scene."

"Yes. But the thing is . . ." Olivia hesitated, and her sisters' attention sharpened.

"The thing is?" Thisbe prodded, and Kyria took Olivia's arm and guided her over to a bench against the wall of the entry. Gesturing for the footman, she handed him her cloak and motioned him away, then sat down on the bench with Olivia, Thisbe providing the opposite book-end.

"What is it?" Kyria questioned her in a low voice. "Are you — well, have you developed any *feeling* for this man?"

"Kyria!" Olivia gave her a horrified look. "No! How can you ask that? I just met him."

"Sometimes it does not take long," Thisbe, usually the most pragmatic and logical of the sisters, interjected.

"The thing is . . . well, when he grabbed my wrist, it jolted me. I actually screamed, I was so surprised. And scared."

"Of course. Who wouldn't be?" Kyria sympathized.

"But then they lit the lamp and I saw who my captor was, and the oddest thing happened. Even though I did not know him at all, and even though he was looking at me quite fiercely, I was no longer afraid."

"Well, I suppose you saw that he was a gentleman and not a ghost or some such. It is what we cannot see that is the most fearsome, ofttimes," Thisbe said.

"But it was more than that. I felt the oddest sensation. This sort of tingle ran up my arm, and for just an instant I felt — oh, I don't know. This sounds mad, I know, but I felt as if I knew him. Yet at the same time I was sure that I had never seen him before. Of course then he made me quite irritated, and the feeling fled. But still . . . there was that instant. I don't know what to make of it."

For a moment both sisters looked at her. Then Thisbe said calmly, "It's chemistry."

"What?"

"That moment of attraction. It is all a chemical reaction. I'm convinced of it. I remember the moment I met Desmond. I have never been so startled in my life by the shiver that ran through me when he turned his eyes to mine. And when he reached out and touched my arm, I felt it all through me. Chemistry."

"No! I'm not going to marry the man!" Olivia cried out in protest. "I told you, I scarcely know him. He was perfectly odious, too. Not only did he ruin my chance to expose that dreadful Mrs.

Terhune, but then he had the audacity to call us the 'mad Morelands.' Right to my face!"

"No!" Kyria's green eyes flamed with anger.

But Thisbe shrugged philosophically. "They all do. It's their narrow minds. One really has to feel sorry for them."

"Well, I don't," Kyria said. "I give them a piece of my mind. And if that is the sort of man Lord St. Leger is, then you are better not to feel anything for him." She reached out and took Olivia's hand. "Come with me to the soiree, Livvy. We'll search for a gentleman good enough for you — well, that's not possible, I suppose, but at least one who measures up as well as a man can."

Olivia gave her a faint smile. "No. Really, Kyria. I'm not interested in Lord St. Leger or any other man. I am fine just as I am. I enjoy what I do, and a gentleman would only inter-fere." She smiled over at Thisbe. "Men such as Desmond are few and far between, I'm afraid. To find a man who respects one's mind and one's career, even shares it — well, *rare* isn't even the word for such a man." She sighed un-consciously.

Beside her, Kyria echoed the sigh. Then she summoned up her usual glittering smile. "It is just as well that I decided never to marry, isn't it? Still, there is fun to be had. Please, do come with me."

But Olivia shook her head, saying, "No. I am a bit tired, I'm afraid. And I must work tomorrow. There is correspondence to be answered, and . . ." Her voice trailed off. "I fear I have forever lost the opportunity to expose that charlatan Mrs. Terhune. Still, there are other avenues to explore."

"Of course." Thisbe patted her youngest sister's hand, and Kyria accepted Olivia's refusal with a philosophical shrug. She was well aware that, despite Olivia's fierceness if a loved one or a cause was threatened, she was a rather shy creature, not at home among crowds. Crushes such as Lady Westerfield's tonight would at worst make her uneasy and nervous, and at best bore her.

Olivia watched as her beautiful sister let the footman help her on with her cloak, then swept out the door. She turned back to Thisbe, but at that moment the twins came in, accompanied this time by Desmond, a quietly good-looking man who usually wore a faint air of abstraction.

"We got the snake in time," Con announced with satisfaction. "Cook never even saw it."

"And we ran into Desmond in the kitchen," Alex added, pulling Desmond forward. "We're ready now, aren't we, Thisbe?"

"Ready for what?" Desmond asked vaguely, and had to be reminded of his promise to starwatch with his wife and the twins. He seemed, however, quite pleased with the notion once he was told about it. "Jolly night for it. Not often you get such a clear sky in the city. Do you have your telescope?"

It seemed the boys did, tucked under the staircase, where it could come to no harm during their jumping from the stairs, and they had also brought a blanket, a lantern and a small sack of fruit for a midnight snack. They asked Olivia to join them, but although she normally would have done so, she demurred, pleading tiredness from her own adventure that evening.

In truth she was not tired so much as desirous of being alone. She wanted to think about the evening and go over what had happened and what had been said. The feeling she had experienced when she looked into Lord St. Leger's eyes had been so odd . . . and though she was certain that it was nothing to do with being attracted to the man, either emotionally or chemically, as her sisters had suggested, she was not sure to what she could attribute that brief frisson of awareness that had run through her.

So she went upstairs and undressed, then sat by the window, wrapped in a brocade dressing gown, and brushed out her long hair. She typically did not require the attendance of a maid, for she wore her hair in a simple, practical style, low on her neck in a bun, that she was able to put up and take down without assistance. She also favored pragmatic clothes, with bodices that buttoned up the front and no whalebone corset that had to be yanked and tugged and tied into place to give her a minuscule waist. It was another of her mother's dicta, adopted by her daughters, not to endanger one's health with constricting corsets for the absurdity of an eighteen-inch waist. Therefore, she rarely needed help in getting undressed, either. Olivia deemed a personal maid an unnecessary luxury for herself, and besides, she usually preferred to be alone with her thoughts rather than listening to a maid's chatter.

Brushing her hair normally relaxed her, but she found that this evening it did not, and her thoughts remained unaccustomedly scattered. She could not seem to concentrate, and she rose more than once to pace about the room. She could not figure out why she had felt as she did when she first saw Lord St. Leger, and it irritated her that she was so concerned with the subject. She kept thinking of things she should have said or done, witty remarks that would have put the man in his place. It was some time before she settled down enough to go to bed, and even then, it took her some time to fall asleep. It was another disagreeable problem to lay at Lord St. Leger's door, she thought. She wished she could see him again, just to give him a piece of her mind.

She spent a rather restless night and arose early the next morning. The only person at breakfast was her great-uncle, Bellard, who smiled with pleasure at seeing her. He was a quiet man usually, but Olivia was his favorite relative, and today he was full of news about the arrival the day before of his latest acquisition, a full complement of French and English soldiers, made out of tin and perfectly replicated down to each tiny ribbon or epaulet the armies of Napoleon and Wellington at Waterloo. Her uncle was a history buff, and his particular pleasure was recreating famous battles in history. On the third floor in this huge house, not far from the nursery, was a huge room given over entirely to tables on which the terrain and participants of such epic clashes as Nelson's victory at Trafalgar, in which glass painted blue carried replicas of the ships involved, and Churchill's win at Blenheim were laid out with exactitude.

A thin man, somewhat hunched over from years of poring over books and tabletop armies, Bellard was often subject to chills, especially in the poorly heated upper reaches of the house, and he was given to wearing a soft cap over his wispy white hair. A beaked nose gave him a look somewhat reminiscent of a bird, but the smile beneath it was so gentle and sweet that no one who saw it ever thought of considering him odd. He was simply Great-uncle Bellard, and his great-nieces and -nephews loved him.

After breakfast, Olivia returned with him to his workroom to review the tin figures he had unpacked, and then she left the house, a plain brown bonnet on her head to match her plain brown dress, whose severe lines were softened only by a conservative bustle in back, below which the garment fell in rows of ruffles of the same material, its one touch of frivolity. Her only ornamentation was a sensible gold watch hanging from a brooch on her chest.

The ducal carriage took her, as it did every morning, and deposited her in front of the door of a modest building containing a few offices. Olivia climbed the stairs to her second-floor office, where the door sported the same discreet title as her business card.

"Hello, Tom," she said as she reached the door, taking out her key to unlock it.

Tom Quick, her assistant, sat on the floor beside the door, his shaggy yellow head turned down to the book in his lap. He jumped up at her words, grinning, and closed the book. "Good morning, miss. 'Ow are you this fair day?"

"Well, I believe, Tom. No need to ask you. You are obviously in good spirits."

"Not from any misdoin'," he assured her quickly.

Tom had been one of her brother Reed's projects, a pickpocket whom he had caught attempting to steal his wallet some years ago. Reed had recognized the bright mind behind the dirty face, and instead of turning the lad in to the authorities, he had provided for his schooling. At her brother's suggestion, Olivia had hired him for her office assistant two years ago and had never regretted it. No one, including Tom, knew his actual age or name;

Quick had been an appellation given him for the speed with which he could pick a pocket. He was, Olivia judged, somewhere between sixteen and eighteen, with a worldly-wise view of life far beyond his years. Slavishly devoted to both Reed and Olivia, Tom refused to leave her, though Olivia was sure that he could have earned more as a clerk for a larger firm. She also suspected, though she had never confronted him about it, that Tom and Reed considered his job more one of unobtrusively protecting Olivia than of actually clerking.

" 'Ow'd it go last night?" Tom asked as she unlocked the door and they went inside.

He went around raising the shades on the windows while Olivia walked over to her desk. "Not well at all, I'm afraid." She described as briefly as she could the contretemps that had arisen at the séance the night before, spoiling her plans.

Tom reacted with appropriate shock and dismay. "That's 'orrible, miss. Wot are you goin' to do now?"

"Forget Mrs. Terhune, I'm afraid. It wasn't even a paying case. I am just so incensed at her foisting those obvious daguerrotypes off as ghosts. Anyone can see that they are flat."

"Anyone except her followers," Tom pointed out.

"I know. I suppose I should let them be deceived, if they are so foolish." Olivia sighed.

"There's some as are born marks, miss, and

that's the truth." He came over and perched on the edge of her desk. "I guess we'll 'ave to start lookin' into somethin' else, wot do you say?"

"I'd love to," Olivia admitted, glancing over her tidily arranged desk. "The only problem is, I haven't any cases."

The business, never robust, had trickled down to almost nothing in the past year. Olivia had spent much of her time conducting investigations on her own, compiling evidence of the tricks used by the mediums.

"You're never thinkin' of givin' up, are you, miss?" Tom looked faintly horrified.

"No. I won't give up. I cannot stand to think of these people fleecing the bereaved, taking advantage of people at their most vulnerable. . . . It is just that I am at something of a standstill. We have no new cases. I have done research until I'm not sure what to look into anymore. I cannot force my way into people's homes and say, 'Look here, let me prove to you that that man is lying when he says he can communicate with your dead mother or husband or whoever.' "

"Well, look on the bright side. We might get a new customer any time now. Until then, we'll just make do."

"Yes. Of course, you're right." She gave him a smile. "I shall get to work writing up my experiences last night, and we can close that file."

She pulled out a sheet of paper and dipped her pen in the inkwell, then settled down to do as she had said. She found it rather difficult, however, to put into words what had happened the night before without it sounding completely foolish and unscientific. No matter how she couched it, she could not get around the fact that Lord St. Leger had grabbed her arm, and she had screamed, and they had wound up getting thrown out of the séance.

Olivia had finally finished sweating through the report and was tucking the file away in a cabinet marked Closed when there was the sound of footsteps on the stairs. She could not help glancing up expectantly, waiting for the steps to stop outside their door, even though she knew that there were two other offices on this floor and more above it, and the odds were the steps would not stop here. Indeed, hardly anyone ever came here, except members of her family now and then.

There was a sharp rap at the door, and Olivia jumped, startled. She glanced over at Tom, who nodded at her with a grin before he jumped up and walked over to open the door. He pulled it open to reveal a tall man standing in the hall. The man looked at Tom, somewhat surprised, then past him into the office, his gaze coming to rest on Olivia.

Olivia simply stared at him, stunned. She had never expected to see this man again. Excitement leaped in her stomach, even as the rest of her seemed frozen. Her reaction annoyed her. She swallowed and forced her legs to move, propelling her up and toward the door.

"Lord St. Leger," she said, pleased that her voice came out cool and calm. "What a surprise. Please, do come in."

St. Leger took off his hat and stepped past Tom, who was regarding him with great interest. He stopped and glanced around the office somewhat awkwardly. "I . . . um . . ."

"Are you in need of some investigating, sir?" Tom jumped in, reaching to take Lord St. Leger's hat and hang it on the rack by the door. "You've come to the right place, then. There's none better than us for tracking down those psychic phenomena."

"Are there any others?" St. Leger asked, faintly surprised.

"Well, um . . ." Tom looked abashed, but quickly recovered. "No, you're right. We're not only the best at it, we're the only."

"Lord St. Leger, please, sit down." Olivia gestured toward the chair beside her desk, ready for a customer to sit down and spill out his problem. She cast Tom a quelling look.

Her assistant cocked an eyebrow but hung back, sitting down at his desk and pretending to be busy sorting papers.

Lord St. Leger went to the chair Olivia had indicated, politely waiting for her to take her seat behind the desk before he sat down. Olivia looked at him, waiting. He looked at her, then away, then cleared his throat. An awkward silence stretched between them. Across the room, Tom moved restively in his seat.

Finally Olivia said, "Is there some way that I can be of assistance to you, my lord?"

"I —" He looked at her and sighed. "Frankly, I don't know. Lady Ol—"

"I prefer Miss Moreland," Olivia said. His eyes, she thought, were really a most extraordinary color, even brighter here in the well-lit room than they had been last night. Silver — or perhaps pewter was a closer color.

"Miss Moreland," he repeated. "I — I am afraid that we got off on the wrong foot last night."

"You might say that, if you consider seizing me and accusing me of being a charlatan and later calling me mad 'getting off on the wrong foot.' "

Faint color stained his cheekbones, and he looked abashed. "I did not mean — I was simply surprised when I realized who you were, and the phrase popped out. It was something I had heard over the years, and, well, in my surprise, I didn't think. I apologize sincerely, and I assure you that I do not think that you — or your family — is insane. I am sure no one does. It is merely a — a silly appellation."

Olivia continued to gaze at him coolly, and finally he went on. "I apologize, too, for accusing you of being Mrs. Terhune's assistant. However, you have to admit that there were circumstances that made it seem that you were." His eyes flashed as he said, "The scene at the séance was not entirely my fault."

When Olivia did not answer, he sighed and stood up. "I can see I am wasting my time here."

"No! No, wait." Olivia popped up, too, and extended a hand as if to detain him, then blushed and let it fall to her side. "I accept your apology. What is it that you want? What can we do for you?"

He hesitated, then sat back down. "I'm not sure — well, what exactly is it that you do here?"

"We investigate the occurrence of certain odd and inexplicable events."

"Ghosts?" he asked with an ironic undertone.

"I have never been called upon to investigate ghosts, my lord. In general, it is the people who call themselves mediums and their practices which I have investigated."

"Like Mrs. Terhune last night."

"Precisely."

"Why?"

"Because I dislike fraud, my lord, and I find it reprehensible that someone deceives people, often those grieving for a dead loved one, by pretending that he or she can communicate with the dead, in particular those departed loved ones."

"Then you don't believe they can communicate with the spirits from beyond?"

"I have never found one yet who did," Olivia returned crisply. "None of them have offered proof that satisfied me."

"Do you know a woman named Madame Valenskaya?"

"I have heard of her," Olivia replied. "I have not met the woman myself."

"Do you think that she can communicate with spirits?"

"I have not investigated her, but based on my experience with other mediums, I would say that it is highly unlikely. In general, Lord St. Leger, mediums employ a number of tricks to make it appear that so-called spirits are in the room with them. They insist on having the right atmosphere in the room, which generally means the room must be in darkness or very low light. Then the 'spirits' visit them in the form of rappings or sometimes as luminous things floating in the air, or even ghostly looking people. They will offer 'proof' that they are not themselves causing these things to occur. This 'proof' usually comes in the form of their having everyone hold hands around a circle, so that someone on either side is holding the medium's hand. They even have the people on either side place their foot upon each of the medium's feet under the table. Then when the rapping comes, the people on either side can vouch that the medium did not use her hands or feet."

"So how do they accomplish the rappings?"

"Some, like the Fox sisters, said that they were able to crack their toes inside their shoes and even their knees, as well, to produce the rapping. They will wear shoes that are too big for their feet, so that they can pull their foot down inside the shoe and crack the toes or even

pull their feet out of the shoe altogether. Then they can crack their toes or raise their knee and knock against the underside of the table. Another common ruse is to have an accomplice in the group, and that person sits on one side of the medium. He will say that he held the medium's hand throughout the course of the séance, but in reality, one of her hands is free. Also, under cover of darkness, the medium can arrange it so that the innocent person on the other side of her is actually taking hold of her accomplice's hand and foot instead of her own. Then she is free to flit around the room doing whatever she pleases."

Olivia, warming to her subject, stood up and went to a nearby cabinet, opening it to reveal a number of items inside. "This bottle contains phosphorescent paint. They can paint it on whatever object they wish to hang in the air in a ghostly glowing way — a popular one is a trumpet. They can put it on a piece of thin cloth, such as gauze, and when they are free of the table, they — or an accomplice who was not even in the room to begin with — can drape this gauze over themselves, and in the dark they give off the appearance of a ghost. I have known intelligent, even scientific, gentleman to be completely won over by the appearance of one of these 'ghosts.' "

St. Leger came over to the cabinet and stood beside her. Olivia was tinglingly aware of his presence, the heat of his large body, the faint smell of shaving soap that clung to his skin. St. Leger looked down dubiously at the length of gauze and the tin toy trumpet and harp that had all been painted with phosphorescent paint. At length he said, "It's absurd. Why would anyone believe these things?"

"Well, they are more impressive viewed in the dark, glowing and seeming suspended in air," Olivia pointed out. "There is heightened tension. People are waiting for the unknown, hoping, and probably a little fearful. And if one believes, as these people do, that the medium is still firmly planted in her chair, then it must seem that these things appear freely, just hanging magically in the air. Even I, I confess, have felt a little shiver down my spine when one has appeared. And I know how the tricks are done."

"What is that?" He pointed to a short black rod, narrow in diameter, with a clamp on one end.

"A telescoping rod," Olivia explained, taking the rod out and pulling it out to its full length of four feet. "They can hold the objects up quite high with this, but then it can be pushed back down to a foot and easily concealed, like the other things in their capacious pockets. You will notice that the mediums always wear rather full garments, with plenty of room for deep pockets inside, where they do not show. Few people will insist on searching a medium's body that closely. It would be considered impolite."

He nodded. "What about this cabinet thing that Mrs. Terhune was locked in?"

"Oh, that is another 'proof' that the medium is not the person committing the acts those in attendance see. The medium sits down on a chair inside the cabinet, and she is tied up as Mrs. Terhune was. In these instances, the medium is skilled at getting out of knots or she has an accomplice who makes sure that the knots are loosely tied, or a combination of both. Then the door is closed and even sometimes locked. The lamp is turned out, so that no one can see, and sometimes the group is encouraged to sing to welcome the spirits. The singing helps to cover any noises the medium makes getting out of her ropes inside the box. Then she'll put on the phosphorescent gauze and leave the box, or even just stand inside it and let her head show over the door, or hold up a painted glove or trumpet or such. Mrs. Terhune holds up pictures of people's heads. It is quite ludicrous to see, except that most of the people there believe they are ghosts. Then the medium ties herself back up, and when the guests open the door again, she pretends to come out of her trance and wants to know what happened."

St. Leger frowned. "It all seems so simple. So obvious."

"It is. But most people don't look at what they see critically or logically. They want the medium to be genuine. They want to believe their loved one can still see them and talk to them.

They want to believe that life goes on after one dies. It is easy to believe when one wants to so much."

"I suppose." St. Leger looked at her thoughtfully. "If you were to go to a medium's séance, could you spot the tricks? Could you expose her?"

"I think so. It might take a few times. Spotting what she does is not as difficult as proving it. I can explain what tricks I think she uses, but usually the victim is so eager to believe the medium is real that I would have to catch her in the act to make the victim believe that it's a trick."

He nodded. Olivia watched him. She could almost see the thoughts turning in his head. She wondered who it was who was being deceived by a medium — presumably Madame Valenskaya, since he had mentioned her — and what relation the victim was to Lord St. Leger.

"What is it you would like me to do?" she asked finally.

He looked at her. "I want you to come to my home in the country for a few weeks."

3

For a long moment Olivia simply stared at him. Across the room, Tom made a noise, quickly covered by a cough.

Finally she said, "I beg your pardon?"

St. Leger colored faintly, realizing how his words had sounded. Stephen did not understand why everything he said to this woman seemed to come out wrong. As soon as he had stepped inside the door and seen her again, he had been touched by that strange, elusive feeling he had experienced when he first looked at her. Then, for some reason, the dream he had had last night had come back to him, making him feel even stranger. It had been a peculiar dream, more vivid and real than any he could ever remember having, and having absolutely nothing to do with anything in his life. It was even more peculiar for his mind to keep returning to it during the day. The whole time he had been here, he thought, he had been extraordinarily inarticulate. It must be, he thought, that he was embarrassed to reveal his family's vagaries to a stranger.

"I am sorry," he said. "I know I must sound . . . odd. I have not told you what the problem is. The thing is —" He paused. "I trust you are discreet, as you say on your card?"

"Yes, of course. Neither Tom, my assistant, nor I would ever reveal anything of which you spoke to us."

"It is not for myself that I worry. But my mother — my mother has been very distraught with grief for the past year. My older brother died, and she took it very hard, of course. This summer she brought my sister to London. And since she has been here, she has taken up with Madame Valenskaya. She thinks that the woman can communicate with the dead. I was not too worried at first. I assumed it was harmless enough. But I found out that she has been giving the woman quite valuable possessions. I fear Madame Valenskaya is taking advantage of her. She manipulates her. I'm certain of it. Somehow she worked Lady St. Leger around to inviting her to our estate in the country, now that the season is over — and Madame's daughter and her patron, as well, a chap named Howard Babington."

"Oh. I see."

"I am not a tyrant. I could scarcely tell her that she could not invite them. She is completely enamored of this woman. . . ."

Olivia nodded sympathetically. "It makes it difficult."

"It occurred to me that perhaps you could investigate Madame Valenskaya. But of course, since she is going to be at Blackhope with us, you would have to come there. However, that might be easier if you could come as a guest, also. She wouldn't have to know that you are investigating her. Is she likely to know what you do?"

"I wouldn't think so. I'm not that famous. Few enough people have taken advantage of my services."

"Then I would be most grateful if you could come. If, of course, you are willing to do so."

"Yes, of course." Olivia saw no point in telling him that the prospect of spending a good deal of time with him in the same house made her heart speed up and her throat turn dry. She was not accustomed to being a guest at country house parties. She was not a social person, as was Kyria, and she certainly wasn't used to spending time in such close proximity to any male who was not a member of her family or Tom.

"It, ah, might actually be easier to catch her out in a house with which she is not familiar," Olivia went on. "When the séances are held in the medium's own home or that of her accomplice, they can rig up various things in the room — wires that let down the objects that appear in midair, trapdoors in the floor through which something or someone can rise up, that sort of thing. The easiest to do in one's own home is to have an accomplice hidden in the next room to do the rappings on the wall between the rooms.

But in your house, there would be no access to any of those things."

"Then you'll do it?"

"Yes. But Tom must come with me. My assistant."

He glanced at Tom, who was grinning from ear to ear at the prospect of an adventure. "Yes, of course, if you wish."

"He can be one of my servants, you know, for helping with the bags and such." Tom looked less pleased at this idea, and Olivia told him, "That way you can investigate through the servants, listen to the gossip. And people talk much more freely in front of servants than others, and they don't question your being in a guest's room, generally."

Tom brightened. "That's right. Mayhap this Madame will have a servant, too, and I can get 'em to talk."

"Yes. That would be wonderful." Excitement was growing in Olivia. She had never had such a splendid opportunity to investigate a medium before — a long period of time and the host's permission. Her eyes shone as she looked up at Stephen. "Lord St. Leger, I appreciate this sincerely."

"Stephen," he said.

"I beg your pardon?"

"My name is Stephen. Surely if we know each other well enough for me to invite you to a house party, you should call me by my given name."

"Oh!" Olivia felt a flush start on her cheeks,

74

and she was embarrassed that such a simple thing should discombobulate her so. "Stephen. Of course. And my name is Olivia."

"Olivia." He reached out and took her hand, bending a little and brushing his lips against it in a courtly fashion. "Thank you. I shall look forward to your arrival. My mother will write you an invitation posthaste."

Olivia firmly squelched the little flutter in her insides that his words caused. He wanted her help, that was all. "What — who are you going to tell her that I am?"

"A friend," he replied, and his mouth crooked up into a grin. "Mother will be so delighted that a duke's daughter is coming that I am sure she will not inquire too deeply into it."

Olivia said nothing, but she had her doubts. Mothers, in her experience, rarely required so little elaboration as that.

Her own family, predictably, reacted to her announcement of her intended journey with a plethora of questions. She told them at the supper table, feeling that it was easiest to get it over with all at once.

Her mother, naturally, narrowed her sharp green eyes and said, "St. Leger? Who is he? How does he feel about the women's vote?"

"I don't know, Mother. I haven't actually asked him."

"Well, what could be more important to know about a man?" her mother countered. Tall, with flaming red hair now somewhat tempered by

75

streaks of gray, she was a commanding woman, and Olivia generally felt inadequate when talking to her.

"Some would say the condition of his pockets," Kyria put in lightly.

The duchess favored her red-haired daughter, so much an image of her in looks, with a grimace. "Honestly, Kyria, one would think you were frivolous, the way you talk."

"Yes, Mama, I am afraid so."

"Who is this chap?" the duke put in mildly. "Lord St. Leger? Do I know him?"

"He's back from the United States." Olivia's brother Reed spoke up. "Younger brother. Inherited his title from Roderick St. Leger. He died some time back in a hunting accident."

"Didn't know the fellow," the duke said dismissively.

"I knew Roderick somewhat," Reed added. "He went to my club." He shrugged. "An ordinary sort, I would have said. I don't know the present earl." He looked at Olivia. "What I am wondering is how you know him. I heard he'd been at his estate ever since he came back to England."

"He is here now," Olivia replied, adding, "I met him at a social gathering a few days ago."

"Social gathering?" Thisbe's husband Desmond asked, looking surprised. "You went to a par — ow!" He broke off and cast a wounded look at his wife, reaching down surreptitiously to rub his leg.

"Yes, Olivia told Kyria and me about him the other night," Thisbe said airily. "We were discussing the, um, party where she met him."

"You mean you barely know the man?" Reed asked, frowning.

"Oh, don't turn big brother on us," Kyria said, shooting him a loving but teasing glance. "As if Olivia doesn't know what she's doing! If Olivia feels that it is all right to attend this house party, then that is all we need to know, isn't it, Mama?"

"Quite right, Kyria." The duchess leveled a stern look at her son. "Reed, dear, Olivia is a grown woman and quite capable of deciding what she should or should not do without having to answer to the men of the family."

"Yes, of course, Mother." Reed sent Kyria a disgruntled glance. "If it were Kyria, of course, I would not say anything."

"Liar," Kyria stuck in.

"Kyria, don't be disrespectful," the duchess told her.

"But Olivia is not as sophisticated as Kyria," Reed said.

"Yes, but I'm not stupid, either," Olivia flared. "I think I can tell whether a man is a villain or not."

She would have liked to tell them that she was going in a professional capacity, not attending a social function, but, mindful of her promise to St. Leger to keep the matter quiet, she felt she could not. She could trust Reed, of course, not to tell anyone, but she wasn't as sure about the rest of them. They were not gossips, but such social matters held little interest for her mother, and her father was rather vague; there was no surety that they would remember that they were supposed to keep the matter quiet. They would all be likely to talk about it among themselves, too, and servants soaked up the gossip. It would soon be all over town. So she kept quiet. Besides, it was, she thought, rather pleasant to have them think that she was actually the object of a man's interest.

"I did not mean that, Livvy," Reed protested.

"I've never heard they were villains," Great-uncle Bellard piped up suddenly, surprising them all. They all turned to look at him as he continued. "Old family. Title goes back to Elizabeth, or maybe it was Henry VIII. Unbroken line, I believe. There are a few legends surrounding them. I'm not sure offhand . . . I think one of them hid King Charles I from the Roundheads. I'll have to look them up." He smiled at the prospect of doing some research. "Their ancestral home is something oddly named. Bleak — no, Blackhope! That's it. Blackhope Hall."

"Ooh," Kyria said, wiggling her eyebrows. "That sounds ominous."

"Really, Kyria, you read far too many gothic novels," the duchess said disapprovingly. "I am sure there is nothing ominous about the place. Old houses frequently acquire the most peculiar names. Isn't that right, Uncle Bellard?"

"Oh, yes, indeed," the old man agreed, nodding happily.

"Well, *I* think it sounds romantic," Kyria said decisively. "You know, the sort of place where one might get swept off one's feet."

"I should hope not!" the duchess exclaimed, and turned to give her youngest daughter a worried look.

"I am not going to get swept off my feet," Olivia retorted firmly, casting her sister a dark look. "I promise."

"I suppose not," Kyria admitted with a sigh. "Still, there's nothing to say you can't make a conquest. Let's go to your room after supper and look through your wardrobe. Surely we can find something that Joan can give some spark to."

"My wardrobe!" Olivia squeaked. "But why? I don't want a spark."

"Nonsense. Whether you want one or not, you deserve one," Kyria retorted firmly.

Olivia suppressed a groan. She had no desire to have Kyria exclaiming in horror over her clothes all evening, but she knew that she hadn't a hope of stopping her strong-minded sister. She gave in with ill grace, trailing up the stairs after Kyria when the evening meal was over.

"I don't see why I can't wear what I always do," Olivia complained, even though she knew it was useless.

Kyria turned and cast an expressive look at Olivia's plain brown skirt and bodice. "Olivia, this is a party. You can't go looking as though you are the family governess."

"I am not trying to 'catch' Lord St. Leger," Olivia retorted huffily.

"Then why are you going?"

Olivia looked into her sister's clear green gaze, and her own eyes fell. "I — well, that is, Lord St. Leger and I are friends. That is all."

"Then it is up to you to change that." Kyria yanked on the bellpull and, when one of the maids popped in a moment later, sent the girl to fetch Joan, Kyria's personal maid.

"I don't understand why you are always trying to set me up with someone when you yourself are so set against marriage," Olivia said feelingly.

"I am not set against marriage," Kyria told her. For a flickering moment, sadness seemed to shadow her face, then was gone as she said, "It simply isn't for me, you see." She went to Olivia's wardrobe closet and threw open the door, continuing, "But for others, it's exactly right. Look at Thisbe, for instance. She's happy as can be with her scientist."

"I can't imagine why you think that I am right for marriage. I have never had the slightest success with men."

Kyria looked at her. "Being an accomplished flirt and being a good wife are entirely different things. Trust me. You are exactly the kind of person who makes an excellent wife, someone whose life is completed by having a husband

and children. You are sweet and kind and generous, utterly loyal and enormously loving."

"But so are you," Olivia protested.

Kyria let out a light laugh. "That you think so, my love, is an indication of your sweetness, not mine."

Kyria went through Olivia's clothes, sighing now and then or shaking her head. "Honestly, Livvy, must you always choose such plain things? Where is that shawl I gave you last year?"

Olivia opened a drawer and pulled it out, caressing it as she handed it to Kyria. It was a beautiful silk shawl, patterned in golds and browns, with brown tassels hanging from it.

"Now, this will dress up your brown silk," Kyria told her, draping it over the aforesaid gown.

"But, Kyria, I won't be needing anything so — so fancy."

"Why not? You will need nicer than this, my dear."

"But it will not be a — a festive gathering," Olivia said. "I — he — we merely have common interests. And it is a small group. His brother, you know, died not long ago."

"A year. They are out of mourning by now. I've seen the girl at parties — small ones, of course. I suspect there will be a party or two, at least. There always is. And there is supper every evening. You have to dress for that, after all."

"Well, yes, I suppose. . . ." Olivia cast a look at

the gown and shawl. It warmed her a little to think of wearing them, of looking, well, if not beautiful, at least not *drab*. After all, this was an occasion where she really did not have to look professional. They were hiding what she was doing under the guise of a house party. She was supposed to look like nothing other than a woman enjoying a social occasion.

"This gown will do, as well, I think," Kyria went on, taking out an emerald-green evening gown, "though Joan will have to pull out all this lace in the bodice."

"But the neckline will be far too low!" Olivia protested.

"The neckline will be fashionable," Kyria countered. "And you have a very nice bosom. It's time you showed it off a little."

Kyria's maid, Joan, a thin, plain girl with a haughty manner, came into the room. She was, according to Kyria, a jewel, having an excellent sense of color and style and being handy with a needle, as well as possessing a deft hand when it came to arranging one's hair, and Kyria was much envied by other young women and matrons for having her. However, there was little chance of any of them being able to entice her away from Kyria, since Kyria had plucked her out of an orphanage at the age of thirteen, recognizing her artistic bent, and had taken Joan's younger and rather slow-witted sister, as well, when Joan had pleaded that she could not leave without her. Joan was intensely loyal to her mistress and quite proud of her position as personal maid to the daughter of a duke, a far higher rung up the ladder of employment than she had ever hoped to reach.

With Joan's help, Kyria went ruthlessly through Olivia's clothes, pulling out the pieces she thought would do and deciding how to give them the desired "spark" — a smattering of lace at throat and cuffs to soften too severe a line, or a brooch or necklace to brighten a dull color, or a bit of embroidery to color a pale gray bodice. But nothing that Olivia owned satisfied either Kyria or Joan as a gown to wear to a dance or party, and they at last brought in two of Kyria's own gowns — a peacock-blue satin and a dark gold silk that were both so beautiful that Olivia could not imagine them on herself — and Joan set to shortening and tucking and taking in here and there to fit Olivia's shorter, slighter frame. Joan, Kyria assured her, was a marvel and would have the dresses done in time for her trip.

"Or she can finish one of them while you are there, of course," she added casually.

"What?" Olivia stared at her. "What do you mean, while I am there? Joan will not be with me."

"But of course she will. You must have someone to do your hair, after all, and since you haven't a maid of your own, this will be the perfect solution. She's an absolute wizard with hair. You'll see."

"But I don't need a maid. That is precisely

why I haven't one. I can do my own hair, and all my gowns are made so I can fasten them without help."

"Yes, I know you are very independent and self-sufficient," Kyria said. "But you simply cannot go to a house party without even one servant. How would it look to Lady St. Leger?"

"As though I am sensible?" Olivia retorted. "No one needs the full-time services of a maid, least of all me."

"Yes, yes, I know your views on the subject. But just this one time? For me?" Kyria smiled persuasively at her. "And think of Joan — she would love a trip, wouldn't you, Joan?"

Joan looked faintly surprised but quickly agreed. "Oh, yes, my lady, a trip would be lovely."

Olivia sighed and, after a few more token protests, gave up. A maid was unnecessary, and she did not, after all, need to appear any lovelier than she really was, but . . . she could not help but think with pleasure of how she would look in the made-over dresses and wonder what Lord St. Leger would think of the changes.

So it was that when she set off the next week for her trip to Lord St. Leger's estate, she carried in her trunks two stunning gowns made over from Kyria's stock and a number of her own clothes remade into far prettier frocks, and was accompanied on the train ride by two supposed servants. It was pure vanity, she knew, that she could not help but admire the new look of her travel-durable plain brown gown, now softened by a collar that framed her throat gracefully and decorated at the shoulder with a jaunty bit of gold braid. Joan had insisted on doing Olivia's hair this morning, and though she had kept the general style of a bun at the nape of her neck to which Olivia was accustomed, she had somehow made the hair around her face softer and fuller instead of pulled back tightly into a knot. It was strange, Olivia thought, how she could look so much the same and yet so much prettier. She was unaware of how her own inner excitement had added a glow to her cheeks and a sparkle to her brown eyes.

Her little party was met at the train station in the village by St. Leger's carriage and coachman. Tom helped the coachman stow their bags, then climbed up to the high seat to ride with him, while Olivia and Joan got inside. The plush seats were comfortable and the carriage well sprung, and Joan soon nodded off as the coach swayed rhythmically along, but Olivia was far too tense and excited to rest. She pushed back the curtain nearest her and looked out at the countryside that rolled by, eager to catch her first glimpse of Blackhope.

Finally she saw it, its light stone walls glowing almost golden in the rays of the setting sun — a sturdy Norman keep with steep blank outer walls, castellated at the top, and behind them the taller upthrust of the round tower, its stone walls broken only by narrow archer slits in the traditional shape of a cross. She drew in her breath sharply, some deep emotion stabbing into her chest.

For a moment the image shimmered before her, and then, as she blinked, it was gone.

Olivia stared in amazement, her heart picking up its beat. The house that lay on the hill in the distance was no ancient castle built for warfare but a sprawling stone mansion of differing levels, obviously added onto and enlarged, its only resemblance to the keep she had seen a moment before the fact that it was built of the same sort of light stone warmed by the dying light of the sun.

She leaned closer to the window, scarcely able to believe her eyes. She closed her eyes and re-opened them slowly. Still the more modern house lay there. There was no ancient Norman keep.

Olivia sat back, clasping her hands together in her lap. She was glad that Kyria's maid was not awake to see the doubtless stunned expression on her face. *What had she just seen?*

She could picture the castle in her mind's eye — flags fluttering from the top of the battlements, the drawbridge down and huge gates open. *It had been so clear, so real!* Olivia leaned over and once again looked out the window. Still no castle sat on the horizon, only the graceful house.

As they drew nearer the house, she stared at it intently, trying to determine how her eye had somehow been tricked into thinking that she had seen an early Norman castle. She had spent too many years around her great-uncle Bellard not to recognize the type of castle she thought she had seen. It had been typical of the sort of structure erected seven or eight hundred years earlier, during the period after the Conquest — a castle built in times of war and unrest, the main purpose of which had been the defense of the lord of the castle, his family and men and the local villagers. Raised over the course of many years on a hill or some other easily defensible land, they were made of stone, with thick, strong walls and sturdy wooden gates, an outer wall surrounding the house itself, which was made of the same thick stone, a single tower rising higher than the rest.

The ancestral home of the St. Legers was clearly not such a castle. There was no outer wall, only the walls of the mansion, one end of it a blocky, almost castlelike structure with a squarish short tower on one end, with another wing added on to it in a style Olivia recognized as Elizabethan, and yet another wing running perpendicular to that one. It was a mixture of at least three different periods and styles, and yet somehow it blended into an attractive whole. Ivy covered one side wall, cut away from the windows and extended its tendrils partly across the front of the house, and despite its size, Blackhope Hall exuded a sense of warmth and hominess quite at odds with its sinister name.

As soon as the carriage pulled up in front of the house, a footman hurried out to open the carriage door for Olivia and help her down. "Welcome to Blackhope, my lady."

He escorted her inside, while the carriage pulled around to the kitchen entrance to unload their trunks and let out Joan and Tom. Olivia walked through the front door into a large high-ceilinged room, which she recognized as having once been the great hall of the original medieval house. A more recent addition of a wide staircase rose to a landing, then split and gracefully arched in opposite directions up to the second floor. Lord St. Leger was coming down the stairs toward her, a smile on his face.

A thrill ran through Olivia, and she realized with some astonishment just how much she had been looking forward to this moment. She wasn't sure why. She had met other men as attractive as Lord St. Leger — certainly others with smoother personalities — but she had never felt this excitement upon seeing any of them. She thought about her travel-stained appearance — crushed skirts and stray soft hairs no doubt escaping from the softer hairstyle into which Joan had fashioned it — and she wished she had been able to freshen up before facing Lord St. Leger.

"Miss Moreland, welcome to Blackhope." He extended his hand to her as he came forward, taking the hand she held out to him. The same sort of jolt ran through her as it had the first time he had taken her hand, a sense of heat and something more, a sort of recognition.

Olivia didn't understand it any more than she had the first time it happened, but she could not deny that she liked the feeling. "Lord St. Leger. Thank you for inviting me. You have a beautiful home."

She did not mention the flash of vision she had had of the old castle; that was exactly the sort of thing that had given her family its common epithet. The sort of thing her grandmother had talked about that had always frightened Olivia as a child.

"I'm deuced glad you came," Stephen confided in a lower voice, his hand still curled around hers, his gray eyes gazing into hers. "I was afraid you might decide not to."

"Nonsense. Of course I came," Olivia replied quickly. It occurred to her that her voice sounded much too eager, and she continued pragmatically, "I am looking forward to this investigation. It isn't often that I have such an opportunity."

"Yes. Naturally. I am fortunate you feel that way." He sounded more formal now, and Olivia regretted her words. Why was she always at such a loss socially?

"Allow me to introduce you to my family. They are quite looking forward to meeting you."

He offered her his arm and led her up the stairs and along a gallery to the double doors of a formal drawing room. There were several people in the room, and all turned toward them with an air of eager curiosity as Stephen and Olivia entered. For a moment, in Olivia's natural shyness, there seemed to be a crowd, blurred and overwhelming, but as Stephen introduced her, they resolved themselves into individuals.

"Mother, allow me to introduce you to the Lady Olivia Moreland. Olivia, this is my mother, the Dowager Countess St. Leger."

His mother, Olivia saw, was a pretty middle-aged woman, her dark hair having turned almost entirely white. Pleasant and plump, she wore the black clothes of mourning, including a black cap, its severity relieved a little by a row of black lace. Lady St. Leger greeted Olivia with a smile, her blue eyes lively with interest. It occurred to Olivia that St. Leger's family must have the same sort of suspicions about his inviting her to this house party that her own family had, and she blushed a little as she returned the countess's greeting.

"My brother's widow, Lady Pamela, the Countess St. Leger," Stephen went on flatly, indicating the woman sitting on a chair just beyond Lady St. Leger. She was a marked contrast to Lady St. Leger, her dress cut in smart lines and of the pale gray color indicative of reduced mourning, decorated with bands of black lace, and her face coolly beautiful and unlined with pain or sorrow. She was a blond-haired, blue-eyed beauty, the sort of woman who made

Olivia feel clumsy and plain, and Olivia could not help but wonder why Lord St. Leger had not mentioned this woman before. She did not seem the kind of woman who would slip one's mind.

"Lady Olivia." Lady Pamela's voice was cool, and there was a look of amused disdain in her eyes. Olivia colored faintly under her gaze, acutely aware of her own travel-stained state.

"And this child jumping out of her skin in eagerness is my sister, the Lady Belinda St. Leger."

"I am not a child," Belinda protested, directing a look of mock anger at her brother. Dark haired like her brother, she had bright eyes of a dark gray-blue, and she smiled merrily, fairly vibrating with youth and high spirits. She turned to Olivia, taking her hand and saying candidly, "I am so happy to meet you. We've all been dying to see you."

"Belinda!" her mother said reprovingly. "Lady Olivia will think you have no manners." But the doting smile she turned on her daughter took any sting out of her words.

"You know it's the truth," Belinda responded irrepressibly.

"Allow me to introduce my dear friend Madame Valenskaya to you," Lady St. Leger said, turning toward the woman who sat beside her on the couch.

"I am ferry happy to meet you," Madame Valenskaya said, inclining her head regally to

Olivia, her voice surprisingly deep for such a small woman, and thickly accented.

Olivia responded, her eyes taking in the woman with interest. Madame Valenskaya was short and stocky. Sharp, button-black eyes, small inside the fleshy face, peered out at Olivia, and Olivia had the impression that Madame Valenskaya was sizing her up just as much as Olivia was analyzing her.

"And this is Irina, Madame's daughter." Lady St. Leger indicated a small, colorless young woman sitting in a chair somewhat removed from the others.

The girl gave Olivia a brief nod and an unaccented "Hello," then glanced away. Olivia was unsure whether Irina was shy or simply rude.

"And Mr. Howard Babington," Lady St. Leger said, smiling toward the man standing beside the window.

He had turned toward Olivia as she entered the room, and he gave her a polite smile and greeting now. This, Olivia knew, was Madame Valenskaya's sponsor into society. Olivia did not know him, which was not unusual, as she did not go out much, but when she had asked Kyria about him, her sister had not heard his name, either, which meant that he was certainly not a member of the upper echelons of London society, if he was even a gentleman at all and not just a pretender like Valenskaya herself.

Mediums commonly had such sponsors,

people who invited them into their homes and introduced them to their friends, who allowed them to conduct their séances in their houses and under the aegis of their good name. Some such sponsors were merely dupes, as fooled by the mediums as their other victims. Others, Olivia knew, were accomplices of the mediums, aiding them in perpetrating their frauds. She had no idea which Mr. Babington was.

A slight man of medium height, he had a pale, narrow face made even thinner by a pointed goatee. His hair was a light brown, as was his beard, and his eyes were hazel. He was, in general, a rather nondescript-looking fellow, neither handsome nor plain, and when he spoke, his voice was as nondescript as the rest of him. He was the kind of man, who, whether through intent or simply by nature, was easy to ignore and even easier to forget mere moments after one saw him.

"Such an honor," he murmured, taking Olivia's hand limply and letting go almost immediately.

"I am sure you must be tired after that long ride from London," Lady St. Leger said kindly. "No doubt you would like to go to your room."

"Thank you, my lady." Olivia accepted the offer gratefully.

"I'll show her to her room," Belinda said cheerfully, popping up from her seat. She led Olivia out of the drawing room, then along the gallery and down another hall.

Belinda linked her arm companionably with one of Olivia's and, leaning in, confided, "We were all agog to meet you. I hope you won't take offense at our curiosity. You see, it is the first time that Stephen has asked a woman to the house. Well, I mean, since — well, since he's been home this time."

Olivia felt her cheeks flush hotly. "Oh, no, you mustn't think — I mean, Lord St. Leger and I are merely friends. There is nothing to — well, to warrant any particular interest in me."

She felt embarrassed by the St. Leger women's assumption that Stephen was interested in her as a female and guilty that she was lying to them, or at least hiding knowledge from them. Yet she could tell them the truth about why she was here even less than she could have told her own family. Lady St. Leger would be horrified and insulted by Olivia's real reason for visiting.

"Of course, Stephen has scarcely left the estate since he returned. He says he has too much to do, learning all the estate affairs." She grimaced. "I don't know. Sometimes I think he's a little uncomfortable here. He was in America for almost ten years. But, then, no doubt you know that. How did you meet him? We've all been wondering like mad. It must have been when he was in London to fetch us, I suppose. But I didn't think he went to any parties. He positively refused to go with us. It must have been romantic."

"Oh! Oh, no, it wasn't — we are merely

friends," Olivia repeated lamely. "We — uh, I met your brother through my brother, Reed. Lord St. Leger came to call on him, and I happened to be there."

Olivia thought to herself that she would have to remember to tell Lord St. Leger about their chance meeting. It had been foolish of them not to have dreamed up a story in advance. Naturally his family would be curious — and would not be distracted so easily, as her own family had been, by a diversion into the issue of equality for women. There were definitely advantages to having a liberal-thinking — and vague — group of relatives.

"So you see," Olivia went on, "it was more prosaic than romantic. Lord St. Leger invited us both, but Reed could not come."

Belinda looked at her assessingly, and Olivia thought that she was not completely dissuaded from her romantic notions by Olivia's story, but then she shrugged and said, "Oh, well. At least it put Pamela's nose out of joint." She smiled a little at the thought.

"Lady St. Leger?" It was Olivia's turn to look at her companion curiously. "What do you mean?"

"Oh! Well . . ." Belinda hesitated, then finished, "I mean, just that she's used to being the lady of the house. You know, the most important female. And you're the daughter of a duke, so of course you outrank her."

Olivia, looking at the young woman's guileless

countenance, had the definite suspicion that Belinda's explanation had not been her original thought. However, she could scarcely press her about it, so she merely smiled.

Belinda stopped at an open door. "Here is your room, my lady."

"Oh, please — I do so dislike titles. I usually go by Miss Moreland," Olivia protested uncomfortably.

The girl's eyes widened, "Oh, but I could not call you that! Mama would be furious with me if I were so rude."

"Well, then, perhaps just Olivia?" Olivia suggested.

Belinda goggled even more. "Truly?"

"Yes, of course. To tell you the truth, I do not feel much like the daughter of a duke."

Belinda's smile flashed across her face. "You are not high in the instep at all. I knew I would like you. I just felt it!"

Olivia chuckled. "The feeling is mutual." It would be, in truth, hard not to like the girl's fresh and candid manner.

If possible, Belinda grew even sunnier, and she gave Olivia's hand a quick squeeze. "This is your room. I hope everything is satisfactory. If not, Mama would be happy to change you around."

"Oh, no. It is a lovely room." It was indeed a pretty place, spacious and elegant, with a set of windows on either side of the bed looking out on the rear garden.

Belinda left soon afterward, closing the door behind her, and Olivia sank down with relief onto a chaise longue. It was more tiring to play a part than she would have imagined, she realized. Nor could she completely stifle a twinge of guilt over the fact that Stephen's mother and sister assumed her to be a woman for whom Stephen had feelings. Well, she had done her best to set Belinda straight about that, she reminded herself. She could not *make* them believe differently.

There was a knock at the door, and Joan bustled into the room, followed by Tom with her trunk. Joan set about unpacking the trunk and putting away Olivia's clothes, while Tom and Olivia held a low-voiced conference. He was, he assured her, settled into the servants quarters, and he had great hopes of soon being in the know of all the gossip. He had already heard that neither Madame Valenskaya nor her daughter had brought a maid nor Mr. Babington a valet, which caused St. Leger's servants to hold them in disdain.

"I'm not sure that the lack of a maid is something we can hold against them," Olivia commented.

"Aye, well, the maids as are 'avin' to do double duty hold it against 'em."

"Oh. I see."

"Yeah. Two of the upstairs girls were arguin' somethin' fierce over which one of 'em had to go help the Valenskayas dress for dinner." He sighed. "Makes my job harder, too. I was 'opin' to get some gossip from their maid."

"Well, perhaps it's an opportunity. What if you were to volunteer to act as Mr. Babington's valet?"

Tom looked none too pleased at the idea at first, but as he thought about it, his expression brightened. "Aye, that's a cunning thought, miss. He might let somethin' slip to me, and it'll set me up right with the lot downstairs, too."

Tom went off with renewed eagerness, and Olivia turned back to help Joan unpack. Joan, however, looked clearly affronted by Olivia's offer. "It's resting you should be, my lady. Dinner is at eight, so we shall have to do your hair and dress in another hour or so. You lie down while I get the wrinkles out of your dress."

Olivia gave in, too tired not to, and she awoke thirty minutes later feeling much refreshed. She arose and washed up just in time for Joan's entrance with her dinner gown, freshly pressed. It was her own emerald-green satin gown on which Kyria had lowered the neckline to what seemed to Olivia a scandalous degree by ripping out the lace trim above it. Still, she had to admit, when she was in the dress, her hair artfully arranged into curls by Joan's nimble fingers, that she did look, well — rather pretty.

Her pride in her appearance lasted only until Lady Pamela St. Leger swept into the dining room after all the rest of them had gathered there. There was no way she herself could compete, Olivia knew, with the woman's narrow waist and the smooth expanse of white chest and bosom revealed by the low-cut black gown. Why, she wondered, looking at Pamela, had she ever worried that her own gown revealed too much bosom?

Subdued by the other woman's blond beauty, it took Olivia some time to notice that the widow's flirtatious comments seemed to fall on deaf ears where Lord St. Leger was concerned. He looked, if anything, bored, and for much of the rest of the dinner, Pamela directed most of her words and glances at Mr. Babington.

Halfway through dinner, the Dowager Countess St. Leger said, smiling, "Madame Valenskaya, I hope we can persuade you to honor us tonight with a sitting."

Lord St. Leger stiffened and shot a glance at Olivia. She turned interestedly to the Russian woman, who had spent most of the meal silently plowing her way through her food.

Madame Valenskaya paused now and looked at Lady St. Leger. *"Da,"* she returned in her guttural accent. "It is you who honors me, my lady. But, as you know, spirits are not always, how you say, ready."

"Of course," Lady St. Leger agreed eagerly, her face alight with enthusiasm. "But it would be so good of you to try."

"Da, da. I will try. For you, my lady."

Lady St. Leger turned to Olivia. "Madame Valenskaya is a gifted medium, my lady. I do not know if you have any experience in such things. . . ."

"I have long been interested in matters of the spiritual world," Olivia told her pleasantly. "If you are about to hold a séance, I would very much like to join you."

Lady St. Leger beamed. "That is so good of you, Lady Olivia. It is just splendid. Stephen? I hope you, too, will join us."

"Of course." Stephen nodded shortly. "If you wish."

So it was that, after the meal, the group gathered in the smaller, less formal dining room, grouped around the table. There was an empty chair at the head of the table for Madame Valenskaya, who had excused herself to go to her room to "attune" herself to the spiritual vibrations of "the other side." Irina, so far so quiet that one would hardly know she was in the room, spoke up to arrange the rest of the seating. She put herself on one side of her mother, Olivia noticed, with Mr. Babington on the other. She put Stephen's mother next to Babington and Pamela next to herself, with Belinda beyond her and Stephen at the opposite end of the table from Madame Valenskaya. Olivia had little doubt but that Lord St. Leger's position farthest from the medium was quite deliberate, buffering the medium from him with her followers. Olivia herself was placed opposite Belinda, and between Stephen and his mother.

Madame Valenskaya swept into the room and

crossed to the head of the table, hands clasped at her waist and eyes turned downward as if in deep thought. At a look from Lady St. Leger, the attending footman left the room, closing the door after him.

The room was quiet as Valenskaya took her seat. A kerosene lamp sat in the middle of the table, casting a soft circle of light around them. Olivia cast a quick glance around the room. Stephen's features might have been set in stone, his gray eyes cool and watchful. Lady St. Leger's face, unlike her son's, was filled with anticipation. Belinda, too, looked excited, but Pamela's expression was more bored than anything else. Irina's face, at the opposite corner from Olivia, was partially in shadows and difficult to read. Babington's countenance, however, shone with something close to adoration as he gazed at the medium beside him.

"Now we will join hands to complete the circle of energy, and open our hearts and our minds to our visitors from the other world," Irina explained in a quiet voice. "Then I will turn out the light."

"Darkness is more conducive to the spirits," Lady St. Leger explained in a whisper to Olivia, reaching out to take her right hand.

All around the table, they joined hands. Stephen's firm hand slipped around Olivia's, and she clasped it, hoping to hide the sudden quiver that had run through her flesh at his touch. Irina reached out and turned down the oil lamp until they were encased in velvety darkness. There was no sound except the soft susurrations of breath around the table. Olivia was vividly aware of the feel of Stephen's skin against her own. Warm and firm, slightly callused, his hand engulfed hers. Her breath came shallowly in her throat; her hand felt hot and tingly, a feeling that was inexplicably spreading up her arm and down into her torso, twisting through her chest and abdomen.

So focused was she on their linked hands that she did not even think about Madame Valenskaya until the woman groaned at the other end of the table. Olivia flushed with embarrassment and was glad for the enveloping darkness that had hidden both her blush and her prior lack of attention to the job at hand.

She peered in the direction of the groan, and at that moment a glowing hand appeared in the darkness above the medium's head. Fingers slightly curled, it moved around for a bit, then slid down and out of sight.

"Spirit? Are you there?" This was Babington's voice, beside Madame Valenskaya.

Olivia wondered why it was not the medium herself who was communicating with the spirits, but then Madame Valenskaya's voice murmured, "Yes."

"Welcome, spirits," Babington said in greeting, enthusiastic but still keeping his voice hushed. Around Olivia, most of the others echoed his words.

"Are you Running Deer?" Lady St. Leger asked beside Olivia.

There was a pause, and then the same throaty voice said, "No."

Olivia felt Lady St. Leger's hand stiffen in surprise in her own. Across the table, Irina said, "Pray, spirit, tell us who you are, then."

Again the voice came, low and halting. "Rod-dy. I am Roddy."

4

Stephen's hand tightened convulsively around
Olivia's as he let out a soft oath, and on the
other side of her, Lady St. Leger gasped, her
hand jerking out of Olivia's grasp to fly to her
mouth.

"Roddy?" Lady St. Leger asked, her voice
trembling and eager. "Roderick, is that really
you?"

"Yes, Mother. I am here. Pamela, my love.
You are looking very beautiful tonight."

"Roderick!" Pamela said urgently. "Where are
you? Let me see you!"

"You cannot," he replied. "I am too new
here."

"Here? Where are you, Roddy?" Lady St.
Leger asked, tears thickening her voice. "Are
you happy?"

"I am among the shades," the low voice continued in its odd, jerky way. "But I cannot rest.
None of us can rest."

"What?" Lady St. Leger's voice registered
alarm. "Why not? Darling, are you unhappy?"

"There are many lost souls here. This house — they cannot rest." The voice grew fainter and more whispery. "They cannot rest because of what was taken away from them. I cannot rest, Mother."

"Roddy!" Lady St. Leger cried out, her voice full of distress. "No, please —"

"Bloody hell!" Beside Olivia, Stephen pulled his hand away from Olivia's and crashed it down flat on the table. "What rubbish!"

"Stephen!" Lady St. Leger exclaimed reprovingly. "No! You must not interrupt."

"He is gone!" Madame Valenskaya proclaimed with disgust. "Our spirits haff left us."

Olivia reached out and pulled the oil lamp to her and lit it, turning it up. The faces of those around the table appeared again, blinking a little in the new light. Lady St. Leger's cheeks, Olivia saw with a stab of pity, were streaked with tears.

"You haff frightened dem away," the medium said accusingly, glaring at Stephen.

"Nonsense. As if there were any here to begin with."

"Is Roderick utterly gone?" Lady St. Leger asked Madame Valenskaya, her voice trembling. "Can you not bring him back?"

"I haff no power over spirits," Madame Valenskaya replied flatly. "He is gone now. Spirits do not stay with unbelievers."

"I must say," Stephen said coolly, "that Roderick's voice sounded uncommonly like yours, Madame Valenskaya."

"The spirits use Madame Valenskaya to communicate with us," Mr. Babington explained. "She is the instrument through which they speak, so naturally the voice is Madame's. However, the words are the spirits'."

Stephen snorted. "As if Roderick would have said anything like that."

"He was unhappy," Stephen's mother said miserably. She turned to the medium hopefully. "Can we not try again? We could do it over. Maybe Roderick would return."

"No," Madame Valenskaya said flatly. "Is too late. He will not come again tonight."

The medium looked at Lord St. Leger significantly. "Spirits will not come if unbelievers are present."

"A convenient excuse, I must say." Stephen turned to Lady St. Leger. "Mother, can't you see that it is all trickery and fakes? That was not Roderick speaking to you."

"Stephen!" Lady St. Leger exclaimed angrily. "You are being impolite to our guests. I invited Madame Valenskaya here, and I won't have you behaving rudely to her."

Stephen's brows rushed together, and he drew breath to speak, but Olivia quickly laid her hand on his arm. "Lady St. Leger, I am sure your son did not mean to be rude." She turned to Stephen with a warning look as she continued. "Nor does he want to frighten away the spirits. He is merely concerned about you. He can see how unhappy the spirit's words made you."

"Yes, of course," Stephen agreed grudgingly. "I cannot believe that Roderick would say anything to make you unhappy."

"Of course not. Poor boy. He must be dreadfully upset to have said anything like that."

Olivia felt Stephen's arm tense under her hand, but he clenched his jaw and kept quiet. Olivia turned back toward the medium, and as she did so, she saw Lady Pamela looking at Olivia's hand on Stephen's arm. Olivia realized belatedly that it was too intimate a gesture to make to a man she barely knew, and she pulled her hand back. Pamela's eyes shifted to Olivia's face, and Olivia saw there a flash of pure dislike before Pamela turned back toward the medium.

"Surely you will not deprive us of the chance to talk to dear Roddy again," Pamela said pleadingly. "I am sure Roderick knows his brother well enough to ignore his bad temper."

"Yes, say you will sit again tomorrow night," Lady St. Leger pleaded. "Lord St. Leger will not interrupt again. Will you, my dear?"

"No. Of course not. I promise that I will be quiet," Stephen replied.

"And keep an open mind."

"So open the wind will rush through it."

"There. You see?" Lady St. Leger smiled winningly at the Russian woman. "Please, say we can have another séance."

"Well . . . for you, my lady," Madame Valenskaya said. She pushed back her chair and rose. "But now, I rest. Irina?"

"Yes, Mama." Irina popped up and stepped around the table to her mother, taking her by the arm.

Mr. Babington went around to the medium's other side, giving her his arm, and Madame Valenskaya exited the room, leaning heavily on both her supporters. Olivia glanced at Stephen, who was watching the scene with a grim expression. He sighed and turned to Olivia.

"Would you care, perhaps, for a stroll around the conservatory before you turn in?"

"That sounds delightful." Olivia felt sure that he wanted to talk about what had just happened. She turned and made her excuses to Lady St. Leger, who answered her somewhat abstractedly.

"I apologize again for my behavior, Mother," Stephen said.

"I know, dear." Lady St. Leger smiled at him. "I do wish that you would give Madame Valenskaya the benefit of the doubt. Such a dear woman."

"You did not use to be so skeptical, Stephen," Pamela said in a teasing tone.

St. Leger looked at her and said in dry tone, "That was before I learned what people were capable of." He turned back to his mother. "I know how much you enjoy Madame Valenskaya's company. I will do my best to, um, restrain my boorish tendencies."

With a small bow to his mother, he offered Olivia his arm. They strolled through the great hall and down the back hall to the conservatory, where wicker furniture, softened by flowered cushions, was scattered among the large number of green plants. It was dark inside, lit only by the sconces in the hall outside and by the moonlight coming in the many windows. Stephen paused to light a candelabra, then led Olivia into the conservatory, making his way to a wicker sofa in the center of the plant-filled room.

"I am sure you are going to tell me that I was foolish," Stephen said. "I know I was. It was that woman's trotting out Roddy like that. I couldn't bear hearing her use his name to perpetrate her schemes. And to play on my mother's grief in such a manner!"

It struck Olivia that he had made no mention of Roddy's widow's grief. She had also noticed the steel in his voice earlier when he spoke to Pamela. However, she had no intention of mentioning either of those things. She said only, "I know. It is despicable. But your mother wants so badly to believe that Madame Valenskaya can contact your brother that we will never be able to convince her simply with reason. We will have to catch the medium in the middle of her deception."

"Yes. It is rather clever of her to have the spirits 'speak through' her. There's no rapping at which one can be caught out. And it sounds like her because the spirit supposedly uses her voice. Pretty difficult to disprove that."

"Yes. But she did the trick with the hand. I

feel sure that was a painted glove stuffed with paper or cloth and held up with a telescoping rod. She could easily hide the glove and rod in a large pocket. Her skirts are full. And you'll remember that she went back to her room before she came to the séance, so she could have slipped the things into her pocket."

"True. But I can hardly stop her leaving the room and demand to search her pockets."

"No. We will have to observe what she does, and when, and then, at just the right moment, light a match and reveal her actually doing the trick."

"Sometimes I wonder if Mother would believe it even if she was confronted with the evidence." He paused, looking thoughtful, then asked, "But why that talk of unhappy shades, these souls that can't rest? That's not the normal thing, is it?"

"No," Olivia admitted. "That was odd. Usually they talk about the peace and beauty of the other side. After all, that is what everyone wants to hear — that their loved one is happy in the afterlife, that there is no more pain and suffering, and that whenever they, too, die, they will join them in that blissful place."

"But for some reason she wants Mother to believe that Roderick is unhappy, that his soul is uneasy. What do you want to bet that it will take some certain amount of money to cause his soul to be at peace?"

"No doubt you are right." Olivia sighed. "I

am afraid that Lady St. Leger would be willing to pay almost anything if she thought it would help her son."

"And completely aside from the money they are going to swindle out of her, there is also the fact that they are causing her pain right now. She is distressed because she thinks that Roderick is unhappy. That he 'cannot rest.' The woman is making her miserable, and she will make her even more so before she's done. She has to make sure that Mother will be eager to pay whatever she asks."

"You're right. I'm so sorry." Olivia laid her hand on his arm in a gesture of sympathy.

He looked over at her, and Olivia could not move, could scarcely breathe. Why did every nerve in her body seem to suddenly come to tingling life?

His other hand came up and covered hers where it lay on his arm. His skin was warm and faintly rough. Olivia felt suddenly hot and melting inside, quivering with sensations she had never experienced before. She thought that she could lose herself in those cool silver eyes, and she was not even sure whether she found the prospect frightening . . . or alluring.

"Olivia . . ." Her name was soft on his tongue.

Olivia looked at him, not trusting herself to speak. He leaned toward her fractionally, then stopped. A muscle jumped in his jaw, and he pulled his hand away, then rose to his feet. Olivia sagged slightly with disappointment, then stood up, telling herself not to be a fool. What had she thought was going to happen, anyway? Whatever fancy hairstyle Joan might give her, she would remain the sort of woman a man did not desire.

"Would you care to go riding with me tomorrow morning?" Stephen asked, his voice neutral, his gaze turned slightly away from Olivia. "I can show you around the estate a bit, if you'd like."

"Yes. That would be very nice." She was not a good rider, and as a result, she rarely went, but she could not bring herself to turn down the invitation.

"Very good, then. After breakfast?"

Olivia nodded. His invitation meant nothing, she told herself. He had to pretend to be friendly with her; he had invited her, after all, and no doubt his family would consider it odd if he did not spend some private time with her.

Stephen picked up the candelabra to light their way, and they left the room. The warm glow of the candles lit a small circle around them, leaving the rest of the large room in shadows. Neither of them glanced around into the dark recesses of the conservatory, and so they did not see the still, dark form standing silently in the corner of the room, hidden by the fronds of a palm tree.

Olivia and Stephen rode out the next morning about an hour after breakfast. She was happy to see that he had had a docile mare saddled up for her, and that he seemed content to amble along talking and pointing out various landmarks on the way. Their path curved around the stand of trees at the end of the garden, then into the meadow beyond. They rode past farms, and Stephen greeted by name everyone they met in the fields.

When Olivia remarked on it, he shrugged and said, "Well, they are my tenants, after all."

"Still, I would lay you odds that there are those who know the names of scarcely any of their tenants."

"Hardly behavior to emulate, I would say," Stephen replied. He glanced at her. "I am afraid you'll find I am not your typical aristocrat. Perhaps it comes from being in America for ten years. But I find I care less and less about one's class. And an estate seems to me more a business venture than some divine right passed down to me."

"Careful," Olivia said with a chuckle, "or people will start to label *you* 'mad,' as well. What you just said sounds very much like my brother Reed who, by the way, I have cast as your friend."

Stephen turned to her with a puzzled look, and she explained. "Belinda wanted to know how we had met, and I felt it best not to say we had created a commotion at a séance, so I said that you came to call on my brother Reed, and I met you there."

"Ah, I see. Very wise, I'm sure. And how is it that I know your brother?"

Olivia shrugged. "I shall let you decide that. Perhaps he belongs to your club. Or maybe you met him through some kind of business. He oversees all our family's finances. He is quite good at it, which is fortunate, for I am afraid that none of the rest of us are. Papa is devoted only to antiquities, and Mama is more concerned about the women's vote and factory workers' wages."

"What about your other brothers and sisters? What are they concerned with?"

"Well . . . Theo — he's the eldest — is fond of adventure. He comes home every year or two, and then he is off again to explore the Amazon or the heart of Africa or somewhere like that. Right now he is in Australia and has been for almost a year. We are hoping that he will come home again before too long. Thisbe, his twin, is a chemist. Kyria's business is the social whirl. And Constantine and Alexander — the second set of twins — are only ten, so mischief is their chief employment."

"Constantine and Alexander? As in the emperors?"

Olivia chuckled. "Yes. Believe me, it could have been worse. Papa wanted to name them Castor and Pollux because of their being twins, you see, but Mother put her foot down about that one."

"I am sure they will bless her when they are older."

"No doubt," Olivia agreed.

"They sound like a lively family."

"Yes, they are — and not a mad one among them."

"Oh, Lord, I can see that *that* remark will continue to haunt me," Stephen commented ruefully. "I am most dreadfully sorry, you know. I didn't mean it. Obviously I didn't even know your family. It just —"

"I know. It just came out." Olivia sighed. "That, I'm sure, is because you had heard it often enough."

"No one really thinks they're mad, I'm sure. It's just a way of talking."

"Yes. I realize it's a jest, or mostly a jest. They mean, I think, not insane, but decidedly odd." She paused, then went on. "And I guess we are. It's just infuriating that what makes us odd in their eyes is that we care more for knowledge than for one's skill at sitting a horse, say, or making social chitchat. We are odd because we care about people who are not in the same class — indeed, we are branded exceedingly peculiar because we don't like the idea of class at all. I am mad because I prefer to be called Miss Moreland instead of Lady Olivia Moreland. My mother is mad because she believes that all children deserve an education. Kyria is mad because she refuses to marry a man just because he has an excellent title and lineage."

Olivia's eyes flashed as she warmed to her subject, her cheeks flushing with the strength of her feelings. Stephen found that he could not take his eyes from her.

"Why are we the ones who are peculiar?" Olivia demanded. "It seems to me that it is the others who are odd. Why is it considered wrong to be devoted to what we believe in? We simply invest a great deal of emotion in the things we do."

"You are passionate."

His words hung on the air between them, and suddenly there was a tension between them, an awkwardness that had not been there before. Olivia, who had been rushing along on her rising tide of indignation, halted, suddenly unable to think of anything but passion in the word's most basic, carnal sense. Her fingers curled around the reins she had been holding loosely as her mind was flooded with images — Stephen's hand around hers, his skin arousing feelings in her she had never known before, the almost electrical shock that had run through her the first time she looked into his eyes, the heat that seemed to blossom inside her whenever he looked at her or touched her in even the slightest way.

"Yes, I suppose we are passionate about our 'causes,'" Olivia said, her voice thin with the effort of keeping it level and unconcerned. She carefully did not look at Stephen. "I am sorry. You must think I am foolish, to get so emotional about what is, after all, only a silly jest."

"No, indeed. I do not think you are foolish at

all." The warmth in his voice made Olivia turn her head to look at him in surprise. There was no levity in his face, only a sincere admiration that jolted her. "I think you are quite remarkable."

She glanced away quickly, feeling a flush rising up her throat. She was, she thought, hopelessly inept in such a situation. Kyria would have been able to take a compliment gracefully. All she could do, she thought, was blush and feel like an idiot.

Fortunately, a woman was emerging from the doorway of the cottage they were about to pass, and at sight of them, she came forward to greet Stephen. By the time he was done introducing Olivia to his tenant's wife and they had all commented on the loveliness of this August day, the awkward moment was past, and they were able to ride on in easy silence.

"I will show you my favorite part of the estate," St. Leger told her, turning his horse from the well-trodden path on which they had been riding. "It will be the perfect place to get off and try the lunch that Cook sent with us."

They struck out across the fields, stopping to unlatch a gate and pass through, a consideration for which Olivia was grateful, as she was sure that had he been alone, Stephen would merely have jumped the low fence, a feat she was sure she would not have been able to accomplish. She could still remember the anguish in the head groom's voice as he had told her that she needed to help her horse over the obstacle, not fight him, and the gratitude she had felt when her father had said placidly, "Oh, what does it matter, Jenkins? You'd best stick with teaching Kyria and the boys. My Livvy's a scholar, not a rider, aren't you, sweetheart?"

They entered the trees beyond the field, following a barely discernible path, and when they emerged from the wood, they were in a small meadow, slanting down slightly to a pond. A grove of trees lined one end of the pond, following its gentle curve. It was a scene of tranquility and beauty, and Olivia drew in her breath in a soft gasp of pleasure.

"It's beautiful!" she cried, pulling her horse to a stop, struck by a deep, intense emotion, which she could neither understand nor describe. It was as if, in some incredible, utterly illogical way, she *knew* this piece of land.

"Do you like it?" Stephen turned to her, his eyes lingering on her face, lit now with an inner glow. "I'm glad. This has always been my favorite spot — where I like to come and think, or just sit."

"It's wonderful," Olivia agreed, urging her horse forward again.

They rode to the trees at the edge of the pond and dismounted. Olivia looked around her, smiling. "I feel so peaceful here. So safe."

The words surprised her even as she spoke them. *Whyever should she not feel safe?* Yet she knew that a sense of safety was part of the feeling that she got from this place, and the sweetness of the emotion inside her was disturbed by a sudden sense of unease.

Olivia pushed the thought away from her. She was being silly. This was simply a lovely tranquil place, and whatever connection she felt to it was nothing more than a normal attraction to a beautiful spot.

Stephen took the hamper from the back of his horse and set it beside the pond, then spread a blanket on the ground for them to sit on. Cook had prepared a bountiful luncheon for them — an array of cold meats, cheeses and fruit, supplemented by thick slabs of dark bread spread with pale yellow butter — and they spent the next few minutes doing justice to her work.

Afterward they sat in contented silence, luxuriating in the warmth of the sun on their backs, listening to the rustle of the leaves as the breeze moved them and the occasional song of a bird. It would be a wonderful place, Olivia thought, to sit and read, or even to curl up and doze in the sun, like a lazy cat. She would have to bring a book here another time. She caught herself on the thought. She would not be at Blackhope that long; she was here merely for a visit, and then she would return to her home.

"It must have been nice, growing up here," she commented.

"Yes. Roderick was four years older than I, so when he went off to Eton, I was mostly

119

alone. I used to like to ride to this pond and sit and read."

Olivia smiled at the echoing of her thoughts. "What sort of things did you read?"

"Oh, tales of derring-do — grand adventure and mysterious happenings. Romantic nonsense, most of it. I was young and full of dreams."

"Is that why you went to America? To pursue adventure?"

He shrugged, and his face closed down, the smile that had curved his lips vanishing. "I suppose. Mostly I wanted to get as far away from here as possible."

His answer puzzled her, and she would have questioned him about it, but Stephen went on before she could speak. "I wanted to make my fortune. Prove my worth. Typical ambitions of a younger son."

"Where did you go?"

"To the West. That was the place to make one's fortune, that was what everyone there said. I tried a few different places, different things, but I wound up in Colorado, silver mining."

"What was it like there?"

"Harsh, cold, beautiful. The mountains are incredibly high and stark, the sky enormous. You cannot look at them without thinking of words such as 'grandeur' and 'majestic' and 'sweeping.' The land dwarfs you, and yet somehow it emboldens you, makes you think that anything is possible."

He shrugged, looking a little embarrassed. "Sorry. I don't usually go on about it so."

"It must have been difficult to leave it."

Stephen glanced at her, surprised. "It was. Most people don't understand that. They think I must have been ecstatic to come home to England, to suddenly acquire the title and estate. I wasn't. For a short while, I even thought about not returning. But I knew the estate would suffer. One cannot really manage effectively from thousands of miles away. And there were Mother and Belinda to consider. So in the end I sold out, and I came back here."

"Do you regret it?"

He did not answer right away, considering her words. Finally he said, "No. I don't regret it. It's a different sort of life, but I suppose it is really the one I was born and bred for. No matter how beautiful the Rockies are, however challenging the land or the work, this is where I belong. Blackhope is my home." A quick grin quirked up the corners of his mouth. "Even with all the lost spirits."

Olivia smiled back. "Do you think we shall have a repeat performance tonight? More words from the spirits?"

"My guess would be no." His face turned serious again. "I think our Madame Valenskaya will make Mother wait for a while. Bring her eagerness to a greater level. I think she will find it too enervating to go into a trance again, or she will declare the spirit guides unwilling to return to the house of a disbeliever. She wants Mother to be so impatient for word from Roderick that she will believe anything, no matter how implausible."

"No doubt you are right," Olivia agreed with a sigh. "I feel so sorry for Lady St. Leger. It must be horrible to wait and hope like that."

"Yes." Stephen's mouth turned down grimly. "That's why I intend to expose these charlatans as soon as we possibly can."

The pleasant mood of the afternoon was gone, chased away by thoughts of Madame Valenskaya and her fraudulent schemes. Stephen and Olivia turned away and began to pack up the remains of the food. He stood up and reached down a hand to Olivia to help her. She took it and rose to her feet.

He did not release her hand immediately, but stood for a moment holding it. Olivia looked up into his face and found him gazing at her in a way that made her pulse speed up.

"I am glad you came here," he said. His eyes glinted silver in the day's light.

"I am, too," Olivia found herself answering a little breathlessly.

He bent closer to her, and her heart knocked frantically against her ribs. She closed her eyes, and then his lips were on hers, soft and lingering. Olivia's fingers curled into her palms. She had never been kissed before, and she found that it was unlike anything she had imagined. His kiss deepened, and heat flooded her.

Her hands came up. She wasn't sure what she intended to do, but when her fingers came into contact with his jacket, they curled into the lapels and she held on fiercely. Stephen's arms went around her, pulling her up into him, and Olivia rose onto her toes, pressing her lips against his. Glorious sensations radiated through her, and she trembled, eager and excited.

At last he released her, and she slipped back down flat on her feet. She lifted her eyes to him, her mouth slightly open with astonishment. Stephen stared back at her, almost as stunned as she.

"I — I —" He stepped back, his hands balling into fists. "I beg your pardon. I should not have done that."

Olivia wanted to protest his words, to tell him that she was quite glad that he *had,* but she caught herself. To say such a thing would not be at all ladylike. Indeed, what she had just done was doubtless not ladylike, either, and she suspected that her unusual upbringing was again at fault. So she swallowed her words and merely shook her head.

"No, please, do not worry. It was — it was —"

"Pray don't think that I brought you out here to force my attentions on you," Stephen went on stiffly, more in control of himself.

"No, indeed, I do not," Olivia assured him. She could think of no way to say what she truly felt without sounding like a forward hussy. Her insides were jumping about wildly, and she pressed her hand against her stomach as if to quiet them.

Stephen stood for a moment, facing her. Olivia appeared soft and vulnerable, gazing at him with her huge dark eyes, her mouth still damp and a dark rose from his kiss. He felt like a cad for grabbing her and kissing her like that, yet he could not deny that, looking at her, he wanted to pull her into his arms once more and kiss her all over again.

"I am sorry," he repeated finally, and turned to fetch their horses.

He packed the picnic hamper on his horse, then gave Olivia a leg up onto hers, both of them doing their best to pretend that the necessary contact between them did not exist. They rode back to the house feeling rather awkward, their infrequent words being directions as to where to turn or stilted attempts at polite chit-chat, such as a query on Olivia's part about a certain tree or Stephen pointing out a low stone wall that was reputed to have been standing since before the Conquest.

Once they were back at the house, Olivia thanked him politely and went straightaway upstairs to her room. It was already midafternoon by the time they returned, so she decided not to try to do anything else, but to simply take a bath and get ready for the evening meal. Since she washed her hair, as well, she spent the next little while running through the tangles with a comb, then brushing out the long mane in front of the low fire.

When her hair was almost dry, she rose and went to the bed and lay down on her side. She was a trifle tired, and her head was still reeling with thoughts of that afternoon. She smiled a little secretly to herself as she had done frequently since their picnic. She relived Stephen's kiss inside her head. She wondered if he had really been sorry that he had done it. More than that, she wondered if it might ever happen again.

As she watched the flames flicker up from the logs of the fireplace, the light seemed to dim, and the room before her subtly changed.

A thick rug lay on the floor, but smaller and reddish in color, and it lay only in front of the fireplace, atop the bed of dried reeds that covered the floor. The fireplace, too, was different, made of large blocks of stone, the opening larger, the fire higher and smokier. Gone was the chair beside the fire where Olivia had sat to dry her hair, and gone, too, the low decorative mahogany table that lay before it. There now, just to the side of the rug, stood only a heavy wooden stool.

A woman sat on the rug, her legs curled under her, running a brush through her long blond hair. Firelight flickered on her hair, turning the pale strands copper and gold. Olivia knew that she should be frightened to see a stranger sitting here in her room, but she was not. All she could feel was a sudden stunned amazement . . . and curiosity.

She stared at the woman, who seemed sublimely unaware of her presence. Her face turned to the side, the woman stroked her hair in rhythmic movements as she hummed a tune beneath her breath. She was a pretty woman, with a squarish face, her cheekbones high and wide, and there was a faint indentation at the bottom of her chin, right in the middle, that gave her a piquant look. It was too dark to see the exact color of her eyes, though they seemed light. Her feet were shod in leather slippers, and on her body she wore a long, slender blue tunic that fell straight from her shoulders to her feet, skimming her hips. Beneath it she wore another, lighter dress of a beige color that showed in the neckline and along the deep-cut armholes of the side. Long sleeves fell to points on the backs of her hands, and at the top, the sleeves were tied to the armholes of the underdress. A belt of gold links encircled her body, just above her hips, fastening in the middle in front and falling down in a straight line to her thighs. Where it fastened, there were three links set with colored stones.

A man came into Olivia's vision, crossing the room to the woman. She turned her head at his approach, and a radiant smile broke across her face. She glanced behind him, then, the smile giving way to an anxious frown.

"Do not worry, my love," he said. "None saw me enter your quarters. Your name will not be sullied."

He wore a gray tunic over an undershirt of blue, and below that, leggings of the same color. Around his hips ran a wide leather belt, and hanging from the left side of it was a sword in a scabbard. His hair

126

was longish and cut shaggily, a darker blond than the woman's, almost brown, and there was a little bit of a curl to it.

Standing behind the woman, he unbuckled his belt and laid the sword aside. Then he knelt and curled his arms around her, laying his head against hers. He kissed the top of her head, and she let out a little sigh and snuggled into him.

"'Tis a sin, I know," she said in a soft voice. "But I cannot help myself. Each day is black unless I see you. I cannot bear to be apart from you."

"'Tis the same with me." His voice was a low rumble, and he nuzzled her neck. "I love you."

"And I love you. I cannot even confess my sins, for I cannot say that I repent."

They kissed, clinging to each other. His hand smoothed down her back and over her hips, and he pulled her closer to him. She turned, her arms going around his neck, pressing her body into his. With one arm around her, he eased her back to the floor.

5

Olivia jerked awake, her eyes flying open. For a moment she stared blindly in front of her. Then, slowly, she sat up, gazing around her at the room. *A dream. She had been asleep and dreaming.*

She rubbed her hands over her face. She felt fuzzy and odd. *What a peculiar dream!* It had seemed so real, as if she had been watching a play, or real people. It had been, she thought, exceedingly odd for a dream. Usually she knew the people in her dreams — even if they did not look like themselves, she was aware of who they were. And she was usually the main participant in her dreams. She was late or running from some horror or doing some task, but it was always herself. But in this dream she had seen an unknown room and people who were strangers to her. She herself had not been in the dream except as an unseen watcher.

The man and woman had been dressed like people from the Middle Ages. She paused, thinking about the woman's dress. The early

Middle Ages, she thought, around the time of King Henry II, for the woman's dress made her think of Eleanor of Aquitaine. And though they had spoken English, their accents had been odd, the words stilted, and she had had trouble understanding what they said. She had once or twice dreamed about a different time or place, but on those occasions she had been reading about that time or place, or studying it in school, or Theo had written her about it. But she had read nothing about the time of Henry II in the recent past.

Unbidden, the thought of an old Norman keep came into her mind — the castle she had thought she glimpsed as the carriage approached Blackhope. A shiver ran through her.

She stood up, rubbing her arms to warm herself. *What was the matter with her?* She could not remember ever having seen something that didn't exist, even for an instant. That, she told herself, was even odder than the dream. If she told anyone about it, they would think her as peculiar as her grandmother.

There was a knock on the door, and Joan entered to help her dress for the evening. Olivia forced a smile onto her lips and determinedly put both the imagined castle and the dream out of her mind.

That night at supper, much to Olivia's surprise, Lady Pamela spoke to her. "I hear that you rode out with Stephen this afternoon,

Lady Olivia. I hope you enjoyed your tour of our place."

Olivia noted that the woman made it sound as if the estate still somehow belonged to her. She smiled politely and said, "Yes, very much. Lord St. Leger told me a bit about his life in the United States, as well, which was quite interesting."

"Really?" Pamela arched one thin elegant brow as she looked at Stephen. "I am surprised you have never told us about it, Stephen."

"I doubted you would find it interesting, my lady," he replied in a cool, formal voice.

Pamela smiled at him. "I imagine you would be surprised what interests me. You must try me someday."

Stephen said nothing, merely picked up his wineglass and took a sip. Pamela turned her attention back to Olivia. "We are very glad that you came to visit, my lady. We have heard so much about your family."

There was a faint thread of amusement running through her voice that made it quite clear what she had heard about the Morelands.

"Indeed?" Olivia said mildly.

"Oh, yes," Pamela continued, a cold light in her blue eyes. "The duchess is quite famous in society."

"My mother is well-known for her many good causes, if that is what you mean," Olivia said pleasantly, gazing back at Pamela with equally hard eyes.

"She is very . . . forward thinking, is she not?"

"Yes, she is."

"Pamela . . ." Lady St. Leger said, casting an anxious glance at Olivia.

"What do you mean?" Belinda asked curiously.

Lady St. Leger looked as if she had swallowed a bug. Pamela's smile was like cut glass.

"She means," said Olivia coolly, "that my mother believes in such things as education for poor children and better treatment of workers in factories and women having the right to vote."

"Really?" Belinda's eyes widened. "But isn't that a good thing? That poor children get educated and that people are treated well?"

"Yes, of course." Olivia smiled and nodded. "My mother has a great deal of compassion, a trait that, I am afraid, is all too often missing in some women of the nobility." She turned her eyes significantly back to Pamela.

Stephen let out a short bark of laughter. "Pamela, if you persist in trying to engage Lady Olivia in a battle of wits, you are bound to lose, you know."

Fire flared in Pamela's eyes, though she quickly hid it by lowering her eyes. "Why, Stephen, I am hurt that you should think I meant anything bad," she said, and when she raised her cornflower-blue eyes again, they were swimming in tears. "I was merely interested in Lady Olivia's family."

"Of course," Olivia said briskly. "I am quite proud of my mother, so I never mind talking about her."

A small silence fell on the table after that. Olivia glanced at Lady St. Leger, who still looked a trifle uncomfortable. In an effort to assure Stephen's mother that she had not been offended by Pamela's remarks, Olivia said, "You have a lovely home, Lady St. Leger."

The older woman brightened and smiled at her gratefully. "Thank you, my lady. I am glad you think so. The house has been here for many, many years, of course, but I did do some redecorating. There were some places that were a trifle chilly — both literally and figuratively."

"I fear that is often so with stone houses," Olivia commiserated.

"Is a sad house." Madame Valenskaya spoke up suddenly, and everyone's eyes turned toward her. "Full of lost souls. I know. I hear dem crying out to me. Soon as I arrifed, I knew."

It was the first time Madame Valenskaya had spoken that evening, having been applying herself with some diligence to her food. But now she looked around the table at the rest of them, nodding her head for emphasis.

Olivia glanced at the others. Stephen's face was carefully blank; he was not going to get pulled into the same sort of mistake he had made the night before. Pamela looked cynical and faintly amused. Belinda was leaning forward, her eyes wide, clearly enjoying the drama

132

of the moment. Lady St. Leger, however, was clasping her hands together at her breast, her expression worried, obviously hanging on to Madame Valenskaya's every word.

"I don't know," Olivia said calmly, keeping her face innocent. "It does not seem a sinister house to me at all. I find it quite spacious and lovely."

"Oh, Madame always knows," Mr. Babington said earnestly, putting down his fork and leaning forward to look at Olivia. "She is very attuned to the spirit world. Whenever we enter a house, she knows if there are lost souls within it. There have been one or two she could not even bear to enter."

"Yes. Terrible places," the medium agreed in her guttural voice. "Here is not bad. But I hear lost souls wailing." She gave a dramatic shiver, adding, "Even de name oozes evil — Blackhope Hall."

"It has been named that forever," Pamela commented. "It comes from some ancient time. I am sure it meant something innocuous at the time."

"I know about the name!" Belinda said, her eyes lighting. "My tutor told me last year. He had me research the history of the house as an exercise, you see. A long time ago, long before the St. Legers even owned it, the house was owned by some nobleman who shut himself up in his castle and spent all his time brooding over his dead wife. The book I read said that is how the house got its name."

"You see?" Madame Valenskaya exclaimed, eager to prove her point. "Another lost soul. There are many."

Olivia noticed that, in her excitement, the medium's accent slipped a bit, her *s*'s losing their sibilance and her *th*'s clearly pronounced. Madame Valenskaya seemed to realize it, as well, for she added, "Is not good place. De spirits wail with pain."

"Madame, please tell us that you will conduct another séance tonight," Lady St. Leger urged, her brow drawn into a frown. "You could help those spirits, perhaps."

"No. Not tonight. Is too soon." Madame Valenskaya put a hand to her forehead dramatically. "I cannot try again. Is too painful."

"Mama suffers terribly sometimes," Irina put in quietly. "Especially when the spirits are restless and tormented."

Watching the pain on Lady St. Leger's face, Olivia had to press her lips together firmly to keep from saying anything. One glance at Lord St. Leger told her that he was having difficulty being quiet, also.

"Perhaps tomorrow night," Olivia said pacifically, hoping to forestall any words from Stephen, as well as ease his mother's distress.

"Yes, tomorrow night," Lady St. Leger said, her words a plea.

Madame Valenskaya nodded, her face that of a martyr. "I try."

"Thank you. You are so good."

After watching the medium's manipulation of Lady St. Leger, Olivia found she had little appetite left. She was glad when the last course was brought in a moment later and they were able to finish the meal.

Little happened the next day. There were country things to do, such as croquet on the front lawn or games in the drawing room, or piano playing and singing in the music room, and Olivia participated, but with a sense of passing time until the main event of the day, the next séance, could take place. Stephen spent most of the day in his office, working on estate matters, so Olivia saw him only at luncheon. She could not help but wonder if he was perhaps avoiding her because of the kiss between them the afternoon before. He had apologized, which was the gentlemanly thing to do. But now she began to wonder if perhaps he had meant his regrets, if he wished that it had not happened. Feeling a trifle blue, she picked out a book from the library late in the afternoon and went upstairs. After taking off her dress, she slipped on her dressing gown over her undergarments and settled down in a comfortable chair to read until time for supper.

The afternoon sun was slipping below the horizon and dusk was falling outside when Joan came into the room, carrying Olivia's freshly pressed evening gown. It was one of Kyria's dresses that Joan had resewn for Olivia, a peacock-blue satin pulled tight across the front and gathered in a bustle at the back, with a spill of lace adorning the skirt from the bottom of the bustle down to the floor.

Olivia went to look at the dress as Joan spread it out on the bed. She could not help but feel a prickle of excitement at the thought of wearing it in front of Stephen. Would his eyes light with pleasure as she had seen men's eyes do when Kyria entered a room? She could not quite imagine it; she was not the sort of woman who lit a fire in men. Still, she could not forget that kiss.

Joan picked up Olivia's brush and comb, and Olivia sat down in front of the vanity mirror. Joan pulled the pins from Olivia's hair and set about brushing it out in preparation for the more intricate style into which she intended to arrange it this evening. Suddenly a loud bang sounded from outside the windows, and Joan jumped, inadvertently hitting Olivia's head with the brush.

"I'm so sorry, my lady," she began, but Olivia was already on her feet and crossing to the window, curious about the sound. The maid followed on her heels. When she reached the window and looked down into the garden Olivia came to a dead stop and stared at the tableau below. Joan, coming up beside her, sucked in her breath in a loud gasp.

Olivia leaned forward, closer to the glass of the window. In the garden, a figure walked along a path in the closing twilight. There was still enough light to see that the person pacing slowly wore not any common sort of attire but a long black, hooded robe of the sort worn by monks. His hands were crossed at his waist, the long sleeves covering them, and the cowl of his robe stood out from his face, concealing it.

As Olivia watched, her skin prickling, the figure reached the end of the path, where it went down a series of steps to the lower garden. He turned and looked straight up at the windows of the house. Reaching up with one white hand, he pushed back the hood a little to reveal the stark white bony face of a skull.

Joan made a sharp noise, clapping her hand over her mouth, and from down the hall there was a woman's shriek. Olivia whirled and ran across the room, stopping to tell Joan, "Call Tom Quick!" before she bolted through the door. She ran down the hall to the stairs, heedless of the fact that she was wearing only a dressing gown and soft slippers and her hair was flowing loose down her back. All down the hall, other doors were opening and people emerging, exclaiming.

Stephen was out of his door and to the head of the stairs a step ahead of Olivia, and they pounded down the stairs together. Aware that he was more knowledgeable about the house and gardens, she followed his lead, bunching up the long skirts of her dressing gown to give her legs better room to run.

He tore through the downstairs hall and out

the rear door to the garden, Olivia on his heels. Taking the steps down to the garden two at a time, he headed toward the path the cowled figure had walked. Olivia hastened after him along the flagstones, wincing when she stepped on the edge of a slab of rock in her thin house slippers. But she did not stop, only hurried doggedly after him as he reached the path leading down to the lower garden, where the "monk" had paced.

There was, not surprisingly, no sign of the robed figure. Dusk had fallen fast, the poor light in which they had witnessed the "monk" now having turned to almost complete darkness. They walked quickly along the path to where they had last seen the figure and stopped at the top of the stairs leading down into the lower garden.

"Bloody hell!" Stephen exclaimed. "We'll never catch him in this light. He could have gone anywhere."

He turned and really looked at Olivia for the first time, taking in her disheveled state. Olivia realized that her sash had slipped loose during her mad dash, so that the sides of her dressing gown hung loosely, a gap down the center at the top exposing the white lace of her chemise. She straightened, raising her chin, and belted the robe more tightly.

"I was about to dress for dinner," she explained with all the dignity she could muster and pushed back her hair with her hands.

Stephen's eyes went to her hair, tumbling down to her hips, thick and brown, and it was a moment before he said, tight-lipped, "Yes, of course."

"Miss Olivia!" They turned, startled, and saw Tom Quick trotting toward them, holding a lantern in each hand.

"Tom!" Olivia said gratefully. "Thank heavens you thought to bring a light."

"It were lookin' that dark, I thought," he agreed, handing one of the lanterns to St. Leger.

"Good," Stephen said. "Let's see if we can catch some sign of him."

They went down the shallow steps into the lower garden. Tom, holding his lantern up to cast as much light as possible, turned to the right. Stephen and Olivia went the other way. Olivia, holding the long skirts of her dressing gown up to her ankles to keep them from brushing the ground, peered carefully to each side of her for any glimpse of their visitor. They wound through the west half of the garden, taking every path they found. Now and again they ran into Tom, searching from his side of the garden, and at last they came together at the very bottom of the garden, at the end of the path. Beyond lay only dark trees and, after that, a meadow. Not surprisingly, they had found no sign of their quarry.

"It's hopeless," Stephen said with some bitterness. "Chasing someone dressed in black through the darkness . . ."

"Especially given the fact that he had all that time to get away while we were running down the stairs and out to the garden," Olivia added.

"I know." Stephen sighed. "We might as well return to the house. We can search tomorrow in the daylight. Perhaps we'll find some trace of him."

They returned to the house to find the rest of the occupants in turmoil. Lady St. Leger, Pamela, Belinda and their guests were all milling about at the foot of the stairs, waiting for them.

"Stephen!" Lady St. Leger pounced on him. "What was it? Did you see him again?"

"I've never been so scared in my life!" Belinda exclaimed, grabbing her brother's arm. Her white face attested to her words, though there was also the irrepressible excitement of a nineteen-year-old shining in her gray eyes. "What was it?"

"I imagine it was someone dressed up in a robe," Stephen replied flatly. "But he was gone by the time we got there."

Lady St. Leger was also still in her dressing gown, but Belinda and Pamela were dressed for dinner. Pamela, icily beautiful, as always, in gray silk and lace, cast a disparaging eye over Olivia's attire. Olivia glanced down at her dressing gown, seeing that she had not managed to keep the hem of it entirely from the dirt; she had also, she realized, stepped on one of the ruffles of her petticoat and pulled it loose, so that it dragged on the ground, dangling and dirty.

"Was there really someone outside in the garden, Stephen?" Pamela asked, her tone faintly derisive. "My chamber is on the wrong side, so I was not able to see this 'ghost.'"

"He was there!" Belinda snapped, whirling toward Lady Pamela fiercely. "Just because you didn't see —"

"It's all right, Belinda." Stephen laid a calming hand on her shoulder. He looked at Pamela. "Yes, I saw him, too. There was someone cavorting about in the garden, though I am sure it —"

"Cavorting!" Lady St. Leger exclaimed. "How can you be so lighthearted about it? It was a horrible, hideous monk, with the face of a skeleton, and he was walking with such a slow, ponderous tread — a walk like doom. Like death!"

Olivia went quickly over to the older woman and put her arm around her comfortingly. "It's all right, Lady St. Leger. I'm sure. Please don't distress yourself. Tomorrow, when it is light, we will make a better search. No doubt it will turn out to be something not very ominous."

Madame Valenskaya spoke up, saying portentously, "Spirits leaf no traces. Can you not see? It was a lost soul. It cried out to me. To you!" She pointed dramatically at Stephen. "How can you ignore it?"

"Bloody hell!" Stephen burst out. "It was

nothing but a man dressed up in a fake monk's robe! But I am sure you already know —"

"Lord St. Leger," Olivia stuck in quickly, "your mother is very distressed. Perhaps you should take her up to her room."

"Yes. Of course." He shot Olivia a grateful look and took his mother's arm. "Let us go upstairs. You should lie down and rest. You will feel better."

"I won't," Lady St. Leger protested. "I'm much too frightened to close my eyes, let alone sleep. I have heard people talk about ghosts, but I never actually saw one before. It was ghastly."

"I'm sure you still have not seen one," Stephen growled.

"It *was* ghastly," Olivia agreed. "Whatever it was."

"When it turned its face up, and I saw that skull —" Belinda shivered "— it nearly frightened me out of my wits."

"You were right to say that this place was full of lost souls, Madame." Mr. Babington spoke up, his quiet voice firmer than normal. "Obviously that was one of the poor shades Lady St. Leger's son spoke about."

"Yes. Of course. Is true." Madame Valenskaya spoke slowly, nodding and looking downcast. "I am sorry, my lady. Blackhope is a dark place, full of unhappy souls."

"Madame, will you sit again tonight?" Lady St. Leger asked, leaving her son's side and going over to the medium and looking hopefully into her face. "Please? I am sure it would be of great help in this matter."

The medium inclined her head regally. "Of course, my lady. I must help you. I will call on de spirits tonight."

Olivia cast a glance at Stephen, who gave her an ironic look in return but said nothing. She felt sure that he realized, as she did, that the only way they could discover Valenskaya's scheme was to let the woman play out her act tonight.

So, after the evening meal, which had been delayed almost to the point of ruination by the "ghostly appearance" and the subsequent turmoil, the household gathered once again around the table in the smaller dining room. They sat as they had before, with the medium at one end of the table, her cohorts on either side and Lord St. Leger as far from her as he could be placed. Once again Olivia sat between Lady St. Leger and Stephen, and even though she was prepared tonight for the sensation that ran through her when his hand folded around hers, the power of it was no less intense. She could not help but wonder what he felt when he took her hand and whether it shook him as much as it did her. Olivia thought of the kiss he had given her the day before; she hoped he could not read on her face where her thoughts lay.

The lamps were turned out, and minutes passed silently as they waited for something to happen. At last Madame groaned quietly, and a moment later, the high tinkling sounds of music began to play on the air. It took Olivia a few moments to recognize it as "Für Elise."

Apparently Lady St. Leger recognized it, too, for she clutched Olivia's hand more tightly and gasped, "That song! That was one of Roddy's favorites. Wasn't it, Pamela?"

From across the table, Pamela said in a hollow voice, "Yes. Yes, it was."

Stephen's grip tightened around Olivia's hand, and she knew that he was struggling to keep from once again interrupting the séance with a loud oath. She squeezed his hand in silent communication, and he returned the gesture, letting her know that he was in control of his emotions.

The music stopped as suddenly as it had begun. There was silence, and then Madame Valenskaya spoke, her voice low and hoarse, speaking slowly, almost as if unused to it. "Mama?"

"Roddy?" Lady St. Leger said eagerly, tears clogging her throat. "Roddy, is that you?"

"Yes, Mama, it is I."

"Oh, darling!" Lady St. Leger stopped on a sob.

"Why are you here?" It was Pamela who spoke up this time, her voice brittle as glass. "What are you seeking?"

"Peace," the voice replied, then let out a ponderous sigh. "I cannot rest. None of us here can rest."

"What can we do?" Lady St. Leger cried. "Can we help you?"

"None can rest in this house until the Martyrs rest," the voice replied in its eerie, measured tones.

"The Martyrs!" Belinda exclaimed.

Olivia had no idea what they were talking about, but she could sense in the tensions around her that at least some of the others did.

"But, Roddy, what do you mean?" Lady St. Leger asked, her voice troubled and confused.

"We cannot be at peace. They cannot be at peace because of the way they were mistreated — put to death, everything stolen."

"No! Roddy!" Lady St. Leger sounded heart-sick. "But we had nothing to do with —"

"No peace . . ." the voice said on a sigh, fading away.

"Roddy?" Lady St. Leger asked, her voice stark with pain. "Roddy? No, don't go. Oh, please — come back!"

There was only silence after her words, broken by the sound of Lady St. Leger weeping. At the end of the table, Madame Valenskaya stirred and groaned.

"What — what happen?" she asked groggily, rustling in her chair.

Irina lit one of the lamps on the table and turned it up a little. It cast only a low light, leaving the rest of the room in darkness and illu-minating the forms around the table in an eerie play of light and shadow. Olivia glanced at the

145

others. Madame Valenskaya was putting on a great show of waking from a trance. Her daughter and Mr. Babington, on either side of her, looked puzzled. Lady St. Leger was crying softly into her handkerchief, and Stephen looked thunderous. Lady Pamela and Belinda looked surprised.

Madame Valenskaya asked again what had transpired during her trance, and her daughter quietly related to her what "Roddy" had told them.

"I'm sorry," Mr. Babington spoke up after Irina finished, his voice diffident. "But I didn't understand — do you know what he meant? Who are the Martyrs?"

"Yes." Madame Valenskaya nodded her head ponderously. "I wish to know, too."

"They were the family who used to live here," Belinda said. "A long, long time ago. King Henry VIII cut off their heads."

Madame Valenskaya let out a dramatic gasp.

"They died for their faith. That's why they're called the Martyrs," Belinda continued. "I don't remember their names."

"Their name was Scorhill," Stephen said. "They owned Blackhope and had for genera-tions. I don't know how far back. But during King Henry's reign, they refused to switch their religion."

"Like Sir Thomas More," Olivia said.

"Yes, just less well-known. The Crown confis-cated their lands and executed them for treason."

"A whole family?" Olivia felt sick, thinking of it.

"Father and mother and two grown sons. If anyone was left, I have no idea what happened to them."

"How awful."

He nodded. "The land stayed with the Crown, of course. Then, during Queen Elizabeth's reign, it was given to our ancestor, along with the title — the first Earl St. Leger. He was one of the Queen's seafaring raiders, and he brought the Queen a good bit of Spanish gold. Blackhope was his reward from her."

"So we had nothing to do with it," Lady St. Leger said, her voice still tremulous with tears. She dabbed at her eyes with her handkerchief. "How can they make Roderick suffer? He did nothing wrong."

Olivia took Lady St. Leger's hand in sympathy. "I am sure he didn't, my lady."

"It's so cruel," Lady St. Leger protested.

"Yes." Olivia glanced at Madame Valenskaya, her expression hardening. "It is cruel. But it will end. I promise."

"It's cruel," Olivia repeated sometime later, pacing the floor of Stephen's study. They had gone there after the séance had broken up and the others had gone on to their rooms. "It's heartless. I cannot believe they would use Lady St. Leger so callously. What do they hope to accomplish, anyway, with all this talk of martyrs?"

"Money," Stephen replied flatly. He, also, was still on his feet, too restless after the evening's events to sit down. "Perhaps they will offer to exorcise all those restless spirits for a fee. Or maybe they are hoping I will simply pay them off to get them away from my mother. God knows, I might just do it if they put her through many more nights like this. Much as I despise giving in to extortion, I cannot stand by and watch her suffer."

"We will stop them," Olivia said flatly. "Let's consider. First, how did they find out about this family that used to live here? The Martyrs. I would not think that is common knowledge. I have never heard of them, certainly."

"They were not terribly important historically," Stephen agreed. "But it's something of a local legend. You know how that is — tales of some ghostly woman who is seen at midnight, and people say she was one of the martyred family. It makes a good story. There is a family history of the St. Legers, and I believe the martyred Scorhills are mentioned there. They might be included in a comprehensive account of King Henry's reign. But, more likely, they picked it up from something Mother or Belinda or Pamela said."

"The same way they learned your brother's favorite songs."

"Yes. But how did they bring off that ruse?" Stephen asked. "I mean, we all heard 'Für Elise.' "

"First they would have found out what songs he particularly liked, probably easier to bring out in casual conversation than one would imagine. Then they just had to find a small music box that played one of the tunes that were his favorites. They wind the music box up so that it will play, then Madame Valenskaya conceals it in another of her pockets or maybe even inside the skirt. She runs a thin wire inside her dress from the switch on the music box to her hand, and when she tugs on the wire, the lever on the music box is pulled, releasing the mechanism, and it plays, fading out soon enough."

He shook his head. "They are clever."

"What of the monk tonight?" Olivia asked. "Is that another local legend? Monks, headless and otherwise, frequently are."

Stephen shrugged. "Not that I can recall. Although, as you said, they often appear in ghostly stories. And a monk would fit with the idea of the Martyrs, since they were killed for not renouncing Catholicism. The Dissolution of the Abbeys was at the same time as the Scorhills' troubles."

Olivia looked thoughtful. "I think they made a mistake with that 'ghost' tonight. However badly it may have frightened Lady St. Leger and softened her up for tonight's séance, it also carries the seeds of their destruction. If we could just find that robe in one of their rooms, it would prove they were behind the little show in the garden."

"I presume it was Babington," Stephen mused.

"I would think so. The monk was certainly not wide and short enough to be Madame Valenskaya, and though it was hard to judge height looking down on it like that, I think it was probably taller than Irina, also. So, unless they have a cohort outside this house working with them, it would have to be Mr. Babington."

"He hardly seems the sort to have the nerve for it," Stephen commented.

"Perhaps that quiet, reticent demeanor of his is another disguise." Olivia shrugged. "Tom can get into his room tomorrow. He offered to take on the job of polishing Mr. Babington's shoes and cleaning his clothes from one of the other footman, so it won't be remarked if he goes in there tomorrow morning. He can search for the robe."

"Yes, if Babington has not already destroyed it. That would be the first thing I would do if I were he — toss it into the fire as soon as I got back and let it burn while everyone is down- stairs talking about the incident."

"Not if you intended to use it again," Olivia pointed out. "How could you be certain that you might not have to trot out the ghost for an- other fright? I wouldn't imagine they think you are going to give in easily."

"I'm not so sure that I would want to have to carry it back into the house, either," Stephen said thoughtfully. "I mean, here I am — I run off into the lower garden. I know there is bound to be pursuit soon. So I strip off the robe and mask — presuming that the skull face is some sort of mask."

Olivia nodded. "That would seem far easier than disguising one's face with phosphorescent paint. After all, then you would have to take the time to wipe it all off before you slipped back into the house, and what if you missed some of it and ran into someone and they saw it? The game would be up."

"That's the crux of the problem — running into someone. The fellow has to get back into the house, and there are going to be people running around outside and in after something like that. One could hope to slip in a side door, and then, if someone comes upon you out in the garden, you can say that you, too, are looking for the 'ghost.' And once inside, you can just pretend to have been in another part of the house and have come to see what all the fuss is. But it would be a little difficult to explain why you are carrying a robe and mask with you."

"True. The intelligent thing would be to take it off in the garden and leave it. Hide it, because you don't want the thing found, for then it's clear that it was a person, not an apparition."

"Right." Stephen grinned at her. "So you scout out a place to hide it before the event, then go there, put the thing away, and go back to retrieve it later."

"The next day?"

He looked thoughtful. "I think tonight, don't you?"

Olivia nodded. "Yes. He is bound to realize that you will start a massive hunt for it tomorrow. So he would not want to leave it. We are much more likely to find it in the daylight, so unless it is in an excellent hiding space, we might very well come upon it. I wouldn't take the chance if I were he."

"Then he will sneak outside tonight to retrieve his robe, if we are right in our assumptions." Stephen's eyes brightened. "What would you say to keeping a watch on our guest Mr. Babington? We might follow him to the hiding place and catch him red-handed."

"I think it's an excellent idea." Olivia smiled back, excitement fizzing up inside her.

They left the study and climbed the stairs, going down the hall past Mr. Babington's room, treading with extreme softness. Stephen stopped in front of the door across the hall and down one from Babington's and silently turned the knob. He opened the door, and they slipped inside, leaving the door open a crack.

The room in which they stood was clearly unused, its furniture hidden under dustcovers, and it was a trifle chilly in the late August evening. Stephen looked around the room, lit only by the crack of light from the hall, then moved about, locating a stool in front of the vanity, which he brought back and set down for Olivia to sit on.

The minutes passed slowly. The house was

quiet, no one stirring. Olivia began to wonder if they had thought of Babington's going out to retrieve the robe too late. Or perhaps they had it all wrong, and it had not been Mr. Babington in the garden this evening at all. She shivered in the growing evening chill and wished she had thought to go to her room and get a shawl before coming here. Indeed, it would have been a good idea to change out of her evening dress altogether, for while its wide, open neckline might set off her chest and shoulders admirably, it did little to keep her warm.

Stephen removed his jacket and draped it around her shoulders, and Olivia looked up, surprised. The coat was still warm from the heat of his body, and she noticed that it smelled like him, a clean, crisp, indefinably masculine scent. She thought of yesterday when he had kissed her, and looking at his face, she was suddenly sure he was thinking of the same thing. Her breath came a little faster in her throat, and she rose slowly to her feet.

The soft click of a door closing in the hall broke in on her consciousness, and she turned back quickly to look through the crack of the door. Howard Babington was walking the hall, his steps careful and soft.

"He's leaving," she hissed, and Stephen opened the door a little wider so he could also see.

Their quarry started down the main staircase, and they left the room, following him with equal quietness. At the top of the stairs, they paused, watching as Babington crossed the large room below them and entered the hall leading to the conservatory and the back door. Stephen, more familiar with the house, went down the stairs first, with Olivia right behind him. The large, open area below them was lit dimly by a few of the wall sconces, their wicks turned so low that Stephen and Olivia were barely able to see their way. They reached the bottom of the stairs and started to tiptoe across the marbled floor in the direction Babington had taken.

At that moment a woman walked across the room. Olivia and Stephen came to a dead halt, staring at her.

She wore a long, narrow dress, belted with a chain of gold rings around her hips and falling straight down the front almost to her knees. Her hair was hidden under a veil that fell back from a low headdress. She did not turn her head to look at them as she moved across their path. It was as if she was the only person in the room. Nor did she pause as she neared the wall. Instead, she walked straight through it and disappeared.

6

Olivia let out a squeak and leaped across the space separating her from Stephen. His arms went around her tightly, and for a long moment they stood, staring at the spot where the woman had disappeared.

"Bloody hell!" Stephen exclaimed softly. "What was that?"

Olivia could only shake her head, unspeaking. A shudder shook her body, and he squeezed her more tightly to him. They looked at each other, and it struck them, finally, that they were standing in each other's arms in full view of anyone who might happen to come by.

Suddenly embarrassed and awkward, they let their arms fall away from each other, and they stepped back. Olivia felt very cold, even inside Stephen's jacket, and she wished she were back in his arms once more.

"Did you see —" he began and stopped, searching for the right words.

"A woman?" Olivia offered. "Yes, I did."

"And did she pass right through that wall?"
Olivia nodded.

"Well, at least I know I'm not mad, unless we've both been struck at once."

Stephen went to a table and picked up a candle, lighting it from one of the sconces, and walked over to the part of the wall where the woman had disappeared. Olivia joined him, though she wasn't entirely sure whether it was from curiosity or from a distinct desire not to be left by herself in the middle of the room.

He held the candle close to the wall, moving it from side to side and up and down, looking for some sort of crack or opening. Olivia shivered.

"It's freezing," Stephen said, and, amazingly, his breath hung on the air for an instant like mist.

They looked at each other again in consternation. It was August, not nearly cold enough for one's breath to condense in the chilled air. Olivia shook her head, as if to disown the reality before them. They moved away from the wall until they reached a place where it was no longer cold.

"I think," Stephen said after a moment, "that what we could use now is a bit of brandy."

He took her arm and led her in the other direction, where his study lay. Once there, he closed the door behind them and lit the wall sconces, as well as the lamp on his desk. Olivia plopped down in a chair, watching him numbly as he crossed to a cabinet and pulled out a bottle of brandy. After pouring a healthy dollop into each snifter, he brought them back and handed one to Olivia.

"I've never —" she began protestingly, but he shook his head.

"This is a time to break the rules," Stephen assured her. "Drink up."

In truth, Olivia felt as though she needed something to calm her nerves, and she took a quick sip. The liquid burned in her mouth and all the way down her throat to her stomach. Her eyes watered, and she let out a gasp. But she had to admit that a moment later she no longer felt as cold or as numb.

"Now . . ." Stephen said, taking a healthy swallow and perching on the edge of his desk. "Can you tell me what we just saw?"

"A woman," Olivia said, pleased that she managed to keep her voice steady. "Who appeared from nowhere and walked across the room in front of us and through a wall, disappearing."

"Succinctly put." He paused. "Can this have been some trick of Madame and her group?"

"Oh! Babington!" Olivia exclaimed, suddenly remembering. "We were following him."

Stephen nodded. "That apparition drove him out of my head. No hope of finding him now. We don't even know by which door he left."

"I guess not. I'll tell Tom to search Mr. Babington's room tomorrow, to see if he hides it there." Olivia sighed and turned her mind to his question. Could Madame Valenskaya have engineered the vision they saw?

What they had seen, she thought, had been far eerier than the "monk" treading the garden path this afternoon. There had been something not quite solid about the woman; she had not been transparent, but she had somehow not looked substantial, either. Most of all, she had not gone from sight down steps into the dark lower garden. She had walked through a solid wall and completely vanished.

"I cannot imagine how anyone could have accomplished such a trick," Olivia admitted, and took another swallow of brandy. "I have seen a medium put on gauze painted with phosphorescent paint and move about the room in very little light to pretend to be a spirit. But this was nothing like that. What we saw appeared to be a real person, someone of flesh and blood. And she walked through a wall! How could anyone make it look as if she had strode right through a solid wall?"

She did not add the most bizarre and chilling thing about the vision they had just seen: that the woman had looked exactly like the woman Olivia had dreamed about sitting in front of the fire yesterday.

She could not think of any way to tell Stephen that without sounding as if she had gone utterly mad. But she was certain it was the same woman. The dress had been different, a deep crimson this time, with gold undertunic and sleeves, a richer, more formal looking gown, and she had worn a headdress and veil, which had hidden her pale blond hair except at the very front, but her eyes, her facial features, the small, lithe body — all were exactly like the woman in her dream.

It was impossible. One did not dream of an unknown woman, then see her so soon thereafter, particularly when that woman seemed to walk straight through a wall. She refused to even think about the fact that at first, when she had seen the woman yesterday, Olivia had thought she really was there in front of the fire. It was only later, when Olivia woke up, that she realized she must have been dreaming. The whole thing made her uneasy in a way she could not begin to express. If it were not for the fact that Stephen, too, had seen the woman tonight, she would have been afraid she had run mad.

"Would it be possible . . . ?" Stephen began musingly, then halted, looking embarrassed.

"What? Go on? It could not possibly be any more bizarre than what we just witnessed."

"You're right. What I was thinking was — if a person were an expert mesmerist, would he or she be able to make someone else believe that he saw something that was not really there? I have heard strange tales of mesmerism."

Olivia sat up a little straighter, intrigued by the idea. "I'm not sure. I have studied mesmerism — it is a fascinating subject. Not all that silly mumbo jumbo about animal magnetism and such. That is why I prefer the term 'hypnotism.' It separates the study from Mesmer's oddities. It is possible to put a person into a sort of half-conscious state. It can be used to remove pain. I have experienced that myself. But I personally have never witnessed any of the phenomena that some have claimed, such as making people act in peculiar ways or do things that they do not remember. The times when I was put into a trance that way, I was aware all the time of what he was saying, and I remembered it afterward, as well. However, there are those who claim it can be used to give one suggestions that one later carries out, not knowing why. If such claims are true, then . . ."

Stephen grimaced. "It sounds absurd."

Olivia nodded. "But no more absurd than someone walking through walls. However, it would mean that Madame Valenskaya or one of the other two would have had to hypnotize both of us and implant the suggestion that we would see such a woman, and also have gotten us to forget that we had ever been hypnotized."

"Unlikely," Stephen agreed. "And how could they make sure that we would see her at the same time? But how else could they have done it? Some sort of mirror arrangement? There was no sign of any mirrors in that room. And I can see no way for a person to appear to step into a wall and disappear."

"And how would they have known to set it up for just that particular time and place? It was happenstance that we were there," Olivia pointed out.

"Not entirely. We were following Mr. Babington."

"You mean, he could have led us right to it? That would indicate they knew we would be following him," Olivia said.

"One could assume we might, I suppose. Clearly you and I did not believe there was a ghost in the garden. They could guess that we would have worked out that Mr. Babington would be the most likely suspect and that he would go out to retrieve his costume, and that we would follow him."

"They could assume that *you* might," Olivia corrected. "I do not think most people would expect me to be helping you in the investigation."

"True. But if they set it up for me, you saw it simply because you were there, too. They wouldn't have had to plan for you."

"Unless it was done by hypnotism, as you suggested. But then they would have had to plant the suggestion in both of us. And they would have had to know we would be there at that time."

"Not necessarily," Stephen argued. "It could have been something that they suggested we would do if we followed Mr. Babington. That way it would throw us off his trail no matter what the reason we were following him — and it would make us witnesses to another ghost."

"A much more believable one," Olivia commented.

"I must say, none of this seems very believable to me," Stephen said wryly.

"No. Nor to me. But we cannot ignore the evidence of our own eyes, either. If we are to judge things impartially, scientifically, we cannot afford blind disbelief any more than blind faith."

"What are you suggesting, then? That this really was a ghost?" Stephen asked.

Olivia glanced at him. "I have as little faith as you do in the actuality of spirits and ghosts. But we must sift through all the information that we have if we are to arrive at an accurate conclusion. It occurs to me — why was she dressed the way she was dressed?"

"Because she was from a different time — or, rather, because we were to be led to believe she was from a different time."

"Yes, but why that time? They were talking about this martyred family tonight, the Scorhills, but if I understood you correctly, they were from the early sixteenth century. Yet this woman's dress was definitely medieval. My guess is from around the time of Eleanor of Aquitaine."

Stephen raised his brows. "You can be that specific?"

Olivia shrugged. "I am fairly confident of it. Within a hundred years or so. Styles did not change as quickly in the Middle Ages. But her dress resembled ones I have seen in drawings and paintings of Queen Eleanor. I have read a good bit of history, and my favorite great-uncle is forever reading and talking about it. He, as it happens, is a great student of Henry II, Eleanor's husband, so I have seen pictures of her more than once. At any rate, I am certain it is medieval, not Tudor."

"Why wouldn't they play up the Martyrs, given what happened in the séance?"

"It would seem to make more sense."

He smiled. "Perhaps they had a medieval costume handy but not a Tudor one. It might not be accurate, but at least it's ghostly."

"A medieval tunic and underdress would probably be easier to sew and to get into, that's true. They are simpler. But this afternoon they used a robed monk, which does seem to fit with the Martyrs, at least to some extent. And if someone is able to pull off as good a trick as a woman walking through a wall, I would think they would bother to costume the ghost correctly."

"What I find hardest to swallow is the idea that Madame Valenskaya and her cohorts have the intelligence to conjure up a trick like that," Stephen said.

"I agree. But if it was not somehow caused by them, then we are left with only the theory that it was real."

They looked at each other. It was not a theory either of them was eager to accept.

Olivia glanced around the room. "There are a number of books here."

"Yes, and more in the library. What are you suggesting?"

"That we do a little research," Olivia replied.

"Into what?"

"Well . . . her gown, for one thing. We could make sure that it really is from the period I think it is. And perhaps we could find some information about the house. Belinda said she found out about the name while she was researching a paper for her tutor. She must have gotten the information from somewhere."

"Oh, I'm sure there must be some histories. People are always writing tiresome tracts about their ancestors. What exactly are we looking for?"

"I'm not sure. Hopefully we will know it when we see it."

They started at one end of the study, and after a few minutes of searching the shelves, they found two histories of England and a study of the English monarchs. Olivia sat down in the comfortable chair in front of Stephen's desk and began to flip through the biographies of the monarchs.

It was not long before she exclaimed with triumph, "Here! Look, a drawing of Queen Mathilde — you know, who fought with Henry over who was the rightful ruler of England. She is dressed in much the same way as our woman tonight."

Stephen, who had settled down behind the desk with one of the histories, came around to look over her shoulder. "Yes. Except for the fur around the cuffs and neck, it looks very much the same."

Olivia turned another few pages. "And here is Eleanor. Still much the same."

"So we must assume that our apparition is dressed as a — what, twelfth-century lady?"

"Yes. She's clearly a woman of some consequence — that girdle she wore around her waist looked like gold links with some sort of stones, perhaps even precious gems. They were unfaceted back then, you know."

"There was some gold in the headdress, as well."

"Of course one would dress as a lady for haunting a place — you may have noticed how rarely ghosts are said to be a farmer or tanner or goldsmith," Olivia said.

Stephen smiled faintly at her statement. "Now that you have placed our lady in time, would you care to take one of these histories off my hands?"

"Of course." Olivia set aside her tome and picked up the one lying on Stephen's desk. Idly she flipped back to the time of the Conquest and began to move forward. "Do we know when this house came to be named Blackhope?" She covered a yawn with her hand.

"I have no idea. Obviously Belinda's tutor was more concerned with the history of this place than any of mine ever were. I don't really know much about it before our family took it over. Somewhere, I know, there's a history of the St. Legers, but it won't help us learn about this house before the time of the Martyrs."

They began to read again, and the room was silent. It was some minutes before Stephen looked up from his reading with a sigh and glanced across at Olivia. She was sitting in the wing chair, feet curled up under her, the book she had been studying lying open in her lap and her head resting against one of the wings of the chair, her eyes closed. Her breasts rose and fell in the slow rhythm of sleep.

Stephen smiled, watching her. There was something about her, he thought, that fascinated him. He found himself thinking about her more and more frequently, and he looked forward to seeing her. She looked lovely asleep, soft and innocent, but he liked, too, the snap of intelligence and wit in her brown eyes, the smile that so often curved her lips, the quick, compact way she moved. He had apologized for kissing her the other day because it had been the gentlemanly thing to do; he scarcely knew her and should not be making advances toward her. However, he did not regret it in the slightest. He had, in fact, enjoyed the kiss thoroughly.

Olivia Moreland stirred his blood; she had from the moment he met her. When he had looked into her eyes that first night, a sizzle had run down through him, a feeling that was not only desire but also some sort of recognition. There were romantics who talked of two people's souls crying out to each other; he had always dismissed such talk as twaddle, but after that moment, he was not so sure. In some strange way, he had felt almost as if he knew her, although that clearly was impossible. There were others, he knew, who would laugh and say that what he felt for her was desire, pure and simple — a physical attraction, a chemical reaction. But he was not entirely sure that that was an adequate explanation, either.

He rose and walked softly across the floor to the small sofa and picked up a crocheted afghan that lay folded decoratively across the back of it. He came back on silent feet to Olivia's chair and laid the small blanket gently over her. She stirred a little and snuggled into the warmth of the cover. He stood looking down at her for a moment, then returned to his seat behind the desk.

Laying the book flat, he propped his elbow on the desk and his forehead on his hand and began reading again. Time passed, and his lids grew heavy. He blinked and started reading again, then stopped again, rubbing his hand across his face. He curled an arm across the book and laid his head down on it.

He leaned against the wall, its sun-touched stone warm against his back, and surveyed the bailey of the castle before him. He pretended to watch the ac-

tivity, but his focus was all on her. She walked down the steps and across the courtyard, a basket hooked over her arm, a ring of keys in her hand. She was not wearing her elegant clothes, merely a plain blue tunic and undergown, and a simple cloth veil on her head. The girdle just above her hips was plaited leather, not gold or silver. But she looked as beautiful as ever to him. His skin tingled for her; his guts clenched in desire.

He knew she could never be his. She was forbidden to him, a married woman and, moreover, married to the man to whom he had sworn fealty.

He watched as she entered the storage building, then swung his gaze around the courtyard. Two servant girls were tending to a tub of wash, and farther away, children chased a hen. Two guards stood at the gates, but there were no men-at-arms idling where their commander could see them. No one watched him.

He strolled away from the gate, moving to the side of the keep. He knew he should not do what he was doing. It was dishonorable, and he hated himself for his disloyalty. But he could not stop himself; he could not stay away from her.

When he was out of sight of the few people in the courtyard, he turned and walked into the same building into which she had gone. It was much dimmer in here, lit only by sunlight creeping in through the cracks of the wooden shutters and door. The door into the cellars stood open, flung back against the floor. There was a dim light below. He moved cautiously down the stairs and into the storage room, making his way through the casks and barrels and crates toward the torch, thrust into an iron holder on the wall.

She was opening a barrel and peering inside when she heard the sound of his steps, and she turned, a look on her face that was part surprise and part hope. When she saw him, a smile broke across her face.

"Sir John!" She started toward him, her eyes alight, then stopped, guilt settling on her face. "We should not — you must not risk it."

He thought that he would risk all for her, but he did not say it. Words, he knew, were easy. He came up to her. Up close, he could see the bruise on her cheek, and his stomach tightened within him.

He reached up and laid a gentle finger beside the bruise. "Did Sir Raymond put this there?" His voice sounded like ground glass, and fury quivered in him.

She nodded, looking away from him, ashamed. She shrugged. "It is nothing. It was not —"

"I hate him!" His voice lashed out. "He is a cruel, godless man. I would like to kill him for hurting you."

He bent and gently brushed his lips against the bruise.

A little sigh, part pleasure, part sorrow, escaped her lips. "But you cannot. He is your liege lord, and you are sworn to protect him."

"I would I had sworn to any other man."

"Then I would never have met you," she reminded him. Her eyes here in the dim light were dark, but he *knew their cornflower-blue color well. They had pierced his heart many months before.*

"I hate the way he so boldly keeps his mistress in the castle. It is shameful, an insult to you. I have seen the slut Elwena flaunting herself about."

"Nay." She laid a finger against his lips, smiling and shaking her head. "It does not matter."

"It matters to me." He looked down at her, love and desire coursing through him. He raised his hands to her face, smoothing them over her soft skin. "Alys . . ."

He moved his hands back, pushing aside the simple veil and sinking them into the pale flaxen mass of her hair. She looked up at him, her lips partly open, her breath rushing in and out. He bent and kissed her, unable to hold back. Pleasure rushed through him like a torrent, a roiling blend of heat and passion and tenderness.

But now, as it happened in dreams, the woman in his arms changed. Suddenly she was Olivia, and it was Stephen who was holding her, not Sir John. Her mouth was warm and damp, her body eagerly clinging to his. Passion surged in him as his hands roamed her soft flesh.

There was a sharp noise; he wasn't sure what it had been, only that it jerked him out of his dream. Stephen awoke with a gasp, his body still boiling with lust. Blinking, confused and dazed with passion, he slowly raised his head.

A few feet away from him, Olivia was sitting straight up in her chair, the book that had been lying in her lap now on the floor at her feet. She was wide-awake and staring at him, her mouth, soft with passion, opened in a startled "O." Her brown eyes were luminous with desire, her cheeks flushed. Yet at the same time, there was a look on her face of mingled surprise and embarrassment.

He gazed at her, unable to speak, and suddenly, with a jolt, he was sure somehow that she knew what he had been dreaming. "Olivia . . ."

She let out a strangled noise and jumped to her feet, the light blanket falling unnoticed to her feet, then turned and ran out the door.

Olivia sought out Tom Quick early the next morning and explained to him her need to have Mr. Babington's room searched for the presence of a black robe such as the "ghost" in the garden had worn the day before.

That task done, she spent the rest of the day assiduously avoiding Stephen. When she saw him in the sitting room with the others later in the morning, she quickly turned and went for a walk in the garden. Though she disliked causing extra work for any of the servants, she had Joan bring her midday meal up to her room on a tray, and then she spent the rest of the afternoon cooped up in her room reading a long and rather boring novel she found there.

The only break in the monotony came when Tom reported to her on his search. He had found nothing untoward in Mr. Babington's room, including a black robe. His words did not surprise her. After they had lost Babington the night before in their amazement over seeing "Lady Alys," she had been sure that Babington would retrieve the incriminating evidence from wherever he had hidden it and get rid of it. Still, she had hoped that Babington might have been careless enough to store it in his room, so Tom's news made her spirits sink even lower.

She would have to tell Stephen, of course, about the results of Tom's search or, rather, the lack of them. But she thought surely that task could be put off until tomorrow. She simply could not face him today — not after that bizarre, licentious dream she had had last night.

It was bad enough that she had fallen asleep in Stephen's study. It was not the sort of thing ladies were supposed to do. Besides, it was embarrassing. Had he thought her rude and uncouth? Had her hair been mussed? Had she talked in her sleep? Worse yet, what if she had snored?

But none of that was as bad as the dream she had had. She had once again dreamed of the medieval woman and man whom she had seen in her dream the other afternoon, the very same woman whom she and Stephen had seen in the great hall. She supposed that was natural enough, as her head had been filled with the woman and the earlier dream, but it still disturbed her to have seen her again. At first it had been like the other dream, as if she were watching a play, and then it had seemed somehow as if she herself was the woman — Alys, he called her — who was speaking and looking at the knight. They had started kissing, and she had felt the onrush of desire, the throbbing hunger that centered in her loins and radiated out through her body.

And then, somehow, she was no longer the medieval lady but herself again, and the man was not the medieval knight, but Stephen. And the heat and passion had been even more intense. She had been alive with sensation, every inch of her tingling and aware. She had ached for him, thrilled to his kiss . . . his touch. . . . Even thinking about it the next day brought a flush of heat that had nothing to do with embarrassment and everything to do with desire.

The passion had grown so strong, the sensations so intense, that finally she had jolted out of her dream and sat straight up, the heavy book in her lap sliding down to the floor with a bang. She had stared at Stephen, dazed and astonished, unable for an instant to separate reality from dream, her loins still heavy with desire.

Then he had raised his head and looked straight at her, and his face had been slack with passion, his eyes hungry and hot. And she had been certain in that instant that he knew exactly what she had been dreaming. Stunned, all she had been able to do was run away.

And she had continued doing so all day long.

She knew, of course, that it was impossible for him to have known what she was dreaming. He wouldn't even have seen her face as she dreamed or heard her say anything revealing, for he obviously had been asleep also, his head resting on his arm on his desk.

But she could not forget the look of passion on his face or the way his eyes had bored into hers. In that moment she had been certain he had seen everything inside her, had felt the blood coursing wildly through her veins, heard the breath coming sharp and fast in her throat, that he had known what lay in her heart and mind.

Since what lay inside her was lust for him, she was humiliated, sure that he must think her forward, licentious, foolish. And no matter how many times she reminded herself that he could not possibly have known, still she could not bring herself to look him in the eyes.

Olivia knew it would be rude to excuse herself from supper altogether unless she were ill, but fortunately, it was impossible for Stephen to actually hold a conversation with her there. Afterward, however, he managed to catch her as she left the room.

"Olivia . . ."

She glanced at him briefly, then away. He looked frowning and serious, and it made her stomach churn with anxiety. "I, um, you must excuse me," she said quickly. "I have a bit of a headache, so I'm going to retire early tonight."

"But —"

She smiled stiffly, still not looking into his eyes. "I'm sorry. Really. Another time. Excuse me."

She turned and walked away quickly, and short of grabbing her by the arm, he could not keep her there. She was almost to her room when she heard quick footsteps behind her.

"Lady Olivia." It was Pamela's voice.

Olivia turned, surprised. Roderick's widow had hardly spoken to her the whole time she had been here, other than to not-so-subtly insult her family. But there was a smile on her porcelain-doll face now as she walked up to Olivia.

"I trust you are not feeling ill, are you?" Pamela said, a hint of concern on her face.

"It's nothing. Just a touch of headache, that's all," Olivia assured her.

"Good. I saw Stephen try to talk to you —" She hesitated, then went on. "I trust you will not think me a busybody, but I have noticed that you avoided Lord St. Leger all day."

"Oh! Oh, no!" Olivia replied, a flush stealing up into her cheeks. "I wasn't avoiding him. I was merely, um . . ."

Pamela let out a light laugh. "It's all right. I am sure no one noticed but me. I, you see, have some experience in that area."

Olivia looked at her blankly. "I beg your pardon?"

"I've known Lord St. Leger for some time. I have seen him at work before. He is a terrible flirt. A charming man, of course, but it's dangerous to take him seriously."

Olivia flushed even more. "Oh, no, you

mustn't think — I am sure Lord St. Leger has not been flirting with me."

Pamela gave her a knowing look. "Well, consider it a forewarning, then. He has trifled with the affections of more than one young lady."

Olivia stared at her. Admittedly, she was a novice in the affairs of men and women, but she had trouble believing that. Stephen simply did not seem like the sort of man who indulged himself in flirtations and toying with the affections of naive young women. *And why was Pamela suddenly so concerned about her feelings?*

Pamela apparently saw Olivia's disbelief on her face, for she went on. "I speak from experience. You see, I fell in love with Stephen many years ago, before I had even met Roderick. Stephen broke my heart. Left me and sailed off for America. Thank heavens, Roddy was there to help mend it. I suppose I should be grateful to Stephen, for without his hurting me, Roderick would never have sought me out to try to apologize for his brother."

"What?" Olivia could not imagine Stephen being so callous.

Pamela quirked an eyebrow and said with some irritation, "It's the truth. Why on earth would I make up something like that? It scarcely reflects well on me."

"Yes, of course. I did not mean to imply . . ." Olivia trailed off to a self-conscious halt.

"Merely a word to the wise," Pamela said, then turned and walked back down the hall.

Olivia, with a sigh, went into her room and shut the door. She felt suddenly sad, as if she wanted to weep. Had she been so wrong about Stephen? Was he really as Pamela said, an accomplished, coldhearted flirt?

She would not have said that he had flirted with her. *Of course, there had been that kiss . . .* Certainly she was no expert on flirtation. And Pamela was right — Pamela wouldn't pretend to have been rejected by someone; it would be an embarrassing thing to admit, certainly not the sort of thing she would make up. Olivia had noticed the coolness that lay between Stephen and his brother's widow, and Pamela's story would explain it.

Perhaps Stephen really was as Pamela had said, a hardened flirt. Perhaps he had broken Pamela's heart and the hearts of other girls, as well. If it were true, then his kiss the other day had certainly meant nothing.

She had already told herself that it had not, of course. But it was a bitter pill to swallow to have the fact confirmed. If he had rejected a woman as beautiful as Pamela, there was little hope he had any real interest in her. Tears filled her eyes, and she blinked them back angrily. It should not matter to her that Stephen did not want her, she knew. Unfortunately, whatever her mind might say, in her heart she knew what Stephen St. Leger wanted was beginning to matter to her very much.

7

When Olivia awoke the next morning, she refused the dress that Joan offered and instead put on the only one of her dresses she had brought that Kyria and her maid had not altered, a plain brown frock with no ornamentation. She also turned down Joan's services as a hairdresser, pulling her hair back into the tight, simple knot in which she had worn it for years.

She was through trying to dress herself up, she decided. She was here purely for business, and the only thing she needed to appear was businesslike.

She marched downstairs to breakfast, determined to put her relationship with Lord St. Leger back on the correct footing. They were colleagues. Working partners. Whatever emotion he might have seen on her face the other night, it was impossible for him to have known what she had been dreaming about. And she would behave in such a way that he would realize that whatever he thought he had seen, he had been wrong.

Her determination lasted until she had finished eating breakfast, when one of the footmen handed her a note from Stephen requesting her presence in his study as soon as possible. She felt suddenly as if her stomach had dropped to her feet, and it took all her willpower to force her feet to turn to the study.

She knocked on the door, and when he called to her to enter, she wavered for a moment, then drew a deep breath and went inside.

"You asked to see me?" she said on a note of inquiry, proud that she was able to keep her voice light and cool. She could not, however, quite look him in the face, so she chose a point just over his shoulder at which to gaze.

"Uh, yes. Please, sit down." Stephen's voice sounded not quite as usual, either.

Olivia stole a quick peek at him. He looked — *could it be nervous?*

"We, um, never had a chance to speak yesterday. I thought you might want to know about the —" he paused and cleared his throat "— research I did."

"Oh?" Perhaps he had not realized what she had been dreaming about, Olivia thought, for the first time looking him full in the face. There was certainly no leering knowledge there. He looked, if anything, rather ill at ease. "What sort of research?"

"Well, I —" He stopped and looked at her searchingly for a moment. "Olivia . . . I . . . I dreamed the other night when I fell asleep at my desk."

It was such an abrupt change of subject that for a moment Olivia could only stare. "Excuse me?"

"The other night. When we were looking through the books, you fell asleep, and I sat here at my desk, reading, and I drifted off, also. I dreamed. When I woke up, I — it seemed to me that you had been dreaming, too."

Olivia felt heat flooding up her throat and into her cheeks. "Yes."

"I dreamed about the woman whom we had seen earlier. The vision."

"You did?" Olivia was startled from her embarrassment.

"Yes. I dreamed about her and a man, someone dressed as a knight. She called him Sir John, and he called her Alys. They were in some place with barrels all over —"

Olivia went cold to the bone. "What?" She took a step closer to him. "You saw them in a storage house?"

He nodded. "Yes. In a castle. In the courtyard, I mean. Then they went down through a trapdoor into a cellar."

Olivia's stomach went hot, and her feet and hands were like blocks of ice. She swayed a little, and Stephen leaped forward to take her by the arms and guide her into a chair.

"Here. Sit down. You look as if you're about to faint." He pushed her head down, squatting beside her.

"I think I was." Olivia looked at her hands;

they were trembling. She would not have been surprised if she had been trembling all over. "I dreamed the same dream."

"Sweet Christ!" There was a long silence. Stephen stood back up. "I thought — my first thought was that you had known what I had been dreaming."

"That is what *I* thought, too." Olivia stared at him. "But it was impossible."

"That is what I kept telling myself all day yesterday. I wanted to talk to you about it, but I could not find you. Did they talk about her husband? Did he ask her about a bruise on her cheek?"

"Yes! He asked her if Sir Raymond had done it to her!"

"Sir Raymond. That is what I heard him say, too." Stephen pushed his hands back into his hair, his expression a little wild. "And then they —"

"Yes," Olivia replied in a strangled voice, blushing to the roots of her hairline as she remembered the couple's embrace and the way the participants had changed into herself and Stephen.

She saw embarrassment in his face, too, but she saw more — a flame that lit his gray eyes and set up an answering heat inside her. Olivia's mouth went suddenly dry, and she didn't know where to look. Just sitting here, she could feel again the passion that had flooded through her; she could taste his kiss . . . his skin.

Olivia wrapped her arms around herself and stepped away. "It's impossible. How could we dream the same dream?"

"Yet we did."

"Madame Valenskaya could not have done this," she said positively. "No one could. How could anyone make us see exactly the same people do the same things in a dream?"

"If an expert mesmerist gave one the suggestion in a trance, said that one would dream about this scene . . ."

"But to arrange us dreaming it at the same time! I cannot believe anyone is that skillful, let alone Madame Valenskaya. She has no subtlety about her, no dexterity. Why, I have heard her accent slip more than once."

"Perhaps it isn't Madame Valenskaya. Maybe Babington is the mesmerist and Madame Valenskaya is just his tool."

Olivia frowned, unconvinced. "Whoever it is, how could he implant a suggestion that you and I would see the same thing?"

"Well, perhaps we didn't see exactly the same people."

"A man with light brown hair, tall and well muscled? His eyes green, with a scar along this cheek, low." She grazed her left cheek with a fingernail.

"I'm not sure how he looked. I felt as if — as if I were he. I saw the bailey, the castle, the woman, everything, through his eyes."

Olivia remembered how toward the end of the

dream she had somehow become the woman. Her voice trembled as she said, "This is absurd."

"It surpasses all logic that I know," Stephen admitted.

"I have never seen, never heard of, any mesmerist this skilled. I don't know of any trick that comes remotely close to this."

"But how else could it have happened?"

Olivia simply looked at him. There was nothing that could have accounted for their shared dream or for the earlier vision of the woman in the great hall.

"There is another thing," Stephen said after a moment. "I — I think I have dreamed about these people before."

"What!"

"While I was still in London, I had a dream. In it, I felt as if I were the same man, as if I were seeing through his eyes. But it was in an old castle. The steps were stone and curved around and up to a tower room. It was no place I'd ever seen before, but in the dream I knew it. It was home. I was fighting — for my life, the way it felt. I held a sword, not a light sword or a fencing foil, but a broadsword. I was dressed in chain mail. And behind me was a woman. I didn't see her — I could not look back, because I was fighting — but I could sense her there, and I knew her. She was — I think she was the lady of the castle and I was sworn to protect her. But there was something more — a deeper emotion, something beyond duty and loyalty. It was the same couple. I am sure of it. I felt as if I were the same man, if that makes any sense." He paused and glanced at Olivia. She looked stunned. "You probably think I am mad."

"No. No, I don't." Olivia stood up. "I dreamed of them before, too. I recognized that woman when we saw her in the hall. I had dreamed about her the day before — her and the man. She was drying her hair in front of the fire in my room — only it wasn't my room, but another room, with rushes on the floor and a bigger fireplace. Then he came in and knelt beside her. It was Sir John. At first I thought she was there, that I was actually lying there looking at her, but then I awoke and realized it had been a dream. When we saw her walk across the room, I knew it was the same woman."

"Why didn't you tell me?"

"Because I was afraid you would think I was insane!" Olivia retorted. "It was so bizarre, and everyone half believes we Morelands are all mad, anyway. I didn't want you to look at me as if I should be locked away."

"I don't think you're mad. I don't think *I'm* mad. I just cannot explain, in a rational manner anything that has happened."

"What should we do?"

"I don't know. I did some research today. I went to Belinda and asked her about that paper her tutor had her write. She went up to the nursery and dug out the books she had used for it. And I found a chap named Sir Raymond."

Olivia gaped at him. "Here? At Blackhope?"

"He owned Blackhope long before the St. Legers took over. He was an ancestor of the Lord Scorhill who lost the place to Henry VIII. Sir Raymond lived here during the reign of Henry II."

Olivia felt as if someone had punched her in the stomach.

Stephen, watching her, nodded. "I know. I had the same reaction."

"Then these people we saw really existed? They lived here in the twelfth century?"

"I don't know. I saw no mention of Sir Raymond's wife or of anyone named Sir John. But it would be unlikely that either of them would be in a history. He was merely the captain of Sir Raymond's men."

"And wives are rarely mentioned," Olivia finished somewhat caustically. "I know."

"However, it was this Sir Raymond that Belinda was talking about at supper the other night. The one during whose ownership the estate got its name of Blackhope."

"The man who shut himself up in the house because his wife died?"

"The very same. That, of course, was put down as legend. But it is fact that this same Sir Raymond rebuilt Blackhope. Apparently at some point, the original Norman keep was destroyed — or mostly so — during a siege. Sir

Raymond built the present house almost directly on the ruins of the original."

"A siege?" Olivia looked at him questioningly. "Such as the battle in your dream?"

Stephen shrugged. "Certainly the enemy was inside the house. And there were fires. I remember the smoke."

"The great hall, where we saw the woman, is the oldest part of this house, isn't it?" Stephen nodded, and she went on. "If it was built on the site of the original, then where that woman walked would have been where the first castle stood. Perhaps she was walking through a doorway in the old house, and that is why she walked right through the — oh, what am I saying!" Olivia flung her hands up to her head in dismay. "There are no ghosts. I don't believe in ghosts. There is no medieval woman stalking through the house! It had to be something that Madame Valenskaya and her group are doing."

"Yet you yourself said you had never heard of anyone being able to do such things."

"Well, that doesn't mean that someone *can't*," Olivia pointed out. "I just don't know how they do it. But it seems too much of a coincidence that these things are happening at the same time that Madame Valenskaya is here conducting séances and nattering on about the lost souls in this house."

"But how would she know about Sir Raymond and his wife? *I* didn't even know about them, and this is my house."

"First of all, we don't know that anything about the wife or this Sir John fellow is true. There is no mention of anyone save a Sir Raymond. Second, Belinda knew about him. She was telling us the other day. She could easily have told the same story to Madame Valenskaya or her daughter. Madame Valenskaya could even have found this history book where Belinda got her information. After all, she, or someone, dug up the story about the Martyrs."

"The Martyrs are quite a bit better known. However," Stephen conceded, "she could have gotten the name from something Belinda said. But there is one problem — I dreamed that first dream about Sir John and his lady quite some time ago. I dreamed it the night I met you, before Madame Valenskaya and her group came here. Before I had ever even seen the woman."

A shiver ran through Olivia. She clasped her hands tightly in her lap and tried to think clearly. "I wish we knew more about Sir Raymond and the house. If only —" She brightened. "I could write to Great-uncle Bellard. He is a tremendous history student. His rooms are full of history books, and he has cronies to whom he writes about all the minutiae of history. If there is anything to be found out about Blackhope or Sir Raymond or the Martyrs, he could find it."

"All right. If you want to write him, I will send a servant with the letter to London to give it to your uncle. I would appreciate any help we can get. I feel as if I have wandered into a mad-house. That charade in the garden the other night seems like the merest trick now."

"Very well. I will write Great-uncle Bellard immediately." She stood up.

"Olivia . . ." Stephen reached out a hand, then dropped it uncertainly. "That dream — what happened — I —" He hesitated, his eyes searching her face.

There was something — a heat, an intensity — in his gaze that made Olivia weak in the knees. She knew she ought to leave the room. He had a devastating effect on her senses, and she could not help but remember what Pamela had told her about his fickle ways. He was dangerous in a way she had never experienced before. It would be safer, much safer, simply to remove herself from his presence.

Yet, as he reached up and curved his hand over her cheek, leaving was the last thing she wanted to do.

"I should not . . ." Stephen said, his thumb softly sliding over her cheek. "But when I look at you, I seem to forget the rules of gentlemanly behavior."

"My family has rarely conformed to rules of behavior," Olivia replied a little breathlessly.

A smile lit his eyes. "Then that is very good for me, isn't it?"

He leaned closer, and as his lips touched hers, all thought left Olivia's head. Instinctively, her lips returned the pressure of his, and he let out a groan deep in his throat. His arms wrapped around her, pulling her up into him, and Olivia went with them eagerly. His body was hard and muscled against her soft curves, and her own body responded to the feel of it.

Their kiss deepened. Her arms went around his neck, and she clung to him, savoring the taste of his mouth, the scent of his skin, the enveloping warmth of his body. When at last his mouth left hers, he kissed his way down the side of her neck, nibbling gently at her skin. His hand slid up her side and gently cupped her breast. Olivia drew in a sharp breath of surprise and pleasure. She wanted to know more, to feel more. She slid her hands slowly up the back of his neck until her fingers intertwined with his hair. It slipped through her fingers like caressing silk, igniting the sensitive nerves of her hands.

He kissed the hollow of her neck, his tongue delicately tasting her skin. Olivia shuddered, heat exploding in her abdomen. He felt her body quiver against him, and he made a low, animal noise of pleasure against her throat. Gently he squeezed her breast through her bodice, his thumb rubbing over the center, making her nipple tighten in response.

His mouth returned to hers, and he kissed her hungrily, their lips melding. Olivia felt as if she would melt against him, her body all fire and hunger. Finally, with a groan, Stephen tore his mouth away from hers, stepping back and half turning away. He plunged his fingers back into his hair, holding on to his head tightly, as if he could thus control his wayward passions.

"Sweet, bloody hell!" he cursed softly. He drew a deep breath. "I think I understand how he felt — that knight — risking it all for her." He glanced back at her. "I apologized before. I suppose it becomes meaningless when I cannot seem to keep from taking liberties. . . ."

Olivia clasped her hands together, trying to bring her own scattered emotions under control. "There is no need to apologize. I —" She looked down, unable to meet his eyes, as she said candidly, "I found it quite enjoyable."

She whirled and hurried from the room, leaving St. Leger standing there, staring after her.

The day was gray, the weather cooler than it had been the first few days she had been there, but Olivia sought the refuge of the garden anyway. A stroll in cool, moist air would be just the thing, she thought, to chase away the fevers in her head and flesh. She had been impossibly bold, she knew — well, not bold, for she was afraid she was more shy than bold; her words had simply been the truth. However, in society, she knew, the truth was often the last thing one should say. Lord St. Leger had doubtlessly been shocked at her words, which were not the sort of thing a lady would say. She had frequently been told that what a gentleman did and what a gentleman expected of a lady were not at all the same thing.

Of course, Lord St. Leger did not seem like other men. He was easy to talk to, straightforward and plain speaking. He did not indulge in the sort of aimless social chitchat at which Olivia found herself remarkably inept. Nor did he talk to her as if she were deficient in understanding, or waste her time with flowery compliments and meaningless flirtation. Indeed, now that she thought about it, he had on more than one occasion been actually rude. He was not at all the kind of man Olivia would have labeled a flirt, and she would have found it hard to believe what Pamela had told her if it had not been for the fact that she could not imagine a woman like Pamela saying that any man had rejected her if it had not been the truth.

She frowned as she walked, wishing she was more adept at this man-woman thing. Someone like Kyria would no doubt know whether St. Leger was a flirt, and what a woman should do and say if a man had kissed her as Stephen had kissed Olivia. A small smile played across Olivia's lips as she tried to imagine any man having the nerve to do such a thing to her sister. She wished quite fiercely that Kyria were there now, so that she could ask her advice.

"Lady Olivia!" A cry came from off to her right, and Olivia turned her head to see Belinda waving at her from the other end of the pathway.

Belinda started toward her, and Olivia turned with a smile to meet the girl halfway. "I am surprised to see anyone else out for a stroll on this gloomy day."

Belinda laughed. "I love the weather. It means autumn's coming, and that is when I love Blackhope the best." She gave a little chuckle and admitted, "Except, of course, for the spring, when I am sure that I love it even better."

"You are very fond of your home?"

"Oh, yes. I love it. Every man I met this season, I would think to myself — would I leave Blackhope to marry him? And, frankly, I did not find any for whom the answer was 'yes.' "

Olivia smiled. "Well, I feel sure someday you will."

"Perhaps." Belinda shrugged.

"So you have never felt that the place was, well, the abode of 'lost souls'?" Olivia asked teasingly.

Belinda made a face. "No. The séances are all very well, you know. I find them exciting. But I'm not sure that I actually *believe* Madame Valenskaya."

"I see."

"You don't either, do you?" Belinda went on. "I can see it on your face, though you try to be polite about it."

"I find it unlikely," Olivia agreed.

"That's good, then, because Stephen doesn't believe it at all, and I don't think he would court a woman who did. He would find her silly, don't you think? Madame Valenskaya makes Stephen furious. He only lets her stay here because it means so much to Mama. I guess you know that."

"Yes. But, Belinda, you must not think that Stephen, I mean, Lord St. Leger, is courting me."

Belinda chuckled. "I don't know why you try to hide it. It's clear that Stephen is head over heels for you. I've seen him watching you when he thinks no one is looking."

Olivia felt her cheeks growing warm despite the cool air. "I'm sure you must be mistaken. Lord St. Leger and I are . . . are . . ."

What were they, really? One could scarcely call what had just happened in Stephen's study as being "merely friends." Yet she could not believe, either, that Stephen was interested in any deep or permanent way, such as Belinda believed. Olivia was there to help him catch a fraud, that was all . . . *Except, of course, for those kisses.*

"Belinda . . ." Olivia said, knowing that she should not be prying like this into St. Leger's life, especially using his young sister to do so, but she could not keep herself from asking. "Do you know anything about Lady Pamela and your brother — Stephen, I mean?"

"Oh, yes, I heard it all long ago. Not at the time it happened, of course, for I was still a child. But later, from things the servants said. Stephen's valet knew it all, you see, better than Mama or anyone."

"Lady Pamela told me that Stephen was a terrible flirt."

"Stephen? Are you serious?"

"She said she fell in love with him long ago, before she met Roderick, and that he broke her heart."

"Oh!" Belinda exclaimed, her eyes flashing. "Pamela is such a shocking liar. She wasn't in love with Stephen. I doubt she's ever been in love with anyone but herself. That was not what happened at all."

"Really?" Olivia felt as if tight bands were loosening around her chest.

"Yes. It was exactly the opposite. Stephen was madly in love with her. It was when he was a young man, just out of university and living in London for the first time. He met Pamela there and fell in love with her. He wanted to marry her. Then the family came to town for the season, and of course he was proud to introduce her to them. But when she met Roderick, she decided she could land a bigger fish than Stephen, so she threw him over and went after Roderick instead. She wanted to be Lady St. Leger, you see, and she knew that Roderick was the heir. It broke Stephen's heart. He left the country because he could not bear to see them together. It caused an enormous rift between him and Roderick."

"Oh! My goodness, how awful."

Belinda's story clarified several things for Olivia. Obviously Pamela's tale that Stephen was a cad who had toyed with her affections, then abandoned her, was untrue, something that Olivia had vaguely sensed but had been unable to understand the reasons for. Now she saw that for Pamela, portraying herself as a victim, even if it meant revealing herself to be rejected, was clearly better than admitting the truth, which revealed her to be greedy, proud and cold.

Unfortunately, the true story did not make Olivia feel much better. It was a relief to know that Stephen was not a heartless flirt. But he had loved Pamela passionately; his heart had been broken by her. It seemed all too likely that deep down, underneath the bitterness and pain, he loved her still. It would not be easy, Olivia thought, for a great passion to cool to nothing. Olivia had seen Stephen treat Pamela with a stiff formality, even coolness, but she was afraid that even that was indicative of the fact that feeling still lurked inside him for her, a feeling he knew to be foolish, even dangerous.

Whatever attraction Stephen might feel for Olivia, she knew, was bound to pale in comparison to the love he had felt for Pamela. Pamela was a great beauty, the kind of woman over whom men had once fought duels and started wars. He had loved her with all the passion and fervor of youth, and that sort of love was never forgotten. The kisses he had shared with Olivia, she knew, while they had been soul shattering for her, doubtless were mild compared to the kisses he had given Pamela. Rather than expressions of the sort of overwhelming love he had felt for Pamela, they were expressions of a cooler, more mature desire — one, moreover, that she feared was at least partially fueled by the desire he had experienced in his dream.

Even worse, Olivia suspected that Pamela wanted Stephen back. He was, after all, now the possessor of the title and fortune for which she had jilted him years earlier, but now he must seem even more appealing to her, because he had acquired an even greater fortune during the intervening years. Pamela would not have any doubts that she could rekindle the fire he had once felt for her. The only reason Olivia could see for Pamela to tell her the story she had told her was to frighten Olivia away from Stephen. Pamela, knowing that Stephen had invited Olivia to stay there, but not knowing the real reason for it, must have assumed, as Lady St. Leger and Belinda had, that Stephen had an amatory interest in Olivia. Olivia did not imagine that Pamela could think her much of a threat, but she had probably decided not to take any chances. By telling Olivia that Stephen was a hopeless flirt, a callous cad who would entice her into loving him, then break her heart, Pamela was making sure that Olivia would back away from him, leaving her a clear field.

If Pamela wanted him back, Olivia thought, how could she ever hope to compete with her? If fighting the memory of his love for Pamela would be difficult, it would be ten times worse to overcome the present reality of the woman.

"It is almost time for tea," Belinda commented, breaking into Olivia's painful thoughts.

Olivia nodded and smiled perfunctorily, and they began to make their way back through the garden to the house, talking of other things.

Inside they found Lady St. Leger and Madame Valenskaya in the informal sitting room on the second floor. Lady St. Leger looked up as they entered and smiled.

"Ah, there you are, dear. Madame and I saw the two of you walking down in the garden." She gave a little shiver. "Too cool and gray for me today."

"Ah," Madame Valenskaya said with a chuckle and a ponderous wink at Belinda and Olivia. "To be young. Yes?"

"Oh, Mama, it hasn't even gotten cold yet."

"I know. But I so hate to see the summer go." Her voice faltered a little, and she looked down hastily at her lap.

Olivia glanced with some concern at Belinda, who was watching her mother, her young face suddenly etched with sorrow. She remembered then that everyone said Roderick had died about a year ago. She had the feeling it must have been about this time of year and Lady St. Leger was thinking of sad memories.

She tried to think of something to redirect the conversation, silently cursing the fact that social chatter was not one of her skills. Fortunately, a footman carried in the tea tray at that moment and strode over to set it down on the low table in front of Lady St. Leger.

Stephen's mother managed to muster up a smile and say, "Ah, Chilton, thank you. Doesn't this look wonderful? Send Cook my compliments."

Lady St. Leger took up the task of pouring the cups of tea, saying, "I don't think we'll wait for the others. They should be here soon. Lady Olivia? Sugar, I believe?"

"Yes, thank you." Olivia accepted the cup gratefully and took a sip, looking over the array of cakes and breads.

Amid the clatter of forks and plates and the bits of conversation, she did not at first notice the odd sound. It was Belinda who paused, cocking her head to one side and said, "What is that noise?"

"What, dear?" Lady St. Leger looked up.

Madame Valenskaya blinked, glancing around the room, and Olivia replaced her cup in her saucer, listening.

"That funny little sound. Almost like a kitten mewling."

"Or a person crying," Olivia countered. She leaned forward, and the noise became a little louder.

"Oh, dear." Lady St. Leger looked concerned. "Someone crying? But who? Where?" She turned to look around the room, frowning. "Perhaps it is one of the maids in the hall."

Olivia put down her saucer on the table and got up to go to the doors into the hall. She looked up and down the hallway, seeing no one, and came back inside, shaking her head. "There is no one there. And I cannot hear it in the hall."

The crying was definitely louder now. The four women were hushed, listening.

"It sounds like a child! But where is she?" Lady St. Leger said, frowning. "It sounds as if — as if she is *here*."

The sobbing continued, hanging eerily on the air, disembodied and forlorn. Madame Valenskaya's voice sounded in the hush, a low, sad whisper. "A lonely soul. She is lost . . . lost."

Lady St. Leger gave a visible shiver, her face turning even paler. "It is a spirit?"

The Russian woman nodded solemnly. "The dead mourn."

Olivia ignored the goose bumps that arose on her arms at the woman's words. "Nonsense," she said stoutly. "It is a person crying right here and now."

She walked around the room and quickly realized that as she moved away from the group the noise became quieter and as she returned, it grew stronger. She stepped past the tea table and Belinda. The sound was loudest here, by the fireplace.

"The fireplace!" she cried suddenly. "It must be coming through the fireplace."

She whirled and ran from the room.

8

Olivia paused outside in the hall, casting a glance at the stairs in one direction, which led down in grand sweeping fashion, then at the less grand staircase at the other end of the hall, leading up. Belinda came hurrying out of the room after her, and Olivia swung toward her.

"What's above the sitting room?"

Belinda hesitated, thinking, then said, "The nursery, I think."

"And below?"

"The small ballroom."

"Up," Olivia decided. On instinct, it seemed more likely to her that someone would use the unoccupied nursery to perpetrate their fraud than a large, open public room where a servant might walk by at any moment.

She took off down the hall and up the stairs, lifting her skirts to run better. Belinda stayed on her heels. They reached the nursery and looked in. There was no one in the large, central schoolroom. Olivia went inside and peered into each of the small bedrooms that opened off it, with Belinda trailing after her. She came back into the central room, frowning. At that moment the weeping sound came again, faint but distinct. Olivia darted into the hall. The sound, she thought, came from the other end of the hall.

She moved lightly and quickly. The sound was becoming louder. Then it stopped, and Olivia broke into a run. The hall was long and narrow and low-ceilinged, with doors opening off either side. It was here that the servants slept, and during the day there was no one up here. Olivia and Belinda's footsteps echoed hollowly on the wood floor. There was no muffling carpet runner here.

Tucked away under the eaves of the house, there were no windows except one at the end of the hall, so it was much darker than it had been on the floors below. The sound came again, a mournful weeping, echoing through the silent gloomy hall. Olivia's skin prickled. Belinda shot her an anxious glance, but she stayed with her as Olivia pressed onward, following the distant crying.

The top floor was a warren of rooms and hallways, and they twisted and turned through the cramped corridors. At one point they reached a closed door at the end of the hall, and they hesitated. Then the weeping came faintly from behind the door, and Olivia pulled it open. It led into yet another hall.

"We must be in the old wing of the house,"

Belinda whispered, intimidated by the profound hush of the corridor in front of them. "Well, it's not actually older, of course. The main wing is the oldest, really, but when they renovated years ago, they only did the main wing. This part of the house is closed off and never used."

Olivia started down the dim hallway, lifting her skirts to avoid the dust on the floors. Belinda stuck to her side like glue. The sobbing came yet again, seemingly from another narrow staircase, and they followed it down and into the corridor below. The crying continued, faint but persistent, and they pursued it along hallways and up and down staircases, past closed doors and open rooms where the furniture stood shrouded in dustcovers. There was utter silence except for the occasional burst of weeping, always somewhere in front of them, and the only light came in around the sides of the heavy draperies, closed to protect the carpets and furniture from the sun.

"I don't like it here," Belinda said in hushed tones.

Olivia had to admit that it was a gloomy, eerie place, where one could easily imagine things jumping out at one. She was growing increasingly uneasy, yet still she pressed on, determined to track down the source of the weeping.

It led them up the stairs again and into another of the cramped hallways under the roof. They hurried along the corridor, the crying floating in front of them, and turned a sharp corner. Something drifted over their faces, clinging and unseen. They shrieked and jumped back, clawing at their hair and faces where it still clung.

"A cobweb!" Olivia gasped, disgust mingling with fright in her shaking voice.

"Let's go back!" Belinda cried, frantically trying to remove all traces of the cobweb.

Olivia took Belinda's hand firmly and started down the hall, listening, waiting for the crying to start again. They reached another set of stairs and stopped. There was no crying. Olivia and Belinda glanced at each other. The minutes seemed to stretch agonizingly in silence.

"It's gone," Olivia said at last, her voice dropping with disappointment. "Blast! We've lost it."

She turned and opened the door nearest her and looked in. It was empty. She stepped across the hall and opened the next door. There was a rickety narrow bed, several of its slats broken and with no mattress. She opened several other doors in close proximity to the stairs and found all the rooms empty or close to it. There was certainly no sign of a person.

Olivia sighed. Whoever had been leading them did not appear to be hiding nearby. She — or he — had probably slipped quietly down the staircase, and there was no telling where the person was by now.

"I suppose we might as well return now," she said.

"Yes. Let's." Belinda glanced first one way down the hall and then the other. "Which way is that?"

"You don't know?" Olivia asked, a little surprised.

"No. I don't really know this part of the house. It has been shut off forever, and Mama would never let us play here, because she was afraid we would get lost. Anyway, it was always sort of . . . scary, really. It's so empty and quiet."

It certainly was that, Olivia had to agree. She, too, looked up and down the hall. "I don't think I could retrace our steps. We've gone up and down and turned down this corridor, then that, so much that I'm completely lost."

"But we have to get back," Belinda protested, panic rising in her voice. "It's getting dark. There's nothing lit in this part of the house, and when the sun goes down —"

"I know." Olivia tried to sound reassuring. It was already getting quite dim; she didn't suppose that it would be long before darkness fell completely, and then they would be trapped wherever they happened to be, unable to find their way out without light. She wished that she had thought to light a candle to bring with her, but, of course, in the heat of pursuit, it had never occurred to her.

"First thing," she told Belinda, taking her hand, "is to go downstairs. These attic corridors are the worst. There are more windows downstairs, so we'll have more light, and if we go to the ground floor, we can find a door that goes outside. That will be the simplest way to get back — just walk around to the main wing."

Belinda brightened at that idea, and they went down the narrow stairs to the very bottom. They struck out along one hall, only to find that it ended in a wall. There was a window, however, and they tugged aside the heavy curtains to let in the light. There was not much of it, for they could see that the sun had slipped behind the trees. Soon it would disappear altogether.

"We must be on the west side of the house," Olivia ventured.

Belinda, looking out the window, nodded. "Yes. We're as far as we can get from the main wing. But I'm pretty sure there's an outside door on this side of the house — and one or two in back, as well. Some old St. Leger — I think it was during the restoration — loved building things, and he kept adding on wings and halls and rooms. And that was after *his* father had already added on to the place."

They retraced their steps down the hall, and at the next intersecting hallway took a right, assuming that it would lead them to the rear of the house. It led, in fact, only to another corridor. They turned left and kept walking, and at last came to a closed door at the end of the hall. When they turned the knob, however, it would not open.

"It's locked!" Olivia and Belinda looked at

each other in consternation. There was no convenient key in the keyhole beneath the knob.

"I suppose they would lock the outside doors," Belinda said. "They wouldn't want people to be able to come in at will."

"No, I guess not." Olivia frowned, thinking. "They are probably all locked."

"We can't be sure."

"No, but we don't want to waste all of the daylight we have left trying to find the outside doors. It would probably be best to find our way back into the main house." She thought for a moment. "All right. We shall look out the windows of a room, and we can orient ourselves in relation to the rest of the house. For instance, if we are looking out on the south lawn, we will know we have to go to our left, because the main wing is east of us, right?"

"Yes. Exactly."

They did as she said, going into the nearest room and pulling aside the drapes from one window. Belinda, peering out, declared they were, indeed, looking out on the side garden, south of the wing they were in and also west of part of the main wing.

They set off down the corridor briskly, for it was almost dark in the hallways now, even though they paused to open any drapes they found along the way. Dusk had fallen outside, and in here, they were increasingly unable to see. Their steps slowed, and even so, they ran into a small table in the hall before they realized they were on it. Olivia put her fingers lightly against the wall as they continued forward, walking ever more hesitantly.

"We won't find it before dark," Belinda said, her voice trembling.

"Perhaps not," Olivia agreed, keeping her voice firm. "But when we literally cannot see, we will sit down and wait. It isn't as if we're in the middle of the woods. We have shelter. The worst is that we'll be a little hungry and thirsty."

"Yes, but it scares me. I mean, when you can't see anything . . . and I keep thinking of that crying. What if it comes back? I wish we'd never tried to find it. What if it can't be found? What if it's something we can't see?"

"I am sure it was a person," Olivia said flatly. They had come to a complete stop. There was not any light to see to walk anymore. The enveloping blackness was rather frightening, she had to admit. She would have felt much more comfortable with a candle or two.

Olivia slid her hand along the wall and felt the recess, then wood, that meant a door. "Look, we've come to a room. We could go inside it and open the draperies, and then we wouldn't be totally in the dark. There would be the moonlight and starlight."

She turned the knob and opened the door. It was pitch-black inside. The draperies must have covered the windows completely, with no gaps, so that not even whatever faint light of stars and moon might be outside could filter in. They gazed into the empty blackness. Olivia could not ignore the shiver that ran down her spine. She closed the door.

"I think I'd rather be out here," Belinda whispered.

"I would, as well." They carefully edged past the door. "Shall we sit down?"

"I'm awfully tired."

They slid down the wall to sit on the floor. Olivia tried not to think about the years' accumulation of dust that might be on the floor. She was also trying not to think of such things as rats and mice that might frequent an unused building. The list of what she should not think about was growing rapidly as her mind lit first on the weeping sound they had followed, then went to the silent woman she had seen walking across the great hall the other night. What would she do if she saw that woman again here, without Stephen by her side or even a candle to light the corridor?

She cleared her throat, more to make noise in the silence than anything else. "We are not alone," she said firmly, not quite sure whether she was reassuring Belinda or herself. "We have each other."

"Thank heavens." Belinda shuddered.

"And your mother knows that we went off to find the crying. She will tell Stephen and the others. They will start looking for us when we don't come back."

"But they won't know where we are. We could

have gone outside or — or vanished." She said the last word in a hushed voice, as if speaking it aloud somehow gave it reality.

"I don't think Stephen will assume we have vanished," Olivia said dryly.

Belinda laughed lightly. "No, that's true. Stephen will not think that the ghosts have taken us. We can count on him."

"Yes. And I think they will search the house before they assume we went outdoors, as well. After all, we heard the sound inside. Surely, after a while, they are bound to realize that we might have wandered over into this wing of the house."

Belinda nodded. Olivia could feel her straightening beside her. "Of course they will. They will find us."

It was then that they heard the rapping.

The knocks were short and fast and came from above them. The hair on the back of Olivia's neck stood up. For an instant neither of them spoke or moved. Indeed, Olivia thought she did not even breathe. Belinda's hand squeezed convulsively around Olivia's. There was silence, and then, just as Olivia began to relax, there came another noise — distant and faint and eerily like a voice.

For an instant Olivia was enveloped in a primitive terror. Then reason reasserted itself, and she jumped to her feet.

"Here!" she shouted, her voice ringing out shockingly loud in the dark. "We are here!"

"Olivia!" Belinda shrieked, rising up, too, in agitation. "No! Don't draw it to us!"

"It's not ghosts, Belinda." Olivia cupped her hands around her mouth and shouted again. "Stephen! We are here!"

"What?"

"It is Stephen! Come to rescue us," Olivia explained. "I'm sure it is. That knocking we heard was simply him walking across the floor above our heads, and then I heard a voice. If we hadn't gotten into a such a state of fear, we would have realized it. It's not ghosts, just people searching for us."

"Olivia! Belinda!" There was the thundering sound of feet on the stairs, and suddenly a glow coming down another corridor toward theirs.

Belinda let out another shriek, this time of joy, and began to cry. "Stephen!"

They ran toward the light, and at that moment Stephen came hurrying around the corner, lantern held high in his hand. He saw them and set the lantern down with a thud, then ran the next few steps. Belinda jumped into his arms. Olivia, running with her, remembered belatedly that while Stephen's sister had a perfect right to throw herself into his arms, it was not appropriate for her to do so.

Stephen, however, shifted Belinda into his left arm and with his right reached out and pulled Olivia to him. For a long moment the three of them stood that way, locked in an embrace of relief and joy. Olivia thought she felt the brush of Stephen's lips against her hair.

"Miss Olivia!" Tom Quick's voice came from the opposite direction, and Olivia turned her head to see him sprinting toward them, his lantern swinging with every step. "I nearly dropped me light, I did, when I 'eard you call. I couldn't picture wot 'ad 'appened to you."

"Tom!" In her happiness, Olivia turned and gave him a quick hug, too. "I am so glad to see you."

"We didn't know wot was goin' on, did we, guv'nor?" Tom went on, addressing Lord St. Leger, a grin splitting his face.

"I had no idea," he admitted. "Mother was having hysterics and saying a ghost had gotten you. It took me ages to calm her down."

He picked up the lantern, and they started walking back toward the main wing as they talked. His arm was still around Belinda, but Olivia had recovered her self-possession enough to stay at a discreet distance from him. Tom Quick strode off in front to light the way, turning back now and again to interject a comment as they explained how they had searched all through the house and had even combed the gardens before deciding to try the unused wing of the house.

"One of the maids said she thought she'd seen you two running up the back stairs to the servants' floor, so we went up there. When we came upon an open door into the old wing, I realized that you must have gone in there."

"It was awful!" Belinda told him. "It's hopelessly confusing, and then it started to get dark, and by that time the crying was gone. Just vanished, and we were lost. We tried to get out the back door to the outside, but it was locked."

"Crying? Who was crying? What are you talking about?"

"Didn't Lady St. Leger tell you?" Olivia asked.

"Nothing very useful. She said you had gone running after some ghost or other, and Madame Valenskaya kept nattering on about 'lost souls' and 'lonely spirits.' All I could think was that you had caught someone pulling a trick and were chasing him. I was afraid he might have hurt you. So I got Tom and some servants, and we started looking for you."

"We heard someone crying," Belinda explained. "But there was nobody in the hall or anywhere around. It sounded as if it were right there in the room. It gave me goose bumps, I'll tell you. But Olivia said it was coming from the fireplace, and then she went tearing out of the room —"

"Of course!" Stephen exclaimed. "Mother said that you were sitting in the rose sitting room."

"Yes, we were," Olivia replied, looking puzzled.

By this time they had reached a set of double doors. Stephen opened one of them, and they found themselves once again in the main part of the house.

"We were so close!" Belinda cried.

"Yes. If we had started on the ground floor instead of the top, we'd have found you pretty quickly."

They walked along the long gallery toward the front stairs. Olivia, her mind still on Stephen's earlier comment, asked, "What did you mean by 'of course'?"

"What? Oh. Just that you can hear things by the nursery fireplace that are said in the sitting room below. Roderick and I used to sit there and listen to Mother gossip with her friends. You have to take up a couple of the tiles there. They come off easily. No doubt the sound works the other way, too."

"I knew it!" Olivia exclaimed triumphantly. "I knew someone was up there, pretending."

"Why did I not know about that?" Belinda asked indignantly. "No one ever told me you could spy on people from the nursery."

"Roderick and I were too much older than you. We were grown by the time you would have been interested in that knowledge. We only found out one day when we were trying to find a hiding place for some 'treasure' or other, and we realized that one of the tiles was loose. It came right off. No hiding place behind it, but we heard two of the maids talking in the sitting room below us."

They reached the great hall and saw Lady St. Leger, Lady Pamela, and Madame Valenskaya and her party all standing at the bottom of the stairs. Lady St. Leger was wringing her hands, and Madame Valenskaya was patting her arm soothingly, when Irina Valenskaya looked up and saw Olivia's group.

"Mother! Lady St. Leger! Look!" Irina cried, pointing.

Lady St. Leger turned, saw them and began to cry, hurrying toward them with her arms outstretched. "Belinda! Sweetheart! Are you all right? I thought something horrible had happened to you. And Lady Olivia! Thank goodness you're here."

"Heavens!" Lady Pamela advanced toward them more slowly, her eyebrows raised sardonically. "You are both covered in dust. Where in the world have you been?"

For the first time Olivia thought of what she must look like, and her heart sank. She was, as Pamela had pointed out, covered in dust. It was on her skirts and hands; she could see that now, in the light. Worse, no doubt it was on her hair and face, as well. She remembered the cobweb that had settled over them and how she had scrubbed at her hair and face, trying to rid herself of it. She must look a fright, her hair all mussed and coated with dust and cobwebs, her face streaked. It was doubly mortifying to look so in front of the poised and beautiful Pamela.

Olivia curled her hands into fists, refusing to give Pamela the satisfaction of letting her hands fly to her unruly hair, as they wanted to. "We have been in the other wing of the house," she said with a calm she was proud of. "I'm afraid it is rather dusty."

"But, my dear, why ever did you want to go in there?" Lady St. Leger asked.

"We were chasing the crying, Mama," Belinda said, adding, "did you know that sound travels between your sitting room and the nursery?"

"What?" Lady St. Leger looked confused. "I don't understand. How could you 'chase the crying'? It was some poor lost soul. It wasn't something you could chase."

"It was a person, my lady," Olivia said with all the gentleness she could muster. "Not a lost soul. A person who went into the nursery and cried by the fireplace, where the sound would come down into your sitting room."

Lady St. Leger stared at her. "But, my dear, why would anyone do such a thing?"

"To convince us, perhaps, that there are lost souls here."

Lady St. Leger gasped. "Lady Olivia! You must be overwrought. It is quite understand-able, of course, what with the ordeal you and Belinda have been through, but you can't have thought — you are implying that —"

"Yes, my lady. I can see no other possibility."

"Disbelievers . . ." Howard Babington spoke up, sighing and giving a sorrowful shake of his head. "They will concoct any preposterous story to keep from admitting what is right in front of their eyes."

"Yes. Someone was in the room with us,

215

crying," Lady St. Leger said. "We all heard it. You yourself checked the hall. It couldn't have come from the nursery. It is too far away."

"You have only to take up a tile at the fire-place —" Stephen began.

"Did you see someone doing this?" Babington asked innocently.

"No. They had left the room. They started the crying again and led us away, into the unused wing of the house."

"That's right, Mama," Belinda interjected. "We followed it until we were lost, and then it just stopped."

"But, darling, if you didn't see anyone, how can you know that it was a person?" Lady St. Leger asked her daughter reasonably. "And Madame Valenskaya was right there in the room with us. She couldn't possibly have done such a thing. You must see that you are being very unfair to her."

"Her daughter and Mr. Babington were not with us," Olivia pointed out.

"But they are right here. They have been with me for some time."

"Sometimes the spirits can be unkind," Mr. Babington said with the air of one imparting a sad truth. "When they are caught here, unable to reach the other world where they belong, they can be bitter. They will play tricks, frighten people, lead one astray."

"Yes." Madame Valenskaya nodded her head sagely. "Is true. I haff seen it. Ferry sad."

"Lady Olivia," Pamela drawled, "while I admire your desire to support Lord St. Leger's views of Madame Valenskaya and her friends, I feel I must point out that they are strangers to this house. How could they have known this trick with the tile in the nursery? I had never heard of it. Did you know about it, Lady St. Leger? Belinda?" At their negative shakes of the head, she went on, raising her eyebrows. "You see? If even we did not know about it, having lived in this house for years, how could these relative strangers have guessed that they could do it?"

"Yes, of course. It would be impossible," Lady St. Leger agreed, pleased. She patted Olivia on the arm, giving her a sweet, understanding smile. "I am afraid you have been listening too much to my son's doubts. Stephen has become much too cynical in the years he's been away. But you can see that Madame Valenskaya and Miss Valenskaya and Mr. Babington could not have done such a thing. It was, I fear, as Mr. Babington mentioned — a restless spirit playing tricks on us." She sighed, turning toward the medium. "We really must try to communicate with the spirits again, Madame. Clearly we must do something to try to help."

"Yes, of course. As you wish," the squat woman replied, her eyelids lowering over a gleam of triumph. "We try again."

Even Lady St. Leger agreed that the séance must be put off until the next evening, as Olivia and Belinda had been through too much that day to participate. Olivia was a little surprised that Lady St. Leger wanted her at the séance at all. She was fairly certain, from a single malevolent glance Madame Valenskaya delivered to her, that the medium would have been more than happy to have her gone entirely.

However, she began to realize that Lady St. Leger was hoping to win her over to the side of the believers and that she felt sure another séance would do so. Lady St. Leger smiled benignly and patted Olivia's hand the next morning after breakfast, assuring her that the séance would straighten everything out for them.

"You will see, dear," she said, giving her a twinkling glance. "And then, perhaps, you will be able to persuade my cynical son."

As for Lady St. Leger, her own faith in the medium appeared to be unshakable. When, that afternoon, Stephen showed Lady St. Leger and Olivia the loose tile in the nursery schoolroom and demonstrated that sound could indeed travel down to the sitting room below, she did for a moment look uncertain.

But then she shook her head and said, "No, Stephen, my love, how could Madame Valenskaya or her daughter or Mr. Babington have done any of that? It is too absurd. Madame Valenskaya is a dear friend. She has helped me so much the past few months. It would be most unkind of me to suspect her of playing such tricks. And, anyway, they are strangers to this house. They could not know about the nursery tile, and they certainly could not have led Belinda and Lady Olivia into getting lost in the old wing. Surely you must see that."

"They could have explored the place," Stephen said. "They have been here an ample amount of time, and it isn't as if we keep watch on them all the time."

"My dear! Of course not — what a thing to say." She shook her head a little sadly. "You have set your mind against the possibility of the spirit world. You should be more tolerant, more open to new ideas."

"Mother . . ."

She smiled, patted his hand and sailed out of the room. Stephen gazed after her in frustration.

"It *is* something of a sticking point," Olivia admitted. "How could they have known of the loose tile? I feel sure they could have explored the old wing and set up that trick, although I'm not sure to what purpose. I mean, Belinda and I would have suffered nothing more than an uncomfortable night, and probably not even that. You would have been bound to search the whole house."

He shrugged. "They gave you a scare. With some, it might have been enough to convince you that there were ghosts, or even make you decide to pack up and leave. They could not have known it would make you more determined to uncover their perfidy."

There was an admiration in the tone of his voice that warmed Olivia, but she pulled herself back to the point at hand. "However, even if it's possible they explored the house, it seems unlikely that they would have thought of prying up all the tiles around the fireplace in the nursery to see if they could be heard downstairs."

"Perhaps Roderick's ghost told them," Stephen said wryly, then sighed. "I don't know how they found out. Maybe they discovered them in the same way Roderick and I did — they could hear faint voices, and they investigated and realized the tiles came up."

Olivia nodded slowly. "It wouldn't be surprising if they were investigating the room above the sitting room your mother uses most to see if they could rig up some trick through the ceiling. And the nursery is someplace people never go, so they wouldn't fear being discovered."

"Possible. Even plausible. But not enough, I'm afraid, to convince my mother."

"Tom went through the other wing of the house this morning," Olivia told him. "He opened the windows and took a lamp to search the dust on the floor for footprints."

"Did he find any clear ones?"

"Much of the halls was a mess, with you and Tom having walked them, and Belinda and I backtracking several times. But he did find in two hallways a single set of footprints in the dust on the floor. Belinda and I were never apart. He also found footprints apart from the two pairs together that Belinda and I made. There was obviously another person up there."

Stephen nodded. "Of course, we were sure of that to begin with. Convincing my mother is another matter. I am afraid it is going to take something much more blatant."

"I know." Olivia sighed. "I should have caught them yesterday. I was foolish. I said right out loud that the sounds must be coming from the fireplace. I didn't even think about the fact that whatever was said in the sitting room probably traveled right back to them. So they knew I was coming after them, and they were able to get away."

"Don't fret over it." Stephen smiled and took one of her hands in his. "You have been doing an excellent job. I couldn't have asked for more."

She looked up into his face, her heart fluttering a little in her chest. When Stephen smiled at her in that way, she didn't know what to say or do. He stepped closer to her, still holding her hand.

A voice came from the doorway. "Oh! My goodness! Have I interrupted something?"

Olivia took a quick step back from Stephen, blushing, as she turned toward the doorway to see Pamela standing there, an amused smile on her lips.

"I am so sorry," Pamela said, her tone indicating she was anything but, and strolled forward into the room.

"Hello, Pamela." Stephen's voice was stony.

"My lady." Olivia glanced around uncomfortably. Pamela had a knack for making her feel wrong and out of place, and the fact that she did so bothered Olivia even more. It was also most annoying that she felt guilty, when she and Stephen had been doing nothing wrong — and Pamela had no rights over him, anyway.

She cast a quick glance up at Stephen, who was looking at Pamela, his face unreadable. She could not help but wonder if, when he saw Pamela, he still felt the same rush of passion he once had. Was it anger or love in his heart — or a combination of both? Whatever it was, Olivia had a sudden urge to get away from the sight of them.

"I — um," she began. "I was just about to go, um, work on something. If you will excuse me . . . ?"

She turned and quickly left the room.

Pamela did not spare a glance at Olivia's retreating figure. She looked at Stephen, her head tilted a little to one side, a slight smile curving her lips, her blue eyes twinkling with amusement.

"Really, Stephen," she drawled. "Don't tell me you are trying to make me jealous."

His eyebrows rose. "I beg your pardon?"

She nodded toward the door through which Olivia had left. "That little scene with the duke's dowdy daughter that I just witnessed. Holding her hand, looking into her eyes. Going riding with her . . . oh, and that touching moment last night when she came dragging in from the other wing, your arm solicitously around her waist."

Stephen gazed at her coolly for a moment. "I am certain it will come as a great shock to you, Pamela, but nothing I have done with Lady Olivia has had the slightest thing to do with you."

Pamela strolled forward, her skirt swaying gracefully, her eyes intent on Stephen's. "Come, now, my dear, you can't expect me to believe that you have any *interest* in the little thing. You forget, I know you."

She stopped in front of him, only inches away. She put a finger on his chest and trailed it down the front of his shirt, saying, "I know your passion. She could never satisfy that. I know exactly the sort of woman a man like you wants."

Her eyes glowed as she looked up at him, the full power of her charm turned onto Stephen. Smiling seductively, she slid her hands up the front of his chest, then went on tiptoe and kissed him.

9

Stephen's hands clamped like iron around Pamela's wrists, and he jerked them down. She blinked at him, her mouth slightly open in surprise.

"Don't make a fool of yourself, Pamela," he bit out.

Her eyes widened, and anger flashed in them. "How dare you! Let go of me!"

"Gladly." He released her wrists and stepped back.

"Are you going to try to tell me that you're in love with that chit?" she cried, her cheeks flushed with rage.

"I am not trying to tell you anything, Pamela. What you do, what you say, what you think, is of no interest to me."

"Of course. You want to hurt me. I realize that. I hurt you all those years ago, and it is only fitting that you retaliate."

"I have no —"

"No." She raised a hand, drooping artistically against the back of a chair. "What I did to

224

you was terribly wrong. I knew it. I regretted it as soon as I had done it. But then you were gone. I could not take it back, however much I wanted to."

"Pamela, please, don't —"

"I must," she said quickly, turning away from him. "I never loved Roderick, not as I loved you. I was foolish, I admit that. I was only a girl, and my head was turned by the dazzle of a title . . . jewels, gold." She sighed. "As I said, I was very young. It did not take me long to discover how little any of those meant when I was sharing my life, my bed, with a man I did not love. I had years to regret what I had done. Every day I wished it was you by my side, not him. Every time he kissed me or touched me, I pretended it was you. Always."

"Stop it." Stephen's voice was clipped. "You are humiliating yourself to no purpose."

He walked over to her and put his hand on her arm, turning her around. Her blue eyes were aswim with tears, and her face was soft and vulnerable, her pink lips trembling.

Grimly, Stephen said, "I am sure that many other men would be entranced by the picture you present. Try it on one of them. Not me. You forget, Pamela. I know you. I know that you are always playing a part, always angling to get the advantage of someone else. No one can really know you, because you would as soon lie as speak the truth."

"I'm telling you the truth right now. I swear it!"

"Then I am sorry for you, for you've lived a very unhappy life, all of it of your own making."

"I have," Pamela agreed earnestly, reaching out to take his hand. "But I learned from my mistakes. I know now that all I want is you."

Stephen grimaced. "I am sure that is true, since the title and wealth and jewels are now mine." He pulled his hand from hers. "It doesn't matter. Whether I believed you or not, it simply doesn't matter. I have no feeling for you anymore."

Pamela stared at him, shocked. "No . . . Stephen, that can't be true. You love me."

"I was infatuated with you, and it was a very long time ago. I feel nothing now." He turned and walked out the door, leaving Pamela staring, openmouthed, after him.

They gathered in the same room that evening for the séance. As they started to take their accustomed places, Stephen said evenly, "I thought, Madame Valenskaya, that we might sit differently this time. I would very much like to sit beside you. I think it would help me understand what you do better. Don't you?"

"No!" Madame Valenskaya's eyes widened in alarm at his words. "I mean, it would not work. I must haff close de ones who believe."

"Indeed."

"Yes," Irina said flatly. "Mr. Babington and I must sit on either side of Mama. It creates a better link, you see, to the spirit world. A disbeliever at her side would break the connection. The chain."

"Then perhaps Lady St. Leger could take your place. You would like that, wouldn't you, Mother?"

Lady St. Leger smiled. "Why, yes, dear, that would be very nice. If that is all right with you, Madame."

"Is not good," the medium said hesitantly.

"Or Belinda," Stephen went on, pleasantly unyielding. "Or Lady Olivia, perhaps."

"No. No. Not her." Madame Valenskaya's eyes cut to Olivia and quickly away. "Irina sits here. And Mr. Babington."

"But Lady St. Leger is a believer. Surely it would not make any difference if she sat beside you."

Madame Valenskaya looked again at Lady St. Leger, who appeared eager to sit beside her. She chewed at her lip and said finally, "Yes. Is all right. Tonight. A, how do you say? Experiment?"

Stephen said nothing, merely held out the chair for his mother. "Shall I sit here beside you, Mother?"

"No, no," Irina cut in quickly. "Your disbelief will still be too near. Your presence will frighten away the spirits."

Stephen nodded and moved down the table to his usual seat. "Then how about a little light? I am so far away it is difficult to see Madame."

"Spirits like dark," Madame protested.

"Indeed? But, surely, does it have to be pitch-black?"

"Yes, why don't we leave a small light on?" Olivia suggested. "A candle — it wouldn't have to be on the table. We could put it on the sideboard over there." She demonstrated by carrying a candlestick to the small table beside the sofa, which had been pushed back to make room for the séance table. "It will be so much easier when the séance is over, don't you think? Not having to scrabble around in the dark, trying to light the lamp."

"That does sound sensible," Lady St. Leger agreed.

"I am not sure the spirits will oblige us," Mr. Babington put in. "That is often the case, I have found, when there are lights about."

"It wouldn't do any harm to try," Olivia responded reasonably.

"Yes, could we?" Belinda spoke up. "I — well, after last night, I'd really rather not be entirely in the dark."

"Of course," Lady St. Leger said quickly, smiling in sympathy at her daughter. "I am sure you would rather not." She turned to the medium, saying pleasantly, "Please, Madame Valenskaya, let us try it with a little light. Belinda and Olivia went through quite an ordeal, and I am sure they would both feel much better if it was not completely dark in here."

"If you wish, my lady," Madame Valenskaya replied, forcing a smile.

Olivia was careful not to look at Stephen, lest a grin of triumph flash across her face. It had been a bit of luck, Belinda piping up with the request for light. It had made Lady St. Leger press for the light, and Madame Valenskaya could scarcely refuse her patroness. Rearranging the seating and having the light would make it easier to catch whatever sleight of hand Madame Valenskaya used — or make her abandon it altogether.

They settled around the table, and the other lamps were extinguished, leaving only the dim light of the lone candle halfway across the room. The people around the table joined hands, Olivia this time linking hands with Mr. Babington, since Lady St. Leger had gone to sit beside Madame Valenskaya. In the dim light, it was at least possible to make out the medium's face.

Madame Valenskaya closed her eyes, and around the table, everyone settled into silence. Olivia watched the medium intently. She saw the woman relax, her head sinking down, then coming back up. "There are many spirits here," she said in measured tones, the accent leaving her voice.

Olivia noticed that there had been no tunes playing tonight or ghostly hands and such appearing. Madame Valenskaya must have been afraid to risk it with Lady St. Leger right beside her and a little bit of light in the room.

"Roddy?" Lady St. Leger asked. "Is that you?"

"Yes. I come tonight. But I — it is difficult. The light . . ." Madame Valenskaya paused, letting out a deep sigh. "I cannot rest. We cannot rest. There are so many of us here. It is very dark here, and lonely."

"Roddy, no! Why can you not rest? What is the matter?" Lady St. Leger cried.

"So much has been stolen," the medium went on in the same flat, ponderous voice. "They cannot rest. The Martyrs cannot rest. None of us can. Until what was stolen is returned to them."

"But what?" Lady St. Leger asked. "What must be returned to them?"

Madame Valenskaya's head sank, and she was silent.

"Roddy?" Lady St. Leger said tentatively. "Please, darling . . ."

Madame Valenskaya jerked her head, then slowly raised it. "He is gone," she said, not yet opening her eyes. "His spirit has left me."

"What did he mean?" Lady St. Leger spoke up. "What are we supposed to return to these people? I mean, we can scarcely give up our lands and house." There was a faintly mutinous look on the older woman's face.

"I think it would be rather difficult to *give* a ghost anything," Stephen put in dryly.

"Wait!" Madame Valenskaya exclaimed. Her eyes were still closed, and she began to sway a little. "I am seeing something — gold, something gold. I see a cross. Yes, a cross, large and gold."

She opened her eyes now. "Forgive me. Is all."

The people around the table looked at each other. Finally Irina said, "Does that mean anything to you, Lady St. Leger?"

"A gold cross?" Belinda asked. "I don't understand. Are you saying the spirits want a gold cross?"

"I don't know," Lady St. Leger said doubtfully. "Do you mean the Martyrs' cross?"

"I do not know, my lady," Madame Valenskaya said. "I saw only gold, much gold — and a cross."

"I think it is clear enough what she is talking about," Stephen said, looking at Madame Valenskaya. "It is the Martyrs' treasure you are speaking of." He looked from her to Irina and Babington and back. "Isn't it?" He leaned into his chair, his face disdainful as he went on. "I presumed you would ask me for money to 'lay' these restless spirits. But obviously it is the Martyrs' treasure you're after."

Madame Valenskaya bridled at his words. "I am not 'after' treasure. I speak for the spirits."

"Stephen!" Lady St. Leger admonished. "Really! How can you say that? Of course Madame Valenskaya doesn't want any money from you."

Olivia, watching the medium, noticed that Madame Valenskaya did not echo Lady St. Leger's words.

Madame Valenskaya laid a hand to her forehead, saying, "I am so tired. Ferry, ferry tired."

She held out her hand, and Mr. Babington took it, helping her up solicitously.

"These sessions are very debilitating for Madame Valenskaya," he said. "She must rest now. It takes too much out of her." He turned to Lady St. Leger. "Perhaps it would be best if we were to return to London."

"What!" Lady St. Leger exclaimed, horrified. "No, you mustn't. Oh, please, Madame Valenskaya, don't do that."

"I am ferry tired," the medium said again in a weak voice.

"It is very difficult for Madame," Babington went on. "The spirits drain her, and it is so much harder, having to fight against Lord St. Leger's cynicism and suspicion. The spirits don't wish to come into such an atmosphere, you see." He cast a reproachful look at Lady St. Leger. "And, I fear, my lady, that you are letting yourself be influenced by your son."

"No! Oh, please . . ." Lady St. Leger looked so forlorn and scared that it hurt Olivia's heart. "Don't leave. You know that I believe in the spirits and what they say. I know Roddy is speaking to me through you. You can't, you simply *can't*, leave now. What will I do?"

Babington made a show of looking uncertain. "I don't know, Lady St. Leger. I cannot allow Madame Valenskaya to wear herself out doing this, especially when she is not believed."

Olivia wondered cynically what he would do if Lady St. Leger simply acquiesced at that point, but, of course, Valenskaya's group knew their victim better than that. After more pleading and a little more dramatic indecision, Madame Valenskaya agreed to stay.

"No surprise there," Stephen said with a grimace an hour later, as he and Olivia sat in his study. It was becoming something of an evening ritual, their gathering there to discuss the events of the day and the progress of their investigation. Stephen usually poured himself a brandy, and once or twice Olivia had joined him.

"They certainly have their act down," Stephen went on. "Pretending reluctance, then letting themselves be persuaded. It is one of the things that makes Mother feel they are perfectly honest. No one who was trying to trick or deceive her would decide to leave, she thinks. She doesn't see how well they twist her around their finger, threatening to take away her access to Roderick so that she will abandon whatever doubts may have arisen in her mind."

"She *was* beginning to doubt this evening," Olivia replied. "She seemed somewhat offended at the idea that the St. Legers should repay the Martyrs for their loss."

Stephen smiled. "That was a slip on Valenskaya's part, I agree. Mother has always been fiercely proud of the St. Legers, and she loves Blackhope. She would not welcome any slight to them."

233

"What is this 'Martyrs' treasure,' anyway?" Olivia asked. "Why do they want it in particular?"

"It is something that was found after the St. Legers moved into this house, hundreds of years ago. The Elizabethans, you know, were great builders, and the first St. Legers here added on to the original house. Part of what we call the main wing includes the additions that the first earl made. They also renovated some of the original house. During the renovations, they discovered a secret room."

"Really?" Olivia asked, intrigued.

He nodded. "A small room between two others. There was a hidden door, cunningly done, and it was only after they had broken through the wall and found the room that they figured out where the door was and how it worked. Anyway, in this room, they found a small box, and in it there were various gold articles, as Madame Valenskaya hinted, including a large gold cross with a cabochon ruby in the center of it. They realized that it must have belonged to Lord Scorhill, the Catholic who was martyred, so that is how it got the name 'Martyrs' treasure.' The secret room might have been a priest's hole, or perhaps he built it for the express purpose of hiding the jewels. No one knew, of course. I presume that Scorhill must have hidden his treasures there, believing he and his family would eventually be released and would be able to return to their house and recover their wealth. Of course, they never had that chance."

"How sad." Olivia thought for a moment. "But why does Madame Valenskaya want that particular treasure? Why not ask for money or other jewels?"

He shrugged. "I suppose this treasure makes a good story — the martyred family, the ghosts not being able to rest, and so on, and they need to draw us into a good romantic story. It has a certain logic, more so than asking for the family silver or the St. Leger emeralds. The casket and its contents are not really as valuable as the jewel collection in the safe, but they do have a certain degree of notoriety that the others do not. And since they are over three hundred years old, that would doubtless add to their value."

He paused, then went on. "However, they have made a mistake in choosing them."

"What?"

"For one thing, they are not Mother's to give. She has several necklaces and rings and such that my father gave her, but like the heirloom jewels, the Martyrs' treasure belongs to the present earl. It is passed down from generation to generation. The first earl decided to keep the secret room, with its cunning door, and he left the casket in the room. Only the lord of the house knows where that room is or how to enter it. It is a bit of knowledge that is passed down from the earl to his heir as soon as the heir reaches maturity."

"So it is a treasure that one would hold on to even more than others."

"Absolutely. I am the only one who could give the casket to them. Mother doesn't even know where it is."

"Perhaps they don't know that only you have access to it. Or they think that your mother will be able to persuade you to give them the box."

"I would hate that. But I can't turn it over to them, even for Mother's sake. I imagine she realizes that, too. You see, it has become something of a superstition, this keeping the treasure safe and secret. The idea grew over the years that the family will continue to live and prosper only if the treasure is kept safe. There was some difficulty when my father died and Roderick became the earl. I then became the next heir, at least until Roderick had a son, so he should have shown me the room and the door and secret mechanism. But I was not here. I was already living in the United States. For a few years, only Roderick knew the secret. If he had died then, it would have been lost a second time."

"What happened? How did you learn of it?"

"Roderick wrote me a letter telling me about the room and the secret mechanism, then sealed it and gave it to his solicitor. His instructions were to give the letter to me if he should die before I returned to England. Which, of course, is what happened."

There was a sadness in his face, and impulsively Olivia reached out and laid her hand over Stephen's. "It must have been very hard for you — both your father and your brother passing away, when you were not even here to say goodbye."

He looked at her, a little surprised, and turned his hand over so that he was holding hers. "Yes," he said. "It was hard. Doubly so because . . . there had been an estrangement between Roderick and me when I left the country. I said some harsh things to him, and he to me, and we were never able to put it right."

Olivia squeezed his hand, her own chest tightening at the sorrow in Stephen's eyes. "I am sure you would have, had you had the chance to speak to him. No doubt he wanted to, as well."

"I think so." Stephen smiled at her faintly. "When I read that letter, it was like his dead hand reaching out to me. After he told me how to get to the treasure, he added a brief note. He said he was sorry for what had happened. He had hoped I would return and we would be . . . close again."

"Oh, Stephen . . ." Tears swam in Olivia's eyes.

He took her hand and raised it to his mouth, tenderly kissing her palm. "You are a remarkable woman, Olivia. Are you aware of that?"

"I am?" She did not quite know what to make of his words.

But then he tugged at her hand, pulling her up and toward him. She went willingly, if a little uncertainly, and he hooked his other hand around her waist, pulling her down into his lap. It felt, strangely, like a natural, comfortable place to be. She leaned against his chest, her head resting against him, and his arms went around her, holding her warmly, securely. She could feel the thump of his heart inside his chest, could smell the distinctive male scent of him. His warmth enveloped her, and Olivia felt as if she was exactly where she was meant to be.

His hand moved at her waist, gliding from her side to the center of her stomach, then back again, and the small movements set up a warm ache inside her. It was highly improper for her to be here like this, she knew, but Olivia had no intention of ending the moment.

Stephen rubbed his cheek against her hair, his breath sighing out. He said her name again, the hunger clear in his voice. He twisted a little, his face coming down to hers, and he kissed her cheek, her chin, then, finally, her mouth. Fire flared between them, replacing the sweet warmth. They kissed deeply, passionately, her arms twining around his neck. His hand sank into her hair, sending hairpins popping from their moorings, and the thick tresses tumbled down over his hand, caressing his skin like silk.

Olivia moaned a little at the unaccustomed sensations flowing through her, and his fingers tightened against her scalp in response, his lips pressing even more deeply into hers. His hand roamed up the front of her dress and back down, spreading fire through her abdomen. He moved it back up, cupping her breast through the cloth of her dress, and her nipples tightened, her breasts suddenly fuller and aching in an exciting way. His thumb traced the circle of her nipple, feeling it grow taut and pointed with desire. With every movement, the pleasure and excitement inside Olivia multiplied. She had never experienced such things, had not even guessed they existed. She moved restlessly on his lap, not knowing what to do, wanting the pleasure to go on, yearning for something without knowing what it was.

The naive movement of her hips against him excited him, and Stephen went to the neckline of her evening dress, caressing the rounded top of her breast, then slipping his fingers underneath the neckline. They slid beneath the thin cotton of her chemise, as well, releasing her breast and sliding over her smooth skin and onto the prickling bud of her nipple. Gently he took the button of flesh between his thumb and forefinger and squeezed and rolled it. Pleasure shot through Olivia in shocking, sizzling darts, taking her breath away. His fingers played over her, and moisture flooded between her legs, startling her. Everything he did was new and surprising; she could not think, only feel the wonderful sensations bombarding her.

Stephen tore his mouth from hers and kissed his way down her throat. His lips touched the top curve of her breast. She made a little noise deep in her throat, her head falling back as if to give him free access to her. He kissed the trembling flesh softly, moving across the smooth orb until his lips reached her nipple. Olivia tightened all over as his mouth grazed the hard bud once, then again. His tongue came out and delicately traced all around the button, finally moving over it in long, lazy strokes. She quivered, her fingers digging into his shoulder.

"Stephen . . ." she murmured, her face soft and languorous, her lips rosy and swollen from his kisses. The sight of her was so beautiful, the sound of her voice so seductive, that his whole body thrummed with desire.

His mouth fastened on her nipple, pulling it into the wet, warm cave of his mouth. Gently he suckled on it, and his tongue danced over the bud, laving and lashing it to an even harder point. He fumbled at the neckline of her dress, dragging it down and exposing the other white orb, centered deliciously by pink. His breath rasped in his throat as he moved to her other breast and began to feast in the same way on it. Olivia moaned, her hands moving restlessly up his neck and digging into his hair. She tugged at his hair, the sharp prickles of pain only increasing the supreme pleasure he felt at having his mouth on her.

Stephen wanted her, wanted to sink into her and possess her. His brain flamed with images of sliding down to the floor with her and pushing up her skirts, of riding inside her to his dark explosion of passion. But even as he thought it, he knew that he could not. Olivia was not the sort of woman that one could just take on the floor in a moment of desire.

With a muffled curse, he lifted his head from her breast and buried his face in her hair, struggling to regain control of himself.

"Stephen?" Olivia's voice was quiet and confused. "What —"

"I'm sorry. God, I seem to be always saying that to you." He lifted his head and looked down at her, clenching his teeth at the wave of hunger that washed over him. She looked so soft, so yielding, so utterly desirable, that for a moment he was not sure he could keep from kissing her again.

He cleared his throat. "This is insane. We must not." He reached out and pulled up the front of her dress, unable to resist a caress of her breasts as he did so. "The, uh, the door is open. Anyone could come in."

"What? Oh!" Red flamed in her cheeks, and Olivia scrambled off his lap, straightening her clothes.

She looked at him, embarrassed and still churning with unspent desire. Was she playing the fool with him? She had no idea what he still felt for Pamela or, indeed, what he felt for herself. Right now, she thought, all she knew was that if he had asked her into his bed, she would have gone in an instant. The thought made her cheeks burn even more brightly.

"I, um, it's time for bed. I mean — I should be — excuse me." She turned and fled from the room.

The séance the next evening was again lit dimly. Madame Valenskaya had seemingly decided to use the idea of the room being lit as another "proof" of her visitations and had taken charge of the lighting by having two oil lamps burning at their very lowest far from the séance table.

"You see," she said in her guttural accent, indicating the lamps with a sweep of her hand, "I haff light so you can see I hide nothing."

The result of the lamps was, Olivia thought, an even more poorly lit séance table than the evening before, but she made no comment, knowing it would merely upset Lady St. Leger, who was obviously eager to please Madame Valenskaya tonight.

"There is no question of that, I'm sure," Lady St. Leger said now, smiling at the medium. "But it is very kind of you, for Belinda's sake."

Madame Valenskaya nodded regally and motioned to them to sit down. They once again took their places as they had in the past, with Irina and Howard Babington on either side of the medium. Linking hands around the table, the group fell into silence. Olivia watched Madame Valenskaya as she went through the same routine she had the night before, her head nodding forward, then after a time rising slowly until her face was lifted up, as if she were communing with the heavens. Her eyes were closed.

As it had the other night, a ghostly tinkling tune played. Olivia felt sure it came from a small music box hidden in some capacious pocket about the medium's person. However, she was not sure how it was activated, for she could see even in the faint light that Madame Valenskaya's hands remained on the table, linked with Irina's and Babington's. The woman must, she thought, be activating the box somehow with her foot. It would not be too difficult to run a wire from the switch on the music box down inside her dress and into her shoe, where she could pull on it with her toes. Or she could run a wire down her sleeve and hold it in her hand to tug at some point, for her hands, of course, were in her accomplices'.

It was a clever thing to do, Olivia thought. By making the eerie music play while having a little light on, they could claim more proof that they were not frauds. Olivia thought she would try to take Madame Valenskaya's hand for some reason after the séance, just to see if she could feel a wire. Of course, the medium could push the wire back into her sleeve when she was finished, or she might have done it with her feet, or it could even be that the music box was hidden in her daughter's clothes and operated by her. Olivia gritted her teeth in frustration.

Apparently Madame Valenskaya's usual spirit guide, the American Indian Chief Running

Deer, was visiting them tonight, for the medium began to speak in a sort of pidgin English, asking them why they disturbed the spirits. Olivia suspected that this monologue was just a tease to make Lady St. Leger more impatient and desperate to speak with her son.

True to form, Lady St. Leger said, after Madame Valenskaya fell silent, "But what about Roderick? Is Roderick there? Can we not speak to him?"

Madame Valenskaya paused for a moment. Then, suddenly, a wind whooshed through the room, chilling them, and the lights in the oil lamps dipped and one went completely out. Belinda let out a shriek. Startled, Olivia looked up the table at Madame Valenskaya. The medium was sitting there, her eyes open now, looking as astonished as the rest of them.

A low, harsh moan issued from the end of the table where the medium sat, and the hair on the nape of Olivia's neck prickled in primitive response. Howard Babington's head was thrown back, and she realized that the sound was issuing from his open mouth. As she watched, he rose slowly to his feet, moving almost as if someone were pulling him upward. His arms dangled at his sides. Then his head fell back down, so that he was facing the rest of them.

"I will have my revenge," he said, his voice booming out, harsh and grating, like the creak of metal against metal. His face looked different

— his eyes filled with a fierce light, his features hard and hate filled, his lips pulling back in an animal snarl.

He had pulled his hands from Madame Valenskaya's and Lady St. Leger's as he stood up. Lady St. Leger stared at him now in horrified fascination, her hand clutched to her throat.

"I will have what is mine," Babington went on in the same deep, rasping voice, his words oddly accented. "I have waited hundreds of years, and I will not be denied. Death cannot thwart me. The whore will pay! No one will escape. They will kneel before me and beg."

His eyes were wide and glowing with hatred, his face almost unrecognizable. He lifted his arms, fists clenched, and from his mouth issued something that could only be described as a howl.

Olivia shivered, goose bumps popping up all over her. She tore her eyes from Babington for an instant to look at Madame Valenskaya, and she saw on the medium's face a look of undisguised horror. Next to Olivia, Stephen pulled his hand from hers and shot to his feet, his chair falling over with the force of his movements.

The unearthly howl ended abruptly, as if cut off. Babington's eyes rolled up, and he began to jerk, as if in the midst of a violent seizure. They all stared with horror as he trembled and shook. Stephen alone was able to move, hurrying around the table toward him. He reached out and grasped Babington's arm as Babington went limp and slid to the floor.

10

Stephen managed to grab the man with his other hand, as well, so that Babington did not crash onto the floor but went down more gradually, Stephen supporting his shoulders and easing his head onto the ground.

As if released from their frozen state, the women stood up from the table, their voices rising in a babble. Stephen knelt beside Babington and loosened his tie and undid his collar. Olivia moved quickly to his side and knelt down with him.

"Is he all right? What happened?"

"I haven't a bloody clue," Stephen replied, taking off his coat and folding it into a makeshift pillow to put beneath the man's head.

"Is — is he dead?" Madame Valenskaya asked, edging closer and peering down at Babington.

Olivia looked up at the medium. Her face was pale, and her hands were clutching her skirts. Her accent, Olivia noticed, had disappeared utterly.

"No. He's still breathing." Stephen took the other man's wrist in his fingers. "His pulse is racing. I don't know what happened. He must have had a seizure of some sort."

"It was the spirits," Irina offered.

Madame Valenskaya stirred. "Yes," she agreed, her voice dropping and reacquiring its guttural accent. "Spirits speak through him. Dey are unhappy."

"I would say unhappy doesn't even begin to express it," Olivia commented dryly.

"Yes," Lady St. Leger agreed, her face troubled. "He sounded quite . . . well . . . mad." She paused, then added, "That was not Roddy. That could not have been Roddy."

"Olivia, ring for the servants," Stephen said. "We need smelling salts. I can't awaken him. And someone please turn on some damn lights."

It was Belinda who turned the lamp's flame higher and brought it over to where Babington lay on the floor. Olivia summoned a footman and sent him running for smelling salts.

When the footman returned a few moments later with the smelling salts, Stephen waved the bottle under Babington's nose. Babington coughed and turned his head away, but his eyes did not open. Stephen slapped his cheeks gently, but that had no effect on him, either.

"Oh, dear, what's happened to him?" Lady St. Leger murmured tearfully.

"I think a spirit tried to speak through him,"

Irina said quietly. "And it seems to have been too much for him."

"Yes. Yes. A spirit," Madame Valenskaya agreed quickly, going back to her chair and sitting down.

Stephen sent a servant for the doctor, then had some of the footmen carry Babington up to his room and put him in his bed. The rest of the group trailed after them, standing in an uncertain clump inside his bedroom door. Olivia lit every lamp and candle in his room. Babington's pallor looked even greater in the increased light.

Stephen glanced at the women. "I will wait for the doctor, and I will let you know what he says."

Pamela looked greatly relieved at this statement and left the room almost immediately. Madame Valenskaya and her daughter hesitated, but it took little persuading to get them to retire, as well.

"I should stay with our guest," Lady St. Leger told her son, giving Babington an uneasy glance. "It is my responsibility as the lady of the house."

Stephen sent Olivia a significant look, and Olivia stepped forward. "But, Lady St. Leger, your son is the head of the house, after all, and I'm sure he is quite capable of remaining with Mr. Babington until the doctor arrives. No doubt poor Mr. Babington would be more comfortable with another man in the room rather than one of us women." She nodded toward

Belinda. "And I think Belinda is in need of her mother right now."

Lady St. Leger looked at her daughter, who was indeed quite pale and frowning with worry. "Yes, I am sure you are right, my lady," Lady St. Leger said, unable to completely conceal the relief in her voice. Everyone, it seemed, felt uneasy in the presence of the eerily silent Mr. Babington.

Olivia eased Lady St. Leger and Belinda out the door, turning back once to look at Stephen. He smiled, saying, "Thank you. I will let you know what the doctor says."

The three women went to Lady St. Leger's sitting room down the hall. "Where do you suppose the others have gone?" Lady St. Leger asked, casting a vague look around the room.

"No doubt back to their rooms," Olivia reassured her. "I think all of us could use a little peace and quiet after that."

"What happened?" Belinda asked, her voice quavering a little. "I've never seen anything like that."

"Nor I," Olivia replied candidly. "I am not sure what happened. Perhaps the doctor will be able to tell."

"It was as if he was another person," Lady St. Leger said. "And that voice — it sounded, well, not human."

"It was very strange," Olivia agreed.

"Do you think it was really spirits?" Belinda asked.

"I wouldn't think so," Olivia said stoutly. "I think perhaps Mr. Babington — well, I don't know what happened to him, but I feel sure there must be a rational explanation for it."

"I cannot imagine what," Lady St. Leger said honestly. Her face twisted in distress. "If the spirits of the departed sound like that, it must mean that they are dreadfully unhappy. I cannot bear to think of Roddy feeling that way."

"My dear lady, I am sure he does not," Olivia cried, her heart going out to the older woman. "I know he would not want you to feel so distressed."

She cast about for something to take her ladyship's mind off the frightening events of the evening. "You know, my lady, I did not know your eldest son. Perhaps you could tell me a little about him."

Olivia soon realized she had hit upon the right topic, for Lady St. Leger immediately brightened and began to describe Roderick to her. Belinda joined in, and they were soon caught up in recounting all the sweet and warm memories they had of the man.

By the time Stephen joined them an hour later, both the St. Leger women were calm and smiling, even laughing, still happily recounting yet another joke that Roderick had played. Stephen's eyebrows sailed up in surprise and he shot Olivia an appreciative look.

"Well," he said, stepping into the room, "you look much better, Mother, I'm happy to say."

"Oh, darling." Lady St. Leger turned to him. "How is that poor man? Did the doctor come?"

"Yes, he did. He checked Mr. Babington over, and he could find nothing wrong — his heart is beating normally, and his lungs sound clear and fine. But he is unable to wake up. The doctor is not sure what happened. He says it sounds as if the man had some sort of seizure and is now in a coma. He suggested that perhaps Mr. Babington had epilepsy. He asked about his medical history, but of course I knew nothing about it, and when we asked Madame Valenskaya and her daughter, neither did they. They said they had only known him for a year. They have never witnessed such behavior from him, but I suppose he could have managed to hide it from others most of the time."

"But will he wake up?" Lady St. Leger asked.

"I don't know. Dr. Hartfield would not say. He said he hoped so, and he said that he will come to check on him. There seems to be nothing to do at the moment except to wait and see that Babington is cared for. I have told the butler to have one of the maids sit with him all the time."

"Poor man." Lady St. Leger sighed. "And poor Madame Valenskaya."

"She seemed rather upset," Stephen agreed.

"Perhaps I should go talk to her."

"I believe she said that she was going to retire."

"Oh. Yes. That would probably be best for us all. Belinda, dear? Shall we go on to bed?"

Belinda agreed, although she said that she would prefer to spend the night in her mother's room. Lady St. Leger, with a smile, said that she would prefer to have company, as well. The two of them went off, and Stephen turned to Olivia inquiringly.

She nodded, getting up, and they made their way downstairs to Stephen's study. Once inside the door, Stephen closed it behind them and turned and pulled Olivia into his arms, holding her closely for a long moment. She leaned her head against his chest, grateful for the support. What had happened with Mr. Babington had shaken her, and her efforts to appear calm and collected and keep Lady St. Leger and Belinda from dissolving into hysterics had taxed her strength. It was wonderful to be able to relax and draw on Stephen's strength, if only for a few moments.

He let out a sigh. "I have been wanting to do this all evening."

"Yes."

He squeezed her a little more tightly, then released her. "I recommend a brandy," he said, going to the liquor cabinet.

Olivia made no protest as she walked over to her usual chair and sank down in it. Stephen brought her a small snifter of brandy and took a seat in a nearby chair. They were silent for a moment as they sipped at their drinks. Olivia let the fire of the brandy trickle through her, warming and reviving her. She took another sip, then set it aside and looked at Stephen.

"All right. What happened?"

He shook his head. "I have absolutely no idea. I was hoping you would."

"No. I have never seen anything like that. Never heard of anything like that." She paused, then went on. "I assume that what he said — about getting back what was his — was directed at the Martyrs' treasure."

"I would think so, given that the chest is what they seem to be after. I presume we are to think it was Lord Scorhill himself speaking through Mr. Babington."

Olivia nodded. "Yes. But how — did you see his face? And his voice!" Olivia could not restrain a shiver at the memory. "He looked and sounded like someone else."

"Someone rather frightening," Stephen added in a massive understatement.

"It is hard for me to believe that Mr. Babington is that accomplished an actor. That anyone is, for that matter. And the fit he fell into afterward also looked very real. The doctor is in no doubt that he is in a coma, is he?"

"No. He is certain of it."

"I cannot help but wonder if it was . . . well, real."

Stephen looked at her. "What are you suggesting? That the Martyrs really do want their gold and jewels back? That Madame Valenskaya is not a fraud?"

"No," Olivia replied hastily. "I am certain that our madame is a fraud, through and through. But I wonder if there isn't something else at work here."

"Such as?"

"I don't know. But look at what has happened. Madame Valenskaya has done several things that I know are absolute fakes. I can explain how they were achieved. The eerie music, from a music box wound up and hidden about her person, switched on at the appropriate moment. The ghostly hand in the air, merely a glove painted with phosphorescent paint. The crying, coming down from the nursery through the removed tile. The ghost capering outside, Babington dressed up in a dark, hooded cloak with a painted mask. As for Roddy speaking through her, it's obvious that it is simply Madame Valenskaya lowering her voice and losing her accent — by the way, did you notice tonight, when she spoke after Babington's seizure, she had no Russian accent at all?"

Stephen smiled faintly. "I caught that, yes. All right, so we are agreed she is a fake and the things she has done are all tricks."

"Yes. But there have been several other things that are frankly baffling," Olivia pointed out. "The woman you and I saw walk through the wall, the dream that the two of us shared — those are very peculiar and, at least to me, inexplicable. And this thing tonight falls into the same category. I cannot believe Mr. Babington was pretending that. How could he have made himself go into a coma?"

"Then what do you think it was? Are you saying he was invaded by a spirit?"

Olivia squirmed a little in her chair. "I find that just about as difficult to believe," she admitted. "But I don't think it was a fraud that Madame Valenskaya was perpetrating. I looked over at her a couple of times while Babington was . . . doing what he was doing . . . and she looked genuinely shocked and horrified. I think it was a complete surprise to her."

"I agree that Madame Valenskaya doesn't have the intelligence or the skill to come up with the visions or the dreams or what happened tonight. But if she is not causing them, where are they coming from? Is there someone else involved? Do you think it could be Babington who has orchestrated these other things somehow? Or that there is someone else, someone not here, but outside somewhere, manipulating it all?"

"I have no idea," Olivia said. "But, frankly, it is beginning to frighten me."

Stephen's thoughts went back to the scene at the séance earlier — Howard Babington's unearthly voice and wild face, his uncontrollable shaking and twitching and eventual collapse — and he nodded. "Yes, you're right. It's very frightening. And I haven't the slightest idea what to do about it."

★ ★ ★

Madame Valenskaya rubbed her hands together as she paced up and down the floor of her bedroom, as she had been doing almost the entire time since Mr. Babington's collapse.

"I don't like it!" she burst out, shooting a glance at her companion that was both wary and ill-tempered. "I've never seen anything like that in my life. And I hope never to see it again."

"Calm down," the other woman said quietly. "I didn't expect it, either, but it will work to our advantage. As long as you can keep your mouth shut. Babington's performance is bound to scare Lady St. Leger into doing whatever the 'spirits' tell her."

"What if she can't get it? You said her son is the one who controls it."

"He will get it. I could see that even he was shaken this evening. And if his mother is scared out of her wits over it, he will do it for her. He hates you, but he will do it just to get rid of you."

The dumpy medium made a noise of disbelief. "I'm not so sure of that. That one's a hard man. I've known men like him before, and there's no scaring or bullying them."

"It will work," her companion said flatly. "As long as you don't lose your nerve."

"I don't know what's so special about this Martyrs' treasure, anyway. I was getting coin and jewels just fine without all this. Lady St. Leger will continue to give me money as long as

I can give her her 'Roddy' to talk to," Madame Valenskaya said, sneeringly mimicking Lady St. Leger's pet name for her son. "I don't know why we have to try to get this gold casket."

"You don't have to know why." The other woman's voice was sharp and disdainful.

"It's not worth it," Madame Valenskaya whined. "I want to leave. I want to go back to London."

"Don't even think about leaving. I have put far too much time and effort into this — seducing that lack-wit Babington into helping us, dragging you along, producing those tricks — to let you ruin it all because you are a coward. You are staying right here, and you are going to keep on giving your séances until we get what we want. Do you understand me?"

"Yes, yes, all right," Madame Valenskaya said grudgingly. "I will stay. And I won't give us away."

"All right. That's better." She gave the medium a last piercing look, then turned and walked out of the room.

Madame Valenskaya closed the door after her and turned the key. Letting out a shaky little sigh, she leaned against the door for a moment, then walked across the room and pulled open one of the drawers. She rummaged around in it for a moment and triumphantly pulled out a bottle of gin. She poured a healthy amount into a glass, her hand trembling so badly that the bottle clinked against the rim. Then she lifted the glass and drank it down greedily, giving a little shiver afterward. The heat exploded in her stomach, and everything seemed better.

Olivia dreamed that night of the woman she and Stephen had seen in the great hall, the woman who, in the dream she and Stephen had shared, had been called Lady Alys. She was dressed as she had been in that dream — in a plain blue tunic and undergown, with a simple veil holding back her hair. She was folding clothes and putting them in a trunk, gracefully bending and turning. She turned and looked straight at Olivia and smiled.

"It's very important, you see, to make sure one's precious goods are saved," she said, her voice softly accented.

She turned back and picked up a gold box, about a foot long and seven or eight inches high. It was ornately engraved along the edges. She set it down on the bed and opened the lid. Inside, golden objects gleamed. Lady Alys lifted out a necklace of gold beads, then a cross the size of her hand, centered by a dark red stone, and laid them on the bed. Inside lay a tangle of gold chains and several rings, some engraved and some with polished colored stones. She opened a large wooden trunk and reached inside, pulling out a belt, or girdle. It was long and made up of links of gold, and in the center of it, three of the links were embedded with polished stones. Carefully she folded the girdle and put it into the golden box, then replaced the large cross and the gold necklace and closed the lid.

There was the sound of shouts, and she turned and ran to the narrow window and looked out. "Soldiers!" she cried, her face filled with panic. "There are soldiers in the bailey!"

Suddenly they were no longer in the same room but in another one with rounded walls and no square corners. A tower room, Olivia knew. There was smoke, and outside the air rang with the clash of swords and the shouts of men. Lady Alys was wearing the same clothes, now dirty and torn and stained with blood. The smoke grew thicker, and the lady coughed, her face taut with fear. Olivia felt the woman's fear, and her own throat tightened.

It was hard to breathe; she felt as if she was suffocating. Olivia's eyes opened, and she realized that she was in her own bed, not some medieval tower room. But still she could not breathe. Something dark and heavy lay in the air all around her, pressing her down, pushing her into the bed, crushing the air from her chest.

Panic filled her. She could not move . . . All around her the air hung like iron, filled with menace. Squeezing her. Killing her.

Olivia finally broke the paralysis that enveloped her, swinging out wildly with her arms. She sucked in a breath and shrieked, tumbling out of her bed, still swinging. There was nothing there. She encountered no resistance except the bedclothes tangled around her. But she was still gripped by the terror that had seized her, and she ran for the door and flung it open, stumbling out into the hall.

Stephen came running toward her from his room, his chest bare, wearing only a pair of trousers hastily pulled on. "Olivia! What is it? What's the matter?"

"Stephen!" Olivia flung herself into his arms, and he held her close, stroking her hair and bending his head to hers, murmuring soothing endearments.

She held on to him, trembling, as her fear slowly subsided. His arms were tight and strong around her, and she wanted to stay inside their safety forever. But finally she stepped back from him, letting out a shaky little sigh.

Olivia glanced around her. Up and down the hall, several other doors had opened, and she found Lady St. Leger and Belinda, as well as Irina Valenskaya, watching them with great interest. Olivia blushed and brushed back her hair with her hands.

"I'm sorry. I've made a terrible fool of myself," she said.

"Don't worry about that." Stephen took her arm and led her back into her room, away from all the interested eyes. He lit a lamp and turned the wick up, giving them light. "Now, tell me, what happened?"

Olivia shivered, cold, and realized for the first time that she was wearing only her nightgown, with nothing underneath. Her blush deepened, and she grabbed her dressing gown from the chair and wrapped it around her. "I — I must have had a bad dream."

"What happened?" His eyes were grave and concerned, and despite the fact that she felt increasingly foolish over her momentary fright, Olivia found herself telling him about it.

"I was dreaming about Lady Alys."

"The woman we saw?" He stared at her. "The one in our dreams?"

Olivia nodded. "She was dressed the same. And she was packing things into a trunk. Then all of a sudden we were in another room — the way things happen in dreams, you know. This room was round, and it sounded like there was a battle outside, and Lady Alys's gown was torn and bloodied and dirty. And there was smoke. It was horrible, choking. But then I was awake and in my bed. But . . . somehow I was still choking!"

"What?"

"I can't explain it. But I could not breathe. It was as if something was holding me down, pressing into my chest, and I couldn't catch my breath. I felt as if I was suffocating. And — and there was this darkness around me. This sense of menace and evil. I knew — I don't know how, but I *knew* — that it wanted me to die. I was terrified."

"My God. And you were awake?"

"I thought I was. I suppose I must have still been dreaming. I guess I awoke, for suddenly I was able to move and breathe, but I had no sensation of waking up. I just started flailing my arms around and screamed and jumped out of bed. Then I took off running."

"Wise girl." Stephen pulled her back into his arms and held her tightly.

"I was so scared," Olivia whispered. "I can't tell you how real it all felt. And I thought — I was sure that I locked the door before I went to bed. Yet when I ran out of the room, the door just opened. It was not locked."

"Do you think there was someone in here?" Stephen asked.

"I don't see how there could have been. If there were, where did he go? But I felt someone — you know, the way you can feel that someone has come up behind you, and you just know they are there even though you can't see them? I felt as if someone — or something — was here. And I was certain that it wanted me dead."

His arms tightened instinctively around her. "Nothing is going to happen to you," he growled. "I won't let it."

He stroked her back soothingly, and Olivia melted into him. It felt so good to stand with him this way; she wanted the moment to go on forever. Wherever his hand moved, she grew warmer. The fear and the darkness were slowly receding. She made a soft noise, part pleasure, part relief, and snuggled closer. She could hear his heart speed up in his chest beneath her head, and his hand where it touched her was suddenly hot. Stephen laid his cheek against her head; her scent was in his nostrils.

"You cannot stay here alone," he told her.

Olivia smiled and leaned back, looking up into his face with a flirtatious expression. "I am afraid, sir, that it would be quite scandalous for you to remain here all night. You are pushing the boundaries right now by coming into my bedroom this way."

"Well, then I suppose I would just have to marry you, wouldn't I?"

His words left her breathless. Olivia pulled away from him. His words were teasing, she knew, and for that very reason, they pierced her heart.

"Don't be foolish," she said shortly, crossing her arms and walking away from him.

He looked at her speculatively. "Would it be so terrible a thing?"

Olivia turned back, holding her head high in a proud, almost defiant pose. "I am sure you would not wish to risk marrying into the 'mad Morelands.' "

"Ah," he said, moving closer to her, his eyes smiling at her, "but, you see, some men prefer a bit of risk in anything they undertake."

There was no mistaking the heat in his eyes or the underlying meaning of his words. Olivia was certain he was about to take her in his arms again, but this time to kiss her, not soothe away her fears. She waited, not moving away, an answering challenge in her stance.

Just before Stephen reached her, Tom Quick barreled into the room, shattering the moment. "Miss! Are you all right?"

On his heels came Joan, a dressing gown wrapped around her, her hair comically rolled up in rags to induce curls, the concealing nightcap half off her head. "My lady! I heard — they said it was you who screamed."

"Yes, I did, but it's all right," Olivia hastily reassured her. "I had a bad dream."

"It was more than a bad dream," Stephen corrected. "She felt threatened."

"By who?" Tom demanded belligerently. "You tell me, miss, and I'll take care of him."

"I don't know. There was no one there. I am sure it must have been merely a dream."

"I think it would be best if your maid slept on a cot here in your room," Stephen said. "I'll have one of the footmen set up a bed immediately."

"I am sure that isn't necessary," Olivia protested, but her heart was not in it. In fact, she knew that if she had to stay in this room the rest of the night by herself, she would not spend any of it sleeping. So she gave in and allowed Joan to sleep in the room, and even accepted Tom's offer to sleep in the hall across her door, just to make absolutely sure that nothing could enter.

Even so, it took a long time before Olivia could go back to sleep, and she awoke several times during the night. Only when the dawn shone in around the draperies was she finally able to fall deeply asleep.

The next morning, after breakfast, Stephen took her arm, suggesting a stroll around the garden. They walked along the paths, coming after a while to the vine-covered bower in the center of the garden. A wooden bench sat beneath the arch of the trellis, for sitting and contemplating the beauty and peace of the garden. Stephen led her to the bench, and they sat down.

"I hope you are feeling better," he said, looking into her face with concern.

Olivia nodded. "Yes. I am sorry to have been such a nuisance. It was foolish, no doubt. Probably the peculiar events of yesterday evening made me have such a . . . a disconcerting dream."

"Perhaps." He paused and looked down at his hands. "Still . . . we have dreamed of these people before. Together and separately. It puzzles me. It seems — I cannot help but think there is some significance to them. I know it sounds superstitious, but . . ." His voice trailed off uncertainly.

"I, too, cannot help but feel they are somehow significant," Olivia agreed. "Yet I cannot understand the dreams. I am not one to believe in signs or portents."

"But neither can we overlook what keeps presenting itself to us," Stephen added. "Why do we keep dreaming of these people? Have you ever dreamed of this woman before?"

Olivia looked at him, startled. "No. Never. Not until I came here."

"Nor have I. Until the night I met you."

Olivia wrinkled her brow. "Are you saying that somehow our meeting set off these dreams?"

"I don't know. It sounds ridiculous." He sighed. "Tell me in detail about this dream of yours. You saw Lady Alys packing?"

"Yes. She was folding clothes and putting them in a trunk. And she looked straight at me and said something about it being important to keep your things safe. I can't remember her exact words — oh, wait, she said 'precious' — to keep what was precious to you safe. It was so odd, it was as if she were talking right to me, and yet I wasn't in the dream, not as a person. It was just something I was seeing. Then she went and got a gold box."

"A gold box?"

"Yes. It was about this big." Olivia gestured with her hands. "And quite prettily engraved around the edges. It was so vivid in the dream! She set the box down on the bed and opened it. Inside it was some jewelry — gold chains and gold and silver bracelets, some rings. She took out a gold cross. It had a red stone in the center of the cross —" Olivia stopped abruptly and looked at him. "It was, well, I guess it was like the cross Madame Valenskaya was talking about, the one you told me was in the Martyrs' treasure. Oh, of course! The gold box! You told me about the treasure box and the gold cross. That must have been why I dreamed about it."

Olivia realized she felt strangely disappointed to think that her dream had had no significance but had simply been caused by things she had heard about the past few days.

"Did I tell you it was gold?" Stephen asked.

Olivia hesitated for a moment, thinking. "I'm not sure. I don't remember your saying it. I was picturing it as a wooden box while you were talking. That is why I did not connect it at first. Is it gold?"

"Was there anything else in the box?" Stephen asked, sidestepping her question.

"Yes. She took out a necklace, as well. It was beautiful, made of gold beads, and the beads looked as if they had some kind of engraving on them." Olivia was gazing blankly out across the garden, recalling the dream in her head, and so she did not see Stephen stiffen at her words.

"She went to another trunk and took out a belt that was made of gold links, and in the center of the belt, where it fastened, there were stones like the one in the cross, three of them, one centered in each link. It was the belt she was wearing when we saw her."

"I didn't notice the belt," Stephen said abstractedly. "But I —"

He stood, reaching down to take her hand and pull her up, too. "Come with me. There is something I want to show you."

11

Stephen whisked her back into the house and seated her in his study, then left. He had refused to answer any of her questions as they walked back through the garden, merely shaking his head and telling her to "wait and see." By the time he reappeared at the study door, Olivia's curiosity was at a fever pitch.

He stepped into the room, carrying a small bundle, and closed the door behind him. Olivia stood up as he carried the bundle over to his desk and set it down. Stephen carefully unwrapped the blue velvet covering from around the object, revealing it at last as a golden box about a foot long and over half as tall. Around the edges of the box were engravings, and in the front it fastened with a clasp that came down over a small bar, which then turned to open and close it.

Olivia stared, her hand going to her stomach. She felt as if someone had knocked the breath from her. The box before her on the desk was the same one she had seen in her dream last night.

"It's the same," she breathed, reaching out her hand toward it, then letting it fall, not touching it. "Oh, Stephen . . . it's *exactly* the same."

Her eyes began to water, and her stomach felt like a chunk of ice. She sat back down abruptly. "This is impossible."

"I know. But when you began to describe it and its contents, I suspected you must have seen this casket."

"But how —" She raised her gaze finally from the gleaming box and looked at him. "I don't understand."

"I don't either. But I want you to look at what's inside." He opened the clasp and raised the lid. There was a pile of golden objects inside the little box, including a small dagger with a jeweled gold hilt. On top lay a large cross, also made of gold, about four or five inches long, and in the center lay a cabochon ruby.

Olivia stared at the cross. She had guessed that it would be in there, after seeing the gold casket, but even so, it made her stomach queasy to see the actual object, exactly like the one she had seen in her dream.

"I did not see the dagger," she said.

"No? What about this?" Stephen pulled out a necklace, long oval gold beads strung together, each bead cunningly etched.

"That's the necklace," she said a little breathlessly. "It was in the box, too."

"It's not a necklace," Stephen replied, holding

it closer to her. "It is a rosary. See, there are different shaped lozenges for the Pater Nosters and the Ave Marias. And each bead, if you'll look, is carved with a biblical scene. It's excellent craftsmanship."

"It's beautiful," Olivia responded. "And the girdle she wore? The jeweled belt? Is it in there?"

"No. I have never seen anything like that. But there are some necklaces and rings and such. Do you recognize any of them?"

He held out the box to her, and Olivia stood up and took it in her hands. As she grasped it, she was suddenly swamped with a strange feeling. Her stomach roiled, and it was hard to breathe. The blood drained from her face, leaving her ashen.

In her mind Olivia saw the woman she had dreamed of the night before. Lady Alys was with the knight she loved. They were outside in a meadow, sitting beside a pond. It was, Olivia realized, the same pond where she and Stephen had gone the first day she was at Blackhope.

Lady Alys was leaning against the knight, his arm curled around her, and they seemed to be lazily daydreaming in the sun. Alys looked up at the knight, her face soft with love. They were facing toward the pond, smiling and talking, absorbed in each other. They did not see, as Olivia saw, another man standing some distance from them, hidden among the trees at the edge of the meadow. His hair was black, as was his small pointed beard. A gold ring glinted on his finger, and the silk tunic he wore was richly embroidered with gold thread at the neck. He was watching the couple, his face stamped with a cold, fierce hatred.

An overpowering sense of evil swept Olivia, and her throat constricted. She could not breathe. She swayed, her eyes rolling up.

"Olivia!" Stephen jumped forward, his arm going around her waist as she slumped into a faint. With his other hand, he grasped the gold box.

He thrust the box onto the desk with one hand, his other arm lowering Olivia gently into her chair. Worriedly, he took her wrist and felt for her pulse.

"Olivia. Please, wake up." Visions of her slipping into the same unconscious state as Babington played terrifyingly through his head. "Sweet Lord, wake up."

He started to ring for smelling salts again, but just then Olivia's eyelids fluttered, and she opened her eyes.

"Thank God." Stephen let out a sigh of relief. "Are you all right?"

"I — I think so." Olivia looked confused. "What happened?"

"You fainted. I'm not sure why. I handed you the Martyrs' casket, and you looked very strange and fell into a faint."

He slipped his hand behind her back and helped her straighten.

"Oh," Olivia said, covering her eyes with her hand. She felt weak and a little sick to her stomach, as well. "I saw something. I'm sorry, I really can't explain it well. But as soon as I touched that casket, I saw Lady Alys." She described the scene to him, along with the man in the concealing woods who watched the lovers.

"Do you think it was the lady's husband?" Stephen asked.

"Sir Raymond? Yes, I think it was. Hatred poured from him. His eyes were glittering with anger and I was just flooded with this horrible sense of evil."

"Evil?" He responded. "There are those who would say her husband was the injured party."

"But you didn't see this man. He was — I don't know, the feeling of evil was so strong. It was more than jealousy or anger. I can't explain it. But it made me feel quite ill."

"I could see that." Stephen moved away and leaned against his desk, stretching his legs out in front of him. He looked at Olivia, whose color was returning.

"All right," he said. "What is happening?"

"I haven't any idea," Olivia replied. "I have never experienced anything like this in my life. What do these things mean that I keep seeing? And why am I seeing them? I would think I was going utterly mad if you had not seen some of them, as well."

"But I have. And I am quite certain that you

273

are not mad." Stephen reached over and took her hand and squeezed it, gazing down into her eyes.

Olivia gave him a wobbly smile in return, her eyes unexpectedly filling with tears. Stephen pulled her to her feet and into his arms, holding her lightly. "No. Don't cry. None of this is worth your tears."

Olivia leaned her head against his chest. It was amazing, she thought, how easy this was becoming. It felt so good to be near him, to let him encompass her with his strength. She was growing accustomed to their chats every evening in his study, to seeing him at breakfast and dinner, to walking with him in the garden or sharing tea with him.

It was foolish, she told herself, weak and foolish. Soon she would be leaving, and she would not see him again. She would return to her normal life, a life he did not share. She would be on her own again, pursuing her enthusiasms with the help of only Tom Quick. She would no longer discuss the happenings of the day with Stephen or see his smile . . . or feel the touch of his hand on hers.

She blinked away her tears, calling herself all kinds of a fool. She straightened and moved from him, turning her back and surreptitiously wiping away her tears. It was time to stop acting like a ninny.

"I'm sorry," she said. Her voice came out a little husky, and she cleared her throat. "I am afraid I have an abominable headache. It makes me a little weak. I do not usually give in to tears that way."

"You have had a good number of shocks the past few days," he said. "We all have."

"I am having a bit of trouble," she admitted. "What I seem to be seeing and feeling goes against everything I believe in. I cannot believe that these visions are real, that these are *ghosts!*" She turned and looked at him, her eyes wide. "In all the investigations I've done, I have never seen a ghost. I have never had a dream like the ones I have had recently, or — or seen people who are not there. And not only that — I have felt so clearly what they were thinking and feeling."

"I cannot explain it."

"Nor I. Even though I do not believe it, let us suppose that Madame Valenskaya or one of the others is amazingly expert in the practice of mesmerism, or hypnotism. And let us even say that it is possible, if one is so expert, to make a person believe they see something that isn't there, or to make them have dreams about a particular subject. And let us also imagine, since we are saying that they can do these other things, that they are able to implant in us the successful suggestion that we forget when and where and how we were hypnotized."

"All right. Given all those unlikely things . . ."

"There are still logistical problems. When and

where did they do this hypnotizing? You had your first dream about this couple in London, before Madame Valenskaya came here. Before you even met her. Isn't that true?"

"Yes."

"And since we have been here, there have generally been other people about, including the servants. I cannot see how anyone could have hypnotized me or you without someone else noticing. Unless they did it in the dead of night. And there have been so many details to the dreams — words and feelings and the minutiae of the people's appearance, what their clothes were, what the box and its contents looked like — and there have been so many visions. How could they have implanted all of that in both of us?"

"It stretches the limits of credibility," Stephen agreed.

"But even if all that could somehow be explained away or believed, there is still this problem — How could I have known what the box looked like or what it contained or what any of the contents were? I had never seen it before, and neither has Madame Valenskaya or the other two. Yet I saw the box and its contents down to the last detail. I knew its size, and I knew that it had engraving around the edge. I knew exactly how the rosary looked, even though I didn't know it was a rosary and thought it only a necklace. Madame Valenskaya could not have described it, because she has never seen it. There is no way she could have seen it before, is there — a drawing or anything?"

"No. She has never been in this house, and as far as I know, that box has never left it. I know my father never removed it, and I don't think Roderick would have, either. As I said, it's something of a superstition in the family. None of us would have risked losing it. And I have never heard of any drawings of the box or its contents. As far as I know, it is not even known outside this family."

"Then I cannot believe these things could have been the product of hypnotism. And if it isn't that, what is it?"

They looked at each other for a long moment, neither of them wanting to actually say it. Finally Stephen sighed and said, "Ghosts? I feel like an utter fool saying it, but I cannot see how any of this could have been engineered. The dreams . . . the visions . . ."

"Mr. Babington's fit?" Olivia offered.

"Do you think it is part of this?"

"I don't know. But it seems to me that we have two sets of events. On the one hand, we have Madame Valenskaya's séances and the things she says — the idea of the lost souls, the Martyrs' treasure, the music and raps and the supposed voice of your brother."

"The monk in the garden. The crying in the sitting room," Stephen added.

"Yes. All of those things can be explained, and

they all pertain to the gold casket. Then we have had an entirely different set of things: the apparition of the medieval woman in the great hall and the dreams you and I have had about this woman and her lover and husband. All of those are disturbingly inexplicable by any rational means."

"That would mean that we have Madame Valenskaya and her daughter and Mr. Babington and their tricks, none of which are real. And an entirely different set of 'spirits,' which do seem to be real. Completely disconnected," Stephen said.

"Not completely, though. The gold casket figures in both of them. And Mr. Babington at the séance the other night — his talking as if he were possessed, the seizure, the coma. That all seemed quite real, as well."

"Yes. This casket." Stephen walked over to the desk and stood for a moment looking down at it. "It was part of the Martyrs' treasure. And that was in the sixteenth century. Yet you dreamed about the medieval woman holding the box and its contents. When you held the box, you saw a very clear vision of the woman and her husband and the strong sense that the husband was evil. And those people appear to be from four hundred years earlier than the Martyrs."

Olivia was silent for a moment, thinking. "Perhaps the treasure that Lord Scorhill hid consisted of family heirlooms. Maybe the box and even the contents had been handed down for generations. They could have felt, as your family does, that they were more precious than even more expensive jewels."

Stephen nodded thoughtfully. "That could have been why they hid them away so securely. They could have taken their other valuables or sent them to family or friends, but they wanted these oldest, most precious objects to stay here in Blackhope where they belonged, even if it meant that no one ever found them again."

"What about the room where your family found the casket? Are you sure that the martyred Lord Scorhill built it?"

"You mean, could it have come from an earlier time? And maybe the Martyrs didn't even know of its existence?"

Olivia shrugged. "I don't know. It just occurred to me that maybe it was wrongly assumed that the treasure belonged to that Lord Scorhill. It seemed the likely explanation, but no one really *knew* that the martyred family built that room or put the gold box in there."

"Let's look at the room," Stephen suggested. "I have to put the box back, anyway."

Olivia stared at him. "But that is the secret room. You cannot show it to me."

Stephen quirked an eyebrow. "Frankly, the secrecy of the room bothers me less right now than a number of other things. Anyway, all you will know will be the location of the secret room. If you turn away or close your eyes, you

279

won't see the mechanism of how the door operates, and, believe me, without that knowledge, I don't think anyone could open it."

"All right. If you are certain."

"Positive." Stephen wrapped the box once again in its velvet covering, then picked it up and tucked it under his arm.

They left the study and went up the stairs to the bedroom wing, walking past the family's bedchambers. Several doors down from the last of the bedrooms used by the family and their guests, Stephen turned a corner and opened a door. Inside lay a smaller chamber than the one in which Olivia was residing, furnished in the style of Louis XIV.

Stephen stepped back to allow Olivia to enter, then went in after her and pushed the door, not noticing that it did completely shut. "We rarely use this room," he told her as they walked to the middle of the room. "It is one of the smaller guest rooms, and it's occupied only when the house is exceptionally full. It is not a favorite room of guests. I remember one cousin who stayed here when I was an adolescent who demanded that my mother move him to another room."

"Why?"

"I'm not entirely sure. I think it was because of the cold."

"It *is* chilly," Olivia commented, rubbing her arms. "I presumed it was because the room was not in use."

"Yes, but even when there is someone staying here and we have the fire lit, it isn't a particularly warm room. It's on the north side, and the fireplace doesn't seem to work well."

"Should I close my eyes now?" Olivia asked.

"Yes."

She did so, and to her surprise, he bent down and kissed her lightly on the lips. Her eyes popped open, and Stephen chuckled.

"Sorry. I could not resist." He hesitated for a moment, then kissed her again, more lingeringly this time. He was still carrying the velvet-wrapped box under his arm, which made an embrace awkward, so after a moment, he stepped back with a sigh. "All right. Close your eyes."

Olivia, feeling a little giddy from his kiss, closed her eyes again and also turned around to face the other direction, just for good measure. Behind her, she heard Stephen crossing the floor.

Behind her, Olivia heard a click, then the swish of something moving. Stephen said, "All right. You can look now."

Olivia turned. Stephen stood beside a narrow door, a piece of the wall, actually, that had swung away from the rest of it. Beyond it lay a small, dark room. She walked over to join Stephen and looked inside the secret room. It was small, the size of her dressing room at home, and it had no furnishings except for a small, narrow wooden table. There were no windows, so that the place lay in a perpetual gloom. Stephen stepped inside the room, ducking to go through the low doorway, and crossed to the table to set the box upon it. He turned to Olivia.

"Come in."

Olivia hesitated, then took a step inside. She stopped abruptly. The room was frigid. However, it was not the cold that stopped her, but the sense of something hovering in the air, heavy with menace and evil. It pushed against her body, its tendrils slithering around her. Thick and black, it tugged at her, curling around her throat. . . .

Dragging in breath with a gasp, Olivia jumped back out of the room. She stared at Stephen, trembling, unable to speak, her eyes wide and her face drained of color.

"Olivia?" Stephen frowned in concern, starting toward her. "What is it? What's the matter?"

She shook her head, unable to formulate what she had felt as she entered the room. Her stomach churned, and she felt weak and dizzy, as she had earlier when she had touched the small golden casket.

Stephen joined her in the bedroom, his arm going around her. "Did you see something again?"

"No. But it was — I felt it. I — there is evil in that room."

"Evil?" He glanced back at the inner room.

Olivia did not follow his gaze. She could not even bear to look into the room again. She turned and walked over to the small straight chair by the door and sank down on it. Stephen watched her for a moment, then turned and closed the section of the wall. Once it was closed, there was no indication of where the line of the door was.

He went to Olivia and squatted down in front of her, taking both her hands between his. "Is it like it was downstairs?"

"Yes. But worse." She looked at him. "You must think me foolish and weak."

"No, of course not. I have never seen you to be either one of those things."

"I feel it. But I couldn't stay there — the feeling was too strong. I felt his presence in that room. I couldn't go inside. It was as though he were pushing on me, smothering me."

Olivia shivered, and the shiver set off a score more inside her, radiating out from her core. She wrapped her arms around herself, unable to stop her trembling. She felt chilled to the bone.

"Here. Let's get you to your room," Stephen said, standing and pulling her up with him.

He put his arm around her and walked her around the corner and down the hall to her room. He found one of her shawls lying across the back of a chair and wrapped it around her shoulders. The room was not cold; it was, in fact, quite pleasant. But Olivia could not stop shivering. He guided her over to the bed and opened the chest that sat at the foot of it. He pulled out a light knitted blanket and wrapped it around her, too. Then he took her in his arms and held her gently, the warmth of his body soaking into hers.

"I'm sorry," Olivia began.

"Hush," he told her, smiling. "I enjoy this."

She chuckled and relaxed in his arms. The shivering had stopped, and for a moment she let herself luxuriate in the warmth. A movement in the hallway caught her eye, and she turned, looking out the door. She stiffened.

Irina stood in the hallway, looking in at them. She said nothing, her face carefully blank, just watching them.

Stephen felt Olivia's movement in his arms, and he, too, looked up, following her gaze. For a long moment, the three of them simply stared at one another. Then Stephen's arms dropped from around Olivia, and he walked over to the door and closed it firmly.

"Stephen!" Olivia said on a gasp, part astonishment, part amusement. "Miss Valenskaya caught us in a compromising position. You just made it even worse."

He shrugged. "It's my house. I don't care to be spied on."

Olivia groaned and sat down on the edge of her bed, shedding the blanket he had wrapped around her. "I wonder what tale she will carry back to the others."

"I find it hard to care." He stopped beside her, his hand wrapping around one of the posts of the bed. "Are you all right?"

"I think so." Olivia shook her head. "It has

been the strangest day. I feel as if I am disconnected from myself."

After a moment, she went on softly. "My grandmother used to tell us that she communicated with my grandfather — after he was dead, that is. And with her dead parents, too. She liked to say that she knew things before they happened. She frightened me terribly." She cast a sideways glance at Stephen. "She, of all of us, was the most deserving of the term 'mad Morelands.' "

"Olivia . . ."

She shook her head, smiling. "No, let me finish. Kyria and Reed and the others always laughed off the nickname, but it bothered me. I think it was because I would think about Grandmother and wonder if it was true. She was an absolute harridan. She bullied everyone. Poor Great-uncle Bellard was terrified of her. Anyway, I remember once she told me that I was like her, that I had the second sight. She said I could see things and hear things that others could not. That was what scared me the most about her, I think. I told myself that everything she said was absurd. I didn't want to be like her. I didn't want to believe any of that was possible. I think that is why I started investigating mediums, discovering their tricks and exposing them."

"You wanted to prove that it wasn't possible?"

Olivia nodded. "Most of all, to prove that I would not, could not, be like her. And now . . ."

"You are not like her," Stephen said decisively. "Whatever you have seen, you are not mad. And you certainly are not a harridan. You are a thoughtful, witty, compassionate and altogether remarkable woman. Don't you remember my telling you that?"

Olivia smiled at him. "Yes."

Stephen moved closer to her, and unconsciously she leaned toward him. His lips brushed hers. "If I stay here any longer," he said, his voice husky, "I really *will* put you in a compromising position."

He kissed her again, a light, firm peck on the lips, then turned and left the room. Olivia sighed and lay back on her bed. Just that light kiss, his very closeness, had her whole body thrumming, and she knew that, if she were honest, she would much prefer to have been compromised.

Supper that evening was subdued. Mr. Babington was still lying in his bedroom in his unconscious state. No one else could bring themselves to be very lively, even Belinda, whose recent scares had made her much quieter. Madame Valenskaya was obviously distressed over Mr. Babington's state, and during the course of the evening, she waxed sentimental over her attachment to the "dear man." Olivia, sitting beside the medium in the drawing room after supper, began to suspect the woman was tipsy.

The following morning, Olivia and Stephen began a search of the library for books regarding Blackhope and the Scorhill family, having already examined all the books to be found in Stephen's study.

"Whatever it is we are seeing," Olivia reasoned, "it has something to do with this house during the Middle Ages. If we could find a history that gave us information about the house during that time, perhaps it would help us."

St. Leger agreed, and they went to the library after breakfast to begin a thorough search. Olivia enjoyed spending the time with Stephen, but after a morning of searching, they had little to show for their efforts.

"I never realized how many arcane and useless books we had in this library," Stephen commented as they sat down at the library table for a rest and a revivifying cup of tea.

"Mmm. The Moreland library is like that, especially the one in the country seat." She grinned. "I think even Great-uncle Bellard hasn't read all the books there." She paused, resting her chin on her hand, elbow propped on the table. "You know, I have been thinking about that dream I had. I keep feeling that Lady Alys was trying to tell me something."

Stephen sent her a quizzical look, and she blushed. "Yes, I know. I sound nonsensical, thinking that some long-dead person — if, of course, she even existed — is communicating with me. But I cannot help feeling somehow connected to her. Why did I dream about that gold casket? And why did she say that to me about holding on to things that are precious?"

Stephen shrugged. "All right, I'll go along. Why?"

"I don't know!" Olivia said in frustration. "That is the problem. But, you know, I have been thinking and thinking about the dream, and I think — I know this will sound odd, but I think some of the things were missing."

"What?"

"They were not in the box you showed me yesterday. That girdle I saw her put in, for instance. And there was a rather pretty chain with a smaller cross hanging on it, as well as a large bracelet — a wide golden band — that were not in your box. Yet there was an elegant little dagger in it that was not in there in my dream."

He frowned. "I don't know that any of that is significant. If the Martyrs' treasure does come from the era of Sir Raymond, then by the time it reached the Lord Scorhill, who was beheaded, any number of things could have been added to or taken from the casket — lost or stolen or sold, even melted down to make some other piece of jewelry. There is no reason to think that all the jewelry would have survived."

"No, I suppose not. And yet, it seemed as if she was trying to tell me something." Olivia groaned, putting her hands to her face. "Oh, dear, I sound idiotic even to myself, thinking that a woman who doesn't even exist is trying to tell me things in my dream."

"At this point, I am not discounting anything," Stephen told her. "You know, it is your mind working in your dreams. I have heard of people who have lost something and in a dream saw where they lost it. They had just forgotten what they knew. Perhaps this is something like that."

"Perhaps."

"What was it she said to you?"

"I wish I could remember exactly." Olivia pressed her hand to her forehead. "You know how dreams are. At the time it seems so clear, and then you begin to forget the exact details. But it was something about keeping the things that are precious to you safe. Or maybe it was storing the things that are precious." She started to speak, then stopped.

"What? What were you going to say?"

"Well, this is nothing, really, but I just had a thought. Maybe some of your really old books are stored. Is that possible? That they've been boxed up and put away somewhere? I mean, it seems likely to me that a book that concerns this time period could be quite old."

"Or very dull," Stephen added. "Which would make it a likely candidate for being stored away. All right. I'm willing to try it. We are nearly through with the books here, and we've found nothing useful. Where else shall we look? The unused wing of the house?"

"I don't know. Do you think there are books there?"

He shrugged. "It's possible. Or there could be boxes of books in the attic, I suppose."

They decided to explore the attic first. After a consultation with the housekeeper as to where such things as books might have been salted away, they climbed to the highest floor, where they went up a narrow staircase into the large attic. It was a vast gloomy room under the roof, lit only by windows at either end. Stephen had come prepared with a lantern, but its circle of light illuminated only the small portion around them, leaving most of the rest of the huge room in shadows.

They started toward the east end of the attic, the bobbing lantern in Stephen's hand casting ever-changing light and shadow over the hodge-podge of objects they passed. There were cabinets and other odd bits of furniture, as well as trunks and hall trees and assorted oddments, including canes, a dressmaker's form that looked heart-poundingly human at first glance, and even a grotesque umbrella stand made out of the foot of an elephant.

When they reached the far end, where the housekeeper had directed them, Stephen put down his lantern on a nearby trunk, and he and Olivia set to work opening the various trunks and boxes around them. They found an assortment of things inside the trunks, usually clothes and shoes and toys, mementos of days past. They came at last to a cache of books, and they went through two trunks, taking out each book and looking at it, then going on to the next. They worked side by side in companionable accord.

Olivia's hands and skirts were soon streaked with dust, and she suspected that her hair and face had gathered quite a bit of dust, too, but, frankly, she didn't care. She felt sure that someone like Pamela would scorn what she was doing, but she was enjoying it. She and Stephen talked about this book or that as they pulled it from the pile, joking and exclaiming over some of his ancestors' reading choices. He looked equally grubby as she, she saw with amused affection, one cheek streaked with dirt and his hair decorated with a cobweb of dust.

They did not find anything helpful in the first two trunks of books, but they continued back the way they had come, opening and exploring more boxes and trunks. They came upon another trunk full of books, and it was there that Stephen at last held up a volume in triumph.

" 'A Compleat Historie of Black Hope Manor,' " he read aloud, and grinned at Olivia.

She let out a squeal and said, "What does it say?"

He opened the front cover and held it closer to the light. "It seems to be a piece of pompous puffery, as best as I can tell, written by one of my illustrious ancestors." He sighed. "He writes about the house, but he begins with the St. Leger acquisition of the place."

"Hardly what I would call 'compleat,' " Olivia complained.

"Yes, well, it looks to me as though his chief objective is illustrating how grand the St. Leger family is. He focuses more on the additions than anything else." He flipped carefully through the aged leaves of the book. "Wait. Look. There is a piece of paper folded and stuck in the back cover. No. It's glued in there, I believe."

Gently he unfolded the fragile paper until it was four times as big as the back cover to which it was attached.

"It looks like a family tree," he said.

Olivia moved closer to look over Stephen's shoulder at the multitude of connected lines. "Your ancestors?"

"I guess — no, look —" His voice rose in excitement. "These are the Scorhills. This name is the martyred Lord Scorhill. See the date?"

"How far back does it go?" Olivia asked, peering down to look at it.

Stephen's forefinger traced the lines back. "Here! Look — Sir Raymond, born 11??, died 1173."

"No descendents," Olivia said, "but here are three bars out to the side. These are wives, are they not?"

"Yes." Stephen pointed to each name, "One unknown, one Gertrude of Rosemont."

Olivia following his finger, finished for him. "And one Alys."

A chill went through her as she looked at Stephen. "We have found her."

12

They stayed in the attic for another hour, looking through trunks and boxes in the spots that the housekeeper had deemed likeliest to contain books. They found nothing else significant, although they did come across a history of the county that seemed to date back to the medieval period and another general history book that they thought might have possibilities.

It was getting on toward teatime when they emerged, dusty and disheveled but still excited by their finds. They carried the books down to Stephen's study and set them on his desk for later perusal.

Olivia looked with a wry smile at her dusty skirts and said, "I fear that first I must clean up a bit."

"We are not exactly presentable for the tea table," Stephen agreed.

Just as Olivia turned to leave, there was a quiet knock on the door, and the St. Legers' butler entered. "There are two gentlemen to see you, my lord," he began, not betraying by even a twitch of his face that he found Stephen's and Olivia's appearance unusual.

"Now?" Stephen looked surprised. "As you can see, I must clean up before I can meet anyone. Who are they? What do they want?"

"As to what they want, I cannot say. One is a Mr. Rafe McIntyre, an American gentleman, I believe. And the other is the Lord Bellard Moreland."

"Rafe!" Stephen exclaimed, looking thunderstruck.

"Uncle Bellard!" Olivia gaped at the butler, then ran past him and down the hall to the entryway. Stephen was close on her heels.

"Uncle Bellard!" she cried again when she saw the small man sitting on a bench not far from the front door, gazing about him with interest, his hands resting on his gold-topped cane.

Beside him sat a much larger and younger man with tousled light brown hair, streaked with gold by the sun. Both men rose at Olivia's entrance, neither of them appearing taken aback by her disheveled appearance or unladylike enthusiasm.

Bellard Moreland smiled in his shy way at his great-niece, setting aside his cane and reaching out his hands to her. "Olivia, my dear."

Olivia hugged her great-uncle as Stephen came up beside them, saying, "Rafe! I never thought I would see you here."

The other man laughed and drawled, "Stephen, old son, how're you doing?"

"Better now that you are here," Stephen replied, laughing. "Olivia, I want you to meet my friend and partner, Rafe McIntyre."

Olivia turned and took a longer look at her great-uncle's companion. He was a tall man, taller even than Stephen, with tanned skin and brilliant blue eyes. He had handsome, even features, and a charming grin that lit up his face when he smiled.

"Mr. McIntyre," Olivia said, extending her hand.

"How do you do, ma'am?" he replied, taking her hand and bringing it up to his lips. His blue eyes twinkled at her as he went on. "You must be the pretty niece that Mr. Moreland here was telling me about."

Olivia could not help but smile back at him, even as she felt a blush rising in her cheeks. "I — I didn't know Lord St. Leger had a partner," she said, then felt hopelessly inept, as she usually did when making conversation with strangers.

Rafe McIntyre, however, was a person who made it difficult to feel inept. He grinned and said, "Yeah, St. Leger tries to keep me hidden."

"Indeed," Stephen agreed, smiling. "But it is a losing proposition, I'm afraid." He turned toward Olivia, explaining, "Rafe and I met in Colorado."

"He saved my neck, matter of fact," Rafe contributed. "I got into a little *contretemps* with a couple of Yankees."

"Yankees?" Olivia looked puzzled. "But I thought —"

"People from the northern United States," Stephen interpreted. "Rafe is from the South, you see."

"Oh. But it's been ten years since the war there was over, hasn't it?" Olivia asked. "Surely there's not still fighting."

Rafe grinned. "Not in any official way. This was just a little private quarrel regarding the other fellow's ancestry."

"It was actually over a card game," Stephen put in. "And Rafe here was a trifle outnumbered, so I stepped in."

"Stepped in with a Winchester, I'm happy to say," Rafe went on. "And we got along, so we decided to pitch in together."

"I see," Olivia replied, although she wasn't entirely certain she did, what with the combination of the American's accent and his vocabulary.

"We were partners in the silver mine. Then I sold my share of the mine to Rafe when I had to return to England," Stephen explained.

Great-uncle Bellard entered the conversation. "Mr. McIntyre and I met on the train up here. We were quite astonished to discover that we were bound not only for the same village but for the same estate."

"Helped to pass the time, having somebody to talk to," Rafe said.

"We had an interesting conversation," Great-uncle Bellard confided. "Mr. McIntyre told me quite a bit about the state of Virginia, where he is from originally. I was intrigued to discover that one of his ancestors was a follower of Bonnie Prince Charlie in his doomed attempt to capture the throne, and he fled to the American colonies after their defeat."

"The McIntyres have always been given to lost causes, you see," Rafe stuck in with a self-deprecating smile that Olivia noticed did not quite reach his eyes.

"But why were you on the train in the first place, Uncle?" Olivia asked curiously. "Not that I am not happy to see you, for of course I am. It's just that, well, it is unusual for you ever to leave London." Indeed, it was unusual for Great-uncle Bellard to even leave the house, but Olivia saw no reason to add that.

"I received your letter," he explained. "About the untoward things that had been happening here and your questions about the history of the house and all that. As it happened, I had already been looking into the St. Leger family — idle curiosity, I'm afraid," he said, with a shy smile to Stephen. "And when you wrote me, of course, I went to see Addison Portwell, who is something of a scholar on old estates. He lent me several of his texts. Highly interesting, I must say. It led me to a wonderful book on the Scorhill family — written by a St. Leger, so naturally I cannot be certain of the accuracy of it."

"Uncle!"

"Oh." The old man realized how his words sounded and looked immediately distressed. "I did not mean any slur upon you or your family, my lord. I simply meant that since the St. Legers were given the estate that once belonged to Lord Scorhill, they would, of course, have a vested interest in, well, showing that the Scorhills were not the best people to have the land. For the St. Legers to be right in owning Blackhope, then King Henry VIII had to be right to take it away from Lord Scorhill, don't you see? It's only natural and quite common in histories, I'm afraid, especially those written immediately after an event. But, of course, it means that one must take great care in reading it not to put one's faith in it entirely."

"Of course," Stephen said, with a smile for Great-uncle Bellard. "I understand perfectly. I am not offended, I assure you, and I agree that we cannot swallow it whole cloth. But I am very pleased that you found some information."

Relieved, Great-uncle Bellard smiled happily. "Yes, it was quite good, actually, and after what Olivia had said in her letter, I hated to waste the time writing it all down and posting it. So I decided to pack up my books and bring it straight here."

"Uncle! That's wonderful!"

"Yes, thank you," Stephen added. He glanced around at the group. "Let us do this — I am sure you two would like to have a chance to settle into your rooms. And Lady Olivia and I, as you can see, have been exploring in the attic, and we could use a chance to freshen up, as well. So why don't I ring for tea for us in my study in a few minutes, and we can talk then about what you've found out?"

It turned out that Great-uncle Bellard and Rafe, politely not wishing to burden Lord St. Leger, had left their things at the inn in the village, but Lord St. Leger, of course, would not hear of them staying anywhere but in one of the many guest rooms of Blackhope. So, after some courteous social sparring, it was arranged that the two guests would indeed stay at Blackhope and a groom would be sent to the village to bring their bags back to the house. Stephen rang for the butler to give him instructions regarding the rooms and the baggage.

Olivia, linking her arm through her great-uncle's, took him off with her upstairs. "I am so happy to see you," she told him, squeezing his arm.

He smiled. "And I, you, my dear. I quite like your young man."

Flustered by his words, Olivia was not sure what to say. "You know, Uncle, I came here because of the medium. I wrote you about that."

"Oh, yes." He nodded happily. "And all the other events. Most interesting, my dear."

"So Lord St. Leger is a colleague, actually. Not my 'young man.' "

"Oh? Pity. He seems to admire you." He switched the topic suddenly. "Very old house

— quite a lot of history to it. Do you suppose Lord St. Leger would mind if I used his library?"

"No, I am sure not. What makes you say he admires me?"

"What? Oh." Great-uncle Bellard looked thoughtful. "I'm not sure, actually, just an impression I had. He looked at you a certain way is all, rather the way your father looked at your mother. Still does, really. As if he had made an extraordinary find. You know."

Olivia chuckled. She knew exactly what her great-uncle meant, and it made her heart beat faster to think that Stephen St. Leger might look at her in that way.

Downstairs, Stephen turned to his former partner. "Rafe." He shook his head, smiling. "I never thought I would see you here."

Rafe grinned. "I got bored, sitting there in Colorado by myself. Some fancy Eastern outfit kept wanting to buy me out. So I thought . . . why not? There are a bunch of things I haven't seen or done yet. There's no more adventure to be had out of that mine. It's just business dealings now, and you know me — I'm not all that fond of sitting around talking about money."

"So you sold it?"

He nodded. "Yeah. Invested in some other things. Went back home for a little while. But it hardly seems like home anymore. Some changes you just can't get past, you know."

Stephen nodded.

"So I thought, why not see Europe? And I caught a boat over here. I figured, since I was in the country, I might as well look you up."

"I'm glad you did." Stephen nodded toward the stairs. "Come on. I'll show you to your room, and I'll get cleaned up. Then we can sit back and discuss old times."

"Sure. Long as you got something stronger than tea."

Stephen chuckled. "I do."

They started up the stairs.

Later, the two of them settled in Stephen's study, sipping glasses of Scotch that Rafe allowed to be "damn near as good as sour mash," while they waited for Olivia and her great-uncle to join them.

"I approve," Rafe said idly.

"Of what?"

Rafe grinned. "Your lady friend."

"What makes you —" Stephen stopped as Rafe let out a chuckle.

"You think I'm blind?" Rafe asked. "It's clear there's something going on between the two of you."

"I'm not sure exactly what is going on. She's, well, she's different."

"I figured that, to have caught you. You always seemed pretty down on high-toned ladies."

"Mmm," Stephen answered noncommittally.

"What's the matter? Miss Moreland not the right sort for you?"

Stephen smiled to himself. "I don't know if you can say that Lady Olivia is any 'sort' at all. She is rather unique. Her father is a duke."

"Yeah? She and her uncle don't seem high-and-mighty."

"Oh, she's not. Not at all. Her family is quite egalitarian. They are something of an oddity. Which only adds to her charm." His face softened unconsciously. "She is witty and independent and intelligent, and when I look at her —"

Stephen stopped and shook his head. "I don't want to make a mistake. I'm not looking for a wife. I decided long ago that I would not marry. My history in that regard is poor, at best."

"But this isn't the same girl that made you gun-shy, is she?"

Stephen grimaced. "God, no. Olivia is nothing like Pamela."

"Then what's the worry? There's no reason to think that this one will break your heart."

"Sometimes it's easier to say that than to believe it." Stephen sighed. "I want her, more than I ever wanted Pamela. There have been a time or two when I barely remembered to play the gentleman. But I can't help thinking, what if this is like that other time, with Pamela? What if it is only lust I feel, and it fades as quickly as my lust for Pamela did after I left England?" He looked up at his friend. "I have always said I distrusted ladies. I'm not sure whether it's simply that or if I distrust myself, as well."

"Sometimes you just have to take a leap of faith," Rafe suggested. "Love isn't a matter of logic. It's feeling."

"I know. But I find it easier to trust my head than my heart." He paused, looking down at the glass of amber liquid in his hand, idly swirling its contents. When he raised his head, his eyes were lit with amusement. "By the way, you will have a chance to meet Pamela. She is also here."

"Here?" Rafe's eyebrows shot up. "Under the same roof? Well, you do like to live dangerously."

"I could scarcely toss her out. She is my brother's widow, after all."

"Interesting situation."

Stephen chuckled. "That's the least of it. Things have happened that are so bizarre I have wondered if I am going mad. Fortunately, Olivia witnessed them, too."

Stephen told his friend and former partner about the medium and her séances, including the one in which Mr. Babington had fallen into a seizure, and also recounted the ghostly apparition he and Olivia had seen, and their dreams involving the same woman.

Olivia and her great-uncle appeared in the midst of this discussion, and Great-uncle Bellard listened with great interest to what had taken place in Blackhope since Olivia had sent her letter to him. Small, bright eyed and balding, with a burst of white hair ringing his head just above his ears, he reminded Olivia of a bird.

He nodded several times and murmured, "Intriguing, most intriguing," during the course of Stephen's description. When Stephen fell silent, the older man reached down beside his chair, where he had set two large books that he had carried into the room and picked up one of them. He put it in his lap and tapped it.

"This is a history of the western counties, written by a rather thorough fellow. Eighteenth-century chap." He sighed a little wistfully. "Too bad. I would have liked to have spoken to him. He raised some very interesting points about the — well, never mind. That's neither here nor there. Thing is, he's a trustworthy historian. In here, I found a passage about the Scorhill family and Blackhope."

He opened the book to where a bookmark held his place. "During the time of Stephen of Blois — if you will remember, he was the king before Henry II, and his was a chaotic reign. He did not have good control over his lords. There had been years of fighting already between him and Mathilde, Henry's mother. Well, it was all very unsettled, especially in the west, with the threat of the Welsh. Many of the barons seized the opportunity to conduct their own private wars amongst themselves — the strong preying on the weak, increasing lands and power, settling old scores and the like. Anyway, it said in here that during this time, the Norman keep of Blackhope was besieged by an enemy of the Scorhill of the time, one Sir Raymond."

Olivia sucked in a sharp breath. Uncle Bellard smiled at her.

"Yes, my dear. I think it must be the same one as your Sir Raymond. The castle was attacked, but Sir Raymond was not at home at the time. He had gone to another noble, his liege lord, actually, hoping to enlist his support in Sir Raymond's ongoing feud with Lord Surton, whose men were even at that moment laying siege to Blackhope. Surton's men took the castle. There were rumors at the time that there was treachery involved, that someone let them into the castle. Whatever happened, they took the castle and a good deal of it was destroyed, by battering rams and by fire. And Sir Raymond's wife — it does not say what her name was — was killed in the siege."

Olivia felt tears prick at her eyelids. She told herself it was foolish, that she did not even know the woman, but she could not help but feel pity and sorrow at her death. "Alys," she said. "Her name was Lady Alys."

"Was it?" Great-uncle Bellard asked and patted his niece's hand. "Well, Sir Raymond upon his return managed to take back the castle, and with the aid of his allies, decisively defeated Lord Surton. So that is how the castle was destroyed. It was, however, rebuilt by Sir Raymond on almost the same spot."

"Now," he went on, caught up in his story, "this is where it really gets interesting." He set the tome back down on the floor and picked up the other book. "This is the history of the Scorhills written by one of the St. Legers. It was written during the reign of Charles I, before the Civil War."

At Rafe's confused look, Bellard added kindly, "I mean ours, of course, not yours."

"Oh. Sure." Rafe grinned. "I'm with you now. The Cavaliers, right? The fellows with the big hats and plumes?"

"Heathen," Stephen joked in what was obviously a long-running line of verbal sparring.

"Of course, as I said, this Cecil St. Leger had a vested interest in the Scorhill family appearing as black and unworthy as possible. In that regard, he is rather harsh regarding the Lord Scorhill, who incurred Henry VIII's displeasure, primarily because of his 'treason' and 'popery.' However, he also has several juicy tidbits regarding Sir Raymond."

"Really?" Stephen leaned forward, intrigued. "What?"

"He accuses the man of having dabbled in the black arts," Great-uncle Bellard said, and sat back, looking pleased at the astonishment on the faces of his listeners.

"What?" Olivia gaped. "You mean witchcraft?"

"He said the man was a witch?" Rafe asked. "I mean, whatever a male witch is."

"Warlock," the historian supplied and nodded. "That is exactly what I mean. He said that Sir Raymond was reputed to be a powerful sorcerer, a wicked and cruel man. Of course, it all sounds like rumors and gossip. There is no way to know the truth of any of it. He does lay out several instances of the man's deceit and wickedness, many of them concerning his dealing with the aforementioned Lord Surton. But chief among them is the claim that it was he who really arranged the 'betrayal' of his own castle. The author puts forth that Sir Raymond not only knew they would attack the castle, but that he actually lured Surton into it, that he paid someone to open the gates to the man's forces, and that he then returned with a much larger force and defeated the invaders, killing his enemy in the process and getting rid of a wife who had not provided him with any heirs."

"How awful!" Olivia exclaimed. "What a wicked man!"

Her uncle nodded. "He certainly was, if these reports have any truth to them. According to this book, he was reputed to be in league with the devil. Supposedly he summoned his dark master and cavorted with him, holding orgies and such and communing with witches. He was feared by all around him, it says, and his death was met with much rejoicing. He was generally held to be cursed by God, as he married twice more and still never produced an heir. The other two wives were also said to have died mysteriously. Since he had no heirs, Blackhope went to a distant cousin, who, this book admits, did his best to restore the house to a proper godly state."

Great-uncle Bellard closed the book and sat back in his chair, watching them expectantly. Olivia did not know what to say. She glanced at Stephen, who seemed to have the same problem. It was Rafe who finally spoke up.

"Well, I have to say, I'd be glad, if I were you, St. Leger, that this fellow wasn't an ancestor."

"I am. The problem is, we know more about him, perhaps, but we still don't know what's going on."

"It looks pretty clear to me," Rafe replied. "This Sir Raymond fellow was one mean son of — excuse me, ma'am — one mean person, and he sold out his own men and gave his castle up to his enemy in order to trap the man and get rid of his wife and her lover. I'm thinking he had more reason to hate his wife than just her not bearing an heir. And since his wife and this knight were killed like that, their spirits remain here, haunting the place. That's who you've been seeing, right? There's your reason. Violent deaths — that's always what sets the ghosts walking in the Tidewater."

"The Tidewater?" Olivia asked, confused.

"In Virginia, ma'am. That's where I come from. The houses may not be as old as those around here, but there are plenty of spirits flitting around them — lonely wives who pace the riverbank, watching for the boat carrying their husband that never came in, people wrongly hanged who still slip in and out among the oak trees where they met their end, girls in white who glide down the staircase at the stroke of midnight . . . that sort of thing."

"But those are stories," Olivia protested.

"Yes, ma'am, and good ones, too," Rafe replied, giving her a lazy grin.

"Rafe always used to keep everyone entertained with his tales," Stephen explained. "But we are talking about reality here, Rafe."

"I don't believe in ghosts," Olivia stated flatly.

"I don't guess it really matters whether you believe in them or not. The problem is, you've seen them," Rafe said.

"He has a point, my dear," Great-uncle Bellard put in quietly. "You know, Livvy, one needs to keep an open mind, even about such things. You have seen the evidence with your own eyes. I have not, but I know that you are not a hysterical girl, nor one inclined to jump to conclusions. When you tell me the kind of things you have witnessed, I have to consider the possibility that they are real."

"I don't want to consider it," Olivia replied honestly. "It's too —"

"Horrifying?" Stephen suggested.

"Yes," Olivia agreed. "I have spent the last few years proving that all the spirits I've witnessed were fakes."

"But this does not make your previous work wrong," Bellard pointed out. "Those were still frauds, just as your Madame Valenskaya is a fraud. But your lady and her knight — I think they are an entirely different matter."

"Then you believe Sir Raymond was a warlock? That he summoned the devil and all that?"

Her great-uncle shrugged. "Well, as to that, I'm not sure. As I said, the source is suspect. It may have been nothing but rumors. Still, I imagine there probably were people who engaged in the black arts, calling up the devil and all." His dark eyes twinkled merrily as he added, "That is not to say that the devil came when they called, of course."

"It seems as though people in the past were terribly quick to label anyone who was different a witch," Olivia argued. "Whenever they didn't understand something, they decided it was sorcery." She paused, remembering the feeling of evil that had hit her like a wall as she stepped into the secret room.

Stephen, as if knowing what she was thinking, said, "Remember when you touched the casket, how you saw Sir Raymond and sensed such a great evil that it made you faint?"

Olivia nodded. "Yes. And in the secret room, as well." She looked up at the others with a perplexed expression. "But that is scarcely objective proof of anything."

"Sometimes you have to rely on your instincts," Rafe said. "You don't have to think to breathe. You don't stand there and debate it if a big ol' bear comes out of the woods at you. You just light out of there. Sometimes you know something without thinking."

"What I wonder," Great-uncle Bellard said,

"is whether anyone has ever seen these people before? Are these people the ghosts of legend here?"

"No. Not that I've heard," Stephen replied. "I didn't even know who they were until we started looking into the history of the place. The most famous occupants were the family that was beheaded by Henry VIII. One would think that, if there were any ghosts here, it would be theirs."

"Certainly that is what Madame Valenskaya has focused on," Olivia added.

"Then Lady Alys and the knight have appeared only at the present, and solely to the two of you," Bellard mused. "That is intriguing, as well."

"Why? What does it mean?" Olivia asked.

"I don't know. This is certainly not my field," her great-uncle said. "But it would seem obvious that there must be some connection."

"*If* we admit that there are ghosts," Olivia put in.

"No," Stephen said thoughtfully. "I don't think we have to say that. Whatever these dreams and visions are, they have definitely occurred. I think we can safely agree on that."

"Yes."

"And you and I have been the only ones who have been recipients of them. Ergo, whatever they are — ghosts, tricks, some bizarre phenomena that we have never even heard of — they are still connected to the two of us."

"That is true."

"It could be because Olivia is in this house. Perhaps that is the vital confluence," Bellard said. "Or it could be the combination of Olivia and Lord St. Leger. Or perhaps it is the mixing of all three — Olivia, St. Leger and Blackhope."

"But why?" Olivia asked. "I mean, obviously the place would have something to do with it. And St. Leger is the lord of the estate, even if it was not his ancestor who was involved in this story. But what would *I* have to do with it?"

"It must involve you," Stephen argued. "If it was only the combination of the house and me, it could have happened anytime these past six months. Indeed, it could have happened years ago, when I was growing up here."

"We are not the only people who have converged at this place," Olivia pointed out. "Madame Valenskaya and her group are here, as well."

"But I thought, from what Stephen told me, you had concluded that what the medium did was all quackery," Rafe said.

"Oh, they are definitely after money or the Martyrs' treasure, and most everything they have done has been a fraud," Stephen agreed. "But there is the matter of Mr. Babington's peculiar behavior at the last séance. We cannot deny that something sent him into a very real state of unconsciousness. And Madame Valenskaya and her group have been here in the house during the time of the visions and dreams. I think we must

313

consider the possibility that they had something to do with them."

"It is rather a lot to ask of coincidence that this medium is here at the same time you are experiencing your 'ghostly' visions," Olivia's great-uncle agreed.

"Of course, Stephen had the first dream before either of us had met Madame Valenskaya," Olivia said.

"But not before she had come on the scene," Great-uncle Bellard pointed out. "She was already involved with Lady St. Leger, was she not?"

"That's true," Stephen admitted.

"When you meet Madame Valenskaya, you will see that she is not capable of carrying off something so skilled," Olivia commented.

"What about her companions?" Great-uncle Bellard asked.

"Her daughter is a veritable mouse of a woman," Stephen explained. "And Mr. Babington has been unconscious the past few days."

"Perhaps it is somebody else, someone who is not even here," Rafe suggested. "He is pulling the puppets' strings, so to speak, and you don't know who he is."

"Yes. We had even discussed that once," Stephen said.

"You know . . ." Bellard mused. "Perhaps it was not by happenstance that Madame Valenskaya latched on to Lady St. Leger. Maybe it was as a result of a careful plan. I would be rather interested in knowing how your mother met this medium. Who introduced them?"

They looked at Stephen, who shrugged. "I have no idea. I don't recall that Mother ever said. I can ask her, of course, but I have to tread carefully where Madame Valenskaya is concerned. Lady St. Leger is very distressed by the existence of my disbelief. The medium has told her that my cynicism stands in the way of the spirits reaching her, you see."

"A common ploy," Olivia added. "It is a handy way to silence critics, making the nonappearance of the spirits the critics' fault."

"Yes, I see."

"I'd like to see this woman in action," Rafe said.

"Yes," Great-uncle Bellard agreed eagerly. "It would be quite interesting to witness a séance."

"I am sure one can be arranged," Stephen said. "We shall broach the subject tonight at supper."

Supper that evening was a livelier affair than usual. Lady St. Leger was predictably charmed by Rafe McIntyre and proud to now have as a guest not only a duke's daughter, but also a duke's uncle. Just as predictably, Lady Pamela spent the entire meal flirting madly with Stephen's former partner. The American obligingly flirted back, but there was a cynical gleam in his blue eyes that made Olivia suspect he knew the true story of what had occurred between Stephen and Pamela. The wry glance Stephen shot at Rafe confirmed her suspicion.

About halfway through the meal, Stephen brought up the subject of a séance. "Madame Valenskaya, I was hoping that you would grace us with another sitting while Lord Moreland is here. Tonight, perhaps?"

Madame Valenskaya turned to him with a startled look. "A — a sitting, my lord?"

"I would greatly appreciate it, Madame," Great-uncle Bellard added.

The medium glanced around vaguely. "Mmm. I don't — I'm not sure."

"Oh, yes, please." Lady St. Leger added her entreaty to the others.

"But Mr. Babington . . . it, um, would seem not respectful, yes?" The medium nodded emphatically with her words, and her cap slipped a little over one ear.

"I don't want to," Belinda spoke up. "It scared me."

"Of course, dear, you don't have to," her mother reassured her. "But the rest of us —"

"Miss St. Leger is right," Madame Valenskaya said and shook her head. She reached for her wineglass and took an eager gulp. "Not good. Not good."

Olivia, watching her, wondered if the medium was tipsy again this evening. She had had her wineglass refilled a number of times throughout the meal. But the drink had not managed to calm her nerves, for Madame Valenskaya was fidgeting with her fork, then her glass, then her napkin.

"Perhaps we could find out what happened to Mr. Babington," Lady St. Leger proposed. "The spirits may know why he acted that way the other evening. Don't you think so?"

"Um. Yes, of course, spirits know all." Madame Valenskaya made a vague gesture with her hand. "But I don't know — perhaps I cannot draw de spirits tonight. Without Mr. Babington."

"Ah, now, Miz Valenskaya," Rafe said, flashing her a grin that would melt ice, his accent thickening with his charm. "You're just being modest. I'm sure that you would do fine on your own. After all, you are the one with the special power, you know."

Madame Valenskaya was obviously not immune to the Southerner's charm, either, for she bridled girlishly and let out a little giggle. "You are too kind, sir."

"You should do it." Even Pamela added her entreaties, now that Rafe had joined in. "The spirits rely on you."

"Yes, they do, I'm sure," Lady St. Leger agreed. "You speak for them, after all."

"Is true." Madame Valenskaya preened a little. "All right. You have persuaded me."

This time Madame Valenskaya did not even go up to her room before the séance. Olivia had the impression that the medium wanted to simply get the sitting over with as soon as possible. Madame Valenskaya had also gotten over her dislike of light. Tonight she brought in two extra candelabras and set them on the table around which they sat.

Lady St. Leger looked somewhat askance at the mass of candles burning in the center of the table. "Won't all this light frighten away the spirits, Madame?"

"Oh, no." Madame Valenskaya made a grand gesture. "They come to me anyway."

They took their places, with Rafe roguishly offering to take Mr. Babington's place by the medium's side. She was happy to oblige him, and Great-uncle Bellard was put in Belinda's usual seat.

Despite her initial hesitation, once Madame Valenskaya began, she relaxed and put on even more show than normal of calling to the spirits, then dropping her head and going into her "trance." She raised her head at last, her eyes closed.

"Mama," she said in a ponderous tone.

"Roddy?" Lady St. Leger spoke up eagerly. "Is that you?"

"You must help me, Mama," Madame Valenskaya went on in the same flat, measured tone. "You must help all of us."

"Of course, my dear. What should I do?"

At that point the candles suddenly guttered low, several of them going out, as if a great gust of air had passed over them. In fact, there had been no breeze at all that Olivia could tell, but the room was suddenly bone-chillingly cold.

A noise came, faint, almost like the buzzing of insects, a low chatter below the level of under-standing. Olivia felt Lady St. Leger's hand tighten around hers, and she was aware of the fact that she, too, was gripping both Stephen's and Lady St. Leger's hands hard.

The noise rose and resolved itself into a sort of breathy whisper, over and over. The sound filled the room, droning insistently, grating at the ears. Finally Olivia picked out the words threading through it: "Mine . . . mine . . . mine."

The noise built, shredding Olivia's nerves until, suddenly, the doors were flung open, crashing against the walls, and the lights blew out, leaving them in darkness.

13

There were shrieks around the table, and Madame Valenskaya jumped to her feet, toppling her chair over backward. Once their eyes adjusted, there was enough light coming in from the hallway to allow them to see, and the medium's eyes were so wide and rounded that the faint light caught the whites around the pupils, making them glint.

"I — that —" the medium gasped, clearly shaken. "It is over. I cannot do it."

Madame Valenskaya turned and fled the room. Her daughter got up, saying "Mama!" in a distressed voice, and rushed out of the room after the medium.

The remainder of the group was silent. The noise, Olivia realized, had vanished, as had the freezing cold.

"Well," Rafe said at last, "you folks sure know how to put on a show."

A ripple of nervous laughter responded to his quip, and Stephen stood up and began to relight the candles.

"I don't understand," Lady St. Leger said, looking puzzled and distressed. "The séances were never like this before. Madame Valenskaya is obviously upset."

"I think," Olivia said carefully, "that Madame Valenskaya has perhaps never had this sort of thing happen until now."

"Would these things cease if we gave the Martyrs back their treasure?" Lady St. Leger asked, frowning, and Olivia could sense the first widening cracks in Lady St. Leger's trust in the medium. "I mean, I don't understand how we *could* give it to them. Bury it at their graves? But, you know, I don't even know where they were buried. They were killed in London, after all."

"Don't distress yourself, Mother," Stephen told her. "There is no way we can give them back their treasure. And even if we could, I feel sure that they do not want it. I doubt very seriously if ghosts have much need for jewelry."

Lady St. Leger smiled faintly at his words. "It is quite distressing. I was telling Madame Valenskaya about it this afternoon, how the treasure is passed from father to son and doesn't belong to me at all."

"And Stephen would never give it over just to ease his mother's distress, would you, Stephen?" Pamela asked in a hard voice.

"Pamela!" Lady St. Leger looked shocked. "I would never think of asking Stephen to do such a thing! The treasure belongs to the St. Legers. It is a family heirloom. It doesn't belong only to

321

one man or one generation. It is something that the current lord keeps in trust for the generations after him."

Pamela grimaced.

"My dear," Lady St. Leger went on gently, "I know it always upset you that Roderick would not let you wear any of the jewelry from that box, but it truly was not his to give, you know."

"I don't care about the jewelry," Pamela said, rising. "Frankly, I find all this talk terribly boring. The séances used to be rather fun, but now . . ." She shrugged and walked out of the room.

"She is right, you know," Lady St. Leger said somewhat sadly. "Madame's sittings are no longer enjoyable. They have become so frightening. I can think of no other word for it. And poor Mr. Babington. . . ."

"Don't worry, my lady." Great-uncle Bellard spoke up for the first time. "I feel sure that this will all be resolved in good time."

Lady St. Leger smiled at him. "Thank you, Lord Moreland." She rose to her feet. "I should go talk to Belinda. I imagine she feels a trifle lonely, missing the séance tonight. But it was fortunate that she decided not to come. I fear it would have scared her badly."

Stephen's mother left the room, and they were back down to the four who had sat together in the study that afternoon.

"Well," Rafe said, "I think we can safely say

that Madame Valenskaya didn't plan or execute any of that. The woman looked scared witless."

"Yes, and she was none too eager to perform the séance, either," Bellard noted. "I think, whatever is happening, it is entirely out of her control, and she has no idea what to do about it."

"You know, Stephen," Olivia said, "if you simply want to be rid of Madame Valenskaya, I think you could achieve that now rather easily. I don't think we would have to expose her fraud to your mother. I think you could suggest that Madame Valenskaya go back to London, and she would jump at the opportunity."

"Especially if you offered her a mite of consolation money," Rafe added.

"Yes, you are probably right," Stephen agreed. "But what about Babington, unconscious up there in his room? And what about all the other things that have been happening? I don't think Madame Valenskaya's leaving will get rid of the rest of it."

"No. But what are we going to do about the rest of it?" Olivia asked. "How do we stop Lady Alys and the others from popping into our dreams? Or keep whatever it was tonight from banging open doors and blowing out candles? I frankly don't have any ideas."

"I wonder . . ." Great-uncle Bellard mused. "Let us just suppose, for the sake of argument, that Madame Valenskaya is a complete fraud and that the dreams, visions and so forth are real. What happened tonight at the séance seemed quite real to me — the cold, the candles going out despite the fact that there was no draft, the doors flying open. Except possibly for the doors, I can't think of any way those things could have been rigged to happen. And this Mr. Babington's coma, at least, is confirmed by the doctor to be real, and from what the two of you say, it did not seem to you as if he were performing when he spoke in that ominous voice. Is that correct?"

Olivia and Stephen nodded.

"What if, despite Madame Valenskaya's lack of any real skill, somehow, in that mishmash of words she mutters or even simply in her calling on the spirits, opening up the room to them, so to speak, she actually somehow opened up a pathway to, well, to another realm, for want of anything better to call it."

"You mean she really did awaken the spirits?" Stephen asked skeptically.

"I'm not sure. But if we can believe there were ghosts from a twelfth-century love triangle somehow locked into this house, isn't it possible that when Madame Valenskaya conducted these séances, she provided a connection to those shades? Perhaps something used her to somehow come into the room tonight, or to pop into that Babington chap and use him to speak for him."

"Uncle!" Olivia shivered. "Now you are really scaring me."

"We cannot discount the fact that you felt an evil presence in this house, as well," Stephen said. "In your room that night you dreamed about Lady Alys, when you touched the gold casket, and in the room containing the casket. You have described it as a 'dark presence,' an overpowering sense of evil."

"That doesn't necessarily mean Madame Valenskaya's sessions brought the presence out," Olivia argued.

"That's true," Rafe agreed. "I think that clearly what stirred this thing up is the feeling between you two. The connection between then and now is the love that this Lady Alys and Sir John felt, obviously strong enough to make them break their vows and risk the sort of tragedy that happened. They are drawn to you two because you have the same emotion."

Olivia blushed to her hairline, and Stephen cast a dark look at his friend. "Rafe! The devil take it! Curb your tongue."

"Sorry, ma'am," Rafe said with a grin, looking uncontrite. "My mama was always shocked at my lack of breeding."

"Mr. McIntyre has a point," Great-uncle Bellard said unexpectedly. "There is a correlation, of course, though one hopes you will not proceed to such an ill-fated conclusion."

Her great-uncle's words left Olivia speechless. She could not bring herself even to look at Stephen. She hoped he would not think she had told her uncle there was anything between them.

Finally Stephen broke the awkward silence, saying, "Whatever has brought this chain of events upon us, what I would like to know is — how do we end it? I personally do not relish living in a house where spirits are apt to appear at any moment."

"It would be rather disconcerting," Rafe agreed with a grin. "You know, I have heard lots of tales about ghosts inhabiting a place, but I've never heard that anyone got rid of them."

"Thank you," Stephen retorted sarcastically. "You are most reassuring."

"There is the rite of exorcism," Great-uncle Bellard suggested.

"I suppose, although I think the vicar might be rather alarmed for my sanity if I suggested it."

"Does that apply to ghosts?" Olivia asked. "I thought it was for demons and such."

Stephen shrugged.

"One theory I have heard is that spirits who died a violent death cannot leave the place where the deaths happened because they are seeking something," Rafe said. "Presumably, if one could provide what they were seeking . . ."

"But how the devil are we to do that?" Stephen countered. "I haven't the vaguest notion what they might be seeking. What could be put right? The siege? Their deaths? We can hardly change something that happened seven hundred years ago."

"Perhaps it is not they who are seeking something. Perhaps it is the evil presence that Livvy sensed," Bellard suggested. "The presence that made itself known at the séances."

"I cannot believe we are even talking seriously about such things," Stephen commented.

Rafe shrugged. "Better than being unprepared."

The conversation wound down after that, and soon Olivia excused herself and went up to her room, followed quickly by her great-uncle. Stephen and Rafe continued to chat in the study, fortified by cigars and brandy, ignoring the strange events of the day to reminisce about the years they had spent together in Colorado and the characters they had known. It was a good two hours before they made their way upstairs to their beds, and the rest of the house lay in quiet slumber.

Stephen got into bed quickly, dispensing with the services of his valet, and soon fell asleep.

He was outnumbered. He was well aware of that. Only the winding, narrow nature of the stairs made it possible for him to keep the others at bay. He was backing up the stairs inch by inch, and at the top of them lay nothing but his eventual death. Still, there was nothing else he could do. His only hope was to protect her. He did not allow himself to think of what would happen when his body fell lifeless, at last, and they were free to break down the heavy wooden door.

All he would think of was keeping her safe.

He could feel her behind him. He felt sure she

was facing outward, the small sack of her possessions in one hand, her dagger ready in the other.
She had never lacked for courage; that was much of
what he loved about her. It had taken courage to
love him, knowing she was risking dishonor and
even death should Sir Raymond find out. It had
taken even more courage to be willing to leave all
that she knew, the life of relative ease and comfort
that was hers as lady of the castle, but that was
what she had been ready to do. They had waited
only for the opportunity presented by Sir Raymond
leaving the castle to visit his overlord. She had
packed what little she would take, waiting for a few
days to pass so that Sir Raymond would have
reached his destination. They had planned to sneak
out of the castle tonight, running for their lives and
their freedom.

But then Surton's men had appeared out of nowhere, and some traitor within had opened the gates
to them, letting the enemy flood in. And now, instead
of running to a new life, they were trapped in the
castle. Doomed to die.

"Get to the room," he ordered, not daring to turn
around. He lashed out with his booted foot and connected solidly with the head of a soldier trying to
climb up the open side of the stairs.

"I cannot leave you!" she cried.

"You must!" he roared, meeting the downward
slash of a sword with the upward swing of his own
and sending the other's sword flying. The soldier
jumped off the side of the stairs to recover his
weapon, but the one right behind him took his place.

"If you love me," he told her fiercely, "you will do this for me. Get to the room and bar the door!"

"No! John! Please, do not make me leave you!"

"Alys! If you love me, go!"

Stephen awakened, panting for breath, his skin damp with sweat. A nameless dread filled him.

Quickly he swung out of bed and pulled on the trousers he had recently taken off. Thrusting his feet into slippers, he grabbed his shirt and shrugged into it as he hurried out of the room. His heart pounded in his chest, and he did not stop to reason as he made his way to Olivia's door.

The knob turned easily in his hand, and he breathed a sigh of relief that she had not locked her door. He eased it open and shut the door behind him. There was little light in the room, only the moon and starlight that crept in around the curtains, but it was enough for his dark-adjusted eyes to see his way to her bed.

Olivia lay sleeping, her dark hair tumbled across her pillow, the fringe of her lashes shadowing her cheek. Emotion tightened in his throat, and he stretched out a hand to caress her face.

Her eyes flew open, and she drew in a sharp gasp of fear. Then she saw who it was, and she relaxed, saying, "Oh. Stephen."

She sat up, her sleepy mind working at half pace. "What is it? Is something the matter?"

"No, I —" He let out a gust of breath. "I dreamed again."

"What? You mean, about —"

He nodded. "The same as the other time. I am on a staircase, fighting to the death, and you — I mean, Lady Alys is on the stairs behind me. There is a door at the top of the stairs, the last point of defense in the castle. I — or I guess it is he — wants her to go there and bar the door, even though he knows that ultimately it will not protect her."

"Oh, no. How sad." Olivia looked at his face, stark with remembered emotions. She turned, sitting a little farther back on the bed and curling her legs up under her. She patted the space beside her. "Come. Sit down. You look exhausted."

He did as she suggested, running one hand back through his hair. "I felt what he felt. He knew he was going to die. But that wasn't what scared him. It was what would happen to her when he did. All he wanted, all he cared about, was keeping her safe."

"He loved her."

"They were leaving the castle. Running away together."

"What?" Olivia turned to look at him, surprised.

He nodded. "That is what was in my head in the dream. That she had packed her things, and they were going to leave the castle while Sir Raymond was away and run off together. Then the enemy attacked, and they were trapped. She was carrying a sack of some sort in her hand. I felt it bump into my legs once as she moved. I think . . . I don't know, but for some reason I think the gold casket was inside it."

"Perhaps that was what she was packing for," Olivia said. "In the dream I had, when she stopped and went to the window. Perhaps she was getting ready to leave with her lover."

"Instead they died."

"It's very sad. I feel so sorry for them."

"The evil cannot be them. There is nothing in them but love."

Stephen turned to Olivia. Her hair fell in a thick silken mantle around her shoulders, inviting the touch of his hand. Her wide, soft eyes glimmered with unshed tears. Her mouth trembled, soft and vulnerable. Desire slammed into his loins like a fist.

"I know how he felt," Stephen said quietly. "He wanted her beyond reason, beyond all thought of duty and honor." His eyes moved over her, dropping down to the soft, hidden promise of her body beneath her nightdress. "I know. . . ."

"Stephen . . ." Her voice was a little breathless.

She felt the caress of his eyes as surely as if he had touched her. Olivia remembered the way his mouth had felt on hers, the teasing, arousing touch of his tongue on her breasts, his hands gliding over her body, heat sizzling in their wake. She wanted suddenly, desperately, to experience those things again. She wanted his hands on her breasts; she wanted to savor the taste and texture of him. Olivia had never known desire until she met Stephen, and now it was an urgent, writhing thing inside her, hammering for release.

He saw the desire in her eyes, felt it slither down through him, sending his own hunger spiraling. He wanted to lay her naked on the sheets before him, her hair fanning out around her. He thought of burying his face in her hair, of setting his hands free on her creamy skin, and passion made him tremble.

"You are so beautiful," he murmured.

Looking into his eyes, their silvery depths darkened with desire, Olivia felt for the first time in her life that she was beautiful. With a boldness she would never have dreamed she possessed, she reached down and grasped the hem of her loose nightgown and pulled it up and over her head, dropping it onto the bed beside her. She faced him, naked, her chest rising and falling rapidly, the pulse in her throat pounding.

Stephen sucked in his breath sharply, time and reason falling away as the dark, heady wine of passion filled him. He said her name, the word falling from his lips like a prayer. His eyes moved over her, taking in her rounded milk-white breasts, centered by pink-brown nipples, her slender waist flowing down into the fullness of her hips. His mouth turned dry; his breath rasped harshly in his throat.

Her nipples hardened under his gaze, and his loins tightened at the sight. He reached out and placed his hands upon her, letting them slide slowly over her shoulders and across the line of her collarbone, feeling the exquisite contrast of the hard bone under velvet-soft skin. His fingertips glided over her chest and onto her breasts, cupping them, and he watched in sensual enjoyment as the nipples prickled and thrust forward, eagerly awaiting his touch.

Olivia lay back against the sheets, giving herself up to the pleasure of his hands. When she thought about it later, she was amazed that she had felt no embarrassment, no shame, only a rippling, shivery delight as his fingers caressed and explored her. She let out a shuddering sigh as his fingers curled around her breasts and drifted downward over the lines of her rib cage and onto the soft flesh of her stomach. His fingertips circled the indention of the navel and spread out over the wider plain of her abdomen, curving out to caress her hip and thigh, then slipping back up the insides of her legs, moving slowly toward the ever-increasing heat at the center of her. He did not quite reach the spot but slid over her thigh and onto her abdomen, gently circling, teasing both of them by moving ever nearer, then gliding away, then slipping back.

Olivia burned for him. She moved her legs

restlessly, unable to ease the ache that grew between them. She reached out to him, her hands going to his chest and sliding beneath the open edges of his shirt. His eyes glittered and his breath sharpened as she moved her hands over his chest, tangling through the hair and seeking out the flat, hard masculine nipples. She caressed the little buds, delighting in the way they hardened beneath her fingertips. She squeezed and released them, damp heat flooding her as a small moan of pleasure escaped him.

He skimmed out of his shirt and flung it aside, giving her free access to his chest, and bent over her, laying a gentle, brushing kiss on the quivering flesh of her stomach. Making lazy circles with his tongue over her skin, he moved slowly, tantalizingly upward until he reached the undercurve of her breast. He kissed the soft orb, his mouth moving lazily, heatedly over her. Olivia waited, tightening all over with each movement of his lips, waiting in an agony of pleasure and impatience, everything within her focused on that one spot that he moved toward yet did not touch. She arched upward, her hands digging into the sheets beneath her, heat pulsing in her.

And then his mouth encircled her nipple, pulling it into the hot, damp cave, and Olivia groaned at the exquisite pleasure she had been so urgently waiting to feel. She moved against the sheets, sighing, as he loved her with his mouth, pulling insistently at the hardening bud, caressing and lashing it with his tongue. And then, when she thought the pleasure in her could not possibly grow greater, his hand slid down her stomach, easing at last between her legs and seeking out the damp, pulsing center of her femininity.

She jerked, letting out a muffled noise of surprise and hunger, and opened her legs to him. Where he touched was like satin fire, and she writhed beneath his hand, digging in her heels and pushing upward against his palm. She moved her hands over his back, the feel of his skin and underlying muscle exciting her even more. She wanted to feel him everywhere, to taste and touch him. Her fingers were halted by the waistband of his trousers, and she slipped beneath it, seeking more. He groaned and moved away.

She gasped at the loss, reaching out for him. Stephen quickly divested himself of the encumbrance of his trousers, shoving them down and off his legs, and then he moved back over her, settling his mouth on her other breast and working the same magic on it. Olivia slid her hands over the sharp outcroppings of his hipbones and down the sides of his hips, curving back up and caressing, then digging in with her fingertips.

Urgently he moved her legs apart, his fingers opening her, exploring the slick flesh and slipping inside. She moaned, moving against him. He caressed the fleshy nub hidden between her nether lips, and his fingers moved within her, widening and stretching her. Olivia whimpered, aching for release. Never in her life had she felt this way — wild and feverish, primitively surging with desire. She ached for him at the very center of her being, longing for a fulfillment she could only guess at. This, she knew, was what she had waited for all her life. This moment. This man. This heated, hungry urgency.

Then he moved between her legs, his hands sliding beneath her hips and lifting her. She arched, the tension in her almost unbearable, as he slid slowly, carefully into her. Pain tugged at her, but it could not breach the onslaught of pleasure as he filled her. He moved within her, slowly building the passion until it was raging inside them, screaming for release. Olivia cried out as desire burst within her, pulsating outward in wondrous waves of delight. He shuddered, and his mouth came down to cover hers, drinking in the taste of her as he rode to the violent, explosive crest of his passion.

He collapsed against her, then rolled to his side, wrapping his arms around her and pulling her with him. Olivia lay with her head resting on his chest, his arms encircling her. Stephen pressed his lips against the top of her head, and she snuggled closer. They did not speak, merely lay in silent contentment. Olivia felt bonelessly relaxed and warm, satisfied to the depths of her soul. No thought, no problem, intruded as she floated in a halcyon realm. For the moment, there was no past love haunting Stephen, no mediums and séances, no ghostly women gliding the hallways of Blackhope or intruding on one's dreams.

There was simply lying in the arms of the man she loved.

Olivia awoke slowly the next morning, drifting to consciousness by degrees, then lay for a long time, savoring the pleasant happiness that still hummed within her. A smile crept across her face as she lay there, remembering what had happened the night before — the joy, then the gentle contentment of lying in Stephen's arms afterward. After a while they had talked a little, whispering to each other, smiling, chuckling easily. They had said little of import, but it had meant everything to her.

She had been falling in love with Stephen almost from the moment they met, she realized now. Despite all the peculiar things that had happened over the past few weeks, she had arisen every morning eager to face the day. She knew now that it had been because she would be spending the day with Stephen.

Olivia had ignored the feelings rising within her until last night, when the realization had exploded within her, the tidal wave of emotion washing over her with as much force as the physical feelings had. She loved Stephen, and she hugged the feeling to herself.

She was much less certain that he returned the feeling, but that was not a matter which she wished to explore. It was enough for the moment to know that he felt passion for her, that he wanted her with the kind of raw, elemental need he had expressed last night. She had no wish to examine whether his feeling for Pamela had been greater than what he felt for her and even less desire to wonder how much of his feeling for her was simply the holdover of passion that they had experienced in their dreams of the medieval lovers.

All she wanted at this moment was to revel in what she had.

Olivia rose at last and went to her mirror, wondering if she looked as different as she felt inside. There was, she saw, something new in her face, a sparkle in her eyes, a faint flush to her cheek, a certain softness to her features, that had not been there before. She hoped it would not be as visible to others.

Joan came in to help her dress, and Olivia relaxed a little when the woman made no comment about how Olivia looked. Olivia went to the wardrobe to choose her dress for the day and stood for a moment, contemplating them. She wondered, with some irritation, why she always dressed so plainly. When she returned to London, she thought, she would purchase new dresses, colorful things that suited her mood.

She chose the prettiest of her day dresses, and when Joan fixed her hair atop her head in an artful arrangement of curls, Olivia made no protest. She went downstairs, rather pleased with the way she looked.

She was not sure what she would do when she saw Stephen for the first time today. She was afraid that a smile might break across her face with such a glowing intensity that everyone would guess what had happened. She felt a little shy and very eager, all at once. What would he say to her? How would he act?

It was a relief to walk into the dining room and find only Stephen there. He was seated at the table, sipping a cup of tea, and he jumped up when she came into the room, a smile lighting up his face.

"Olivia!" He came around the table, and for an instant she thought he was going to take her into his arms, but then his gaze flickered over to the footman standing beside the sideboard, and he hesitated, then merely held out her chair for her.

He remained behind her chair for a moment, and his hand brushed briefly over her shoulder. He walked back around to his own chair, saying, "Would you care for some tea?"

"Yes, thank you."

The footman was beside her chair immediately, pouring her a cup, then retreating to his post. Olivia looked across the table at Stephen, glad there was no one else here to witness her smiling at him. She could not seem to control her face. If anyone had been here, she felt sure that they would have guessed immediately what had happened.

They went to the sideboard and dished up their meal, then sat and ate, chatting as they did so about the most mundane of subjects. It scarcely mattered to either of them what they said. All they wanted was to look at each other. Olivia wondered if he would come to her bed again that night, and even as she did so, she saw a light flicker in his eyes that assured her he would. She colored and looked down at her plate, smiling to herself.

Rafe came in after a time and joined them. He seemed to notice nothing unusual and made conversation in the same easy way he had the day before, inquiring politely how Olivia had slept. Olivia had to clamp her lips shut tightly to keep a giggle from escaping, but she managed to nod and return a polite reply.

They were, apparently, the last to come down to eat, for no one else joined them. After the meal, the three of them made their way through the great hall to the formal drawing room, where the footman had said Lady St. Leger was waiting for her guests.

They were somewhat surprised to find only Lady St. Leger in the room, and she explained that though she had breakfasted with Lord Moreland and Belinda, she had not seen them since.

"Lord Moreland, I believe, wanted to see the library," she said, and Olivia chuckled.

"Yes. I am sure that he will spend most of his time there. My great-uncle is a dreadful guest, my lady, if you wish conversation — wonderful if what you desire is solitude," Olivia told her.

"I find Lord Moreland quite charming, my dear," Lady St. Leger said with a smile. "He is such a knowledgeable man. There is scarcely a topic about which he cannot talk."

"And what of Belinda?" Stephen asked.

"She is, I hope, practicing her piano. She neglected it a good deal in London, I'm afraid."

They continued to chat in this general way until they were interrupted by the sound of hurrying feet outside in the marble-tiled hall. As one, they turned curiously toward the door.

Irina Valenskaya rushed into the room, saying, "Mama?"

She stopped and glanced around the room, which clearly did not contain her mother. She turned to Lady St. Leger and asked abruptly, "Have you seen my mother this morning?"

"Why, no," Lady St. Leger replied, looking puzzled. "What is wrong, child?"

"My mother!" Irina exclaimed, looking distraught. "She's gone!"

14

"What?" Lady St. Leger's hand flew to her throat, and she paled. "What do you mean?"

"She has vanished!" Irina cried.

"Vanished?" Stephen stood up, going over to the young woman. "Here. Sit down. Calm yourself, and tell us what happened."

"I can't sit down!" Irina cried. "Don't you understand? Something has happened to her! She isn't here!"

"Are you sure?" Lady St. Leger asked. "You know, it is a large house."

"I looked in her room. She was not there when I went down to breakfast, and I was a little surprised, for we usually went together. I decided she must already be in the dining room, but when I got there, she was not. No one was there. I thought I must simply have missed her somehow, so after I ate, I came in here, but there was no one, so I went back upstairs and looked in her room again. It was still empty. I thought she might have gone to my bedchamber, but she was not there, either. I looked into Mr. Babington's room, but the maid said she had not been in this morning. I waited in her room, thinking she would return, but she never did. So just now I returned to the dining room to ask the footman if Mama had said where she was going when she left breakfast. He said that she had not been in all morning!"

Madame Valenskaya's absence at any meal was indeed odd, Olivia thought, but she did not say so. She crossed to Irina, saying in a calming voice, "I am sure Madame Valenskaya is all right. Perhaps she is in some other room, or she's taken a walk in the garden."

"Before she ate breakfast?" Irina shot her a disbelieving look. "That is not like Mama at all."

"Oh, dear!" Lady St. Leger clasped her hands together, her brow knitting. "Surely nothing can have happened to her! There can't have been another calamity!"

"No doubt she is perfectly fine, my lady," Olivia reassured her.

"Begging your pardon, ma'am," Rafe said to Irina, "but are you sure she didn't take off? She looked pretty green last night after that séance."

"Mama would never leave without me!" Irina cried. "Certainly not without at least *telling* me."

"Of course not," Lady St. Leger agreed. "I am so afraid — I mean, with what happened to Mr. Babington, I fear that something has happened to her. I don't understand why the séances have turned so — they are so different than they were at first."

"Don't worry," Stephen told her. "We will search for her. Mother, you stay here, in case Madame Valenskaya should happen to seek you out. Rafe?"

It took only a look toward the man, and Rafe was by his side. "Where shall we start?"

"Why don't you and Irina go through this side of the ground floor? The ballrooms, the conservatory, both dining rooms. Olivia and I will take the west side. I shall send a message to the stables, as well, and set a couple of footmen to searching the gardens."

Rafe nodded and steered Irina out the door. St. Leger yanked at the bellpull, and when a footman appeared, gave him instructions to search the kitchens, the gardens and the stables for the missing medium. Then he and Olivia started down the hall. Their first stop was the library, empty of people except for Olivia's great-uncle Bellard. When he heard of their quest, he was quick to join them. In the music room, they found Belinda, who was quite happy to leave her piano practice and help them search, as well. The small salon, near the rear of the house, and the smoking room, proved empty.

They returned to the base of the stairs as Rafe and Irina came in from the other side. In response to Stephen's raised eyebrows, Rafe shook his head.

"We have been all through this side. You know, Steve, my lad, you have far too many rooms in this house," Rafe told him. "There is no sign of her. I talked to the footman in the dining room again, and the fellow swore up and down that she hadn't been in this morning."

"Something has happened to her," Irina insisted unhappily. "It must have."

Stephen started up the stairs, with the rest of them following. Stephen sent Rafe and Irina down one side of the corridor, and Great-uncle Bellard and Belinda down the other. He took Olivia's arm and headed to the end of the hallway where the medium's room lay. They walked into Madame Valenskaya's room, which was indeed empty of her person. However, the woman's clothes were still there, many of them flung messily across the chair and dresser.

"At least she hasn't packed a bag and taken off," Stephen said. "That was my first thought when Miss Valenskaya said she was gone."

"No, it doesn't look like it. Although she did seem very shaken last night."

They went next into Irina's room, finding it empty, as well, and after that into Mr. Babington's, thinking that perhaps she had come in to check on her friend. There was no one there except Babington, lying still and silent in his bed, his eyes closed. The maid who had been assigned to sit with him looked up and started to rise from her chair at their entrance, but Stephen waved her back down.

"How is he doing?" Stephen asked. He, like

Olivia, had been in to check on Babington every day since his accident, but there had been no change in him.

There still was not. The maid shook her head, saying, "He's the same as ever, my lord. The doctor should be here before long, if you want to speak to him."

Stephen nodded, and he and Olivia left the room. They looked down the hallway, where the others were advancing toward them room by room, obviously finding them empty.

"What about the unused rooms?" Olivia asked, gesturing toward the smaller corridor that crossed the one in which they stood.

Around the corner, along the other hallway, lay several guest rooms, presently not in use. Stephen shrugged. "I suppose we must, to be thorough, and then we'll start on the upper floors. I am beginning to think, though, that she might have wandered into the unused wing of the house and has gotten lost."

"Yes, or perhaps it is part of some elaborate trick."

Stephen glanced at her, a sardonic smile on his lips. "Why, Lady Olivia, do I detect a note of cynicism in your voice?"

"A veritable symphony, where Madame Valenskaya and her daughter are concerned." Olivia replied.

His eyes were warm as they rested on her face. "I have a great desire to kiss you right now, my little cynic."

Olivia's face warmed under his regard, and she glanced away, murmuring, "You make me forget what we are supposed to be doing."

"Sorry," he replied in a voice that held little regret as he took her arm and started around the corner.

They looked into the nearest room, then the one across the hall from it. The other members of their search party were just coming around the corner to join them when Stephen opened the door of the chamber containing the secret room.

The door into the secret room stood open.

Stephen stepped inside, Olivia coming in after him, then turned and stuck his head out the door. "Rafe. Keep the others here."

Rafe nodded as Stephen closed the door and turned. Outside they could hear the others' voices rising in query and Rafe's firm reply.

Stephen and Olivia looked at each other, then at the opening in the wall. The small room beyond was utterly silent. Stephen started quietly for the door, Olivia right behind him. There was a sick feeling of dread in the pit of her stomach.

He stepped inside the room, and despite her dislike of the place, Olivia moved in after him, then drew in a sharp breath as she saw what lay inside.

The gold casket was not on its small table, but on the floor on its side, treasures spilling out of it, only inches from the outstretched hand of the still body beside it. The woman who lay there was obviously dead, but it was not the stocky form of Madame Valenskaya that lay on the floor, face contorted in the rictus of death.

It was the slender body of Pamela St. Leger.

"Good God." For a long moment, Stephen simply stared at Pamela, not moving.

Then he crossed the few steps to her body and knelt down beside it. He reached over and curled his fingers around Pamela's wrist, automatically searching for a pulse, although the coldness of her skin made it clear there would be none.

"She is dead," he said quietly.

"Stephen . . ." Olivia went to him, sympathy overcoming the rising nausea in her stomach. This woman, so beautiful in life, now so pitifully dead, had been a woman he had loved madly. However much Pamela had hurt him, she knew regret and pain must be eating at him now.

"I am so sorry," she told him, laying her hand on his shoulder.

"I never would have dreamed . . ." he said in a low voice.

Olivia forced herself to look down at the body. Her stomach lurched, but fortunately it did not revolt. Pamela's face was contorted; it was no great stretch of imagination to say it was a mask of terror. She saw, though it scarcely registered, that there was no blood upon her anywhere, nor any blood upon the floor.

She shivered. The room was unbearably cold, and its heavy atmosphere lay on her like a weight.

Stephen stood up and slipped his arm around her shoulders, and they walked from the room. Olivia put her arm around his waist, and they stood that way for a moment outside the secret room.

"Do you think — how did she die?" Olivia asked.

"I've no idea. There are no marks upon her. No blood. No sign that she was strangled. But her face!"

"I know. She looked . . ."

"As if she were terrified. Poor greedy fool."

"Do you think that Madame Valenskaya did that to her?"

Stephen sighed and sat down on the edge of the bed, shoving his hands into his hair. "Since she is missing, she would seem to be the likely candidate."

"But if Madame Valenskaya killed her for the money, why wouldn't she have taken it?" Olivia wondered. "And why was Pamela here? Was she —" Olivia paused, trying to think of a delicate way to phrase her questions.

"Stealing the Martyrs' treasure?" Stephen suggested bluntly. "I can think of no other reason for her to be there, with the casket lying beside her. She has complained more than once that her widow's jointure was scarcely enough to live on. Roderick left her well provided for, but for a woman like Pamela, that was not enough. She was bitter that because she had not borne an heir, she no longer had any hold on the estate. She had proved often enough that she was mercenary, yet still it makes my mind reel to think she would stoop to this."

"Perhaps it was Madame Valenskaya who was stealing it. Perhaps Pamela just happened upon her and —"

Stephen cast her a quizzical look. "There is no need to try to whiten her misdeeds. I know the sort of woman Pamela was better than anyone."

"But how did she get into the room to get it? Either of them?"

"Perhaps Roderick told Pamela. He was besotted enough to have done anything she wanted, at least when they were first married. I don't know if he came to realize her true nature before his death."

"But if that were true, she could have taken it any time. Why choose now, with a houseful of people about?"

"She might have feared I would relent and give it to Madame Valenskaya's 'restless spirits.' Or perhaps she just finally realized that she had no hope of seducing me into marrying her and regaining the money and estate she had lost by Roderick's death."

"Oh." Olivia could think of nothing to say to that. She could not deny a spurt of elation at the knowledge that Stephen had not been tempted by Pamela, but it shamed her, too, that she could be thinking of such a thing when the woman lay dead only a few yards away from her.

Stephen clenched his jaw, then stood up, his face determined. "I think it's time we got a few answers."

He opened the door and beckoned for Rafe to come inside. "Thank God you are here," he told him. "I'm going to need you."

"What is it? The Valenskaya woman?"

"No. Pamela. And she is dead."

"What?" Rafe stared at him blankly, and Stephen led him to the secret room. He stared for a moment, then turned back to Stephen. "What are you going to do?"

"Send for the constable, for one thing. The doctor will be here soon to look in on Mr. Babington, anyway. He is the coroner, too, so he can examine her. In the meantime, I intend to talk to Miss Valenskaya. I need you to stay here and guard the door, if you will."

"I'll make sure no one gets in," Rafe assured him.

The three of them went back into the hall, Rafe closing the door after himself and positioning himself squarely across it. Irina moved forward tensely.

"What is it? Have you found my mother?"

"I need to talk to you," Stephan said, avoiding her question. He glanced at his sister and Olivia's great-uncle, who was also standing there. "Rafe will explain to you. Come, Miss Valenskaya."

Stephen took her by the arm and almost forcibly led her away, taking her down the stairs and to the drawing room where his mother sat. Irina peppered him with questions as they went, which he did not answer. Irina grew more agitated by the moment, and Olivia felt a little sorry for her. It seemed cruel not to tell her that he had not found her mother dead, at least, but she felt sure that Stephen wanted to keep the woman's nerves on edge in the hopes that she would be more likely to break down and tell them the truth.

By the time he ushered Irina into the formal drawing room, Irina's fingers were dug into her skirt, and she was fairly shrieking, "Why won't you tell me what happened?"

"Your mother was not there, Miss Valenskaya."

"Then what —"

"Stephen, what on earth is going on?" Lady St. Leger asked, rising from her seat.

He looked at her, and his face softened for a moment, "Mother, I — I am sorry to upset you, but I can no longer stand by and allow you to continue this nonsense. Someone is dead now, and —"

"Dead!" Lady St. Leger stared at him, her face paling, and Olivia moved quickly to her side. "You can't — who? Madame Valenskaya?"

"No, it was not Madame Valenskaya." He looked at Irina as he said, "It is Pamela."

Olivia quickly took Lady St. Leger's arm as she let out a gasp and swayed. Olivia tugged her down into the chair she had just recently vacated.

"But how — what happened to her?" Lady St. Leger asked faintly.

"I'm not sure. There wasn't a mark on her. But I think it is safe to say that someone killed her."

Stephen turned to Irina, his face implacable. She stared back at him, openmouthed, unable to move.

"I have said nothing about the absurd show you and your mother have been putting on —" he began.

"We have not —"

"Don't bother!" Stephen snapped. "I haven't time or patience for your games anymore. Pamela is dead now, and I will find out what happened. How did you come to latch on to my mother as the victim of your schemes?"

"I — I —" Irina opened and closed her mouth several times, looking at Stephen like a rabbit found in the open.

"Mother?" He swung around to Lady St. Leger. "How did you first meet Madame Valenskaya?"

Tears glittered in her eyes. "Stephen, how can you talk about such things at a time like this? Pamela is dead!"

Olivia took her ladyship's hand in hers and squeezed it comfortingly. "I know it seems very hard, my lady, but Stephen is only trying to find out who hurt Pamela and why. He must."

"But what does it have to do with Madame Valenskaya?"

"Surely you can see that it has everything to do with her," Stephen told her. "Pamela was found with that treasure your medium kept harping about. I don't think it was coincidence. Who introduced you to Madame Valenskaya?"

Tears flowed down Lady St. Leger's cheeks, and she sniffled, wiping at them with her handkerchief. "I met her at Lady Entwhistle's. It was just a small dinner party."

"Why did this Entwhistle woman invite you?"

"I — I don't understand. She just sent me an invitation. I was a little surprised. I only know her slightly. I wasn't inclined to go."

"Why did you, then?"

"Pamela was terribly bored. And she persuaded me that it would do us both good to get out, and since it was such a small party, it would be perfectly all right, even though it had not been an entire year. So we went. Madame Valenskaya was there, and she was persuaded to hold a séance. It was so illuminating. I had never realized it was possible to speak to someone one had lost. She spoke straight to me. She said that I had lost someone dear to me. And the raps sounded out Roddy's name."

"Pamela." Stephen's jaw tightened. "That scarcely sounds like Pamela, to be interested in something like that."

"Yes, I was a little surprised, too, I confess," Lady St. Leger said. "But I think it was more that Pamela wanted to get out, you see." She sighed waterily. "Poor girl. She was overbalanced by Roderick's death. I had never thought she cared overmuch for him, frankly. She was a cold sort of woman. I shouldn't say that about the dead, I know, but it is the truth. But after he died, she cried and cried for days."

"I suspect it was more losing the status and fortune of being Roderick's wife than losing Roderick himself," Stephen told her bluntly.

"Stephen! What a thing to say!" Lady St. Leger cried.

"It is the truth, and we both know it. But I have no intention of letting whoever killed her get away with it. Whatever her faults, Pamela did not deserve to die." He swung back to Irina, barking, "Was Pamela in on your scheme? Did she help you lure Lady St. Leger into your trap?"

Irina shrank back from him. "No! I —"

"Stephen! What are you saying?" Lady St. Leger cried.

"I think Miss Valenskaya knows," Stephen said grimly. "Did you know Pamela before you met my mother?"

"Lady Pamela!" Irina squeaked out, her hands writhing in her skirts. "How could I?"

"I don't know how! That is what I'm trying to find out. Why was Pamela killed, clutching the Martyrs' treasure? Was she stealing it? Or was your mother? Or you? Which one of you killed her?"

"Stephen!" Lady St. Leger exclaimed, shocked. "You cannot mean —"

"I can. I do. Miss Valenskaya, I don't know where your mother went, but it seems obvious that she disappeared because she knew Pamela was dead. The likely reason is that she herself killed her."

"No!" Irina took an involuntary step backward. "Mother would never —" She licked her lips nervously and cast an imploring look at Lady St. Leger. "Please, my lady, tell him. . . ."

"Enough!" Stephen roared. "I am done with these charades. I will turn you over to the constable when he gets here — and your mother, too, whenever we find her. Perhaps a night in gaol will help you to realize —"

"All right!" Irina cried, trembling all over. "I will tell you! I never hurt Lady Pamela! I barely even spoke to her!" She brought her hands up to her face. "I never — she talked to my mother. I don't know how they met, but she came to us. She was angry about how little money she had. She said that the St. Legers had cheated her, that after all she had done, she had been left penniless."

"Penniless!" Lady St. Leger looked indignant. "Why, Roderick left her a very generous amount of money, everything that was not entailed. He could have done no more!"

"She said she was being punished because she had not borne any children. And she kept on about this box."

"The Martyrs' treasure?"

Irina nodded. "Mother was content with doing the usual sort of thing, the rappings and harps hanging in the air and all that, getting gifts from Lady St. Leger. She was quite happy to be invited to stay here and enjoy the earl's generosity, of course. But Pamela wanted that treasure. She could talk of nothing else — how her husband had kept it from her, how he had refused to let her have any of the jewelry. She said he had kept it hidden from her and wouldn't even tell her how to get into the place where he kept it. She came up with this scheme to pry the box away from you. She was sure that even if Stephen didn't want to give it to us, he would eventually do it because he wouldn't want Lady St. Leger to be unhappy. She said that even if you would not give the box up, with all the talk about the jewels, you would be bound to at least go there to look at them. She had never been able to catch the first Lord St. Leger going to where they were stored and taking them out. She thought she could keep an eye on you and —"

"And catch me opening the secret room!" Stephen exclaimed, and his eyes flew to Olivia. "That must be what she did. The day that you and I went in there, she must have been watching, and we didn't notice."

"I should have known she was up to something!" Irina exclaimed, bitterness tingeing her voice. "There was this smug look to her the last few days. She must have found it and didn't even tell us. She was going to take it all for herself."

"Until someone stopped her," Olivia said quietly.

Irina looked alarmed. "It wasn't me, my lady! I never knew she'd found the box, let alone that she was planning to steal it."

"I suppose not," Stephen agreed. "I rather think it was your mother."

"Mama? No!" Irina wrung her hands together. "You don't understand. It couldn't have been. Mother would never —" She stopped, looking around her uncertainly. Then she straightened, lifting her chin, her hands clenching into fists at her side. "I don't believe you!" she cried defiantly. "Mama has not killed anyone. Something terrible has happened to her, I just know it!"

She burst into tears after that, and, covering her face with her hands, she ran from the room.

Stephen watched her go, then turned toward Lady St. Leger. "Mother, I am so sorry."

Lady St. Leger's eyes swam with tears. "I have been a fool, haven't I?"

"No, not a fool," Olivia assured her, putting a comforting arm around her shoulders. "Many people have been deceived by people such as Madame Valenskaya and her daughter."

"I thought Roddy was talking to me." The older woman's mouth trembled. "I wanted it so much, I made myself believe it." She looked up at her son. "You tried to tell me, and I wouldn't listen. Both of you did. And now Pamela's dead, and all because I brought those people here."

"It is not your fault that Pamela died," Stephen said firmly. "Pamela died through her own greed. I don't know who killed her, but I am sure that it stemmed from the fact that she was stealing the Martyrs' treasure."

Lady St. Leger sighed. "Nevertheless, I cannot help but wish that I had never invited Madame Valenskaya here." She rose slowly. "I think I will go to my room now."

"Let me help you," Olivia offered, walking with her toward the door.

Lady St. Leger smiled at her. "Thank you, my dear. You are very sweet. It is no wonder that Stephen is head over heels about you. We must go see to Belinda. No doubt she will be quite distressed."

She curled her hand around the crook of Olivia's arm and walked from the room, her pace slow but her head held high.

Irina gained the sanctuary of her room and closed the door after her, turning the key in the door. She relaxed, and her face changed, losing its distress and turning cooler, harder. She wiped the tears from her cheeks with her hands and began to pace the room.

"Where the devil are you, Mother?" she muttered to herself.

It had been a shock when Lord St. Leger told

her that Lady Pamela was dead, but she was certain that her mother had not killed the woman. She had, she thought, managed to convey her own loyalty to her mother yet evidence that little touch of doubt at the same time. She needed, after all, someone else to take the blame if St. Leger and his constable should decide that it was Irina herself who had taken Pamela's life. Irina didn't know how Pamela had died, but she thought that it served her right for trying to steal the treasure right out from under their eyes.

Imagine! It wasn't hers, anyway. Like everything else here, it belonged to *him*.

Irina had never been very concerned about her mother's whereabouts. She had felt sure that the old woman, scared as a rabbit after the séance last night, had simply taken off, hoping to hide her departure for a few hours by leaving her things behind. It had been all Irina could do to hold her here the past few days, anyway. Ever since Babington had fallen into that seizure, she had been terrified.

Irina had put on the act of confusion and distress about her mother's disappearance simply because the others would have found it most bizarre if she had not, and also to buy herself some time. She needed to remain longer at Blackhope, and St. Leger would scarcely have wanted her to if she told him that Madame Valenskaya had simply fled from sheer terror.

But now, of course, with Pamela's death,

everything had changed. She had had to reveal their duplicity to St. Leger, and of course he would not allow her to remain now. Even Lady St. Leger would not want her in the house. Right to the end, Pamela had proved to be a thorn in Irina's side.

Pamela had only been after money, of course, as had her mother, but Irina knew herself to be different. She had a larger purpose, and she must stay to see it out.

The problem, of course, was how to do it. She closed her eyes for a moment, wishing for guidance. *He* was here, yet she could not speak to him, ask him what to do.

She brought out her cards and began to shuffle them, then laid them out, hoping for answers. They were difficult to read today, as sometimes happened. There was *his* card, of course, the Magician, and the Tower, as well, signifying destruction. There would be, she was certain, the result he was hoping for, but what she wanted was answers to what she should do, and the cards were hazy on that topic.

Outside in the corridor, she heard now and then the sounds of people moving and talking. The constable would have come, no doubt, and she had little desire to meet him. The best thing she could do was to stay here, out of sight. The less St. Leger or any of the others thought about her, the better.

Hours passed, and she moved restlessly about the room. It had grown quite silent in the hall.

Finally, unable to wait any longer, she opened the door and looked into the hallway. There was no one there. She was tempted to slip down to the room where Pamela's body had been found. It had been there that the golden casket had been kept. Perhaps there . . .

But, no, she knew it would be futile. St. Leger would doubtless have placed someone there to guard the door. It was even possible that the constable or doctor was still there. Instead, she walked across the hall to Babington's room.

One of the maids sat beside his bed, working on some mending, and she looked up at her entrance.

Irina smiled at the woman. "I will sit with Mr. Babington for a while. You may go. I will call you when I need you again."

"Yes, miss. Thank you, miss." The maid got up, putting her mending back into the bag by her chair. "Isn't it terrible about Lady St. Leger?"

"Mmm. Dreadful."

The girl gave a dramatic shudder, then bobbed a curtsy and left the room, closing the door softly behind her.

Irina went to stand beside the bed, looking down at the still form of Howard Babington. Her lip curled in contempt. What a puny, incompetent nothing the man was! It irked her to think of all the time and effort she had wasted seducing him.

She laid her hands flat on his chest, saying,

"You were too weak a vessel, alas. There was not enough strength in you to house my dark lover, was there? I should have chosen a better man. You were unworthy of such a powerful presence. But how am I to get him back now?"

She let her head fall back, her eyes closing, as she said, "Come to me now, my love. My dark prince. Fill this unworthy body again and let me know you."

She began to chant, ancient, secret words falling from her lips. The air around her grew cold, and the sound of a great wind filled the room, though nothing stirred.

Irina stiffened, stretching up on her tiptoes, then jerked violently and fell hard onto her knees. She knelt for a long moment, recovering herself. Slowly she rose and gazed about the room. Her face was different from before, her eyes cold and hard as stones.

Her voice, when she spoke, came out a low, rusty growl. "I will have what is mine."

She turned and walked back to her room, going to a drawer in her dresser. She shoved aside the lacy underthings, going to the leather scabbard that lay beneath. She slid out a knife from the scabbard, and it gleamed. A smile as cold as death lifted her lips.

"I will have what is mine," she repeated, and put the knife back in its scabbard, shoving it up the sleeve of her dress.

Then she turned and walked out the door.

15

Olivia walked into Stephen's study, and he looked up and smiled at her. Then he stood up, came around his desk and pulled her into his arms, laying a soft kiss on the top of her head.

"You are an angel to look after Mother and Belinda," he said.

"It is no hardship. I am fond of them," Olivia replied, stepping back.

"How are they doing?"

"I think they will be fine. Belinda has had some hard knocks this week, but she is young and resilient. It will take Lady St. Leger more time. She blames herself for setting the whole thing in motion by bringing Madame Valenskaya here, and she feels much taken in, I fear."

Stephen sighed. "I hope she will not dwell on it too much."

"I left them in Lady St. Leger's room. Your mother is lying down, with a cloth dipped in lavender water on her head, and Belinda is reading to her. I'm not sure either of them is attending much to what is on the page, but at least it keeps their minds off what happened." Olivia looked up at him, concern in her eyes. "What about you? How are you faring?"

"I am all right. It was foolish of me not to guess that Pamela was involved in their scheme. Obviously someone had given them a large number of facts about Roderick and the family. Who better than a member of the family? And I knew Pamela's mercenary nature better than any of them."

"You could not have known," Olivia said firmly. "Disloyalty, I think, is too far from your nature for your mind to leap to that sort of conclusion. If anyone should have thought of her involvement, it is I. It is my field of expertise, after all, and as an outsider, I should have been better able to look at the situation logically, impartially."

She knew, in fact, one reason she had not even considered Pamela to be in league with the medium was that she had been too wrapped up in her own jealousy of the woman. She had had difficulty looking at her as anything but the woman Stephen had once loved and might still.

Olivia took a breath, summoning up her strength. It was not a subject she wished to pursue, but for Stephen's sake, it had to be done. "You must be feeling a great deal of sorrow. You were, after all, in love with her."

Stephen looked at her, startled. "You knew that I —"

"Pamela herself told me that you were in love with her, although her story was far from the truth. Belinda told me later what had really happened between you — how much you had loved her and how she had broken your heart."

"I thought myself madly in love with her," he agreed. "She was beautiful."

"Yes, she was."

"She was even lovelier at eighteen — fresh and blooming. I was a complete fool. I had no idea what sort of person lay beneath her looks. Looking back on it, I have to be thankful that she jilted me. If she had not, I would have married her and been miserable these past ten years, no doubt. I was filled with hurt and rage at the time, of course. I rashly ran off to America, hating my brother, hating her. But before long, I realized what I had escaped, and I was thankful. I only wish my brother had not had to endure marriage with her."

Olivia looked at him, perplexed. Stephen glanced down at her and smiled. "Why do you look so? Did you think I had been pining away for her all these years?"

"Well, I — I mean, you loved her, and she is — was — so beautiful. I — did you not?"

"Lord, no. I was infatuated with her looks. I scarcely knew her, really. As it is with young girls making their come-out, we were all chaperoned. I danced with her. I exchanged the kind of polite chitchat that one does. We managed to sneak away enough to share a few kisses. But that was all. I would like to think that if I had actually talked to her, spent time with her, I would have realized what she was like. As it was, I was in love with an image. Nothing more. It died quickly once I was away from her. When I returned, I wanted nothing to do with her. I looked at her and felt nothing."

"Oh." Olivia supposed it was awful of her, with the poor woman dead, but she could not help feeling a burst of joy at Stephen's words. "I see."

"I am sorry she died," Stephen went on. "As I would be sorry for anyone. But I do not mourn her as a lost love."

Stephen took her hand and raised it to his lips. "You are —"

"Ah, there you are," said a voice behind them, and Stephen released her hand and turned.

"Lord Moreland. Come in."

For once Olivia was less than happy to see her diminutive great-uncle. *What had Stephen been about to say?*

"I hope I am not intruding."

"Of course not, Uncle," Olivia lied. "Come, sit down with me."

His bright bird eyes went from her face to Stephen's as he came over to the chair Olivia had indicated. They sat in front of Stephen's desk, and Stephen resumed his seat behind it.

"I wondered what news you had had," Great-uncle Bellard said. "Has the constable come? Has Madame Valenskaya been found?"

"Yes, the constable and the doctor have both been here. They removed Pamela's body. As for Madame Valenskaya . . ." Stephen shrugged. "Rafe has joined Tom and the servants in searching for her, but they have found no sign of her yet. I am inclined to think she probably got well away from the house before we even knew she was gone. Perhaps she even had some sort of conveyance waiting for her. It seems far too organized and efficient for the woman, but it may be I am entirely wrong about her, and she is so clever that she carries on a perfect masquerade as a fool."

"Do you think she killed Lady Pamela?" Great-uncle Bellard asked.

"I have no idea. I am not even sure that Lady Pamela *was* killed. According to the doctor, she was not shot, nor stabbed nor beaten nor strangled. He is inclined to believe she died of natural causes, probably a heart attack. I did not tell him, of course, that she was in the act of stealing the Martyrs' treasure. But given that she was, perhaps the fear of being discovered or the excitement of it caused her heart to fail, though no one has ever seen any indication in her of a weak heart."

"And one has to wonder if Madame Valenskaya would have been able to kill her," Great-uncle Bellard added. "After all, she was much older than Lady Pamela, who was young and fit."

"And Madame Valenskaya had been drinking," Olivia pointed out. "I noticed two nights in a row that there was alcohol on her breath."

"And why, if they fought over the casket, were there no signs of a struggle, either in the room or on Pamela?" Stephen mused. "Why, having bested her, would the woman not have seized the casket and taken it with her?"

There was a rumble of voices and the sound of footsteps outside, and the three of them turned toward the hall. A moment later, a strange trio appeared in the doorway: Tom Quick and Rafe McIntyre, each with a firm grasp on one arm of Madame Valenskaya, who stood dispiritedly between them.

She was dusty and bedraggled, her hair straggling down from its knot.

"We found her hiding in the unused part of the house," Rafe said, steering the woman into the study.

"I was not hiding," the medium protested, pulling herself a little straighter and trying to regain the threads of her dignity. She jerked her arms from the men's loose holds. "I was lost."

"Is that right?" Tom asked, grinning. "Then why'd we find you inside that wardrobe?"

"I was frightened when I heard you approach." Her eyes darted about the room. "Where is my dear friend, Lady St. Leger?"

"You needn't look to her for help, Madame. She has finally seen how you have deceived her these past few months," Stephen said.

"What? You lie! I haff never —"

"Be quiet!" Stephen snapped, and, startled, Madame Valenskaya subsided, looking at him warily.

"You have worse problems now than Lady St. Leger discovering the game you and your group have been playing on her. Lady Pamela is dead."

Madame Valenskaya gaped at him, her face turning white. "Dead! Oh, no! Oh, no! They have killed her!" The medium's Russian accent had completely deserted her now. She looked frantically about the room as if she was once again going to hide. She grabbed Stephen's arm. "You must help me. You must protect me."

Stephen took her arms and none too gently deposited her in a chair. "What do you mean, 'they have killed her'? What are you talking about? Who killed her?"

"They will kill me, too. You must help me," Madame Valenskaya repeated, rolling her eyes about in a dramatic way.

"Really, Madame, I have a little trouble believing these histrionics," Stephen told her sternly.

"No! I am telling you the truth! You must believe me!" Madame Valenskaya looked panic-stricken, and despite her melodramatic way of acting, Olivia had no trouble believing the woman was indeed terrified.

"Then, tell me, of whom are you so frightened?"

"Irene!" Madame Valenskaya said at last,

looking around nervously, as if her daughter might suddenly appear in the room with them.

"You are saying that your daughter killed Lady Pamela?" Stephen asked skeptically.

"Yes! Yes! It had to be her. She — she's — you don't know her. She looks timid and retiring, but that is all an act. It is what she wants people to think, so they won't see what's really inside her. But she is powerful! It was all her idea — it always is. I am only an actress, you see. That is what I did all my life, and I made a living at it. But then Irene came up with this idea, you see — a way for us to make money. I used an accent. In America, I was French, and in France, I was Russian. And here, as well, I was Russian, as it worked so well. Irene pulled Mr. Babington into it, as well. She — she convinced him to join us, to let us use his house."

"So you're saying that it was Irina — *Irene* — who set up the tricks?" Olivia asked. "Painting the glove with phosphorescent paint? Hiding a music box about your person and turning it on?"

Madame Valenskaya gaped at her. "How did you know? Yes, she learned how to do all that and showed me. She and Howard rigged up some things in his ceiling, too, so that harps and such would hang from it, looking like they dropped from the sky. She was smart. But she always wanted something more. She would cast stones and lay out those cards." She gave an outsize shudder. "It scared the devil out of me, I tell you, what I would hear coming from her room sometimes."

"What do you mean? What did you hear?" Rafe asked.

"Voices . . . chanting . . . and once, in one of the upper rooms at Babington's house, I saw this, this star sort of thing done in chalk on the floor. It fair gave me the shivers, I'll tell you."

"She was dabbling in the black arts?" Stephen asked.

Madame Valenskaya nodded her head emphatically. "And after that is when she came up with this idea. This thing about Blackhope."

"Here?" Stephen looked surprised. "This house specifically?"

"Yes. She went on and on about it. She looked into everything about the estate and who lived here. She was happy as could be when Pamela came to town. She arranged it so she could meet her, but Lady Pamela wasn't any too interested in the séances. She said she didn't believe in that nonsense, you see. Irene was furious, only then Lady St. Leger arrived, and Irene learned how it was with her, how she mourned her son, the one that died — more than that Lady Pamela ever did, I'll warrant you! So she cooked up this scheme to get Lady St. Leger. She got Lady Pamela involved in it, promised to give her some of the money, you know. So Lady Pamela told us all about things at the house and about her dead husband, so I could make Lady St. Leger think I was talking to him."

"Very clever," Stephen said sarcastically.

Madame Valenskaya paused and looked at him, seeing the contempt and anger on his face. She lifted her chin and said with some defiance, "We weren't doing anything all that wrong! It made her ladyship happy to think she was talking with her Roddy, and that's a fact."

"And the fact that you were lying to her, playing on her grief to extract money from her, makes no difference, is that it?"

"We didn't hurt her!" Madame Valenskaya contended. "She wanted to hear those things, and she had plenty of money. It wasn't as if we took much. She'd give me a ring or a bracelet or some such thing."

"Nice little items you could sell or pawn."

"She never missed 'em, she had so much."

"But what about Blackhope?" Olivia asked, dragging the two combatants back to the subject. "Did your daughter set it up for you to come here?"

"Yes. She worked it around, her and Lady Pamela, so that Lady St. Leger invited us to come here, thinking she'd come up with the idea herself."

"But why?"

"It was because of what Irene was doing," Madame Valenskaya said obscurely. "She wanted to find that treasure, her and Lady Pamela both. Irene thought up tricks to make the lot of you think there were ghosts here — the monk in the garden and like that. Lady

Pamela told her about the place in the nursery where you could take off a tile and talk and sound like you were right in the room below. Her husband had told her about you and him playing with it, you see."

"Yes, of course. I should have realized she was lying about that."

"But why did your daughter want the treasure so much?" Olivia asked. "I mean, there are more valuable things in this house, as I understand it. Why that particular box?"

"Because of — of what she was doing. What I told you —" She glanced around again nervously.

"Madame Valenskaya, don't worry," Stephen said. "We will not let your daughter do anything to you."

"Maybe you won't be able to stop her!" Madame Valenskaya said. "You were right there when that happened to Mr. Babington, and you couldn't stop that, now could you?"

"You're saying that . . . Irene did that to Mr. Babington? Put him into a coma?" Stephen asked.

"Course she did. Or, rather, what she conjured up. She — see, something's latched on to her. She never was a sweet girl. I mean, she always looked out for herself first and the devil with anybody else. But she wasn't . . . *obsessed,* the way she is now. The last few months, all she can talk about is Blackhope and getting in and getting that treasure and all. And she got all secretive-like, locking herself up for hours in that room, you know, the one where I saw that funny star thing."

"She is practicing witchcraft."

"More than that. She summoned something up. Something awful and wicked."

"What do you mean 'something'?"

"I don't know." Madame Valenskaya lowered her voice. "Spirits, I think. Evil ones. Maybe even the devil. That's what's been coming into the séances lately. Nothing like that ever happened before. I swear it. Something took hold of Babington that night, something powerful evil. Didn't you feel it?"

"Yes, I did," Olivia agreed. "What do you think it was?"

"I don't know! I don't want to know. I told her I didn't want to do it anymore. And she told me I had to keep on. She threatened me if I didn't. But I couldn't! It was too scary. I was afraid of what was going to happen next. That's why I ran away. I wasn't thinking straight. I didn't know what I was going to do." She looked at Olivia a little ruefully. "The fact is, my lady, I'd had a mite too much to drink last night. I didn't think about what I was going to do once I'd got there. I just wanted to get away from her. To hide. So last night, in the middle of the night I got up and —"

She stopped, her face growing visibly paler.

"Yes?" Stephen urged, leaning forward, his eyes fixed on the woman's face. "What happened?"

Madame Valenskaya swallowed and said, "I saw Lady Pamela going down the hall, all quietlike. She was in front of me, going the same way I was. I didn't know what to do, but she looked so odd, the way she was sneaking along, so I followed her. She went into this bedroom around the corner, and I went after her and opened the door a crack and peeked in. There was a door in the wall, and it was open into another room, and there was a candle in the room. I could see that. I guess Lady Pamela was in there, because I didn't see her anywhere else. But — but then all of a sudden that little room was filled with this awful oily black smoke. And — and it scared me so bad, I nearly dropped my own candle. I closed the door and I ran. That's — that's when I did get lost in that other part of the house. I hid when I heard them coming because — I don't know what I thought. I was scared."

She paused, then added mournfully, "I wish I'd never come to this house."

No one added what they all thought — that everyone else in the house no doubt wished the same thing.

Stephen sighed, then said, "You had best take her back to her room, Tom."

"No!" Madame Valenskaya screeched. "You can't send me back there. Irene will be furious with me. There's no telling what she'll do to me!"

"I'll stand guard outside her door," Tom offered.

Madame Valenskaya sent him a contemptuous glance. "As if you could thwart her!"

"I will be talking to 'Irina' in the meantime, Madame Valenskaya," Stephen said sternly. "I will get to the bottom of this and be rid of you both. Now, I suggest you go to your room, or I shall have to fetch the constable to investigate the fraud which you and your daughter have perpetrated upon my mother."

Madame Valenskaya subsided at that threat, apparently fearing gaol even more than her daughter. She went docilely with Tom out the door. Rafe volunteered to bring Irene down to the study and strode out of the room after them.

Stephen and Olivia looked at each other. "We are talking about possession now?" he asked disbelievingly.

Olivia shrugged. "I don't know that it is any more bizarre than any of the other things we have seen."

Great-uncle Bellard spoke up. "If we believe that those who have died can remain in a house in some form, as your Lady Alys and Sir John seem to have, then I would think it's not that hard to believe such a lingering spirit could somehow enter a living human being. You have accepted that Olivia sensed a sort of lurking evil. What if it tried to enter Mr. Babington? You said that he looked and sounded unlike himself."

Olivia nodded. "That is true. It was . . . eerie. It was Babington, and yet it wasn't. Still . . ."

"I know," Stephen said. "I cannot accept it, either."

"Yet we can scarcely deny what our own senses have told us," Olivia argued. "It is hard not to think that we have been drawn into this centuries-old struggle between a couple in love and her husband."

"It makes no sense. And even if it were true, how are we to stop it?"

"I have one idea," Olivia began tentatively. "The other time when I touched the casket, I — for want of a better word — *saw* Lady Alys and her husband. What if I were to hold the casket again? Maybe we could see more. Maybe we could find out what really happened and what we could do to stop this haunting."

"No," Stephen said quickly. "I won't allow it. You remember what happened to you last time you held the casket. It made you ill. You fainted."

"It was the shock," Olivia argued. "I was not prepared for it, but this time I will be. I am sure it won't affect me so badly. Please, we must try it."

They argued the point back and forth for several minutes, with Great-uncle Bellard coming down on Olivia's side. Stephen was unconvinced, however.

"You didn't see what it did to her," he pointed out to the older man. "I did. I don't want to have her hurt again."

"But it is my choice, isn't it?" Olivia asked.

"And you will be there to help me, should anything happen. I had a headache afterward, but that was all. I think that would be a small price to pay to find out what is going on."

At that point, Rafe appeared in the doorway, looking a little uneasy. "Now the daughter is gone."

"What?"

He shrugged. "I can't find her. I looked in her room and then in Babington's. A maid said she had been in there earlier, that Irina had told the maid to leave and she would stay with the patient, but she's gone now."

"Damn. Well, I suppose we had better set up a full-scale hunt for her."

"Stephen . . ." Olivia went over to him. "I think it's even more important that we try our experiment. What if Madame Valenskaya is telling the truth? No matter how much we don't want to believe in the idea of her daughter conjuring up some evil and setting it loose in the house, I think it is scarcely something we can ignore. Please, let me try."

Reluctantly Stephen gave in.

Rafe and Great-uncle Bellard left to search for the missing Irene, and Stephen and Olivia made their way up the stairs to the bedroom leading to the secret room, where a footman still stood guard.

They stepped inside, and Olivia cast an uneasy look toward the wall where the secret door was now closed, indistinguishable from the rest of the wall. She did not want to step back into that room where Pamela had died.

Stephen, seeing the direction of her gaze, said, "Don't worry. We won't do it in there. I'll bring the casket out here."

"I am surprised you left it here," Olivia replied, relieved that she would not have to go into the secret room. Even before Pamela had died in there, she had found it almost unbearable to enter it.

"I wasn't sure what else to do with it. I expect that Pamela did not tell 'Irina' how to get into the room. She would have wanted to keep the treasure all to herself. Besides, with the guard outside, no one could enter here. I can't keep the footman on guard forever, of course. I presume I shall have to move the treasure down to the safe, which I obviously should have done much sooner than this."

Olivia sat down beside the bed, and Stephen went over to the wall and opened the door into the inner room. He emerged a moment later, leaving the door into the room open. He walked over to where Olivia sat and set the golden box down on the bed.

The two of then looked at it for a moment; then Olivia stood up and put her hands on the box. Nothing happened. She stood that way for a moment, feeling slightly foolish.

"Perhaps if you touched one of the pieces inside . . . ?" Stephen suggested.

"All right." Olivia undid the clasp and opened

the lid. She hesitated for a moment, then reached in and picked up the rosary.

As her fingers curled around it, a jolt ran through her, shocking her. Stephen saw her flinch, and he reached out instinctively, his hands curling over hers. He, too, felt the shock of sensation, the warmth that suddenly flowed into him.

They stood, hands locked together, suddenly engulfed in a world long dead.

16

Stephen and Olivia smelled smoke and the scent of fresh blood; screams pierced their ears. It was as if a scene were playing out in front of them, and yet, strangely, they not only saw but also felt what the people before them felt.

Sir John and Lady Alys stood on a set of winding stairs. He was protectively below her, wielding his sword with ferocity against a small band of soldiers who were trying to push past him up the stairs. Behind him, Alys drew her dagger from its scabbard on her belt. Jewels winked in the hilt, but the blade was not decorative. She gripped it firmly, facing out, ready to jab at any man who tried to come at them from the side, where the steps were close to the ground.

Fear surged in her, along with the heated excitement of battle. She knew they had little chance. The enemy had gotten inside the bailey before they even knew they were besieged. Only treachery from inside could have managed it. This was the advance guard. Soon the rest of the men would have dis-

patched Sir Raymond's remaining soldiers and, unless distracted by the prospect of looting, would join the men here, and then they would swarm up the steps.

The only safety lay in the tower room upstairs. It was the last bulwark of defense, high above the rest of the great hall, reached only by a set of narrow, twisting stairs. At the top of the stairs, a heavy wooden door opened into the round tower room, and it could be shut and barred with a heavy plank.

One could hold out for some time in the tower room, protected by the stone walls and thick wood, but eventually the door would be breached and death would come pouring in or, if not, one would die a slower death of thirst and hunger. It was possible, of course, that one could provision the room and thereby last longer, if the door held, but there were no provisions there now. There had been no warning, no time to prepare. Alys had barely managed to make it to these stairs leading to the room, carrying a hastily packed sack of her goods; she had reached it only because John had come running to meet her as she emerged from her room and had dragged her with him to the stairs, laying out around him with his sword.

"Go on!" he growled at her now. "Get up to the room."

"I cannot leave you!" How could she run to safety, knowing that he stayed here below to perish under the enemy's swords? "You must come with me."

A soldier tried to come from the side of the stairs.

There was no rail to the side low on the stairs here. It made it easier to defend, but it was also possible to put one's hands on the stairs and try to swing up, which was what one of the enemy tried to do now. Alys jumped forward, bent down and stabbed her dagger into his hand. He fell back with a yowl of pain.

"My lady! Help!"

Alys looked out across the great hall. A woman was pelting toward the stairs, some distance in front of a pursuing soldier. She was dressed far better than a servant, and she was comely, as well, her hair a fall of raven-black. It was her husband's mistress, Elwena, and she held a boy's hand in hers as they ran with the speed of the terrified across the hallway.

"Help me, my lady! Please!"

Without thinking, Alys went down on her knees at the edge of the stairs, as low as she could get without impeding Sir John. Elwena reached the side of the stairs and lifted the child up. Alys caught him under the arms and swung him up onto the stairs, setting him back against the wall. Then she turned.

Elwena grabbed the stairs and tried to scramble up onto them, perilously close to John's swinging sword. Alys reached down and grabbed her arm, pulling with all her might. The enemy soldier reached Elwena and grasped her by the belt, jerking her backward.

Behind them the little boy screeched with fear, "No! Mama! Mama!"

Elwena turned, a dagger in her hand, and struck swift as a snake, sinking the dagger into the break between the sleeve and tunic of the man's chain mail. The tip sank into flesh to the bone, snapping off, and the soldier fell back with a roar of pain and rage. She turned and jumped at the stairs again, straining to lift herself up, her face contorted with fear. Alys lay flat on the stairs, almost beneath John's feet, and grasped the woman's belt as the soldier had done, straining to pull her up.

On the floor, several feet away, the wounded soldier staggered to his feet, clutching his wounded shoulder. He bent and picked up the sword he had dropped, and with a cry of fury he flung it at Elwena, as she dangled above the ground. The sword caught her in the side, cutting into her, then clattered down to the floor. She shrieked with pain and would have fallen but for Alys's grasp of her. Alys struggled to keep hold of her, letting out a groan of dismay as Elwena began to slide back.

With a bitter oath, Sir John struck with all his strength, slicing into the neck of the soldier in front of him. Blood spurted as John pulled back his sword and with his foot shoved hard against the dying man, who staggered backward, crashing into the men behind him, and they fell, stumbling on the stairs. The soldier on the outer edge slipped on the blood, and John encouraged him over the side with a swift kick to the jaw. In the instant of peace this afforded him, he put his sword in his left hand and reached down to hook his hand in Elwena's girdle and yank the woman up onto the steps. He turned just in time to dodge a blow from an enemy sword that clanged uselessly onto the stone. Switching his sword back into his right hand, he started to fight again with renewed fury.

"Mama! Mama!" The boy was still crying, and he flung himself on the woman, sobbing.

"'Tis all right, precious. Hush." Elwena leaned back against the wall, her face gray.

"We must get you up the stairs," Alys said, bending and putting her arm around the woman. "We are right beneath his feet. He needs more room to fight."

Elwena nodded and pushed herself up with her hand as Alys lifted. They managed to stagger up a few steps before Elwena fell back to the ground. Having given John some breathing room, Alys knelt now beside the woman and examined her side. She was bleeding profusely. Alys dug into the sack she had dropped on the stairs as she had gone to help Elwena. She pulled out a linen shift and pressed it hard against Elwena's side.

"'Tis the best I can do for now," she told the other woman. "Mayhap 'twill stanch the blood."

Elwena nodded, not wasting breath on words. She leaned against the wall, one arm around her young son. Alys looked at him with pity. He appeared to be no more than four or five years old. Even if he survived this day, in all likelihood he would be an orphan, for if Elwena's present wound did not kill her, the soldiers would when they breached the tower room.

Alys glanced back at Sir John. He was still

holding off the soldiers, though he was slowly retreating upward. She murmured a prayer for him under her breath, then turned back to Sir Raymond's mistress. "We must go up the stairs."

Elwena nodded. "Help me up."

Again she managed to stand with Alys's help. Alys sheathed her dagger and picked up her sack, curling her other arm around Elwena's waist. Slowly they went up the steps, Elwena leaning against Alys, and the boy following behind them, keeping a death grip on his mother's skirts. Every few steps they paused, and Elwena sagged against the stone wall for a moment. Then they started again.

The stairs seemed endless, and the sounds of battle were still a din in their ears. The stairs curved, and soon they could no longer see down to the bottom, where Sir John fought on. Alys's heart ached at leaving him, yet she had to help the wounded woman to the room above them.

They reached the door at last and stumbled inside. The room was lit only by a cross-shaped window open to the outside air. It was little used and contained few creature comforts — dried rushes spread across the floor, a simple pallet for a bed, a small stool beside it, and on the stool, a cheap candle in the form of a bowl of animal lard with a thick wick stuck in.

Alys helped Elwena over to the crude pallet and eased her onto it. She set down her sack and knelt beside the woman. Gently she pulled away the shift she had pressed against the other woman's waist.

The blood was, she saw, still flowing freely. The wound needed to be cleaned, she knew, but she had no water with her, and so she left the wound as it was, pressing the makeshift bandage back into place. Taking out a nightshift, she used her dagger to tear off a long strip from around the bottom, and this she used to wrap around Elwena's waist, tightly binding the bandage to her.

Elwena lay half-propped up against the wall, panting from her exertions. "You helped me," she said after a moment, her voice wondering.

"Yes, of course. You were in trouble."

"You are his wife. And I —"

"I know." Alys shrugged. "That does not change the fact that you were in trouble. I could scarcely stand by and watch them rape and kill you."

"There are some as would," Elwena told her.

"Perhaps. I am not one of them."

Elwena looked at her oddly. "I was not kind to you. I strutted in front of you with my finery."

"I know." Alys paused, then added honestly, "I hold no grudge against you, Elwena. I am not jealous. I was only glad that the nights Sir Raymond went to you, I did not have to endure his lust. I pitied you that you had to."

Elwena lifted her chin proudly. "I don't need pity. I was able to take anything he did, and I made a good life for me and for Guy."

"I am sure you did the best you could for the boy," Alys agreed candidly.

She got up and went to the door, sliding the bar up and opening the door to look out. The sounds of battle were growing closer. That could only mean that Sir John was still alive, and she offered up a small prayer of gratitude. After replacing the bar, she came back and squatted down beside Elwena. The woman's son was sitting quietly by his mother's head, one hand on her hair, patting it. His other thumb, she noticed, was firmly planted in his mouth, and his eyes had a haunted look. He knew, she thought. With a child's instinct, he saw that his mother was in grave danger.

Alys glanced at the bandage tied around Elwena's waist. The blood had soaked clear through it and was spreading out to stain the whole side of her dress, as well. She was mortally wounded, Alys knew; the only question was how long she would be able to hold out before she died.

Elwena opened her eyes and looked at her, and Alys started a little guiltily, as though Elwena would be able to guess what Alys had been thinking.

"Do you love him?" she asked, surprising Alys.

"Who?" Alys said, though she was certain Elwena did not refer to Sir Raymond.

"Sir John. The captain. There's them as say you do."

"Who says it?"

"He said it once, when he was drinking."

"Sir Raymond?" Alys asked, stunned by the other woman's statement. "But he never —"

"He would not admit it to anyone. It would damage his pride too much. I am sure he didn't mean to tell me, probably doesn't even remember it.

He will find some way to make you suffer without anyone knowing why."

"I fear he will be too late," Alys remarked.

"I don't know. Perhaps he was not."

Alys looked at Elwena sharply. "What do you mean?"

"The castle has been overrun. We will all die. And by chance it happens when Sir Raymond is not here."

"No!" Alys said automatically. "It is his own! His home. And all the rest of the people . . . he could not . . ." Her voice trailed off as she considered. "To kill all these people — the soldiers, the servants — just to get his revenge on me? Even he could not be that evil."

"They say he dances with the devil in the woods."

Alys's hand curled instinctively about the cross she wore on a chain around her throat. "You think he would kill even you?"

"You think he cares for me?" Elwena's smile was bitter. "Because I give him pleasure? He gives me things, yet he counts me no more than he would the loaf of bread he eats or the shoe he puts on his foot."

"Wait." Alys raised her hand to silence her and cocked her head, listening. "'Tis closer — the fighting." She stood up and hurried to the door, leaning her head against it. Again she lifted off the bar and eased the door open.

They were so near that she could see them now, only a few feet below her. Blood streamed down the side of John's face, and his arm moved more slowly. He stumbled a little as his foot sought the stair above him, and Alys gasped, fearing he would fall. But he righted himself and moved on.

He was tiring. Soon he would stumble and fall, and then the swords would come flashing down.

"John!" she called.

"Alys! What are you doing? Get back in the room. Bar the door!"

"Not without you!"

"Are you mad?"

"I will not leave you. I told you that."

Sword rang against sword. John cursed. He could feel the air from the open door behind him. He eased back, making his strokes weaker, and the lead soldier pressed on eagerly. John continued to mount the steps, moving more quickly now. His opponent followed, outstripping the soldiers behind him. John did not need to glance back; his feet were on the landing. He jumped back, landing inside the room. Alys swung the door shut, but John's opponent jumped, too, crashing into the door and sending Alys stumbling back.

He pushed his way inside, and Alys slammed the door behind him, pulling down the bar. John came forward, swinging his sword, all pretense of weakness gone. Two quick, hard blows sent the man stumbling back, and John lashed out with his foot, catching him behind his heels, and swept upward, sending him crashing to the floor. John rammed his sword home in the man's throat.

He pulled the sword out and turned to face Alys.

Blood and sweat mingled, streaming down his face. "God's blood, woman! I told you to close yourself in here! Do you know what you risked?"

"Only what you risked for me," Alys replied.

He dropped his sword and swept her into his arms, holding her close.

Outside, the soldiers crashed uselessly against the door. John glanced toward it, and his mouth twisted in contempt. "They'll try the battering ram next, but they'll find the staircase is built too close. 'Twill take axes."

He dropped down onto the floor and leaned against the wall, casting a glance toward Elwena. "Why did you save her?"

"I could not let them kill her."

John looked at her and smiled. "No. I suppose you could not. She would never have done the same for you."

There were noises outside of men coming and going, and then the sounds of someone hacking at the door.

"Battle-axes," John judged. "I'll have time to rest."

But then there were more rustlings at the door, and men shouting at one another. And then, faintly, they smelled smoke. Alys turned to John, alarmed.

"What is that? What are they doing?"

"They must have lit a fire against the door — piled kindling and got it started. They hope it will burn through the door, make their job easier — or smoke us out."

"It will be much quicker, then, than I had

thought." Alys glanced around. "The flames will set these rushes on fire."

He nodded and began pushing the dry rushes away from the door and toward the center of the room.

"Wait." Elwena motioned to them to come nearer.

"What is it?" Alys went over to kneel beside her.

"I can get you out of here," Elwena said.

"What?" She must be delirious, Alys thought, from loss of blood.

"No. 'Tis the truth. I know a way out. But you must promise me — promise me you will take my boy. Care for him. Promise you will raise him as your own."

"Of course I would care for him." Alys looked over at the big-eyed child sitting beside his mother. "But we cannot leave. There are soldiers —"

"There is a secret door."

Alys stared at her. John came over and squatted down beside them.

"What are you saying? There is a passage out of here?"

"Yes. A secret staircase that goes down inside the wall. The stone is not solid. There are two sets of stone, and a narrow passageway in between. I have gone up and down it, meeting Sir Raymond in here. He loves secrets. He had it built long ago, before you even came here."

Hope flared in Alys. "Truly? Then we will go. But you will come, too."

"No." Elwena met Alys's eyes squarely. "I would only slow you down."

"We cannot leave you to them."

"You must," she retorted firmly. She turned her face up to John's, saying, "You know what I say is true. You must leave me here. I will not live. You know that. And you could not move quickly with me. We would be caught before we left the bailey."

John nodded and looked at Alys. They both knew that Elwena spoke the truth.

Elwena went on. "We will change clothes, my lady. And — and leave something of yours. They do not know you. They will think I am you, and then they will not search. They will say that the lady of the castle died. And then he will believe it."

Elwena looked significantly at Alys, and Alys understood her meaning. If Sir Raymond thought she was dead, he would not look for her, and she and John would not have to spend their lives in dread, waiting for him to find them. She and John had been willing to run because it was their only chance at happiness; they could not stand to remain here, unable to love each other freely. But they had known the risks; Sir Raymond would have hunted for them, and even given the few days' head start they would have had, it was likely that he would have tracked them down and killed them. Even if they had gotten away, they would have had to live all their lives looking over their shoulders, afraid he would find them.

Elwena was offering them freedom. Tears filled Alys's eyes. "Thank you."

"I ask only that you take my boy with you. Take Guy and raise him."

"I will." The tears spilled over onto Alys's cheeks, and she knelt beside the woman and took her hand in hers. "I promise you. We will raise Guy as our own."

Elwena offered her a small smile. "Thank you, my lady."

As it turned out, it seemed too much trouble for the dying woman to exchange her clothes with Lady Alys. Alys simply removed her outer tunic and pulled it on over Elwena's bloody clothes, fastening one of Alys's girdles around her hips. Then she pulled her other simple tunic from the sack and slipped it over her head, fastening it with the ordinary leather girdle she wore. She took off her veil, too, and refastened it so that it neatly hid all her hair.

She decided to leave the golden box here, too, with much of the house's treasure inside it. She took out her best jeweled girdle and put it in her sack, along with a handful of bracelets and rings, and the small leather purse containing a few gold and silver coins. They would need something for their future, a little bit of money to get away and to start their new life, perhaps purchase a small holding of land somewhere far from here. She would leave the large, showy gold cross Sir Raymond had given her as a bride gift, and the other necklaces and bracelets and rings. That should be enough treasure to convince the marauding soldiers they had found the body of the lady of the castle.

Alys took the small gold cross on a chain from around her own neck and hung it around Elwena's.

She removed her wedding band and placed it on Elwena's finger, along with two other of her rings. Then she handed the woman the cunningly carved rosary. It cost her a pang to give it up, for it was beautiful, and she had brought it with her from her father's house, so it in no way had anything to do with her husband. She had prayed upon it many a time, her fingers rubbing over the engraved beads until it was a wonder there were any pictures left. But it was her prized possession, and nothing would convince Sir Raymond that her body had been found as the presence of the rosary with it would. Besides, she knew, Elwena would have far more need of it as she lay dying than Alys would, running away.

She put it in Elwena's hand, and Elwena's fingers closed around it, instinctively rubbing the sacred gold beads. Alys reached inside her loose shift and untied the leather thong she wore there around her waist and pulled it out of her clothing. From the thong dangled a small, engraved gold ring, a token given her months ago by Sir John, which she had worn daily against her skin, a secret reminder of him and of their love. Smiling a little, she caressed the trinket, then slipped it on her finger in place of her wedding band.

Elwena pulled out a small leather pouch and handed it to Alys. "Take this. It is for the boy. Everything I have saved for him."

Alys nodded. It was heavy for its size, and it clinked with the sound of coins. She put it in the sack along with the rest of her possessions.

"Put the casket on the far wall, my lady, far from me."

Alys was puzzled, but she did as the woman asked. As she had worked, John had stripped the outer tunic from the soldier he had killed. Though stained with the man's blood, it carried the emblem of Surton's men and would allow them to pass whoever they might meet outside with much less problem.

"Put your tunic on him," Elwena said. Her voice was growing weaker. "And change your sword with his."

"He's one of their own," Sir John pointed out, though he did as she bade, struggling to get the tunic on the dead body and buckling his own sword belt around him. "They will know him."

"I will take care of his face," Elwena replied grittily.

"There won't be enough bodies here. They're bound to wonder what happened to the other two," Alys said.

Elwena shook her head. "Doesn't matter. Many will tell them I'm a witch, for there are a number who believe it." She flashed a smile reminiscent of her old cocky grin. "I didn't discourage it. They will probably think I flew from the window. It doesn't matter what they think or make up to explain it, as long as they trumpet it around that the two of you are dead. And they will. It will be a matter of pride for them to have defeated Sir John and to have killed Sir Raymond's wife."

"She's right. They will want to believe that you

and I are dead, and that makes it easy to dismiss whatever doubts they have. Come, my love, we must go. The fire is growing," he said.

He was right. The air was becoming thicker with smoke, its acrid scent tickling her throat, and one could feel the heat near the door. John laid his sword beside his enemy and picked up the other man's weapon. Alys picked up her sack.

Elwena hugged her son to her for a long moment, then spoke quietly and firmly to him. He nodded solemnly, tears streaming down his face, and Elwena hugged him again and kissed him. Alys came over and took his hand, and he stepped away from his mother.

Alys bent down to the other woman and handed Elwena her own dagger. She could not leave the woman without some protection, and Elwena's dagger had snapped off in the arm of the soldier. Elwena's fingers gripped the hilt, and she offered Alys a small smile.

"Take the candle," Elwena said, nodding toward the stool. " 'Tis dark in there."

Lighting the candle was a difficulty, for there was no lit candle or burning fire in the room. But John sheathed his sword and picked up one of the longer rushes and carefully slid it between the wooden door and its frame, low to the ground, so that it reached the outer side of the door and caught the flame burning there. Then he pulled it back with even greater care and dipped it into the bowl, lighting the crude candle. He turned to Elwena.

"We are ready."

"See that stone?" Elwena pointed to the wall across the room from her. "The fifth one up from the floor? It is smaller than the others. Pull it out."

John did as she said, edging his fingers into the cracks around the rock and wiggling it out. To his surprise, it came easily, and inside the hole was a lever. He reached in and turned it, and there was a click.

"Now push the wall to your left — low — and it will go out. Just put the rock back in its place and when you get on the stairs, shove the door closed. No one will know the door's there."

He reached down and pushed, and, amazingly, the heavy stone slid back and to the side, leaving them a small opening. He replaced the small rock in its hole, covering the lever. Then he crawled through the opening, finding a set of stairs curving downward, so narrow that his shoulders brushed both sides.

Alys turned and said, "Goodbye, Elwena."

Elwena nodded. "God speed, my lady."

Alys guided the boy through the door, then crawled in after him. They slid the door closed and started down the stairs. The light of the candle was little enough in the gloom of the staircase, and they moved carefully down the steps. The stairs seemed to go on forever, an endless, curving path of uneven stone.

But at last they reached the bottom and stood before the blank stone wall. There was a lever set into this wall, also, and, taking a breath, John lifted it. With a click, the door unlatched, and John inserted his fingers into the crack between the stones and pulled back. The door slid open easily.

Cautiously, John eased his head out, then the rest of his body. He motioned for Alys and the boy to follow. She did so, clutching Guy's hand tightly.

It was still day. It amazed her. It seemed as if so much time had passed that it should have been night. But it was only late afternoon, the sun casting long shadows across the bailey. The scene was chaotic. There were fires dotting the courtyard — sheds burning and stacks of hay, whether set by carelessness or pitch-flame arrows or for sheer perversity, she was not sure. The storage shed had been broken open and the tuns of wine rolled out. Soldiers, obviously having partaken of the contents, staggered around, shouting and laughing boisterously as they carried out other goods from the shed. There were no longer screams around the castle. The battle, it seemed, was over, except above them in the tower.

There were people about, but they paid no attention to them. John wrapped his hand around Alys's arm and strode off purposefully, dragging Alys with him as if she were a captive. The boy, his hand firmly in Alys's skirts, trotted with them. They looked neither to left nor right, and Alys kept her head down.

They did not pause until they reached the shelter of one of the sheds that lay in front of the castle wall. Protected by the shed on one side and the wall on the other, they stopped and looked around. No one, it seemed, had noticed their progress or, if they had, they had paid no attention to it. With John wearing Surton's mark, it seemed that no one questioned them.

"We shall slip along the wall here and out the rear gate," he whispered to her. "If anyone should stop us, I'll silence him quick enough. All right?"

Alys nodded. She looked up at the tower. There was smoke billowing out of the small window. It seemed far too much for the burning door to be creating. And in that instant she knew what Elwena had done. She had said she would take care of the soldier's face, and now Alys realized that she had meant to burn it. She must have pushed the rushes against the door and set them on fire, and soon the rushes, the pallet, the enemy soldier, all of the room, would have been on fire, everything burning but the stone.

Alys had not thought of it at the time, but now she saw that Elwena's black hair would have given her away as the woman who had run across the great hall, not the lady of the castle who had fought her way up the stairs. She had doubtless decided to set the room ablaze in order to conceal her identity and that of the soldier. Alys shivered at the thought and hoped that the smoke had overcome her, or that Elwena had plunged her own dagger into her heart before the fire took her.

John nudged Alys, and she nodded. He took off along the wall, moving swiftly through the lengthening shadows. No one stopped them or even seemed to notice them. They reached the door in the wall, standing wide open. No one guarded it, and they *slipped through it and out into the field beyond. They ran then, John picking up the boy and carrying him.*

They ran across the field and into the woods beyond, escaping to a new life.

17

Slowly the scene disintegrated, as if turning into smoke, and once more Stephen and Olivia were standing beside a bed, the golden rosary between their locked hands.

Dazed, Olivia lifted her eyes from their joined hands and looked at Stephen. He was staring at her with the same sort of amazement as she was certain was on her face.

"Did you —"

"Was that —"

They spoke at once and stopped together. Olivia let out a shaky little chuckle. She sat down on the chair behind her, feeling rather weak.

"Are you all right?" Stephen bent over her solicitously.

"I — I'm not sure. Did we just see what it seemed we saw?"

"We can scarcely deny it. The battle . . . the flight . . . my God."

He straightened up, shoving his hands back through his hair in a familiar gesture. "They did not die."

"No. Do you suppose he never knew it? Sir Raymond, I mean. Do you think he believed them dead and so didn't hunt for them, as they hoped? He did marry twice again after that, though from what was said about him, I don't suppose that the thought of bigamy would have deterred him from doing what he wanted to."

"No. I imagine not. And what an odd alliance — Lady Alys and his mistress."

"She sacrificed herself to save her child. She knew it was his only chance." Tears swam in her eyes. "It must have been a horrible death. I cannot imagine how she got the courage to set the rushes on fire, knowing the pain it would bring to her."

"That was why she wanted Alys to put the casket on the other side of the room, so the fire would not spread to it. She must have scraped all the rushes together close to her and that soldier. Otherwise, the heat would have damaged the box and its contents —"

"But the rosary — it was in her hand — it must have been the center of the fire — and it survived intact." Olivia looked down in awe at the rosary, still wrapped around her hand.

Stephen's gaze followed hers. "It would take —"

"A miracle?" Olivia asked, looking up at him.

So focused were they on the rosary and the past that neither of them heard the door open quietly. In fact neither of them heard a thing until an unearthly voice growled out, "Bitch! Whoremonger!"

Before Stephen could turn, something thudded against his back, and he went down hard onto his knees. Olivia jumped to her feet, gazing in horror into the contorted face of the woman she knew as Irina Valenskaya.

Only it was not Irina Valenskaya anymore, but a strange distortion of her, her height, her clothes, her hair, her face — but with the ice-cold eyes of a stranger.

And Stephen, on his knees, had the hilt of the knife she had plunged into him sticking out of his back.

Olivia screamed. In the next instant, Irina was on her. She grabbed Olivia by the shoulders and shoved her hard toward the open door to the secret room. Olivia staggered and fell, and then Irina was on her, her hands around Olivia's throat, choking her. Olivia struck out with her clenched fist, the rosary still wrapped around it, and connected with the woman's cheek. Irina's hold loosened, and Olivia slid back, struggling to get away from the woman's clutching hands.

She managed to get onto her knees, but then Irina slammed into her again, knocking her down. They rolled across the floor, kicking and hitting and scratching.

Stephen, the knife still in his back, managed to get to his feet and stagger across the floor to them. He reached down and grabbed Irina around the waist, pulling her off Olivia. Olivia struggled to her feet as Irina, insanely strong, turned and hit Stephen with all her force in the stomach. He staggered back, and she wrenched herself away from him. Irina grabbed the golden casket from the bed and slammed it into the side of Stephen's head. He staggered sideways and went down. Irina, still holding the casket, charged at Olivia again. She slammed into her, and the two of them tumbled backward into the small inner room. The casket fell from her arms, and the contents spilled out over the floor.

"Mine!" Irina roared in a harsh, deep voice, the same voice that had rushed out of Howard Babington days before. "Bitch! I will have what's mine!"

She straddled Olivia, her hands digging into her throat, painfully strong. Olivia struggled, her hands around the other woman's wrists, trying in vain to pull them away. She could not breathe. The darkness seemed to swirl around her, a harsh buzzing filling the air. She gripped the rosary, its beads cutting into her hands.

And then suddenly power rose up inside her, filling her with a strength she had never known. She smashed her fist once, twice, hard against the other woman's throat. Irina's hold loosened, and Olivia rolled hard to the right, sending Irina toppling to the side.

"I am not yours!" Olivia cried, crawling to her

feet. Her hand touched metal and closed around it. It was the hilt of a dagger, and it felt familiar in her hand. "For all eternity, I do not belong to you!"

Olivia surged up, her arm swinging forward just as Irina leaped at her. The dagger sank into Irina's chest. Surprise flashed across Irina's face, and a fierce, primitive shriek burst from her mouth. The evil of centuries past burned out of her eyes at Olivia and then was gone. Irina collapsed on the floor.

Olivia stood for a moment, staring down at her foe, stunned.

"Stephen . . ." She broke from her trance and started out of the room.

The outer door burst open, and Rafe's voice shouted, "Stephen? Olivia? Who screamed? What the devil happened to the footman out here? He's knocked out." His footsteps advanced into the room. "Good God! Stephen!"

He hurried toward his friend, unconscious on the floor. Then he looked up and saw Olivia walking toward him, a blood-stained dagger in her hand. Behind her, on the floor lay Irina. He gaped at her.

"Stephen . . . help him." Olivia managed to say, then fainted away at Rafe's feet.

When Olivia came out of her faint, she opened her eyes to see Belinda hovering over her. "Belinda?"

"Oh, thank goodness!"

Olivia sat up slowly, feeling a little dizzy. She was lying on her own bed. "How did I get here?"

"Rafe carried you," Belinda answered. "He sent for me to look after you, and he went back to stay with Stephen."

"Stephen!" Olivia gasped and swung her feet off the bed, about to stand up. "Where is he? Is he —"

"He's alive," Belinda assured her quickly. "We sent for the doctor. Rafe had some of the footmen carry him to his bed. He — he's still unconscious."

"I must go to him."

"No. Wait. You are too weak," Belinda protested.

Olivia ignored her, getting out of bed. "I am fine. I fainted, that's all."

"But you should rest —" A single look from Olivia silenced her, and she followed Olivia out the door.

Olivia strode down the hallway and into Stephen's room. She stopped just inside the door at the sight of him. His eyes were closed, and his face was as pale as the sheets. Her heart hammered in her chest. She went closer to the bed, looking across it to Rafe.

He shook his head at her, saying, "He hasn't awakened yet. It looks like he got quite a blow to the head." He gestured toward the side of Stephen's face, where bruises were beginning to form on his cheek.

"I bandaged him up," Rafe went on. "You get

pretty good at that kind of thing out in the mountains, where there's no doctor around. The blood stopped flowing, at least."

Lady St. Leger sat on the other side of the bed, looking pale and worried. Rafe pulled up another chair for Olivia, and she sat down, her eyes fixed on Stephen.

The minutes passed by at a nerve-racking slow pace. At last the doctor came and shooed everyone but Rafe out of the room, saying that he might need the other man's help. The constable arrived, as well, and took Olivia into another room to ask her a seemingly endless number of questions. She answered abstractedly, her mind on Stephen and what was going on in his room.

When at last she was able to return to his side, she found the doctor gone and Stephen still sleeping in his bed. Lady St. Leger, who was once again seated beside his bed, said, "Dr. Hartfield patched him up. He said he should be all right. By some miracle, the blade apparently missed both his heart and his lungs."

"Thank God."

"He gave him laudanum for the pain."

Stephen continued to sleep through the evening and into the night, whether from the concussion he had received or from the laudanum, Olivia was not sure. She could not leave his bedside. *What if he were to die from this?* She did not think she could bear to live if he did.

It was in the pale light of dawn that Stephen finally stirred, his head rolling from one side to the other on his pillow.

Olivia, watching him, leaned forward hopefully. She put her hand over his where it lay on the counterpane and whispered, "Stephen . . . my love . . ."

She recalled then that his mother was also in the room, and she glanced across the bed. Lady St. Leger was asleep, her head lolling against the wing of the chair.

Stephen's hand turned under hers, and his fingers curled around her palm. His eyes fluttered open.

"Stephen!" Olivia had to swallow back the lump in her throat. "My lady, he is awake."

Stephen gazed at Olivia, his eyes hazy, and a slow smile spread across his face.

"Hello." He started to sit up, then winced with pain. "Ow! What the devil? Oh. Oh!" His eyes widened, and he stared at Olivia. "My God! Olivia! Are you all right? Where is Irina?" He glanced about as if he expected her to still be lurking about somewhere.

"She is dead. I killed her."

He tried to rise again and sank back against the pillows, biting back an oath. "What did she do to me?"

"She stabbed you in the back," Olivia said.

"Oh, darling!" On the other side of the bed, Lady St. Leger dabbed her handkerchief at her eyes. "Thank goodness! Dr. Hartfield said you would be all right, but I was so afraid you would not wake up."

"The last thing I remember was Irina swinging that box at my head."

"She connected," Olivia told him. "Then she came after me and tried to strangle me again."

"She was so strong!" Stephen marveled.

"She was insane," Lady St. Leger put in tartly. "The magistrate came by yesterday evening. From what the constable told him, he is going to rule that Lady Olivia killed the woman in self-defense, which of course she did. It's just a miracle that she was able to overcome her. The constable is of the opinion that Irina was trying to steal the Martyrs' treasure from you. That is why she attacked you."

"I see." Stephen's eyes went from his mother to Olivia, but he said only, "And what about the others? Madame Valenskaya and Mr. Babington?"

"They will be going back to London tomorrow. Rafe and Olivia felt sure that you would not wish to press charges against them because of the scandal it would mean." Lady St. Leger paused, then added, her voice husky with tears, "I am so sorry, Stephen. I know it is for my sake that you don't want to charge them. You would hate for the world to know what a fool I was."

"Don't worry about it, Mother." Stephen patted her hand. "You were not a fool. You were merely a grief-stricken mother taken in by a pack of charlatans."

"But to think that you were nearly killed because of my folly!" Lady St. Leger cried, her voice breaking. "I shall never forgive myself."

"But I didn't die." Stephen smiled reassuringly.

Lady St. Leger got to her feet. "I must go and tell Belinda and Rafe. He bandaged you, you know. The doctor said he did an excellent job."

The older woman stood up and hurried out of the room. Olivia suspected that she might stop for a good cry in her own room along the way. Olivia felt like indulging in the same thing herself.

Stephen squeezed her hand. "Are you all right?"

"Oh, yes, I'm fine. She didn't really hurt me much." Her hand went unconsciously to her throat. "Babington has come to."

"Really?"

"Yes. I don't know if it was because of my killing Irina or what, but he woke up yesterday evening and seems all right, even though he's a bit hazy about things. It looks as though he was largely a dupe in this whole thing, used by Irina and —"

"Sir Raymond's spirit?" Stephen suggested.

Olivia nodded. "I think so. Yesterday, the way she was, the way she spoke. I could see him looking out of her at me."

She shivered, and Stephen squeezed her hand, bringing it up to his lips to kiss. "I am sorry you had to face her."

"It was frightening, but — no doubt this will sound as mad as the rest of it — but when I was fighting her, I was still holding on to the rosary, and suddenly I felt more powerful. It seemed as if Alys was there with me, inside me somehow, helping me. Is that possible?"

Stephen nodded. "I believe it." He paused, then added, "Do you think the evil is gone now?"

"Yes. Perhaps it's just wishful thinking, but when I plunged that knife into Irina, I saw the evil in her eyes wink out. I think that when I killed her, it somehow killed him, too. It's all tied up with Alys helping me, I think, as if she finally overcame him. Does that make sense?"

"Not rationally, but, yes, it makes sense, considering everything."

At that moment Lady St. Leger came in, followed by Belinda, Rafe and Great-uncle Bellard, and the subject was dropped. It was not until several days later that Olivia broached it again.

Stephen had made rapid progress in the days since the attack, growing stronger, first sitting up, then walking, even taking on the stairs. It was clear that it would not be long before he had completely recovered. Olivia had realized as he improved that she was rapidly running out of any reason to remain at Blackhope. Madame Valenskaya and Mr. Babington had left. There was no longer a pretense of a house party. Nor was there any business for her to conduct. She had stayed, telling herself that of course she could not leave while Stephen was still recovering from his wound.

But it was clear now that he was close to recovery, and even that tiny excuse was gone. She supposed Lady St. Leger must be wondering why she stayed on but was too polite to bring up the matter. It made Olivia's heart ache in her chest to think of leaving Blackhope. Leaving Stephen. She thought that when she went, it would feel like leaving part of herself behind.

She and Stephen were sitting in the conservatory a few days later, surrounded by pleasant green plants and looking out at the garden. Olivia had been reading to him, as she had grown accustomed to doing during his convalescence, but she had abandoned that a few minutes earlier and they had fallen into silence, simply looking out at the late afternoon play of sun on the garden.

Olivia said quietly, "That day, when we held the rosary and saw . . . what we saw . . ."

She paused, and Stephen turned to look at her. "Yes?"

"I noticed something."

He looked at her questioningly.

"Lady Alys pulled a ring out from under her dress and put it on."

"Yes, I saw it."

"It was a ring that Sir John had given her."

"Ah. I didn't realize that."

"I knew it somehow. I could feel what she was feeling, even as I was watching it."

"Yes. I had that sense with him. And what about that ring?"

"I knew it."

"What?" His eyes narrowed, and he looked at her searchingly.

"The design — the etching — I have seen it before. Many times."

"What do you mean?"

"It is a family heirloom. Of my family, I mean. The Morelands. I'm not sure how it came down through the family. Great-uncle Bellard might know the exact lineage of it. But it has been in my family for years." She looked at him. "I think that Lady Alys was my ancestor. I think she and her knight made good their escape and built a home, had a family. And I am descended from her. I think that is why we connected with them — I because she was my blood and you because of Blackhope."

He was silent for a moment, absorbing this news. Then he reached out and laid his hand over Olivia's, saying, "There is more than that between us, my love."

Her heart flip-flopped at his use of the endearment, but Olivia told herself not to be foolish. She did not look at him; she did not dare, for she thought if she did, he must see what lay in her heart.

"What do you mean?" she asked, her gaze steadfastly on the windows.

" 'Twas love that connected us — John's and Alys's, yours and mine."

She looked at him then, startled. "I — um —"

"I love you," he said simply. "I want us to be together always, as they were."

"What?" she said, dumbfounded. "What are you saying?"

He smiled. "I want to marry you, Olivia. I am asking you to be my wife."

Joy burst in her, and she felt as if she might fly all apart in her happiness. She hardly dared believe his words.

At her continued silence, he said, "If you are worried about the proprieties, I have already obtained permission from your nearest male relative present to pay my addresses to you."

"Uncle Bellard? You have spoken to Uncle Bellard about this? Before you said anything to me?"

He looked a little puzzled. "I thought that you knew. That you understood. That night in your room — I would never have come to you if I had not thought we would marry."

"Are you sure?" Olivia asked anxiously. "My family is — well, I know you know Uncle Bellard, but, taken as a whole, my family is rather daunting."

"The mad Morelands?"

"Yes."

"After what has happened the last few days, I think any antics that your family may perform would seem quite mild in comparison."

A giggle escaped her lips. "Yes, perhaps so."

"Are you going to make me wait forever for an answer?" he asked teasingly. "I beg of you, Olivia, put me out of my misery."

"But, Stephen, think. I — you must be sure. What if what you feel is just because of *them?* Lady Alys and Sir John. We felt what they felt. What if you think you are in love because you felt his love for her? What if we, like Irina, were *invaded* by their spirits?"

A smile quirked Stephen's mouth. "Ah, but you forget, I don't believe in ghosts."

Olivia smiled faintly.

Stephen reached over and took one of her hands between his. He leaned forward, looking at her earnestly. "Do you think that is what you feel for me?" Stephen asked quietly. "Only an overflow of her feeling?"

"No," Olivia admitted quietly. "That is not all I feel."

"Then why should I be any different?" he asked. "Olivia, look at me. Believe me, what I feel for you is not some secondhand love from another time and place. Yes, we are connected to that couple somehow. It does not make our love less. It makes it more. We are fated to be together. Even if their love somehow spanned generations and found itself in us so many years later, it is still a real love. And isn't our love all the more wonderful and miraculous for having that connection?"

He raised her hand to his lips and kissed it

softly. "I am very clear that it is you I love, not some medieval woman. And," he added with a grin, his eyes lighting wickedly, "the desire I feel for you is very much in the present."

He kissed her on the mouth, his lips hard and possessive, and when he drew back, Olivia's breath was rapid and her cheeks flushed.

"The only question, Olivia, is do you love me? Will you marry me?"

"Yes! And yes!" Olivia cried, joy burgeoning up inside her. "I love you, and I will marry you."

He laughed aloud, and pulled Olivia out of her chair and into his lap, nuzzling her neck. She let out a little shriek of mock indignation, remonstrating, "Stephen! You are still recuperating. Think of your wound!"

"Damn my wound!" he responded, his lips sending shivers of delight through her. "I'm done recuperating." He lifted his head and looked down into her face. "But I do think we should repair to the bedroom."

And with that he kissed her. Olivia wrapped her arms around him and kissed him back, giving up the argument.

About the Author

Candace Camp is the bestselling author of over forty contemporary and historical novels.

She grew up in Texas in a newspaper family, which explains her love of writing, but she earned a law degree and practiced law before making the decision to write full-time. She has received several writing awards, including the *Romantic Times* Lifetime Achievement Award for Western Romances.